OTHER ANTHOLOGIES BY
ALFRED HITCHCOCK

Tales to Make Your Blood Run Cold

FOR CHILDREN

Ghostly Gallery
Haunted Houseful
Monster Museum
Daring Detectives
Supernatural Tales of Terror and Suspense
Witch's Brew

ALFRED HITCHCOCK'S

TALES TO MAKE
YOUR HAIR
STAND ON END

ALFRED
HITCHCOCK'S

Tales to Make
Your Hair
Stand On End

Edited by Eleanor Sullivan

MAX REINHARDT
LONDON SYDNEY
TORONTO

British Library Cataloguing
in Publication Data
Alfred Hitchcock's tales to make your
hair stand on end.
1. Horror tales. American
I. Hitchcock, Alfred   II. Sullivan, Eleanor
813'.01'0816   FS   PS648.H6
ISBN 0-370-30584-1

Printed in Great Britain for
Max Reinhardt Ltd
9 Bow Street, London WC2E 7AL
by Redwood Burn Ltd, Trowbridge
First published in Great Britain 1984

ACKNOWLEDGMENTS

Grateful acknowledgment is hereby made for permission to reprint the following:

Hush, Dear Conscience by C. B. Gilford; copyright H. S. D. Publications, Inc., 1974; reprinted by permission of Scott Meredith Literary Agency, Inc.

Death by Misadventure by Elijah Ellis; © 1963 by H. S. D. Publications, Inc.; reprinted by permission of Scott Meredith Literary Agency, Inc.

The Death Desk by S. S. Rafferty; copyright H. S. D. Publications, Inc., 1975; reprinted by permission of the author.

The Room at the End of the Hall by Helen Nielsen; copyright H. S. D. Publications, Inc., 1973; reprinted by permission of Ann Elmo Agency, Inc.

Kisses and Chloroform by Donald Olson; copyright H. S. D. Publications, Inc., 1974; reprinted by permission of Blanche C. Gregory, Inc.

A Left-Handed Profession by Al Nussbaum; copyright H. S. D. Publications, Inc., 1975; reprinted by permission of the author.

Second Spring by Theodore Mathieson; copyright 1959 by Theodore Mathieson; reprinted by permission of the author.

Bank Night by Arthur Porges; copyright 1966 by The Diners Club, Inc.; reprinted by permission of Scott Meredith Literary Agency, Inc.

The Contagious Killer by Bryce Walton; © 1965 by H. S. D. Publications, Inc.; reprinted by permission of the author.

The Man Who Came Back by Edward D. Hoch; copyright H. S. D. Publications, Inc., 1973; reprinted by permission of the author.

Bad Actor by Gary Brandner; copyright H. S. D. Publications, Inc., 1973; reprinted by permission of the author.

Pigeon in an Iron Lung by Talmage Powell; copyright 1956 by Flying Eagle Publications; reprinted by permission of the author.

Alfred Hitchcock Photoquiz by Peter Christian; © 1980 by Davis Publications, Inc. reprinted by permission of the author.

King of the World by John Lutz; copyright H. S. D. Publications, Inc., 1973; reprinted by permission of the author.

Contents

Introduction

You have only to scan the Alfred Hitchcock Photoquiz in this new Hitchcock anthology to realize—if you hadn't before—that the Master of Suspense was partial to cool-looking blonde leading ladies. You needn't, however, be a blonde to have more fun reading the twenty-four tales accompanying Peter Christian's challenging quiz, though a look through the Contents at the titles of the stories and the names of the authors—whose reputations speak volumes about their ability to make your hair stand on end—should convince you that, whatever you hair color, whether you're a lady or a gentleman, you're unlikely to remain cool while reading this hairraising collection.

Good reading.

Hush, Dear Conscience

by C. B. Gilford

The impact jarred her forward against the steering wheel because she hadn't fastened the seat belt, so she didn't see quite clearly what was happening out there in the night, in front of the windshield, in front of the headlights. Only that there was a dark shape . . . a mass . . . a body. The car bumper seemed to catch that body . . . fling it . . . toss it . . . straight ahead. Then the most horrible part of it all: the car didn't stop. No message seemed able to travel from her brain to her right foot, to tell it to leave the gas pedal and press instead on the brake, because the car, still plunging forward, caught up with the flung body and this time struck it down. The entire vehicle lurched as the front wheel, then the rear wheel, passed over the thing, ground it into the pavement.

Stop . . . but it took so long! She wanted to stop . . . and yet, of course, she didn't. The car had a momentum, a life, a will of its own. It went right on. Bodies—flesh—meant nothing to it; a machine, metal and rubber and glass. So she had to rouse her own will. That thing back there on the road was akin to her, brother flesh. Flesh, blood, pain . . .

Her foot finally found the brake. She stood on the pedal. The car reeled under the sudden leash, tried to escape it, veered first toward the guardrail on the left and then toward the trees on the right. She fought for control, insisted on the brake, her hands pulling upward on the wheel as if it were a pair of reins. The rear end bucked, tires squealed on the asphalt, and then at last the machine halted. She sat there, rigid, numb, her hands unable to relinquish the wheel.

It was a long time before she managed to unbend, let go. Her brain was absolutely blank, all the cells frozen. Time passed. Awareness returned only slowly. Her left hand groped for the door handle, worked it, pushed. Her left foot exited, found the pavement. Her body followed it, emerged from the now motionless machine. At first she merely stood there in the road, without orientation or purpose.

There was silence everywhere. All night noises had ceased—insects, birds, animals, even the wind—all interrupted by the sudden crash and crunch of violence. The grey-black asphalt road was almost invisible. She was alone, apart, suspended in time and space and dark. Alone, except for . . .

What had she hit? Who?

The awful mystery immobilized her for a long time—whatever, whoever, it was back there, a hundred feet or farther, where the road curved into the deeper gloom. *I know this road,* she thought. *I know it like my own hand. That's the bad turn, where all the headlights can do is to sweep across trees and the dirt of the embankment . . . I know that. I've driven this road at night a thousand times . . . and I usually slow down . . . because I know how it is. An object can loom up in the headlights suddenly . . . and there isn't time to stop . . .*

An object. No, a . . . a person. No . . . a dead person is an object.

She found herself walking, her high heels thudding dully on the asphalt. Away from the red glare of the taillights, she was quickly swallowed in warm darkness. There was no moon, only fuzzy stars, providing just enough illumination to distinguish sky from ground, until she came closer to the thing; fifty feet, perhaps.

She halted then, terrified in a new, different way. Off to one side, half hidden in tall grass, it was so still, shapeless, silent; a thing slightly blacker than the rest of the night, a slightly denser shadow.

She could not physically move any closer, although she willed herself to do so. No movement, no life, what was the use? What could she do?

"Are you alive?"

The sound of her own voice, words suddenly shattering the silence, startled her, magnified her terror. There was no answer! Because there was no life in that thing on the ground!

She ran back to the car, a familiar island of light and safety. She leaped inside, slammed the door as if against some pursuer. The engine still idled. She shifted into gear; the car leaped gratefully.

A quarter of a mile—less than that—a continual curve, and just on the other side of the woody knob was *home*. The car turned into the driveway. The garage door rose by radio-magic; the car slipped inside. She switched off the engine, but she did not go into the house. Instead she sat there, staring at the bare white of the garage wall, dazzling, blinding in the headlights.

I should go back, a voice, her own, kept repeating inside her brain. *I should go back . . . or call . . . somebody . . . a doctor . . . an ambulance . . . the police!*

Yet the terror, like cold hands, would not let her go. It would allow her neither to get out to inspect the front end of the car, nor to go inside to telephone, nor to turn off the headlights. Not even to scream.

So the awful thought had to stay inside her skull, echoing, reverberating: *I'm a hit-and-run driver!*

At dawn she finally stirred. Her body ached as she climbed stiffly from the car and walked out of the garage into the early summer dawn. Vaguely she was aware of the sunrise glistening on the dew, of the fragrance of earth and vegetation, of the bird song in every tree. The world of the new day was so different from the world of last night that she wondered, hopefully, if she had dreamed the night.

She walked on the graveled drive, trying to work out the stiffness. Her clothes, she noticed, were certainly from the previous evening. A short-skirted green dress and matching green pumps were not quite appropriate to the dawn.

Everything was so quiet. Shouldn't she have heard a siren? Not necessarily, of course. Not many cars traveled Tanager Lane, so perhaps the discovery hadn't been made yet. Therefore, she could return to the spot herself, and . . . and what?

The thought was like running into a solid wall. What would she do if she went back now? Take a long look at the body? Call the police? Admit her guilt? Then try to explain why she hadn't called last night? Perhaps if she had called then, something might have been done. Now it was surely too late. *I'm afraid we'll have to arrest you, Mrs. Rand . . .*

She went into the house, through the inside garage door to the kitchen. She put coffee on to perk, went to her bedroom and changed into shorts, a thin, cool blouse, no shoes. All her movements seemed to be slow, robot-like. When she returned to the kitchen, the coffee wasn't ready, but she waited patiently. When it was done, she sat down with a cup. Black, the stuff was bitter, and burned her mouth and throat. It didn't matter. What was she waiting for, a police or ambulance siren?

What she heard, after a long, long time, was the ring of the telephone. She listened for a while, hoping it would stop, but when it went right on, she rose with resignation and lifted the instrument from the wall.

"Hello . . ."

"Jen? Jennifer?"

"Yes." The voice sounded only vaguely familiar. "Is that you, Brad? Where are you?"

"Of course it's me. Who else would dare call you at this ungodly hour? I'm in Denver, where else? Look, I didn't wake you, did I? I know how you like to get up early in the summer, so I risked it. I was worried about you."

"Worried?"

"I shouldn't have let you take me to the airport and then drive home alone."

"Oh, that."

"Yes, oh that. I know you're an independent widow, and you go where you please, when you please. But you don't have to be my chauffeur."

She knew she should say something, take up the argument perhaps, but she didn't feel like saying anything.

"You are all right, aren't you, Jen?"

"Yes . . ."

"You sound kind of funny . . ."

"No . . . I . . . I'm all right."

"Sure?" Brad said insistently.

"Sure."

"I didn't wake you?"

"No, I was awake."

"Are you absolutely wide awake?"

"Yes."

"Will you marry me?"

She stared at the opposite wall. Finally she answered very deliberately, "No, Brad, I can't marry you." Then she hung up.

It was only a minute, perhaps two minutes, before the phone started ringing again. Leaving the sound behind her, she ran from the kitchen, barefoot, out into the garage.

The car sat waiting. In the daylight now, she walked around to the front of it.

Last night had been no dream. There was a dent in the chrome, and the yellow parking light embedded in the fender had a cracked glass. She had hit something. Something . . .

She got in, started the engine, wheeled out of the garage. It took only a minute. It wasn't far; back around the curve, to that place. To the place where she had hit *something*, cracked the light, and dented the chrome.

There was nothing there. She stopped, got out, walked barefoot back and forth—on the road, into the grass. Not even bloodstains. Shouldn't there have been blood? Or do bodies, smashed by automobiles, bleed only internally?

There was *nothing*.

She didn't tell Brad about it until late September, at the end of summer. She'd waited three months to tell him about what had happened on the night he'd left for Denver and she'd taken him to the airport.

He listened seriously, sympathetically, and when she finished, he had a ready explanation for the mystery. She had hit some kind of fairly large animal, hadn't killed it, but had injured it, and the creature had crawled away, into the woods somewhere. Had it died or recovered? Well, three months later that would be pretty hard to establish, but there was one happy certainty: what she had hit was an animal. A man, a human being, wouldn't have crawled off into the woods.

Then Brad smiled at her indulgently, took her into his arms, kissed her, and chided her for not having confided in him earlier. "You see, Jen, I could have saved you months of doubt and worry. You need me. Isn't that clear to you now? So why don't you marry me?"

She looked at him. Brad Richmond: not quite handsome, but rugged and very masculine; middle thirties; successful in his business. Divorced long, long ago; needing a woman; needing love. Lonely; just as she was.

"Jen, it's not right, your living way out in this wilderness all alone."

"Wilderness! When the leaves fall, I can see a dozen other houses. And I like this place . . ."

"I know."

Yes, he knew. She'd had six happy years here with Evan, and this was her home. When Evan had died in that car crash, Mike had died with him, and ever since, she had resisted acquiring either another husband or another dog. So she had lived here very much alone.

"Marry me, Jen," he insisted.

"Do you want to marry a hit-and-run driver?" she challenged him.

"What do you mean?"

"I mean that it doesn't matter how it turned out. Morally, that is. I hit something in the road. It wasn't my imagination; the car was dented. I hit something . . . a living creature . . . and I ran away and left it . . . to suffer pain . . . or to die."

"Because you were scared," Brad argued. "Simple psychology. Your husband died in a car accident. That's always been there. You can't forget it. So when you were involved in an accident, you panicked."

She shook her head. "Since Evan was killed in a car, all the more reason for me to do the right thing . . ."

He tried to take her into his arms again. "Honey, I'm not going to hold it against you. Nobody's going to hold it against you."

She walked away from him. "*I* hold it against me," she said.

It wasn't until January that the man came. She was dragging home a fallen tree limb off the wooded hillside, thinking how self-sufficient she was, able to swing an ax and cut her own kindling, when she saw him in the driveway. She had left the garage door open because she had exited that way, and now he was standing there, staring at her station wagon.

She might not have been alarmed otherwise. She was accustomed to living alone, not nervous or easily frightened, and this was daylight; but the man was looking at her car. It was that fact alone—some terrible intuition warned her—*was he . . . ?*

She dropped the tree limb. She wanted to run in the opposite direction, away. She might have, but while she stood frozen and undecided, he turned from her car and looked instead at her.

They were a hundred yards from each other. She could not see his face, nor his eyes, yet his gaze held her and would not let her run. When she moved finally, it was toward him, slowly, pulled helplessly along as if by some malign magnet.

Thus her first picture of him didn't come to her suddenly, but gradually as she drew closer. He wore a ragged topcoat against the chill, and his body was small and thin. Wisps of long, stringy brown hair grew from under his red stocking cap. In the beginning she imagined his narrow face was contorted into some kind of sneer, but then she saw that it was his real face. His left eye was a mere slit. Below the slit a scar ran down toward his mouth, and seemed to yank the left corner of it upward, showing half his teeth. He's ugly. The unkind words started to pound inside her brain . . . ugly . . . almost deformed . . .

She stopped a dozen paces from him. He seemed perhaps to be smiling at her, but it was a horrible, twisted smile. Panic urged her question.

14

"What do you want?"

"Mrs. Jennifer Rand?" His voice was soft, with a strange, small lisp. The scar, the twisted upper lip, made him do that, perhaps.

"Yes." She tried to keep her own voice level and calm. "Who are you?"

"Danny Korth."

The name meant nothing.

He let her puzzle over it for ten or fifteen seconds. Then he added, "I'm the man you hit with your car six months ago."

Then she knew; everything that her conscious mind had denied knowing all this time. That had been a human body crumpled on the asphalt. Rolled into a little ball . . . dark clothes and a mop of dark hair in the darkness of the night . . . so that it had seemed to have no shape, no human identity. So that she could fool herself into believing that it was something other than human. Yet her subconscious had known better, hadn't it? Somehow there was no great, enormous surprise concerning this man's arrival. Deep down, she had always expected him to appear.

"You remember, Mrs. Rand?"

She nodded. The panic had evaporated. In its place, resignation and despair, her secret companions of the past half year.

"You stopped the car; you came back to look. Maybe you thought I was dead, or you hoped I was. Then you went home. You didn't report the accident. You didn't call an ambulance. You just went home."

She nodded again, hypnotized by his one eye, a blue orb, bright, glittering.

"I might have died. I almost did. Instead I was left this way." One thin hand made a vague gesture toward his face, and then he took a step toward her. His body dipped and swayed as he took that single step. His left leg was several inches shorter than the right.

What could she say? That she was sorry? Make excuses? Explain? Nothing seemed adequate. Everything was up to him. He had chosen to return. "What do you want now?" she asked meekly.

She was certain then, by the way his lips contorted, that he was grinning. "Right now," he replied, "I'm cold. I want to go inside and have a cup of coffee."

She had no mind of her own. She'd be safer here outside. With that limp of his, she could run away from him. Inside the house, when no neighbors or passersby could see or hear, he could corner her. Small and deformed though he was, he was surely still stronger than she . . . and he could beat her, or pull a knife, or a gun. But it didn't matter. This was her destiny, what she deserved. There had never been any escape from Danny Korth, and there wasn't now.

She led the way, through the garage, through the kitchen. "The living room's in here—"

"I'll have my coffee in the kitchen," he said.

"May I hang up your coat?"

"I'll just throw it over a chair."

He did exactly that, and the red stocking cap. His brown hair looked dirty and uncombed, ugly as the rest of him. Because he'd been wearing no gloves, he began to blow on his hands to warm them. She tried not to watch what he was doing, but turned and busied herself with the preparation of the coffee.

"Nice little place you have here," he commented after he sat down.

She stood staring at the coffee pot, not looking at her visitor.

"And you live here all alone."

She did not even tense her shoulders. Although she could not guess his next move or words, everything he said, once he had said it, seemed precisely what she had expected of him. She knew he was staring at her now. "Why don't you take off your coat?" he asked finally.

She obeyed, throwing the garment on a chair as he had done. Then she faced him. Sooner or later, she knew, she would have to face him, and so she looked at him; directly at his drooping eyelid, and the scar, and his twisted mouth. He had never been handsome, or even passable, so he had never been much—but of course he was less than that now, less than nothing . . . hideous . . . a monster.

"I went back to the scene of the accident the next morning," she found herself telling him. "You weren't there. Where did you go?"

The grin again. "Curious about that, are you, Mrs. Rand?"

"Yes, I've been curious ever since. I knew I'd hit something, because there was a dent in the car. I finally decided that it must have been an animal that crawled away."

"And that satisfied your conscience, huh?"

"Not completely. I hadn't wanted to hurt an animal either."

"I'm glad to hear that, Mrs. Rand. Now that we've met, I see you're a person with a conscience."

He was mocking her, of course, but she had no right to take offense, so she accepted the mockery.

16

"Where did you go?" she asked again.

"Oh, I'll tell you, Mrs. Rand. That's why I came back. To tell you all about it. But first you'd better sit down."

She obeyed. She'd had a sense of foreboding all these six months, and now it overwhelmed her.

"After your car hit me," he went on, his one-eyed gaze forcing her to look at him, "you stopped the car and walked back. I was conscious. I knew you were there. And you asked me, 'Are you alive?' "

She bit her lip. How well she remembered. Those had been her words.

"I was in great pain, Mrs. Rand, but I heard that question very clearly. And I caught the tone of your words. What you really meant to say was, 'I hope you're dead, because then you can't testify against me.' Oh, I knew what kind you were right then. Rich woman in a big car. I've always hated your kind, the rich people in the big cars, because I've spent most of my life walking. And I hated you especially, for hitting me and not caring, preferring to have me dead. I hated you so much that I didn't answer your question. I didn't groan to let you know I was alive. And I was right about you, wasn't I? Because you drove away, didn't you? And no ambulance ever came. You left me there to die. Leaving the scene of an accident is a serious crime, Mrs. Rand."

"Yes, I know."

She searched the horrible mask of his face for a clue. "Is that why you're here? To blackmail me?"

He grinned, a distorted death's-head. "How about coffee?"

As before, she moved at his command. When she brought only one cup, he said, "Won't you join me?" Then she poured two. She brought cream and sugar, but the visitor drank his coffee black. "You're not drinking," he pointed out. Obediently she sipped from the cup.

"Let's put it this way, Mrs. Rand," he said finally. "I got an idea while I was lying there on the road, while you were wishing I was dead. I thought to myself, even if she calls the police or an ambulance or anybody, she'll tell them it was an accident, and because she's a rich lady they'll believe her. And her insurance will take care of me. I'll bear the pain, and the insurance company will bear the expense, and not one damn thing will happen to her. So I said to myself right then, I'm not going to let it be that way."

He stopped and sampled the coffee. "That's good and hot," he remarked. "It's cold out there today."

She waited, like a prisoner waiting for sentencing.

He took half a dozen sips of coffee before he continued. "I decided I was going to come back to see you someday. My buddy and I—"

"Your buddy?" she asked.

"That's right. My buddy and I, we had a pickup parked just off the road near there. I guess you didn't see it. Anyway, he took me to a hospital. Then he came back a couple of days later and checked the car. We had the license number, you see. The car was in your garage. It still has the same license. And my buddy checked you out. We found out your name. You're a widow and you live alone in this house. We figured we could report you to the police any time—"

"You still can," she interrupted.

He nodded, sipping more coffee. "We still can. And don't you forget that, Mrs. Rand."

He was a huge, malevolent spider sitting there spinning his web around her, and she tried to fight her way out of it. "So you intend to blackmail me," she said weakly. "Couldn't you have gotten more from the insurance company than you could from me?"

His reply was calm, easy. "We can always go back to the insurance company if we have to." He banged his cup down hard, startling her. "You forgot what I said a minute ago. Letting the insurance company handle it is too easy on you. I want to deal directly with you. I want you to pay."

"I'm not rich—" she started to say.

"There are things besides money."

She blinked at him. "I don't understand."

"Look at me," he commanded her.

Was the expression on his face a grin? The way that scar drew up the left corner of his mouth, baring his teeth, made the expression seem a grin, but considering the business on which he had come, surely it couldn't be.

"Look at me, Mrs. Rand. What amount of money could make up for this?" With his hand he gestured to his face, to the drooping eyelid, the pale scar, the twisted mouth. "How much, would you say?"

"My insurance," she began, "goes to a hundred thousand—"

The palm of his gesturing left hand came down hard upon the table, rattling the cups. "Shut up about insurance!" he shouted at her. "I don't want payment from them! I want it from you!"

18

She cringed before his anger.

"I don't have that much money—"

"Money!" The shout became a scream. "I don't want just money!"

She stared, in terror of him. "What do you want, then?" Her question was a mere whisper.

"I want a life," he answered quietly.

"What?"

"I want a life."

"My life . . . you came here to kill me . . ." An even lower whisper.

He was shaking his head. "Not *your* life, Mrs. Rand. *Mine*. The life your car smashed. The life I had before. A normal life."

Now she could whisper only with the greatest difficulty. "How can I . . . ?"

His one-eyed gaze was stern upon her, like that of a judge pronouncing sentence; and indeed, what he demanded was a barbaric kind of justice. "I want all you have. This house. The car. Your bank account. And you."

She bit back a scream.

"You," he repeated. "You, Jennifer."

When Brad arrived that night, unexpectedly—they didn't have a date—she had recovered from the worst of her hysteria, but she must have looked different to him. She knew, in fact, that she did. She had glanced briefly into a mirror and had discovered there a near stranger, with pale cheeks and haunted eyes.

"Jen, what's the matter with you? Are you sick?" He grabbed her shoulders, but she shrugged off his hands and backed away. "Jen!"

"Brad, go away. I shouldn't have answered the door."

"I'd have battered it down if you hadn't. What's happened? I'm not going away, so you'll have to tell me."

Finally, she told him Danny Korth's story.

Brad was enraged, seemingly almost on the verge of violence; but she saw him struggling to remain cool, to think. Brad had always been the calm sort, inclined to being methodical, figuring things out, all the angles, then deciding the best way to proceed; but he was visibly shaken now—he hadn't found the best way quite yet.

"Where's this Danny Korth right now?" he wanted to know when her recital was finished.

"Out in the car."

"Your car?"

"Yes. He said he wanted to ride in the car that struck him down."

"He's stolen it."

"Oh, Brad, I hope he has. I hope he takes it and keeps it. Then maybe I'll never see him again."

He nodded grimly. "Yes, I suppose it might be cheap at that."

"But I know I won't get off that easy," she argued. "He'll be back."

"And then what?"

"I don't know."

"Jen, I'm going to call the police. We'll have this man arrested."

"For what?"

"He's trying to blackmail you."

"Do you want him to tell the police I ran away from an accident?"

"You can deny it. You've had the car fixed. What can he prove? It would be his word against yours."

She shook her head and looked at him longingly. Why hadn't she married him a year ago, when he'd first proposed? Then she wouldn't have been living here, wouldn't have been driving that road, wouldn't have struck and crippled Danny Korth. "I'm guilty, Brad," she insisted. "I'm responsible for that man being in the condition he's in. I've ruined his life. Don't you see? It isn't just a legal position. It's moral. I'm morally guilty, so I've got to pay. The full price."

"Meaning?"

"He said I've ruined his chances to lead a normal life. Like any other man, he wants a home, a woman—this house and me . . ."

"Now wait a minute!" Brad came toward her, but she backed away again, evading him. He didn't pursue her, but he was biting his lip and clenching his fists. "Okay, so he's got your car. Let him have it. But as far as a home is concerned, or a woman . . ." He stopped, appalled at what he was saying. "He's not going to get you!"

While they stood staring at each other, they heard the sounds from outside, the roar of a car engine, tires on the gravel drive, the garage door opening and shutting, then sounds inside the house, footsteps, ominous, uneven footsteps; and then Danny Korth appeared.

Korth spoke as if he owned the place. "Who's this guy, Jennifer?"

"This is Brad Richmond," she responded automatically. "He's my very good friend. And he knows who you are."

She saw Brad staring at the apparition, at the maimed leg, the awful, smashed face; but he recovered quickly. Brad had a strong survival instinct, an ability to cope; it had made him successful in business. She saw it in operation now. He was intense, but not hysterical as she had been.

"Jennifer and I are very good friends, Mr. Korth," he began. "Although there are no formal plans, we have discussed marriage. So I consider her problems to be mine also."

The man leaned against a wall, giving his body the support his shrunken left leg could not manage. He said nothing.

"It seems you are a problem, Mr. Korth."

The warped face seemed to grin.

"Mrs. Rand told me the story you told her. You claim you were the victim, and you were rescued by a friend in a pickup truck. The truck, you claim, was parked off in the woods. Where was your friend at the time of the accident? With you, or somewhere else? And what were you doing in this area late at night, wandering in the woods, or walking on the road?"

The solitary blue eye stared back at the questioner mockingly. A red tongue darted out and licked the perpetually curled lip. "Scouting," Danny Korth said.

"What do you mean?"

"The neighborhood looked pretty good. And all the houses were off by themselves. We thought we might find something—"

"You mean you might find an empty, isolated house to break into?"

"Maybe."

"Why didn't you explain that to Mrs. Rand?"

"She didn't ask."

"You're a burglar by profession, Mr. Korth?"

"I didn't say that." Danny Korth limped across the room and sank into the most comfortable chair, facing the fireplace. He appeared tired. "Anyway, what's the difference? I'm a human being. Jennifer ran over a human being, left a human being to die in the road."

"Stop calling her Jennifer!" Brad lost his control for a moment. He turned away, fighting himself. He could easily throw the intruder out of the house, of course. Or even kill him. He looked as if he wanted to, but he turned to Jennifer. "Why don't we call the police? This man is a criminal."

"You can't prove that," Korth interrupted.

Brad sat down. He was better now. He stared at Korth for a long time, then he started the questions again. "You say this friend took you to the hospital. What hospital? What doctor took care of you?"

"What difference does that make?"

"The doctor and the hospital didn't do a very good job on you."

"I was in pretty bad shape."

"Oh, sure. But plastic surgery works wonders these days. A halfway decent doctor could have—"

"Brad, stop!" Jennifer shouted. "Why do you want to torture him any more?"

"I don't want to torture him. I want the facts. Don't we have a right to the facts? Look at this man, Jen. Sure, he's crippled, and he knows you hit someone or something on the road. But the connection hasn't been proved. How do we know *you* did that to him? That scar on his face—it looks like an old scar to me."

"Are you a doctor?" Korth demanded, but not angrily, just wearily. "Do you know the difference between old scars and new scars?"

"No, but I'll bet I can find someone who does know. Will you submit to a physical examination?"

Korth leaned back in the chair. "No. Why should I? Jennifer believes me. I don't give a damn whether you do or not."

Brad turned to her. "Do you believe him?" She nodded.

"Don't forget, friend," Korth volunteered, "how I first identified myself to Jennifer. When she got out of her car, she came back to look. And I heard her say, 'Are you alive?' Her exact words. Ask her. How else am I supposed to know that if I wasn't the one lying there in the road?"

Brad glanced at her, his eyes full of pain and helplessness.

She nodded again. "Go away, Brad. There's nothing you can do."

"And leave you here with him?"

"Yes."

"What are you worried about, friend?" Korth interrupted. "Do you think I'm going to rape her? Maybe I used to be a burglar, although I couldn't be even that anymore, in the shape I'm in. But I'm no rapist. I'll sleep in the guest room till Jennifer and I are married."

"Jen!" Brad crossed the room and grasped her shoulders roughly. "You're not going to marry him?"

"What else can I do?"

"Let him go to the police. Let them put you in jail for a year. That would be better than—"

"That wouldn't help Danny."

"Jen, you can't do this! You were going to marry me."

"That was a long time ago, Brad. We missed our chance. I have other responsibilities now."

"Jen, I won't let you. That's final."

"Please go, Brad . . ."

"I'm not stirring."

She faced him squarely, resolutely. "Then I will have to call the police. I'll have to tell them Brad Richmond is here in my house against my wishes and I want him out."

He backed away from her.

"You're crazy," he breathed. "That creep sitting there is a crazy man, but you're crazier than he is."

He turned then and burst out through the front door without saying good-bye, without saying another word. She went to the door and closed it as his car drove off. Then she turned back to confront Danny Korth.

"All right," she said submissively.

"You think I'm a rapist too?" he asked.

"All I know about you is that you're the man I injured."

"Good. That friend of yours—maybe he'll try to blow the whistle on me, accuse me of rape. I'm taking no chances. I really will sleep in the guest room. We'll do this all nice and legal, because I want everything you own, Jennifer, besides you. Go along to bed now. We've got things to do tomorrow, like getting the marriage license and planning the honeymoon. I'm looking forward to that, Jen . . . the honeymoon."

She went obediently to her bedroom, and left him sitting there in her favorite chair, watching her fire, totally in command of her house.

Danny Korth had appeared on Tuesday. Now it was Thursday; the license and all the other preliminaries had been accomplished, and the wedding awaited. Danny had been busy. "Judge Verone will marry us at four o'clock," he informed her. "I have overnight reservations down at Sandbury, then we'll drive south, take our time. Florida is always crowded at this time of year, but we'll find something. I want to bask in the sun." She hadn't argued, but had gone obediently to the bank and drawn out sufficient funds for the trip.

She'd packed, under Danny's watchful eye. "That pale green suit," he'd said, "that will do nicely for the ceremony," and he'd supervised the rest of her wardrobe, including several bikinis for the Florida beach. All in all, five bulging suitcases, every one she owned. He, of course, had no luggage, but he said he'd pick up what he needed on the way.

It was three o'clock and Danny was loading her suitcases into the station wagon when the phone call came. It was Brad. She hadn't seen him since Tuesday.

"Thank God you're still there," he began. "Are you all right?"

She knew what he meant. "Yes, I'm all right."

"Good. I'm headed your way right now—"

"No, don't," she interrupted, and told him the wedding plans.

He stopped her before she could finish. "Hold off. Stall him till I get there. You got that, Jen?"

"Brad, what's the use?"

"Listen, I've been doing some checking. I think I've checked every damn hospital and clinic within a hundred miles. I've been going through records, looking for the name of Danny Korth. The people have been pretty cooperative. And I've had some help—a police captain I know. No Danny Korth. You got that? Well, maybe he used another name. But we know the date of the supposed injury, June twenty-fifth, right? But there's no record of that kind of injury then or for several days after. You understand?"

"His friend could have driven him farther than a hundred miles," she argued wearily.

"Sure. But why? Why should he, when he was in pain, when he could have died? It doesn't make sense."

"Brad . . . it doesn't help . . . I'm guilty . . ."

"You listen to me! Stall him! Don't leave the house! I'll be there in thirty minutes—maybe twenty. You stay there! I love you . . ." He hung up.

She walked away from the phone, stopped at a mirror, and gazed at her reflection there. She was wearing the pale green suit. Her hair was neat, there was the proper amount of makeup on her face, but she did not look like a bride. Rather more like a condemned prisoner ready to be led off for sentencing. Well, that was what she was, wasn't she? A guilty prisoner . . .

A life sentence. She saw herself shudder. If she had killed Danny Korth, and had phoned the police and ambulance immediately, she would be free today. Who could have testified that she'd been driving too fast? If she had injured him and then phoned, she would have been remorseful surely, but essentially free. She had instead injured him . . . and run . . . abandoned him to suffer and perhaps die. So now she was not free. But a life sentence!

Yet there was justice in this, wasn't there? All that she had robbed him of, she was providing him now. Or all that she could.

"Jennifer, it's time to go." Danny's voice came from the kitchen.

She obeyed automatically. She met him in the kitchen.

"The bride looks beautiful," he said.

Was he mocking her? How could she ever know?

He held the door for her, and she walked out into the garage. There sat the station wagon which had been her undoing, the rear deck full of her honeymoon luggage. The groom opened the front door on the passenger side. She climbed in. The big garage door, on command from the button on the wall, yawned wide and the cheerless January sunshine streamed through. Her gallant escort hobbled around toward the driver's side, but before he could arrive in his place, she snatched the keys out of the ignition.

He didn't discover the loss until he was seated behind the wheel. She could sense that he stiffened.

"Jennifer," he asked after a moment, "where are the keys?"

"I have them," she said.

"Give them to me."

"No."

There was a silence, a kind of test of wills. It was he who spoke again finally. "What's happened?" he asked calmly.

"Brad Richmond phoned. He's been checking hospitals. There's no record of any Danny Korth, or of anybody else being treated for your kind of injuries around June twenty-fifth."

"So now you don't believe me." His voice remained quiet, confident.

"What hospital were you taken to? What doctor treated you?"

"I can't answer those questions. Not even for you, Jennifer. There are people I have to protect."

"Then I won't marry you." She was amazed at the steadiness in her voice, at the sudden steadiness inside her, at her sudden decision and determination. Would Brad be proud of her? She hoped he would. Brad's approval was important, the only thing now onto which she could hold.

Danny didn't stir. "You're not going to pay me what you owe me?"

"Not until I'm absolutely sure I owe you."

"I already gave you a full description of the accident. How could I know all that unless I was there?"

"Somebody could have told you about it."

"Who?"

"The person I hit, before he died. That friend of yours in the pickup truck. Maybe you were the friend. Maybe you drove the victim away."

He laughed softly, mockingly. "Brad Richmond must have put that crazy idea into your head."

She didn't wither under his mockery as she had before. "Maybe he did," she told him. "But I want more proof."

He laughed again. "What more proof can I give you?"

She hesitated, only very briefly. "How well do you remember being hit?" she asked.

"What do you mean?"

"I remember the details very vividly." Her confidence grew as she talked. "What the pedestrian looked like when I first saw him. How the car hit him. All that. How well do you remember it?"

"I've already told you."

"You told me about afterwards. How I got out of the car and walked back, and what I said. But how well do you remember the actual details of the impact?"

He was wary. She wasn't looking at him, refused to look at him directly, but she sensed that he was on his guard, being very careful about everything he said. "It's obvious where I was hit," he answered slowly. "My leg . . . my head . . ."

"Yes, but how? What part of my car hit you? Did you fall? Were you thrown? Did the car run over you? Which side of it?"

"Jennifer, it all happened so suddenly, I—"

She continued to stare straight ahead, at the garage wall. "I won't accept that, Mr. Korth. You've already told me, remember, how very conscious you were of details afterwards."

"That was different." She had him on the defensive now. He wasn't mocking her; he was trying to soothe her. "There's a difference between things that happen suddenly and things that happen when you've got time and a good reason to notice carefully."

"It happened suddenly to me, too," she argued swiftly, without mercy. "The picture of it is in my mind. It will always be in my mind."

26

"All I saw was headlights. I was blinded. I didn't even know which way to dodge."

"You must have been struck on your left side."

"Of course."

"What else?"

"I don't know."

"I want proof."

"Proof!" His mood had suddenly turned nasty. Perhaps he would do her some kind of violence, but she had to take the risk. "Proof!" he yelled. "Look at me! Look at my destroyed body!"

"But that isn't what I remember . . . Show me what I remember . . ." Her voice trailed off.

He was panting there beside her. His hot breath was on her cheek. "I don't understand."

She was in a kind of trance by now, staring through the windshield at the blank garage wall beyond. On the blank wall, shadowy memory-pictures began to form. "Show me," she urged him softly, "if you're the one who fits the picture."

He hesitated. "You mean . . . get out there and stand in front of the car?"

"Yes . . . yes . . . maybe that would do it . . ."

He tore at the door handle, lunged out, limped around to the front of the car, then stood there, glaring back at her. "How do I look?" he screamed. "Do I fit your picture?"

Yes, he did! Although the garage was filled with sunlight rather than the glare of headlights, the nightmare memory seemed to take shape around him. Her expression must have revealed her horror, for he seemed to grin in triumph.

One last detail, small but important . . .

"Throw up your left arm," she shouted back at him, "in front of your face. Don't look . . . try to protect your face . . . don't look . . . hold it there . . ."

He followed instructions with precision.

She knew her car, how instantly it could respond. They key into the ignition . . . turn . . . the engine roaring into life . . . the flick of the gearshift lever to Drive . . .

Then his scream! As the lunging car, even lacking her foot upon the accelerator pedal, pinned him against the garage wall.

She was screaming too; sliding along the seat to her left, trying to get her foot on the pedal, so she could push down hard and finish the job.

Then there was Brad, his big shoulders filling the open driver's door, his arms trying to pull her out.

"I want to kill him . . . that's the only way . . . end his suffering. Then I'll go to prison!" she cried.

"Hold it, Jen! Just hold it, will you please!"

Somehow she listened. Somehow she obeyed, and froze.

Brad's shoulders and arms withdrew. "Korth!" she heard him snap.

The man confronted them both, his one eye wide and bright with terror.

"Korth, tell the truth now!"

"It wasn't me," he panted. "I got this . . . this leg . . . this face ⸴ . . from a truck . . . four years ago. Jennifer killed my dog . . . I buried it in the woods—I'll show you where. I knew she thought she'd hit a human being when she asked 'Are you alive?' That's how I got this idea to get even. I loved that dog—the only thing that ever loved me . . ."

Together they watched him limp off, down the road from whence he'd come. They'd offered to take him to the bus depot, or to the airport, or anywhere, but he had refused. He wasn't a cripple, he had snarled bitterly, he could manage for himself. They had offered him money, but he'd refused that too. He wasn't helpless. He'd get by.

"Do you think he'll be back?" Jennifer asked.

"Never," Brad said. "You're free."

"I killed his friend. I'll never be quite free. I want to leave this place. I never want to see it again."

"I'll take you away," Brad promised.

Death by Misadventure

by Elijah Ellis

We drove along in a silence as unfriendly as the autumn day that sprawled like a cold, gray blanket across the hilly farmlands south of the river.

We were on our way to look into a possible murder.

Brief scurries of rain hissed against the windshield of the county car. The grizzled sheriff of Pokochobee County, Ed Carson, was at the wheel. I sat beside him on the front seat and wished mightily that I was back at my new office at the courthouse, in Monroe. The office with the shiny new lettering on the frosty glass of the door: *Alonzo Gates, County Attorney*.

But I didn't get elected last year on a platform of sitting on my tail at the courthouse. I'd promised the voters that I, personally, would investigate every major crime committed within the sacred borders of Pokochobee County.

Now I was stuck with it.

So was Sheriff Ed Carson, who liked it even less than I did. He hadn't at all expected that I meant to fulfill that campaign promise. Otherwise, he probably wouldn't have called my office that morning to let me know there had been a violent death in the county, the first since I'd taken office two months before.

I glanced out at the half-drowned countryside and shuddered. I asked Carson, "How much farther?"

"Couple of miles," he grumbled. He was older than me. In fact, I was still wearing knee-pants when he was first elected sheriff, a job he'd held ever since. This rainy morning he had on his usual garb of wrinkled khakis, five-gallon hat, boots with badly run-over heels, and a gunbelt, complete with .45. In deference to the weather, he'd brought along a shabby poncho that looked like it might have been used in the Civil War.

What could you expect? I asked myself. To my mind the sheriff was a kind of living fossil, left over from the nineteenth century. So was

Pokochobee County, for that matter—but I was the fair-haired boy who was going to change all that.

Now I said briskly, "Give me the run-down again on this case. A Mrs. Reiseman called your office at ten-thirty this morning, and . . . ?"

Carson gave a sigh that ruffled the moth-eaten fringes of his pepper-and-salt moustache. "I told you once. Milly Reiseman called. She said she found her husband, Tom Reiseman, laying in a shed behind their house with his head caved in. He'd gone out to the shed earlie, this mornin' to chop some kindling. My deputy was out in that neck of the woods, and I radioed him to get over to the Reiseman's place and take over." He paused, then he added acidly, "Then I called your office. For no good reason I can think of, you decided you had to come along to see."

Luckily, just then the radio under the dashboard buzzed. The sheriff snorted, unhooked the mike, and said, "Yar?"

"Ed? This is Zach. Listen, I got here a couple minutes ago. Tom Reiseman's deader'n that old doornail. There's an axe beside the body, but there ain't no way I can see where it could be an accident. Somebody's clobbered him. Over?"

"All right. I'll be there in a couple minutes," Carson said. He hitched the mike back on the prongs projecting from the radio. He hit the brakes of the county car, turned off the highway onto a graveled section-line road. He said, "Damn it, I was afraid it would be like that."

I waited for him to clarify his statement, but he didn't.

Finally I asked, "What do you mean?"

"Tom Reiseman." The sheriff scowled at the bumpy, muddy road ahead. "He was pretty much of a no-good."

I waited some more. I took off my horn-rimmed glasses and tapped an ear-piece against my front teeth, my way of counting to ten when I'm angry, but darned if I was going to ask the sheriff any more questions. I tried to dredge up from my memory what, if anything, I knew of a family named Reiseman.

I vaguely recalled that a Frank Reiseman had been in high school during the time I was there. And, yes, Frank had an older brother named Tom. I'd never known Tom, except by reputation as one of the county's moonshine-drinking and hell-raising set.

And there was something else, something a friend of mine had mentioned in a letter to me, something about a girl.

Oh yes, Milly Thomas. She'd been planning to marry Frank, and then suddenly she'd married Tom instead. There'd been a bust-up between the brothers.

I forgot my vow not to ask any more questions of the sheriff. "Listen, whatever happened to Frank Reiseman? The younger brother of the murdered man?"

Carson lifted a horny finger from the wheel, pointed at a small white house up ahead and to the left of the road. "That's his place, there. Lives there alone." We passed the little house, which stood on the crest of a gentle ridge. Carson added, "See the old house yonder, down in the valley? That's Tom's place."

I said thoughtfully, "I take it Frank and Tom made up their quarrel, then . . . about Milly."

The sheriff shook his head. "Nope."

I whistled softly. The houses were maybe a mile apart, no more than that. "You think Frank . . . ?"

"I ain't thinking," the sheriff growled.

At the bottom of the ridge we left the road, bumped across a muddy field to the shambling, unpainted house that squatted in a grove of autumn-bare trees. Carson slowed the car to a stop near another county car in the bare front yard before the old house.

We got out and picked our way across the yard. Carson's deputy, Zach Mullins, came from the house to meet us at a corner of the ramshackle front porch.

Mullins shook his head somberly. "Bad, Sheriff. You want to go on around to the back and look at the body before you see the folks inside the house?"

Carson said, "Yar. What do you mean, 'folks'?"

"Well, the wife, Milly. And Frank Reiseman is here. Milly called him, she says, just after she called you. And he got here, he says, just a minute or two before I did. And Milly's paw is in there, old Allen Thomas. He's been livin' here the last few months. He's awful sick, according to Milly. Bad heart. I didn't see him. He's in bed, spends all his time there, and ain't expected to live much longer. Milly's afraid this business will finish him off."

Carson sighed. "Well, Doc Conley will be here pretty soon. He's coming out quick as he can get away from his office."

Indian file, we trooped along the side of the house to the rear. There was a dilapidated shed attached to the back of the house. There was an open doorway in the side of the shed nearest us. Through it I could see a man's body sprawled face down on the earthen floor inside.

"Let's stop right here, a minute," Mullins said. "There's just the two ways into that shed. This door here, and another that opens off the kitchen inside the house. That's all."

Carson was bending forward, peering at the ground around the open doorway. After a moment, he said, "Oh, boy."

"Uh huh. It's plain enough there ain't nobody gone in or out this way. Not since the rains last night, anyhow. Soft as that ground is, a chicken couldn't cross it without leaving tracks . . . and there ain't no tracks."

I said, "There's no other way into the shed, except through the house itself?"

Mullins nodded. "Yep. That's how it is. Milly Reiseman, she admits she ain't been out of the house all morning." He spat on the muddy ground. "Damn. You'd think her and Frank would've done a better job of it. . . ."

"All right," the sheriff said sharply. "We won't go into the shed till Doc Conley gets here. Let's go back around to the front."

In silence we retraced our steps to the front of the house. A cold gray drizzle began to fall from the sodden sky. Thinking about the blood-spattered body lying back there in the shed, I swallowed thickly, and wished again that I was in my warm, comfortable office in Monroe.

Zach Mullins deadpanned, "Say, Mr. Gates, that sure is a purty trench-coat you're wearing. Tailor-made, ain't it? But ain't you afraid you'll get it wet?" I couldn't think of a good answer, so I just scowled at the deputy and let it go at that.

Carson said, "Zach, you head on back to town. Stick around the office."

After the deputy had left, I turned to Carson. I said, "Just like that, huh? You don't ask him what he found, what these people said to him—nothing. Good lord. Is this your idea of a homicide investigation?"

Carson looked up at the sky. He said mildly, "If Zach'd had anything new, he'd have told me." He brought his bleak blue eyes down from the weeping heavens, and focused on me. He started to speak again, but then shook his head, and clumped up the steps to the porch. I followed.

The door opened at once. A dark, heavy-set man stood there glaring at us. His beard-stubbled face glistened with sweat. He was about my age, thirty or so, and wore the usual faded blue-jeans, workshirt, and denim jacket.

"Morning, Frank," the sheriff said, speaking in normal fashion.

Frank Reiseman nodded curtly. He stood back from the door as Carson and I went inside. The large living room we entered was clean enough, but nothing could hide the threadbare shabbiness of the furnishings. A small, plump woman sat on an ancient sofa over near a rough-stone fireplace. As she rose to her feet, swaying slightly, I noticed a dark bruise on her right cheek. Her mousy brown hair was pulled back into a bun at the nape of her neck.

Another time, another place, she might have been pretty.

She wasn't now.

Carson introduced me, and Milly Reiseman vaguely gestured for us to sit down. The sheriff sat beside her on the sofa. I pulled a cane-bottomed chair around facing them. Frank Reiseman put a hip on the arm of the sofa nearest Milly. He looked taut as a bowstring.

There was a lever-action .22 rifle hanging on pegs above the fireplace. I was glad that I was between Reiseman and the rifle, and also glad that the sheriff had on his .45.

For a couple of minutes Carson made small-talk. Milly nodded automatically. Reiseman stared at the far wall. I waited impatiently for the sheriff to get down to business and start asking questions.

Then he said, "Well, Milly, what happened here?"

Reiseman stiffened. Milly shook her head violently. "I don't know, Mr. Carson. I just don't know." She moistened pale lips, blinked unseeingly around the room. "We had breakfast. I took a plate to my Paw—he can't get up anymore, even for meals. After awhile, Tom went out to the shed to chop some wood for the fires—been awful cold and wet the last few days."

"What time was that, Milly?"

"Time? I don't know. Around nine or nine-thirty. I don't know. I was busy straightenin' up the house and all. Then about ten-thirty I wanted to ask Tom to drive into town for some things. I went to the kitchen, and to the back door that opens into the shed. I opened the door, and . . ." She broke off, scrubbed her hands over her face.

Reiseman swore softly, gave me an angry glance.

"She's done told you all this on the phone. And told it again to the deputy. She . . ."

"Let her tell it again, Frank," the sheriff said. "Milly?"

She spoke through her fingers. "I seen . . . I seen Tom there, on the

33

floor of the shed, near the door to the yard. His head was all caved in. Blood spattered."

"Did you go into the shed?" I asked.

"No. No. There wasn't any use. He was dead. Anybody could see that. His head. . . ."

"All right. What did you do then?"

"I don't rightly remember. I think I screamed. And I run into my Paw's room and told him. But he's so sick, I don't think he even knew what I was sayin' right then. And I kind of remember going to the phone and callin' the operator in Monroe, and she. . . ."

"She connected you with my office," Carson finished. "Uh huh." He switched his attention to Frank Reiseman. "How'd you find out about this?"

"Why, Milly called me, right after she'd spoken to you. I came right over. I looked in the shed, then I scouted around the house and the yard a few minutes, thinking whoever had done it might still be hanging around, but I didn't find anything. About then Zach Mullins drove up. That's all."

Carson said mildly, "What made you think Tom'd been killed by somebody? Instead of it being an accident?"

Reiseman gulped and looked even sicker than he had before. "Man don't accidentally smash in the back of his head with an axe, Sheriff. I figure some enemy of Tom's came across the fields and went inside the shed from the back, without Milly seein' him. Plenty of people around the county that didn't like Tom." He paused. He repeated, "Plenty of people."

I wondered who he thought he was trying to kid. I remembered the smooth, wet, untracked earth outside the door to the shed.

I glanced meaningfully at the sheriff. He shrugged his shoulders slightly. He got up, stepped to the fireplace, and casually lifted down the .22 from its pegs. He turned the rifle in his hands, worked the lever. A bright cartridge was ejected. It bounced across the bare wooden floor. Carson ejected six more shells, emptying the rifle's magazine.

"Nice little gun," he said.

Reiseman snorted. "You didn't have to do that. I ain't plannin' to pull down on you, Sheriff. No reason to."

"Course not." But I noticed that Carson didn't reload the rifle before he put it back on the pegs over the fireplace.

I'd had enough of this farce. I rose, walked over to stand above Milly Reiseman. "How'd you get that bruise?"

She quickly raised a small, work-reddened hand to cover her right cheek. "I . . ."

Reiseman broke in. "I'll tell you how she got it. My dear brother knocked her around. He had a habit of doin' that. Ever'time he got drunk, which was about every other day."

"Frank," Milly cried. "Stop it."

Reiseman made a brusque gesture. "I ain't telling anything that ever'body in the county doesn't already know. Tom was a bum. He treated you and your old man like dirt. If you wasn't so stubborn, you'd have left him long ago."

"Stop it, I said." Milly Reiseman was on her feet now. "He was my husband, whatever else he was."

The two glared at each other. Milly Reiseman evidently had more backbone than I had expected.

Reiseman blurted, "I guess you loved him dearly, huh?"

"Loved him?" Milly gave a short laugh. "I hated his insides, but he was still my husband."

The sheriff and I stood back and looked on in silence. They were making my case for me, and very likely buying themselves tickets to the state prison, if not the electric chair. But I felt a bit disappointed. It was so open and shut. There was no challenge to it.

Just then, to my annoyance, Dr. Conley arrived, breaking the spell. Another couple of minutes, and I felt sure we'd have had a confession.

Dr. Conley strode into the house, cocked a bright eye at each of us in turn. His gaze lingered on Milly. "Why don't you sit down and unwind?"

"I'm all right," Milly croaked.

"Ummm," the doctor said dubiously. Then to Carson, "Well?"

"It's at the back of the house, Doc."

Reiseman muttered, "I'll show you," and stalked out of the room into a dim corridor. About halfway, Milly stopped at a closed door and put her hand on the knob.

"I'll stay here with Paw," she said.

There was a soft cough from the room. Milly opened the door. Looking in, I saw a withered old man propped up on pillows on the bed across the sick-smelling room. He was wearing only long-handled grey underwear. There were soiled places on the elbows and knees.

35

Milly hurried to him, exclaiming, "Oh, he's kicked the covers off again." She pulled a quilt up over the scrawny old body.

Dr. Conley followed Milly into the room. He took up one of the old man's toothpick arms, felt for a pulse. He shook his head. He put his black medical bag on the bed, opened it, and delved inside.

The old man's eyes fluttered open. "I've got to . . ."

"You've got to lie back and relax, Mr. Thomas," the doctor said. He placed a capsule between the bluish lips, followed it with a sip of water from a glass on the bedside table. He stood back, watching the old man. He said, "Milly, you stay here with him. He ought to drop off again in a minute."

Then Dr. Conley came back out into the hall. He grimaced. "Really not a damn thing I can do. Damn it."

As we followed Reiseman on along the corridor, I heard again the soft, futile coughing from the bedroom. We reached the kitchen, with its wood-burning stove and iron sink that was complete with an attached pump. Frank Reiseman threw open a door in the back wall. He turned to us, muttered, "In there."

The sheriff, Dr. Conley, and myself went into the shed. Reiseman stood in the doorway. The shed was a dingy, dirt-floored enclosure with cobwebs festooning the corners. There was a jumble of old boxes and discarded furniture. Along one wall was stacked a pile of roughly trimmed tree limbs.

The body lay spread-eagled, face down on the earth, near the door that gave on the back yard. Murky gray light filtered in through the opening, but did little to break up the shadows. A blood-smeared axe lay a couple of feet from the body. After one look I turned away.

Dr. Conley gave a low whistle and dropped to his knees beside the body, bending close to the crushed-in head. After a moment, he said, "Now, that's funny."

Carson, who was examining the dirt floor, looked up. "What's that, doc?"

"Just a minute."

Carson grunted, turned his attention back to the ground. I watched him. He straightened up, looked thoughtfully at a heavy chopping block that stood just inside the door to the yard. Beside the block was a small heap of freshly-split kindling, and a quart jar half full of a clear liquid. I picked my way around the body and the kneeling doctor, and bent to

36

sniff at the open jar. Moonshine whiskey. "Uh huh," the sheriff said. "Looks like he came prepared to spend the mornin'."

"He never took a step without a jug of 'shine with him," Frank Reiseman muttered from the kitchen door.

I put my back against the wall, out of the way, and looked again around the shed. I noticed idly that there was a rusty length of wire stretched across the width of the shed, about seven feet above the ground, with a few dirty rags dangling from it. My eyes dropped down from the wire to the body. Dr. Conley was busily probing with a short metal instrument from his bag. I looked hurriedly away.

Carson came over to stand beside me, watching the doctor. "Well, it's easy enough to figure out what happened here—up to a point," the sheriff mused. He pointed at a deep round depression in the earth near the center of the shed. "That's where the chopping block usually stands, right, Frank? Yes. But this mornin', what with it being so dark, Tom moved the block over here by the door, where he could get more light. You can see the scuff-marks on the ground, where he walked the thing across. Then he split a piece of kindling or two, and probably had himself a snort of 'shine to keep his strength up. He'd laid aside the axe. So he has his drink, facing out toward the yard there, and then he sets down the bottle and straightens up, and then. . . ."

"Then someone lets him have it with the axe," I said. "Fine. Brilliant deduction, Sheriff. All that's about as obscure as the nose on your face."

I pushed away from the wall, turned slowly to face Frank Reiseman. "So why don't you tell us about it, Reiseman? Was that how it happened? You came through the door where you're standing now. Your brother didn't hear you. You came up behind him, picked up the axe, and that was that."

Reiseman just stared at me. "Are you crazy? I wasn't even here."

"No? What're you trying to do—pin it all on Milly? Come on, man. Whoever killed your brother had to come through the house. He couldn't have come in here from the yard. Not unless he flew. Milly admits she was in the house all the time. No one could possibly have passed through without her knowing it. So what's that leave?"

What little color was left in Reiseman's face drained away. His beard-stubble stood out black against his chalk-white face. "You can't mean that."

I walked toward him. "Come on, come on. If it wasn't you, it was Milly.

You or her. Or both of you. That's really how it was, wasn't it? Tom gave her a bad time this morning. When he came out here to the shed, Milly called you. You rushed over. You saw the bruise on her face. You decided you'd had enough. Milly agreed."

"No! No. You're crazy." He started to back into the kitchen.

Carson snapped, "Don't, Frank. Stay right there."

Reiseman stopped. He shook his head helplessly.

"Trying to lay it all on Milly," I said. "What kind of animal are you?"

Reiseman sank down to his knees, still shaking his head and mumbling, "No, no."

From behind us, Dr. Conley said mildly, "I don't think he did this."

I whirled around, glared down at the bandy-legged little doctor. He pursed his lips thoughtfully. "Whoever hit Tom with that axe was several inches shorter than he was. Frank there was as tall as Tom, if not an inch or two taller."

Carson blinked at the doctor. "What're you gettin' at?"

"Simple enough. The wound is in the back of the skull. Not the top where it would be if, say, Frank there had swung the axe. No, no, it just won't do."

I said slowly, "Then it was Milly."

"Oh, for—can you see that little woman coming out here and using an axe to kill her husband?" Carson growled. "Especially when there was a loaded rifle in the living room, ready to hand."

Frankly, I couldn't see it. In fact, I now had to admit to myself that I'd never been quite able to believe that Frank Reiseman had killed his brother. There were too many things wrong with it.

"I guess the man committed suicide," I said.

The doctor shrugged. "Don't see how. Nope."

We stood there, the three of us, glaring at each other. Reiseman came slowly back to the kitchen door. I said doggedly, "It must have been the woman."

Dr. Conley told me, "Even she's too tall. I'd say the murderer was about, oh, four feet, not much more'n that."

I gave up.

Suddenly we heard Milly Reiseman calling frantically from inside the house. We hurred into the kitchen just as she appeared in the mouth of the hallway across the room. "Doc, it's my paw. Come quick. He's . . . I'm afraid he's . . ."

Dr. Conley brushed by her, went along the hall and turned into the old man's room. He said, "Stay here," and shut the door behind him.

Milly turned to Frank Reiseman. She rubbed a palm across her forehead. She looked dazed, uncomprehending. Reiseman hesitated a moment, then he abruptly put his arms around her, and she pressed her face against his chest and began to cry.

Carson and I moved further along the corridor. "About time that happened," Carson muttered, nodding toward the man and woman.

I said bitterly, "What I want to know is who killed Tom Reiseman?"

"I've got a piece of an idea, but. . . ."

The door of old Mr. Thomas' bedroom opened. Dr. Conley poked his head out and said, "Ed? Would you come in a minute? I need your help."

Carson went into the bedroom. The door closed again.

I lit a cigarette and took a deep drag. I needed it. Down the hall, Frank Reiseman was speaking softly to Milly. She had quieted down some. I sighed. What a day.

Carson came out, followed by the doctor. "Milly, it's all over. Your paw's gone. Just now."

"I'm glad," she said gently. "He was so old, and worn out, and tired." She entered the silent bedroom. Reiseman went with her.

Dr. Conley said, "There was just nothing to do, nothing." Impatiently he stalked away. "I'm going to phone for the wagon," he tossed over his shoulder.

"Well," I said. "What do we do now?"

Carson stared into space a moment. Then he shook himself. "We catch ourselves a killer," he said. "Come on."

He led the way back to the dim, shadowy shed. He paid no attention to my questions. In the center of the shed he stopped, put his fists on his hips. "Uh-huh," he said. "That's how it was."

"What?"

He wheeled on me. "Use your eyes, man. Tom moved the chopping block from its usual place to over here by the door. He was half-drunk, judging from the amount left in the jug, so he stumbles around here, swinging that axe around. Don't you see it?"

I blinked at the body, the axe, the chopping block. Either the sheriff was insane or I was. Dr. Conley joined us now. The sheriff pointed a horny finger at him. "Doc. You said the wound was in the back of Tom's head."

"It is."

"All right. Watch, both of you."

Carson bent, picked up the stained axe. He took up a position just beside the body, facing the chopping block. Slowly he swung the axe up and back. At the top of the swing, he paused. Finally I saw what he was getting at.

The wire! The wire that stretched across the shed, a foot or so above the sheriff's head. The shaft of the uplifted axe rested against the wire now.

"Got it?" Carson said. "The first few times Tom missed the wire. But then he started a full, overhead swing. The axe handle hit the wire, and tore itself out of Tom's hands. The axe spun around the wire, and the head of it whacked right into the back of Tom's skull."

Dr. Conley snapped his fingers excitedly. "Yes. That would explain the position of the wound, the uniform depth—yes!"

Carson lowered the axe. He faced me. "Satisfied?"

For a long minute I studied the scene. "Satisfied."

Carson relaxed. "All right. Let's get back to town. Doc? You'll stay here?"

"Yes. Of course. So Tom did commit suicide after all, even if unintentionally."

"You could put it that way," Carson agreed.

A few minutes later, the sheriff and I left. Just before we did, he carefully took down the wire clothes-line, twisted it into a series of loops. "Milly won't be wantin' this around here," he said. When we got to the county car, he tossed the coil of wire into the back seat. "We'll throw it out on the way."

We drove toward town in silence, but not the same kind of silence as during the trip out. We passed the ambulance headed for the Reiseman place.

"Too bad about the old man," Carson said.

"Um," I replied. Another mile passed behind us. Up ahead was the bridge spanning the rain-swollen river. Monroe was four miles north. I lit a cigarette. "That was one nice piece of theorizing you did. Too bad it isn't true."

Carson slowed the car. His shoulders tensed. He kept his eyes on the rainswept road ahead. "What do you mean?"

40

"Oh, hell," I snorted. "Let's have the truth. Like maybe an old man who knows he's dying, an old man who can't stand the thought of leaving his daughter with a drunken bum. So he gets out of bed and crawls on his hands and knees—getting the knees and elbows of his long-handled underwear dirty in the process—crawls from his room, across the kitchen to the shed. The door's open, and he can see the man he hates standing at the end of the shed with his back turned. He sees an axe lying on the ground. He picks it up, raises himself up on his knees, and swings with whatever strength there is left in him. Then he somehow gets back to his bedroom before he collapses, but he's so weak that he can't tell anyone what he's done."

The county car bumped across the bridge. I looked down at the rushing, swirling muddy water below.

Carson said, "Why, that's . . ."

"The truth," I said. "He told you, didn't he, when Doc called you into the bedroom, just before he died?"

"Try to prove it," Carson said bitterly.

I leaned over the seat, picked up the roll of rusty wire from the back seat. I worried the wire between my fingers, then gave it a tug. It snapped easily.

I snapped it again. And again.

"What now?" Carson asked.

I gathered together the pieces of rusty wire, rolled down my window, and tossed them out. The pieces sailed over the bridge-railing, plunked into the river. I rolled the window up again. "I'll be glad to get to town," I said. "Get some hot coffee, and maybe a shot of rye to chase it with."

The sheriff tramped down on the gas pedal. "I'm buying."

The Death Desk

by S. S. Rafferty

I've been bouncing around the newspaper trade for almost thirty years—layman in Buffalo, police beat in Chicago, wire editor in Baton Rouge. I've been in a lot of city rooms and must have filed five tons of copy but, like all reporters, I have one yarn that has never seen the light of print. Some reporters will tell you they didn't print a certain story because they couldn't prove it, even though they knew it to be true. In my case, it wasn't just a lack of proof; I couldn't even figure the damn thing out. Now that I have, it's too late to do anything about it. Even if I could, I wouldn't.

I didn't have to go far to observe the whole thing, because it happened right under my nose in the city room of the *Frankport Post-Union*, up in New England back in the early '30s.

The *Post-Union* was a morning and evening paper with separate editorial staffs for each edition. I worked the night shift on the rewrite desk, which wasn't bad when you considered that Ted McCoy, the managing editor, worked on the day side. Of course the day crew had a large circulation and got all the prestige, but I was too old a newshand to put up with McCoy's testy ways and daily tantrums; but try to explain that to young Bobby Hawks.

Poor Bobby had been slaving on the night obit desk for almost fourteen months and hadn't moved a quad's width toward advancement. Now, all young fellows starting out usually are assigned to write obituaries. It's good training in using the five W's properly and learning the paper's stylebook. However, fourteen months on obits was unheard of—it was cruel and inhuman punishment.

The kid brought it on himself, though. Bobby's problem was not seeded in incompetence; contrarily, he was the best obit man the *Post-Union* had ever had.

His career had been crippled by his own enthusiasm and deferred by his initiative. He was imprisoned, seemingly forever, in a job he performed too willingly, too well.

Even the location of the obit desk, tucked away in a far corner of the city room, symbolized Bobby's isolation from the other men who handled hard, front-page news. In the cynical and sarcastic minds of the night crew, Bobby was a joke. While the rest of us worked from 6 P.M. through 2 A.M., McCoy had assigned Bobby to the "trick shift." All of us knew the "trick" was to stay awake from four in the afternoon till four the next morning. It made little sense to keep the kid there for two hours after the morning paper had been put to bed. Even if a late story came in, Bobby couldn't do much about it anyway, except leave it for the daymen when they came in at seven to work up the afternoon editions.

"You know what that kid's trouble is?" Cal Slocum, a sportswriter, asked one night when we were drinking our dinner break in a "speak" about two blocks from the paper. "He's too naive."

"I don't know, Cal," I said. "I know what you mean—the conscientious thing—but there's something about that young guy that's, well, foreboding. I covered an execution once in Louisiana and the guy had the same kind of ice-blue eyes, the same intentness on the task at hand.".

"Look of the doomed, huh?"

"No, I meant the hangman. Same kind of eyes."

"Probably gets that way from all the undertakers he talks to. You know they send him Christmas presents?"

"Why not, Cal? For the first time in ten years the obits come out with the right ages and addresses—a definite improvement."

"Sure, but McCoy knows that too. The kid's stuck."

Well, if he was stuck, he was making the most of it. A few weeks later, I learned that Bobby had written several articles for a funeral directors' trade journal. I managed to get hold of one and was surprised to learn that he could write rather well. The subject, "The Obituary, Your Best Public Relations Tool," was a little bizarre, but showed crafty inventiveness. I know now just how inventive Bobby really had been.

I decided to play Dutch uncle when Fred Norris, the night editor, came down sick and took a leave of absence. I took over the night slot in the interim, but that didn't allow me to elevate Bobby to straight news. I didn't want McCoy on my neck. I did have a talk with Bobby, however.

"You ought to quit, Bobby," I told him on my way home one night. "Not right away, but make some plans. I know several people who have their own slots on papers around the country. I'll write them and see if they have any openings."

"Thanks just the same, Mr. Bowers, but I've got to make it here. I grew up in this town, I grew up reading this paper. I think it can be better. Thanks anyway, I'll remember this." He looked up from his typewriter, those cold blue eyes staring off somewhere else as if planning a dream.

Three days later I came in to work to find a message waiting from Ted McCoy. I reported to his office a little tremulous and a bit excited. I was thinking that maybe Fred Norris had died and I was getting his job. I should have checked with Bobby. Although Fred wasn't exactly kicking, he was alive, and McCoy was in a rage.

"Did you print this?" he snorted, tossing the morning edition's obituary page onto the desk in front of me. I read it quickly:

MRS. JAMES BERNOIT

Mrs. Mary Bernoit, 70, wife of James Bernoit of 215 Spring Street, died last night in St. Helena's Hospital. She had been a patient there since March 10. Funeral services will be announced.

I breathed a sigh of relief. Bobby had not let me down. The style and form were correct. "Yes, I edited this."

"Then where the devil is the rest of it, survivors, affiliations? It's half an obit."

"Well, that's all Hawks could get from the hospital."

"The hospital! Didn't he get this from an undertaker?"

"No, sir. You see, Hawks had an idea that we shouldn't wait for an undertaker to give us information. He just calls the hospitals and picks up the latest deaths."

The smile on McCoy's face eased my tension, and for a moment I had a glimpse of hope for Bobby.

"Now that's what I call running an obit desk." McCoy was beaming. "Tell that kid he's doing a great job."

"Well, Mr. McCoy, since you brought it up, don't you think a bit of reward is in order? Maybe I can start breaking him in on the county desk. You know, he really can write."

The grin and the beam went behind a cloud of rumbling anger. "Are you nuts? Are you out of your ever-lovin' mind? I finally have someone on that desk who does a good job, and you want to take him off. For ten years, I've had phone calls from irate families because we'd left out the fact that some joker was a Mason or an Elk or a Grand Exhausted Rooster. I used to get mail canceling subscriptions, but I don't get them anymore, and that's the way it's going to stay. I swear the only thing some people read in this town are the obits."

Well, that was the end of that, and I urged Bobby again to take my offer of looking around for him. He refused.

We started to slip into early winter and with it, the specter of influenza. Bobby was busy from the moment he set foot in the city room until I put the paper to bed. During that time, he had published another article for an undertakers' trade journal: "The Chig Beetle, Nature's Undertaker." It would never be confused with dynamic journalism, but it did show an ability to make a story out of nothing—absolutely nothing.

In a sense, this seemed to be Bobby's long suit. He could work within rigid confinements and still succeed. I have always admired people who can whip something up out of the materials at hand, like an inventive short-order cook. The only problem was that short-order cooks never become great chefs, nor do hack writers become great editors, even if they do sign their work "R. Southgate Hawks."

By midwinter, I thought I noticed a change in Bobby. At first, I analyzed it as occupational ennui, because he spoke very little and went about his business mechanically. Yet it was more than psychological.

"It's his stupid getup," Cal Slocum said, laughing at my lack of observation. "You're so busy you haven't noticed it. The dark suit, the black tie and piped vest. Do you know he wears a homburg on the street?"

"So the kid's conservative."

"The boob is dressing like a mortician, and he gives me the creeps. Have you talked to him lately? He gives you this low, soft monotone, like he's very sorry for everything. You ought to have a talk with him."

I never got the chance. At ten the next morning, I was roused from sleep by McCoy's telephone snarl. "Get down here!" I got down there.

Ted McCoy was more confused than angry when he handed me the typed copy:

CHARLES DONOVAN

Charles Donovan, 67, of 75 Cottonwood Road, a retired railway clerk, died at 8:15 this morning in St. Luke's Hospital after a long illness. He is survived by his wife, the former Mary Herrig, and a son, George. Funeral arrangements will be announced.

"Well?" I asked him.

"Well? What do you mean 'well'? We found this in the hold-over copy box this morning. Everyone thought it missed yesterday's afternoon edition, but when a rewrite man finally got through to the hospital at 9:30, we found out that Donovan had died *this* morning—an hour and a half ago. How could Hawks write an obit at 4 A.M. about a man who didn't die until five hours later?"

I told him I didn't know and he told me to "get Hawks the hell down here."

I called and he got the hell down there.

"Where did you dig up that outfit?" McCoy commented on Bobby's attire in surprise.

"I'm sorry, sir, but on my salary, it's about the best I can do."

"Looks like you're going to bury someone." He said it offhand and then caught himself. He checked his pause and picked up the Donovan announcement.

"Would you mind explaining this, Hawks? Where did you get this information?"

"From a Mr. Demos. Nick Demos, I think he said. I assumed it was the Demos Funeral Home."

"To my knowledge, Hawks, there is no Demos Funeral Home in this entire city."

"Maybe it was from the suburbs, sir. Is there anything wrong? Is the copy incorrect?"

"Oh, it's correct, all right. Charles Donovan died this morning at 8:15, hours after this copy was written—that's what's wrong."

"I'm sorry about the error, sir. Mr. Demos said at 8:12. I took an editorial liberty and rounded it out."

"I'm not talking about a three-minute error, you idiot. I'm talking about a story written before the man died. What are you, a clairvoyant or something?"

"No, sir, at least not to my knowledge. I simply answered the phone and took down the facts. I'm pleased they were right, sir."

McCoy looked at him with confusion and then dismissed him after telling him to take his dumb homburg off in the office.

At least three weeks had passed when McCoy again summoned Bobby and myself from slumber.

"Hawks," he said, holding up another piece of copy paper, the one Bobby had put in the "hold" box earlier that morning, "this is insane. How in the world could you have known that R. J. Riggs was going to die this afternoon and write an obit ahead of time?"

"You have every reason to be angry, Mr. McCoy. I know the guidebook is quite explicit about getting the time of death right, but Mr. Demos wasn't quite sure and it was very late. I'll watch it in the future."

"Watch it, my foot. I'll tell you something, Hawks. After the Donovan obit, I had a reporter check with the State Licensing Bureau. There is no mortician practicing under the name of Demos. In fact, there is no Nick Demos listed in the city directory or the phone book or voter registration lists or anywhere else. What does this guy say when he calls?"

"Well, Mr. McCoy, it's hard to say. After working eleven or twelve hours a day, I get kind of fuzzy. When the phone rings, and I answer it, there isn't anyone on the line right away. There's a lot of electrical sounds, clicks and things, like a connection is being made. Then Mr. Demos comes on and says, 'I have one for you, my boy.' I'll tell you, Mr. McCoy, he has the deepest voice I've ever heard, and yet it's quite soothing. Well, then he just gives me the dope and I type it up. He doesn't say anything else, except, 'I'll be speaking with you again.' "

McCoy sent him back to work, and the next day had the phone at Bobby's desk changed to a new extension number. During the rest of the winter, Bobby placed three predeath obits in the hold box, but there were no more conferences with McCoy. The rumors spread throughout the building, and before spring not one soul would go within five feet of his desk. Lou, the counterman at the Diamond Luncheonette, asked him to please let him send the coffee up gratis rather than drink it in the restaurant. He continued to wear his mortician's outfit, with the addition of spats and a red carnation in his lapel.

By mid-June, Bobby's isolation was tantamount to Coventry. Then it happened. McCoy didn't call us in the morning this time. He was waiting for me when I came to work.

"Get Hawks and come to my office," he said in an agitated tone that was far from anger. Ted McCoy was visibly nervous. When we showed up at his office door, he motioned us in. His face was drawn and ashen, his words thick and slippery.

"Hawks," he said, taking a paper from his pocket, "when did this come in?"

Bobby looked at the copy:

(Date to come)

THEOPOLIS MACOPOLIS

Theopolis Macopolis, 56, . . .

"I should have tossed this away, sir. It was careless of me. I know you like desks kept neat."

"Don't play games with me, Hawks This was found on your desk this morning. What did Mr. Demos say?"

"Well, he came on and said, 'I have another one for you. His name is Theopolis Macopolis,' and then something happened to the connection and the line went dead. I just put in 'date to come' in case he called back when I wasn't here."

"Do you know who Theopolis Macopolis is?"

"No, sir, I don't. Sounds Greek."

McCoy lowered his head solemnly. "Hawks, I am Theopolis Macopolis."

"But, sir, your name is Ted McCoy, or Theodore McCoy."

"I changed it years ago. There isn't a soul in this world, not even my wife, who knows my real name. Heaven help me, Hawks, didn't he say anything else? Mr. Demos, I mean."

"Not another word, except—"

"Except what? Look, son, you can tell me. I'm a pretty tough guy after thirty years in this business. I can take it, son."

"Well, he said, er . . . that the party was 56 years of age."

"And I'm 56. He didn't say anything about next Tuesday, did he? I'm supposed to fly to Chicago next Tuesday. No, he wouldn't do that, would he? He only tells you hours in advance, doesn't he?" He tugged his tie open and unbuttoned the neck of his shirt.

"Well, sir, Mr. McCoy, sir, I can see that this has upset you and I'm sorry. Now, he did say he was going to call back, didn't he? Maybe he will tonight."

McCoy winced at the word "tonight."

"Now that I really think of it, Mr. McCoy, it couldn't be you," Bobby went on.

"How do you know that, son?"

"Because if it were a person of your importance, he would have called the city desk, not me. It stands to reason that—"

McCoy gave us a weak smile. "That's right. No, wait a minute. There was no one here except you when the call came in. He had to talk to you, he always talks to you. Look, I don't want you here tonight. Take it off. In fact, you're starting on the day crew tomorrow morning. I need an assistant anyway, and you might as well learn from the best. Now go home and take it easy. And stop wearing those dumb clothes. Go down to the cashier now and draw an advance on your new salary. I'll call them."

Well, if Bobby's stock went up, mine went down. Fred Norris recovered and came back as night editor, so I called a few friends around the business and finally landed a Sunday feature writer's berth with a Jersey paper. I continued to follow Bobby's career via the "People and Places" column in *Printer's Ink*, and I have to admit I envied him. In his first year under McCoy's tutelage, he became the youngest city editor in the country. Then there was the Pulitzer for "best makeup" and, two years later, "best reporting under a deadline." That was followed by the announcement that R. Southgate Hawks, on the death of Ted McCoy, had been made managing editor of the *Frankport Post-Union* and a director of its parent, the Post Communications Company.

I was telling a fellow scribe named Todd about Bobby's meteoric rise in journalism one Saturday night when we were waiting for the final page proofs to come up from Composing.

"It was a trick, plain and simple," Todd said. "He probably got McCoy's real name from his birth record. You can change your name, but the records remain the same."

"Oh, I figured it that way too. But how do you explain predicting the time of death?"

"Luck."

"Five times? And a couple of them almost to the minute?"

"Wait a minute. Who did obits on the day side?"

I thought about it for a few minutes. "A girl. College kid. Carol something."

"And she came in earlier than the rest of the day crew, right? So they dream up a scheme. She gets the deaths after they occur and she puts the copy in the holdover box rather than sending it through the city desk."

"That's possible. I never thought of that."

"And I'll go you one better. I'll bet this Carol is either sitting in a top job at the *Post-Union* right now or she's married to R. Southgate Hawks."

It was a good theory, but it didn't hold water when I finally got back to Frankport. One thing I can say for Bobby, he always keeps a promise. Back when I told him I would try to get him a job on another paper, he said, "I'll remember this," and he did. He sent me a letter offering the night editorship and a healthy raise. I jumped at it.

I was on the old job for two weeks and was surprised to see so many new faces in the city room. In fact, none of the old night hands were still there. Bobby had made the paper into a dynamic news machine that kept me busy and happy.

In the old days under McCoy, editors and subeditors were serfs. However, Bobby's regime gave us new status. We were even invited to a Christmas reception at the Hawks home, and I looked forward to it because I hadn't seen Bobby since I arrived. He now lived in a rarefied atmosphere of mergers with other papers and the management of three radio stations in the state.

I drove out to the Christmas reception with Millie Hogan, editor of the women's page. She had been lured away from a New York sheet and considered our boss in the same category as gods and saints. I gave a low whistle as we turned into the long drive that arced in front of the Hawks' Tudor mansion. "He's come a long way from the obit desk," I said.

"Who?" Millie looked confused. "Mr. Hawks? R. Southgate Hawks actually worked the obit desk?"

"Not only worked it, he lived at it for fourteen months. And I was the guy who was going to get *him* a new job."

"You'll have to tell me about that," Millie said as I turned the car over to a parking attendant and we entered the main hall of the house.

The reception line was moving slowly, and I had a chance to get a good look at him. Seven years hadn't changed him much. He was more mature and expensively dressed, but he still exuded that same intent manner, that inner ability to make do with the things at hand. The short-order cook had indeed become a master chef.

Millie whispered that the woman to Bobby's right was his wife.

"Hey, is her name Carol?"

"No, Martha."

Well, that exploded that theory. Mrs. Hawks wasn't the type of woman you would expect a rising media czar to marry. She was a plain woman, in dress and in features. There was a sense of calm control about her, and when I shook her hand, I was impressed by its firmness. Bobby, or rather Mr. Hawks, asked me how things were going on the night side.

"Well, it's a lot different than the old days," I said jokingly, but he didn't laugh.

Once through the line, I joined Millie at the eggnog bowl.

"What did you say to Mr. Hawks?" she asked me between sips. "He looked a little angry."

I mumbled an "I don't know" but I had an idea. "Martha Hawks looks a little out of place, doesn't she?"

"It's got to be true love, let me tell you. I'm relatively new in town, but they tell me that he gave up a passel of beauties when the late Mr. McCoy made him city editor. He was considered 'the catch' in this town."

"Did she ever work on the paper? I don't remember her."

"No, I did an interview with her last year. Nothing extraordinary. Born upstate and came here about ten years ago. She was a nurse at St. Luke's for a time."

I have never brought up Bobby's tenure on the obit desk to anyone again. I like my job. As for how they did it, I have convinced myself that she simply asked doctors the prognosis on terminal cases and then took a rough, professional calculation on the time of death. Of course, there is the alternative which I won't allow myself to think about.

Yet every Christmas, when I go to that reception and shake hands with Mrs. Hawks, the awesome thought creeps into my mind. Those strong fingers, cold and firm, the arms lean and sinewy . . . a pillow . . . a weakened, terminal patient . . . I always dismiss the idea immediately. That is, until I shake hands with R. Southgate Hawks and look into those determined blue eyes—the eyes of a man who can make the most of a limited situation.

The Room at the End of the Hall

by Helen Nielsen

You must begin by accepting the premise that there really are spirits. David Cabell hadn't reached that state of mind when he took on the job of night clerk at the old Reardon Hotel, but he was of a sensitive and romantic nature and, therefore, capable of learning. Calvin Wyatt, to the contrary, was a cynic, and that was his downfall. Others, like Ara, the full-blooded Apache, who was the head maid at the hotel, never questioned the rumors of ghostly visitors who had long frequented the north wing of the third, and top, floor of the old building. On the night the two coeds from Tucson evacuated a room in panic, she accepted the situation like the stoic she was.

"It's always risky renting rooms in that wing," she said. "Especially this time of year."

The time she referred to was Pioneer Week, an annual promotion of the local Chamber of Commerce, planned to double the tourist trade with every lure from dancing in the town square to the rodeo and quarter-horse races at the fairgrounds. For the greater part of the year the Reardon Hotel, an establishment of sixty rooms, twenty baths, and the second-floor shower (where cowboys still came on a Saturday afternoon to pay one dollar for wash-up privileges before going out on the town), was the home of about twenty-five pensioners taking advantage of the low monthly rates, and a dozen or so students at the local junior college who were equally attracted by the economy factor. Occasionally a scholar of Americana, aware that the Reardon was one of the oldest big hotels in the territory, would check in long enough to imbibe an atmosphere unspoiled by commercialism. The management was frugal. Safety and health standards were meticulously observed, but modernization had ceased with the installation of electricity and plumbing fixtures of the Taft era. There was no air-conditioning, no swimming pool and no room service. The one elevator was a collector's item; even the blotter on the registration desk was bordered with advertisements of stable and harness shops long defunct. It was what the younger residents called a real funky place. The oldsters merely watched the television in the lobby and waited for time to pass.

David Cabell wasn't a student, although the black-rimmed glasses he wore for nearsightedness gave him a scholarly appearance. He was twenty-two years old, recently home from Vietnam, and had taken the low-paying job as an interim occupation while awaiting admission to the University of Arizona. During the first week of his employment he discovered, in a small storeroom behind the office, several dust-covered boxes containing the yellowed sheets of old registration books dating back to territorial days. An imaginative mind could conjure up an exciting past for the old relic of a hotel and lighten the ennui of a long night's desk duty, broken only by a routine hall check every two hours.

There were two floors to check above the first floor, which consisted of the lobby, office, storerooms and a small independently operated cafe that had once been a saloon. For the most part this check consisted of searching the hall baths, the shower and any unlocked room for derelicts who sometimes came in through the fire-escape doors which must, by law, remain unlocked. Also, fire hoses were sometimes pulled off the mountings (an undergrad's macabre sense of humor), and a keen nose was required to sniff out smoke from any guest who might have dozed off while smoking a cigarette. The second floor check was routine, but even from the first night David sensed something strange about the north wing of the third floor. It wasn't the lighting, which was as garish as that of the other floors. It couldn't have been the sound of his footsteps—the shabby carpeting was identical throughout the building—but there were sounds. It might have been that the elevator groaned more when straining up to the higher level, and that the wind rattled the iron fire escapes more at that height.

After the first few nights it might even have been his imagination, stimulated by what he had learned from the old records. The north section of the hotel was the original building, and the third floor had been the deluxe section where men with important appendages to their names—"Senator," "Judge," "Doctor" or "Colonel"—had left their signatures upon the registration books. According to the floor plan, there were four suites with baths and four singles with lavatories on this corridor. The two best rooms, 327 and 329, had doors opening onto an open balcony

53

where the city and mountain views were unsurpassed by any other rooms in the hotel. It was strange, therefore, that only one of the permanent guests lived in the north wing, and even stranger that, according to the records, no transient had been booked into a room in this corridor in almost a decade. It was as if the area were off limits for everyone except the one resident guest, whom David never saw, a Miss Melanie O'Farrell.

That was prior to Pioneer Week when the new manager, Charles Gerber, a hard-nosed businessman, lifted the unwritten ban on the north wing and put the two coeds from Tucson into room 328.

"I've checked it out with the other hotels," Gerber said. "Every year they turn away people that we could have for the taking. I'm not going to sit here with seven vacancies because of some old superstition that a ghost walks in the north wing. Just keep an eye on those fire doors, David. Keep out the hippies and we'll have no night visitors."

In retrospect, it seemed to David that Ara disapproved the policy change but, like all of her race, was loathe to show emotion before the White Eyes. Perfectly disciplined, the Apache conducted herself with the dignity of a lady whose homeland had fallen into the hands of a hostile power which she serenely knew would one day self-destruct.

David took a key from the row of pigeonhole boxes on the wall behind the desk and handed it to Ara—who promptly handed it back.

"This is for room 329," she said. "That room can't be rented."

David examined the key and saw his error. He replaced it with the key to 328, but Ara's comment aroused Gerber's attention.

"Why can't we rent 329?" he demanded.

"Because it's reserved for Miss O'Farrell," Ara said.

Gerber checked the board where all rooms and prices were listed. There were blue tags for monthly residents, pink tags for weekly residents and white tags for the day rates. There was no tag for 329—merely a notation: Do Not Rent This Room. Gerber pulled the blue tag for 327. "Melanie O'Farrell," he read aloud, "double with bath. Oh, I see, O'Farrell has a suite."

"No suite," Ara insisted. "She's holding one room."

"Holding? How long has she been holding it?"

Ara shrugged. "I don't know. I've only worked here fifteen years. Miss O'Farrell was here when I came. She lives in 327. Once a week I change the linens in 329, but it's never used. 'I'm holding it,' she says."

Gerber studied the plan and shook his head in disbelief. "It's the best room on the wing. Well, as long as she's paying for it, I guess she can hold it as long as she wants. Make up 328 for the college girls. Fifteen years! David, there really are some kooks in this hotel!"

Gerber was right about that. The permanents included every phase of near-senility, from the quaintly fey to Major Randolph whose night dreams sometimes exploded into wild battle cries. In the younger set was one Calvin Wyatt, student, who had traded his sports car for a station wagon because he could keep a full-size bed available at all times behind the front seat. Calvin had splurged on a red silk shirt and boots to wear during Pioneer Week, when anyone caught without some vestige of Western attire could be hustled off to the local jail. He had the room next to the one Gerber reserved for the night clerk, and David knew that plenty of action went on in that room as well as in the station wagon. Husky and swarthy as an Indian, Calvin was attractive to the ladies, and David, who could afford only a string tie and a silver belt buckle for his gesture to local custom, envied him the knack. Another resident was old Mr. Clancy, a retired miner, who still toiled over mysterious maps and brought strange-looking packages to his room, which unnerved some guests lest they be chemicals that might blow up the hotel. Both Clancy and Calvin were within earshot of the desk when Gerber made his decision that dispatched Ara to the north wing. Clancy was at the soft drink machine. He drank at least six bottles every day because, he said, it eased the gas on his stomach. Bottle in hand, he approached the desk as Gerber hurried off to other duties.

"That Ara," he said, shaking his head knowingly, "she knows more than she tells. She knows about Melanie O'Farrell."

Clancy waited until David asked, "What does she know?"

"Well, that she wasn't always called *Miss* O'Farrell, for one thing. She was called a lot of other things—especially by the church ladies on the hill. Melanie—that's what she was called professionally."

"Professionally?" David echoed.

"Melanie had the finest stable of girls west of St. Louis!"

Calvin brightened eagerly. "Do you mean call girls?"

Clancy nodded. "A dying art," he said sadly. "Nowadays, the trade's overrun with scabs. Miss Melanie was a real pro. She started in the cribs. Then, when the fort was enlarged and business got more brisk, she built a house of her own. Finest house in that end of town. You can still see it, but it's a place for roomers now. It's these deterioratin' values. Nothin' is quality anymore. Melanie, now, was quality. She brought out a piana from Chicago and built a stage in the front parlor. Had live entertainers from San Francisco—even New York. You might go so far as to say she was the cultural director of the territory. Leastways, hers was the only house in town that didn't smell of liniment and beans."

"Where did she come from originally?" David asked.

"Don't rightly know. Some used to say Denver, some New Orleans. I figured it was from someplace in the South because that's where Blackman came from."

"Brett Blackman—the outlaw?"

Clancy beamed his appreciation of an attentive audience. "That's right. Melanie was Brett Blackman's girl before she worked the cribs or ran the big house. She was his girl when he and his gang robbed a gold shipment practically off the steps of the Denver mint. Fifty thousand dollars in new twenty-dollar gold pieces, and they would have got clean away if a little rat named Sanders hadn't informed, to save his own hide. The law picked off the gang one by one—there was three of them, includin' Sanders. Finally, a couple of months after the robbery, they got Blackman in an ambush. Shot him right out of the saddle as he was ridin' hell-bent for leather toward this very town. Never did find his share of the gold. Twenty-five thousand dollars and they never found a dollar of it! When Melanie built the house about three years later there was talk that she'd gotten the money, but I figure she made it like anybody makes it—hustlin'." Clancy cackled at his own wit. "That's the only way to make it—hustlin'—one way or the other."

"If she made so much money," Calvin challenged, "where is it now? A rich woman wouldn't live in a dump like this."

Skepticism pained Clancy. "Oh, she made it, all right," he insisted. "Only one thing goes faster than money, son, and that's time. And maybe Melanie don't see the Reardon with the same eyes as you. Maybe she sees it like it was when the carpets were thick and red, and there was a big crystal chandelier hangin' in the lobby. Why, there used to be a big paintin' up in the third floor corridor of a lady wearin' nothin' but a red rose behind her ear! It was a fine place in the old days."

Already, David's imagination was beginning to form pictures of the past glory. "Does Miss O'Farrell ever come out of her room?" he asked.

"Scarcely," Clancy said. "Mostly, she just stays up there with her memories, I reckon. Sends out for her meals. I've even known her to hire a car and go for drives in the country a whole day at a time—but not lately. Guess she's content. Sooner or later, no matter how hot the blood's flowed, a body gets content. Not the mind—the body. Now, David, you better take this old windbag up to his room or I'll talk all night." Clancy belched loudly and placed the empty bottle on a stand beside the dispenser. "Sure relieves the gas," he said.

That was the last night Melanie O'Farrell had the north wing to herself, and the first night David saw the ghost.

It was almost midnight before David made the first hall check. He covered the second floor and then took the grinding old elevator up to the third. Last of all, he approached the north wing. It might have been the result of Clancy's tale, but something made every sound magnified. The air seemed warmer, too—almost balmy—and with a tantalizing scent in the air. Was it magnolias? Orange blossoms? Something muskier, he decided. He found a window and struggled with the catch but it was stuck tight. He reached the corridor leading to Melanie's room just as the bulb in a no-longer elegant ceiling fixture sputtered and burned out. Now the corridor was lighted only by the neon glow of the night sky reflected on the small panes of the balcony door. The light moved as the door opened inward and a woman stepped in through the doorway.

She was small and slender. Folds of sweeping chiffon couldn't conceal the beauty of her body. Her face was shadowed, but the light silvered her hair. She might have been an apparition until, seeing David immobilized at the far end of the corridor, she spoke. "I'm sorry if I frightened you," she said. "I just stepped outside for a moment. I thought I heard someone coming down the street."

Her voice was soft and surprisingly warm. David recovered his equilibrium and said, "There's likely to be a lot of night traffic this week. It's the pioneer celebration."

"Is it really that time again?" There was a touch of weariness in her tone. "That means we'll have that noisy parade. Perhaps those were the horses I heard."

David still hadn't moved.

"Is there something wrong?" she asked.

He had to answer, and he couldn't tell Melanie O'Farrell that he thought she was a ghost.

"The ceiling light burned out," he said.

"I hadn't noticed. You needn't replace it on my account, Mr. Cabell. I'm going straight to bed now."

Fluttering one hand in a gesture of dismissal, Melanie O'Farrell opened the door of 327 and stepped into her room. The door closed and only a teasing fragrance remained outside in the hall. David turned uneasily away.

"Brett Blackman, 1873 to 1906. Believed to have been the son of a prominent Southern family whose fortunes were lost in the War between the States. Blackman had a brief but colorful career as the leader of the Blackman gang which terrorized banks and railroads at the turn of the century."

Calvin read slowly, tracing one finger under the words in the book. Above the words was a faded photograph of a fairly handsome man with a thick black moustache sweeping sorrowfully toward his chin and shaggy black eyebrows balancing the brim of a dark Stetson. David took the book from Calvin's hand and studied the likeness of Brett Blackman more closely. "He looks more sad than mean," he declared.

"But Clancy was right about the Denver mint robbery," Calvin said. "It's all in the book—even the part about nobody ever having recovered Blackman's share of the heist."

"It wasn't called a heist in 1906."

"Don't split hairs. You should appreciate the fact that I am uncharacteristically cracking a book instead of chasing chicks."

It was true that Clancy's gossip had a strange effect on Calvin. Armed with a stack of library books, he invaded David's domain behind the desk the following evening. Each one contained a bit of the legend of Brett Blackman. One had a photograph of a young woman standing on the porch of an impressive Victorian mansion with only the smiling portion of her face visible under the shadow of the roof overhang.

"Well?" Calvin asked.

David squinted at the pictures. "I can't be sure from this. The woman's dressed differently—and she's sixty-five years older than the woman I saw in the hall last night. If I really did see a woman."

"*If* you saw a woman! You told me that you finally saw Melanie O'Farrell last night."

"I guess I did. It was dark and kind of spooky."

"*Spooked*, you mean. You were spooked on old Clancy's story. I've got a theory about the haunt in the north wing—and all the pensioners in the hotel swear by it. I think the whole thing's the work of the Indian maid, Ara."

"Indian medicine?"

"No, I don't believe in Indian spooks any more than any other kind. But I've noticed that the service room, where all the linens and cleaning stuff are kept, is way down in our end of the second floor, and that's about as far from the north wing as you can get. The Apache's no fool. She makes up those stories herself to save all those footsteps going up to clean the rooms."

"You must be sick!" David said.

"Maybe—but there's nothing wrong with my vibrations. Oh, wow, look at that and look at those!"

Calvin snapped the book shut and leered openly as the two coeds, who had checked in earlier in the day, pranced in through the street doorway. They were rigged out for the festivities in the tightest of Western shirts and jeans. One had honey-blonde hair to her shoulders, the other had a cap of brown curls, and both had the latest in rotary mobile power.

"They can haunt my corridor any day," Calvin said. He was all smiles when the girls approached the desk, but it was David who grabbed the key from the box and followed them into the elevator.

"I'm the operator here," he said. "Going up, ladies?" He managed to close the door before Calvin could join them.

"If any of the guests in this hotel bother you," he said, as the elevator ground upward, "let me know."

"I think he was cute," the dark-haired girl said.

"I think the elevator man is cute," remarked the blonde. "What do they call you, elevator man?"

"Mostly 'Hey, you.' "

"I heard someone in the lobby call you David," she told him.

"That was probably Goliath."

With such brilliant repartee, the girls were shrieking with laughter when the elevator reached the third floor. They had spent some time at the old Crystal Palace bar at the square and caught the holiday contagion. Explaining that there was no light in the hall, David offered to walk them to their room but the first floor buzzer began to nag and they produced a pencil-flash to prove they were prepared for minor emergencies. They certainly weren't afraid of the dark, or of anything else within reason.

Ghosts were not within reason.

It was four hours before David saw the girls again. He was making his rounds on the second floor, directly under the stairway to the north wing, when they came screaming down the stairs wearing near-transparent nightwear and panicked expressions. Babbling with fright, they told an eerie tale of someone, or something, that had opened the locked door to their room and stood watching while they slept.

"Something in white!" cried the honey-blonde.

"That smelled of perfume!" the dark one insisted.

By the time Gerber, whose apartment was adjacent to the stairway, reached the scene, doors were opening all along the second-floor corridor. There was no way of getting the girls back to that room and the only room vacant on the lower floor was the one David used. It had no bath—only a lavatory—and was located next to the noisy fire-escape door, but they accepted his offer without question. He gave them the key and went on upstairs with Gerber to inspect the hastily vacated room. They had left the lights blazing but all was quiet. Gerber tried the key in their door. It had been years since these locks were used and Gerber's grip was strong. There was the sound of breaking metal and a piece of the lock clattered to the floor.

"I'll get a locksmith up here tomorrow," Gerber said. "You can see for yourself, there's nothing wrong with this room. Nightmares—that's all it was."

"There were two of them," David protested.

"At that age, nightmares are contagious," Gerber said. "I'll take their suitcases down. You finish your hall check."

David stepped out onto the balcony from which Melanie O'Farrell had come the previous evening. It was four feet wide and had a wooden railing extending its full length. Three doors opened onto the balcony—the one from 327, the one to the hall through which Melanie O'Farrell had come the previous night, and the one leading to the long-reserved 329. Draped from inside, no light showed at the third door. He tried the knob and found the hardware so rusted from disuse that the knob wouldn't turn. Retracing his steps, David locked the balcony door, then stepped back into the hall, closing the door behind him. There was no light at the transom of Miss O'Farrell's room, which seemed strange after all the noise the girls had made in exiting. There was no light at all except from the balcony door. The air seemed heavier in the hall. A great flush of warmth came over him, and then he could smell the perfume again—strong and musky. Compulsively, he ran back to the lighted corridor at the head of the stairway. There he paused as the sound of laughter welled up from the darkness behind him—a woman's laughter, low and teasing—but it was the sound of the spirited tinkling of a piano that sent him racing down the stairs.

David made no more hall checks that night. He sat it out with his chair backed against the key boxes and his eyes fixed on the brightly-lighted lobby. He watched three old films on the television set, and was engrossed with the test pattern when his relief came on duty.

Off duty, he went to sleep on a couch in the storeroom. It was mid-morning when he awakened. Because the storeroom had no windows, the door had been left open into the office, and whoever was on duty must have taken someone up in the elevator because there was no one at the desk. Something like a shadow standing before the reservation board caught David's eye. He stepped to the doorway and the shadow turned quickly. It was a woman in full Pioneer Week regalia: dressed all in black, tight bodice, long flowing skirt and a wide black hat. Tiny, black-gloved hands grasped the long handle of a black parasol that was used as a cane. The body could have been that of a girl, but the hair piled high under the hat was silvery-white, and the still lovely face was webbed with lines. The sable-brown eyes still sparkled with vitality. Embarrassed at being caught on the wrong side of the desk, she edged toward the key box on the opposite wall.

"I thought I saw something in my box," she said, "and there was no one behind the desk."

The voice was that of the woman David had encountered in the third-wing corridor—Melanie O'Farrell. It could be no other.

"I didn't mean to frighten you," David said. "I was asleep in the store-room. Did you hear the noise in the hall outside your room last night?"

He watched her face for reaction. She cleverly turned her head. "No," she answered. "I heard nothing last night. I took a sleeping pill before I went to bed."

"The guests across the hall from you thought someone broke into their room. They were terrified."

"I shouldn't wonder. Well, since there's no mail, Mr. Cabell, I shall go for my annual promenade around the square and see what nonsense the city fathers have come up with this year." A fey smile played at the corners of her generous mouth. Still using the parasol as a cane, she stepped forward smartly. "If I don't break my neck on these fool heels," she added ruefully. "I only wear them during Pioneer Week. At least they're authentic."

"You look lovely, Miss O'Farrell," David said.

She dazzled him with a full smile that wiped fifty years from her face, and swept magnificently across the lobby.

Later, David met Calvin in the coffee shop and told him of his meeting with Melanie O'Farrell. "She's beautiful!" he said. "You wouldn't believe a lady who must be eighty, at least, could be so beautiful. And I mean *lady*. She can't be the Melanie in the book."

"Why not?" Calvin challenged. "Nobody said Melanie wasn't a lady. You heard what Clancy said—she brought culture to the town."

"Did you hear about the girls moving out of 328 last night?"

Calvin grinned over his coffee cup. "Every weird detail—and it's great! They're next door to me now. And don't accuse me of spooking them last night, even if it does sound like a fun idea."

"We can't blame Ara. She wasn't even in the hotel."

Calvin grew thoughtful. "That's right, she wasn't. Maybe it was old Clancy."

"Motivation?"

"At that age, who needs motivation? Anything to break the monotony. Besides, the girls could have been dropping pills and had a bummer."

"Maybe."

"You're really bugged about that north wing, aren't you?"

"Forget it," David said.

"Okay, I'll change the subject. I found another book on Blackman and it tells what happened to the stoolie who sold out to the law. Three years after Blackman's death, Sanders was found dead in a Nogales hotel with a .22 slug in his forehead. That's a woman's gun."

"Gamblers used them. They were called sleeve guns."

"But look at the possibilities! Sanders caused Blackman's death, and Melanie was Blackman's girl. The gold disappears. Melanie works in the cribs—figuring Sanders will turn up someday. Through the grapevine, every strata of society has one, she learns where he is and hits the trail. Sanders dies. Melanie builds a big house."

David cried, "Now you're making out she's a murderess! How venal can you get?"

Calvin sipped his coffee thoughtfully. "Life," he said, "is very venal. Anyway, for your sake, because you're obviously a romantic soul, let's say she killed him for revenge and built the house with the crib profits. That still leaves $25,000 in twenty-dollar gold pieces unaccounted for. Do you realize what they would be worth today? Many times the value!"

"Calvin," David said, "forget about the gold. That was sixty-five years ago."

True to Gerber's expectations, the old hotel was filled to capacity by noon. When the Grand Parade started at two o'clock, Major Randolph appeared in full uniform to ride with the cavalry veterans, and Mr. Clancy, in miner's garb, marched with a pack mule laden with chilled drinks, drinking and belching all the way.

Caught up in the spirit of the celebration, David never did finish his sleep. Once he caught a glimpse of Calvin carrying a six-pack of beer into the coeds' room. He still had the book in his pocket but it was obvious that he was imbibing more freely of the beer.

David snatched his evening meal from a vendor at the park, where the marching bands had been replaced with an electric rock group and people of all ages were dancing in the street. When it was time for his shift to begin, he returned to the hotel and was surprised to find Miss O'Farrell standing at the same place behind the registration desk where he had found her earlier in the day.

"Miss O'Farrell," he scolded gently, "there's no mail until tomorrow."

Startled, she grasped the desk top for support. "Oh, I must be confused," she said. "It's been a long day. I'm a little tired."

He offered to take her up to her room, and she accepted eagerly. Once the elevator was in motion, she seemed to regain vitality.

"There was a gallant Captain Cabell stationed at Camp Verde when I was young," she said. "Was he kin of yours?"

"I doubt it, ma'am. My people were teachers, mostly."

"Oh, dear! Still, there is a resemblance." She reached out and caressed his cheek with one hand. "The captain wore a fine beard. You would look handsome with a beard, Mr. Cabell. I'm so pleased that men are wearing them again. There's nothing more pleasing to the eye than a splendid young man with a beard."

David was on the verge of asking her if she really was the Melanie of Calvin's books, but the elevator reached the third floor, the doors opened, and Miss O'Farrell, as if rejuvenated, stepped out smartly before he could even offer his arm in support. When the tip of the closed parasol caught in the worn carpet, she pouted.

"It was so much nicer when the carpets were red," she said, "and when there were gay paintings on the walls. It's all so shabby now."

Then the illusion took over. Before David's eyes, Melanie O'Farrell was young again. Her hair was black, her eyes were flashing and the long skirts swished invitingly as she pranced down the red-carpeted corridor toward her room. From the wide staircase came the laughter of women and their gentlemen of the evening as they eagerly mounted the stairs to the north wing. The mystery was no longer a mystery. Carriages from Melanie's house must have brought her most talented girls to entertain the powerful men of the territory. The scent of their mingled perfumes filled the suddenly warm air, and from somewhere came the sound of a piano. It was as if David had penetrated a shim into the far side of time, and the strangest thing was how very natural it all seemed.

He returned to the lobby and spent the next few hours taking guests up to their rooms. He told no one of what he had seen.

It was many hours later, after the lobby was empty and David was making himself a cup of coffee in the office percolator, that he became aware of a man standing in front of the desk. He was at least six feet tall. His eyes were shadowed by the wide brim of a dusty black hat, but a black moustache accentuated the long line of his face, and sideburns reached almost to the edge of his collar. He wore frontier dress: a long black coat, string tie and a brocade vest. For all his size, he gave the impression of great weariness. Placing a small package wrapped in brown paper on top of the desk, he began to drum the counter with gloved fingers.

"I'm sorry," David said, "we don't have a vacant room tonight."

"I have a reservation," the man insisted. "B. Black of Denver—"

"I don't see how that's possible."

"Well, look, sonny. Look."

It was impossible not to obey. David searched the reservation board, where every room was tagged, and noticed a white slip showing at room 329. On it was written: B. Black.

"Oh, no," David groaned. "Gerber couldn't have sold that room!"

The man didn't wait for confirmation. He had already stepped into the elevator. It was irregular, but he could register in the morning. Catching sight of the package on the desk, David scooped it up on his way into the elevator. "You were forgetting your package," he said.

Black grabbed the parcel. "That wouldn't do. It's for my wife." He opened his coat to take a coin from his pocket and David noticed that he wore a pair of long-barreled pistols in a black leather gun belt strapped around his hips.

"Hey, those are beauties!" he said. "Peacemakers, aren't they? They sure do make realistic replicas of those old guns!"

Black closed his coat and dropped the coin into David's hand as the elevator doors opened at the third floor.

"I'm obliged," he said.

"Your room is at the very end of the corridor—"

"I know where my room is, sonny."

As Black stalked down the corridor, David realized that he wore high Texas-style boots and drop-shank spurs that made no sound when he walked. Before he could try to understand this, the elevator buzzer drew his attention to the indicator. He was wanted on the second floor. He closed the doors and started down.

Gerber waited at the second level, bouncing with anger. "I told you to watch that fire door!" he screamed. "Do you know what those girls in your room are doing? Every young buck in town's been traipsing in and out of that room! They've got beer and reefers and different-colored pills. I've called the police."

In the hall behind Gerber, doors were opening one by one. He stopped shouting and hustled David back to the room next to the fire escape where the girls, one dazed and one nearly hysterical, were being comforted by three young men.

"It was Calvin Wyatt's fault," the noisy one sobbed. "We were having a nice little party—everybody cool—and then Calvin dropped something that made him wild. He jumped up and yelled: 'I've got it! I know why that old lady spooks the north wing! She's got the gold in that room!' "

"Calvin said that?" David asked.

"That's what he said. Then he couldn't get the door open—it was stuck—so he kicked it open and ran out, yelling something about the spooks protecting all that gold. He's crazy, man!"

"Where is he now?"

"Who knows? The last we saw of him he was climbing up the fire escape to the roof!"

"Oh, no!" David groaned. "He can't go into that room now!"

He shoved Gerber aside and ran back to the elevator. The first floor buzzer was signaling—probably the police—but he had no time for them. Calvin was high and on his way over the roof to drop down on the balcony outside room 329, and the room was occupied. David ran the elevator up to the third floor and was racing toward the north wing when the sound of a gunshot exploded from somewhere in the front of the building. He stopped, listening. There was no further sound but, suddenly, the corridor that had once been warm and fragrant became dark and chill. He walked slowly to the balcony door and opened it. It was there that he found Calvin Wyatt's body.

He had fallen back against the stucco wall, his legs spread-eagled and a look of stark terror in his eyes. One hand clutched at the front of his shirt. David knelt beside the body and pulled the hand away. There was a round hole burned through the shirting, but there was no blood. The doctor who arrived later explained that Calvin had died of a heart attack. The pills, the sprint up the fire escape and over the roof, the drop down to the balcony, any one of these, he claimed, could have killed him. Guests in the room vacated by the girls admitted to hearing someone on the balcony, but denied hearing a gunshot. What David heard was shrugged off as an auto backfiring in the street.

A cigarette stub found on the balcony accounted for the burned hole on Calvin's shirt.

Only David knew otherwise. During the excitement that followed the discovery of Calvin's body, two doors remained closed: the doors leading to Melanie O'Farrell's room and the room reserved for B. Black. It was daylight before the balcony was cleared and David could make his own search.

He found no bullet hole or shell casing, but there were chips of paint at the threshold of the balcony door that led into room 329, and the knob that had been rusted shut turned easily in David's hand. He opened the door and stepped inside the long-unused room. The draperies were drawn but daylight from the balcony doorway was enough to show that someone was in the bed.

"It's all right to go in now," Ara remarked at his shoulder.

She had come silently with fresh linens on her arm. She brushed past David and opened the draperies, and they could see then that it was Melanie O'Farrell in the bed. A gentle smile softened her face and one arm was thrown out across the empty space beside her as if in a loving embrace. David felt for her pulse. She was dead. There was something more. The sheet on the empty side of the bed was wrinkled, as if it had been recently occupied, and the pillow still bore an indentation from the weight of a head. David picked up one long black hair from the pillow.

He telephoned the desk from Miss O'Farrell's room, and there he found the brown wrapping paper in a wastebasket and the bottle of perfume on the dresser. The musky scent was everywhere. When he returned to the other room, Ara had smoothed out the sheets and was putting a fresh case on the pillow.

"It will be all right to rent these rooms now," she said.

Nobody thought it strange that Melanie O'Farrell had died in her sleep. She was a very old lady, and if she chose not to die in her own bed that was her business. Some would say that she had reserved the room all these years for that purpose. David told no one about her visitor. There was no registration card for B. Black, and he knew that it was Melanie, not Gerber, who had placed the reservation slip in 329. Everything fell into place when he searched the old registration books for the night Brett Blackman was killed. Two rooms had been reserved for Mr. and Mrs. B. Black of Denver. The rooms were 327 and 329. Mrs. Black's signature was on the registry—Mr. Black never checked in.

No gold was found in either of Melanie O'Farrell's rooms; but David, who was learning to keep silent about some things, like Ara, could appreciate Calvin's terror when he wrenched open the door to the room at the end of the hall and was met by the blazing Peacemaker in the hand of a gunman who had waited sixty-five years to complete a rendezvous. There are times when even a ghost needs privacy.

Later, David took breakfast in the coffee shop and left a tip for the waitress.

"Hey," she called out as he was leaving, "you've got to be kidding! The service wasn't that good!"

David hastily replaced the coin Black had given him with a quarter. He just wasn't up to explaining how he came by a twenty-dollar gold piece—Denver minting, 1906.

Kisses and Chloroform
by Donald Olson

Birdella Lampkin approved of the neighborhood, admired the house, a truly baronial edifice secluded behind hedges of yew and privet, and couldn't have been more impressed with her prospective employer, a middle-aged gentleman of aristocratic bearing who looked as if he had been swaddled from infancy in the richest of Harris tweeds.

"Permit me to say, Mrs. Lampkin, that your credentials seem quite as impeccable as—ahem—yourself." It was the way he colored slightly as he said this that assured Birdella she was on solid ground; these little expressive nuances were often more eloquent than the spoken word—but then he fingered his lips and looked gravely hesitant. "There's a chance, however, that you might find this case not altogether . . . commonplace? Your patient might prove too heavy a responsibility."

"Mr. Deacon, sir, I've handled more than my share of difficult patients."

One could believe it to look at her; that air of efficiency and professional tenderness did not require a uniform to identify Birdella Lampkin as a Nurse on Duty, and one could picture that full-figured body responding with a minimum of wasted effort to any midnight crisis.

Deacon smiled, yet managed to convey a look of well-bred melancholy at the same time. "My wife Jane—your patient, should you take the case—is physically unimpaired. At present she's in a nursing home, but you're no doubt aware that most of them provide only short-term psychiatric care. My only alternative is to commit her elsewhere. Frankly, Mrs. Lampkin, I haven't the heart for that. I want Jane here, in her own home."

He went on to explain that his wife was tormented by paranoid fantasies, seemed to be living wholly in the past, talked of people he'd never heard of and places he'd never been. "She insists she lives in Seattle, and that she's been kidnapped. Kidnapping is an *idée fixe* which no amount of therapy has succeeded in dislodging. And all her fantasies focus upon me as the archenemy. Her doctor has suggested that if I insist on bringing her home I at least make sure that she doesn't even see me until she has oriented herself to being here. So you see what I meant by a heavy responsibility. You would be the only person Jane would be allowed to see—perhaps for as long as two weeks. Jane will probably look upon you as her jailer—you must be absolutely firm. She may even transfer the antipathy she now feels toward me to you."

Birdella was shrewder than she looked. "I assume, sir, you're actually hoping such a transference will occur?"

He lowered his head. "Frankly, yes."

"The fee you've proposed is more than ample, Mr. Deacon. I'm sure it will compensate for any little discomforts I may have to put up with."

Deacon gave her a look of vast relief. "Jane means everything to me, Mrs. Lampkin. I want her to have the best of care."

Birdella was not surprised that Mr. Deacon found her so eminently satisfactory. She had that combination of brute strength and geniality that were the most persuasive of recommendations for the sort of private-care nursing cases in which she specialized; angels of mercy are all very well in their way, but a few weeks of tussling with a fractious or bedridden patient and most relatives looked at a prospective nurse's muscles more critically than at her tender smile.

It was suggested that she get what she would need in the way of personal effects and report back for duty at ten the following morning, by which time her patient would have been transported from the nursing home.

Birdella was delighted with her accommodations adjoining the suite occupied by her patient, and she felt once more that inevitable tingle of excitement which always accompanied the hope that this would turn out to be the Ideal Situation, that vaguely defined but always yearned for case which would somehow elevate Birdella Lampkin to another and more luxurious plateau of life: a Cinderella complex is not uncommon among women of her tedious profession.

Yes, indeed, this was all very encouraging, and she anticipated a huge catalog of fringe benefits, which included those comforts and conveniences in plain sight, such as the color TV and queen-size bed, as well as certain yet to be discovered emoluments, of both major and minor importance, for Birdella was a resourceful old girl and not above a bit of discreet filching here and there—nothing too noticeable; perhaps a piece of two of really good old sterling tucked away in a dusty sideboard, a bit of antique jewelry or crystal; and she was attuned by now to the wiles and whims of elderly patients so that she was expert at guessing the most popular hiding places for secret caches of money; the undersides of bureau drawers was always a good place to start looking.

Before we condemn Birdella for these shocking aberrations of professional conduct we should remember that private nursing lacks many of the perquisites enjoyed by employees of big corporations; a girl has to look after herself and think about her own old age when, who knows, she might be reduced to as helpless a state as her present patients and become herself the victim of younger predators. So, all things accounted for, Birdella embarked upon her new case with the highest of high hopes, which were not by any means diminished at sight of her patient.

Jane was as bird-frail as Birdella was beast-husky; a scared-looking twirp of a woman and doped to the teeth, too, from the foggy look she gave Birdella.

"Who are *you?*"

"I'm your nurse, dearie. Birdella Lampkin. Call me Bird."

Tears rolled down Jane's cheeks. "Then help me. Please. I don't need a nurse. I need the police. I've been kidnapped. You must help me."

"That's why I'm here, sugarplum. Let's begin by turning that pillow over, shall we, like a good girl?"

"Please! Listen! Where am I?"

"Why, you're in your own home. Tucked safely in your own little beddy. Ain't that nice?"

Frightened blue eyes swarmed over everything in the room with the panic of lost children looking for something they might recognize.

"No, no, no. Not my home. Never been here before. Where's Roddy—and Jennifer?"

Roddy and Jennifer were names Mr. Deacon had alerted Birdella to expect, and so she nodded sympathetically. "Roddy and Jennifer are fine, sugarplum. Roddy and Jennifer are just hunky-dory . . ."

The addled woman shrank back into her pillow. "How can you be so—good heavens!—you must be one of them!"

"Now, you just calm down. Sooner you do, sooner you'll be able to leave your rooms and see your sweet hubby."

"My husband is *dead.*"

"Oh, sugarplum, what a thing to say."

The blue eyes were glittery with tears. "They took me away and kept me drugged for two days. I don't even know what they look like. It's all a nightmare . . . please help me."

Pathetic, Birdella mused, but that was about as far as she would allow her compassion to carry her; emotional involvement, as she always told her younger colleagues, is professional suicide; and for all her whining and weeping, this little sugarplum wasn't going to be any trouble at all. Not like some she'd had—Mr. Braithwaite, for instance. Talk about cuckoo; and old Mrs. Feather and Edna May Murphy. This was going to be a holiday compared with them.

It turned out to be something less than a perfect joy, however, to be in absolute charge of her patient; fine not to be troubled with meddlesome busybody relatives, but also unduly confining. She felt more like a bodyguard than a nurse.

Though constantly solicitous, Deacon was true to his word and never ventured into the patient's room, nor did the household staff, which consisted of a young woman introduced to Birdella as Ruth Van Ness, the housekeeper-cook, and a husky young fellow named Jungquist, the gardener. At least he was supposed to be the gardener although Birdella wondered how he kept his job, considering that he spent most of his time wandering about the premises like a watchdog—sometimes, at night, she suspected he was even watching her. One of the fringe benefits of this household was a well-stocked refrigerator to which, around midnight, Birdella quickly got into the habit of making furtive trips when she thought the others were all asleep. Twice she had run into Jungquist, but all he'd done was give her a surly grin.

It was a curious household, quite different from any in which Birdella had worked, and the most curious thing about it was its air of quiet neglect and gloominess, an air of things deferred and suspended, an air which she assumed was created by that climate of morbidity surrounding most invalids. Deacon, for instance, rarely left the house and seemed to spend most of his time reading, working crossword puzzles, and watching TV—all very much like a relative in a waiting room while surgery is proceeding behind mysterious swinging white doors. He would react with evident pleasure when Birdella, trying to get a feel for the situation, would interrupt these dreary pastimes with a jolly word and smile.

"She's asleep, poor darling," Birdella said, accepting Deacon's invitation to sit down. "You know, I really don't see how it could do her a bit of harm if you were to peek in on her now and then."

A faint wrinkle of concern puckered Deacon's brow.

"I made the doctor a solemn promise. I don't think it would be proper to violate it."

"Oh, I agree. But, goodness, this could go on forever."

He looked at her. "Nothing, my dear Mrs. Lampkin, goes on forever."

There was nothing in his expression to confirm the ambiguity of this remark. "She keeps insisting her husband's dead," she said.

"He is. Her first husband, I mean. Her mind seems to have slipped back to the time before we met. So you see, although it all sounds like madness, there's a curious sort of logic to her behavior."

He went on to explain that Jane's first husband had been extremely rich and it was Deacon's theory that Jane felt somehow guilty for sharing her first husband's wealth with another man. "I suggested this to one of the psychiatrists. He didn't agree at all."

While he spoke, Birdella was reading his face as if it were all small print, designed to conceal some underlying, stupendous fraud. Birdella was very experienced at deciphering such physiognomic small print, but in this case she found Deacon's face almost entirely illegible. She decided there would be no harm in doing a bit of cautious probing, and she asked him if it was only her advertisement in the newspaper that had prompted him to contact her.

He looked surprised. "I'm afraid I don't follow you, my dear."

"Most of my cases, you see, come through personal recommendation. A satisfied relative, you know, is the best advertisement."

"I can't quite agree with you there," he objected. "To me a person's face and manner are the most reliable recommendation."

This sounded like so much baloney to Birdella, who was encouraged to go on and ask about children. Deacon shook his head. "No. Jane and I have no children. Roddy and Jennifer are Jane's children by her first marriage." He looked unusually solemn. "They live in Mexico now."

"So far away. Have they come to see their mother since her—illness?"

Deacon studied his hands. "Er—no. I regret to say there's been a slight coolness between them. You can guess why."

Heading toward solid ground again, Birdella smiled. "They disapproved of your marriage."

"Quite natural, I suppose, that they should resent me."

"Why? They ought to be grateful their mother has such a wonderful companion."

72

"Oh, they're all for that. It's the money part."

Birdella nodded, even more safely. She knew all about that. More than once she had been close to the center of family money squabbles, the direct cause in a couple of them. Twice she had managed to ingratiate herself with her elderly employers right up to the brink of marriage, only to have litigious relatives raise such a fuss she had emerged from the legal hassles with little to show for her efforts. Then there had been other situations that bordered on the Ideal but never quite made it, until here she was, trying not to gaze at Deacon too calculatingly, trying to promote her cause without making it too obvious what she was up to, being extra careful this time because, after all, it was only a hunch on her part that the reason Deacon kept strictly away from his wife wasn't because of any promise to a doctor but because, for all his sweet talk about "dear Jane," he really couldn't stand the sight of her.

As for dear Jane herself, Birdella, for all her ambitions, couldn't help feeling a bit sorry for her, because there was something so chillingly real about the poor creature's fantasies.

"I'm *not* mad, Birdella. I swear this is all a plot. I *was* kidnapped out of my home. Drugged, gagged, and blindfolded. It *sounds* insane, I know. But I can prove it. Call Jennifer! Call my daughter in Seattle. She'll tell you the truth. She'll tell you my husband—her father!—is dead. Whoever this man is who kidnapped me, *he is not my husband!*"

To placate her, Birdella promised to call the number Jane gave her, and she did have to admit to a most uneasy feeling in the pit of her huge stomach after she had left the room. Mere ravings were one thing but there was something so convincing about numbers, and for a few moments she actually debated placing the call. Then she decided it would be wiser to mention it to Deacon. If he acted funny—but no, it was ridiculous, and she wasn't even mildly surprised when Deacon treated the whole thing with a shrug and a laugh.

"Didn't I warn you she could be very persuasive? Jane's an intelligent woman but she's living in the past. Ah, you're still a bit dubious."

"No, really. It's like you say—she makes it sound so real."

Deacon lifted the phone and held it toward her. "Call Seattle."

"No! Honest, I don't for a minute be*lieve* . . ."

"I'd still feel better if you did. Here."

Still protesting, Birdella placed the call, only to be told there was no such number.

Immensely relieved, she wasn't quite so cordial the next time she spoke to Jane.

"But it's true!" the woman cried. "You must have asked for the wrong number. Or else they tricked you."

"Now you relax, sugarplum. You better start getting that pretty head of yours together or you ain't ever going to be leaving this room."

"I won't ever leave it alive. You think I don't know that."

Birdella turned away with some half-angry rejoinder. She didn't like to hear talk of death. So many of her patients talked morbidly of their approaching deaths; they seemed to exist under a cloud of presentiment which set the tone and texture of everything they did and said. For some reason, Jane made her think of Edna May Murphy; they'd been a lot alike, delicate little wrens, nervous but iron-willed, daintily poised on the edge of doom and having no idea what to do about it, except weep and wring their hands and plead for help.

"I'm not terribly optimistic," she confided to Deacon a couple of days later. "She seems totally obsessed. It may have been a mistake to bring her home, sir."

"One hopes for miracles."

"Life is the only miracle."

"A brief miracle."

"Yes. Brief. May I ask, then—if she shows no improvement—you still plan to keep her at home indefinitely?"

"My dear Mrs. Lampkin, I would rather see her dead than in an institution."

This quite took Birdella's breath away; her only reply was a sharp grunt of protest at his remarks.

He looked her straight in the eye. "I'm serious. Half a life is worse than none at all."

There were many things Birdella could have said at this point, but she was not about to risk a wrong move or a wrong word—not with the Ideal Situation at stake. Things must be allowed to mature slowly.

"Life is sacred," she reminded him piously, "no matter how damaged."

"Oh, I agree—philosophically," and on this ambiguous note the conversation ended.

Jane continued to be a problem, twice trying to escape from her suite; on the second occasion Deacon was sufficiently ruffled to speak harshly to Birdella.

"You were hired to watch *her*, you know. Not the rest of the household."

She took exception to this. "I wasn't snooping. I always get myself a midnight snack. Ask Jungquist. He's the one who's always lurking about downstairs."

"I have no objection to your midnight snacks, Mrs. Lampkin. But please take the trouble to lock your patient's door before leaving her rooms."

To avoid clashing with the tale-bearing Jungquist she made a point thereafter of delaying her trip to the kitchen until she could feel fairly sure that he was asleep, and so it happened, a few nights later, that she was surprised to hear voices issuing from behind the kitchen door. Usually it was open; tonight it was shut. She paused, wondering whether to go back upstairs, and as she stood there she heard Jungquist's voice suddenly raised in anger; she moved closer, pressing her ear to the door.

"I still don't like it," she heard Jungquist say. "It's stretching it out too long."

Deacon: "A plan is a plan, you idiot. We do it my way."

Jungquist: "But the longer we wait to put the pressure on 'em the more chance they've got to get onto us."

Deacon: "No one's getting *on*to us. We're in this for a cool half million. It's no time to lose our nerve."

Jungquist: "I still don't like that nurse dame sticking her nose into everything."

Deacon: "Stop worrying about her. I put the fear of God into her the other day."

Jungquist: "By the time she knows she's been used we'll be halfway to Rio."

Birdella felt a succession of emotions—the only one she didn't feel was fear; she was too furious for that.

For the next couple of days she kept not only her patient but the other three under close watch, without giving herself away, which isn't to say that she utterly dismissed the idea of revealing everything to Jane; she considered every aspect of this and finally decided such a move would be worth precious little in cold cash. Besides, it would be more fun to outsmart the rascals.

A noticeable flurry of activity cued her to make her move a couple of days later, shortly after she'd seen Jungquist leave the house carrying a briefcase.

Deacon had just picked up the phone and started to dial a number when she sauntered into the study. He looked annoyed. "Something wrong, my dear?"

"Not a thing. Just thought we might have a little chitchat."

"Later, all right? I'm tied up at the moment."

"Busy day, is it?"

"Rather. If you'll excuse me—"

"Like hell I'll excuse you. But if you're so busy I won't waste your time beating around the bush. That dame upstairs is no more your wife than she's insane. You did kidnap her."

She grinned at the look on his face. "You blabbed a little too loud the other night in the kitchen."

Deacon smirked. "And your next remark, I assume, is going to be: 'The cops will be arriving any second now.'"

"Not necessarily. That's up to you."

"I figured you for a cool one, Birdella. I was wrong. You're solid ice."

"I've written out a complete statement. It's in a safe place, along with your descriptions and fingerprints."

"So Florence Nightingale turns into Birdella Vulture."

"Let's not call names, sweetie. Mine is the only face she's seen. Per your plan. My fee as a patsy is a hell of a lot higher than my nurse's fee. You're cutting me in."

He bowed. "So be it."

"And we're going to get rid of dear Jane," she added.

"Nothing doing. I want no blood on my hands. That's why I planned this caper like I did."

She smiled. "There'll be no blood, sweetie, on anyone's hands. Not the way I do it."

"You talk as if you'd done it before."

"Many times."

"You're lying."

"It's funny, you know. I thought that's why you'd hired me. I thought you'd heard about my unique way with my patients."

"You'll have to explain that."

"No harm in your knowing. Some relatives with a hopeless invalid on their hands hire a nurse to dispense tea and sympathy. Others hire me—to dispense kisses and chloroform."

Deacon's amusement didn't quite cover his shock. "Birdella, the hit woman. That's one for the books."

Birdella looked modestly flattered. "Folks don't talk about it but you'd be mighty surprised to know how many mercy terminations are handled in this country every year."

"Mercy terminations?"

"You know what I mean. Well, land sakes, somebody's got to do it. Not many doctors, of course. They've got too much at stake. Not that there's anything *wrong* with it, whatever the law might say. Goodness, we're doing these poor old things a favor by putting them out of their misery."

"You're a monster of mercy, in other words."

She treated this epithet with the cool disdain it merited. "No point in being finicky about it. I decided that a long time ago. One of my employers—a real sweet old gentleman—begged me to put his poor suffering wife out of her agony and, well, it just went on from there. Word gets around—you'd never believe how many cases I have to turn *down*."

Deacon listened to all this with a frozen smile. "You know," he said, "I almost believe you."

"It's the gospel truth, whether you believe it or not."

"And you'd kill a woman like her?"

"Why not?"

"Well, you'd have to stretch the definition a bit to call that a 'mercy termination.' "

Birdella gave him a roguish, sly look. "In a mercy termination, dearie, it's usually the surviving relative you're bestowing mercy on. *They*'re the ones that have suffered."

"From greed, I suppose?"

"Motives aren't my business. Just methods."

"You always use chloroform?"

"It works, dearie, it works."

"That's not what I mean. Suppose the fuzz start making connections. You pulled any of these 'mercy terminations' in this area?"

"Not right *in* Philly, no."

"You mean, nearby?"

"Up north."

"Man or woman?"

"You've got a morbid curiosity, dearie."

"I've got a half million dollar investment to protect, *dearie*."

"Woman. Does that satisfy you?"

"Who hired you to—terminate her?"

"Her young hubby. Who turned out to be a lousy welsher."

"So what did you do—terminate him, too?"

"No profit in that. I don't do anything unless I'm paid to do it—like you're paying me, sugarplum. Now, if you're satisfied with my qualifications let's get down to brass tacks. When's the payoff?"

"Tonight. In Scranton."

"Not here?"

"The geographical details are an important part of my plan. We're leaving here soon as Jungquist gets back."

She gave him a playful but vicious jab in the ribs. "You're a trio of sweethearts, you three. You were going to take a powder and leave me here to guard the little lady. Why, I wouldn't even have been paid my nursing fee!"

Deacon looked at his watch. "You'd better start earning your fee right now; we shove off in twenty minutes."

Birdella smoothed the white uniform over her watermelon hips. "Dearie, what I got to do won't take me no more than five."

Leaving him sitting there, she went straight to her room and came out a moment later with her "termination kit," and after listening outside Jane's door she opened it a crack and called softly: "Sleeping, sugarplum?"

No answer. Good. So much tidier when they were asleep; no frantic tussling. She tiptoed into the room and prepared her ministrations. Holding what she called her "permanent derespirator" in her right hand she slipped her other hand deftly under the recumbent woman's head.

Then she gave a startled yip and jerked upright as the light came on behind her.

Deacon, flanked by Jungquist and the Van Ness woman!

"What are you doing here?" she bellowed.

"Observing your *modus operandi*, Mrs. Lampkin." He flipped open an I.D. wallet. "Time to unmask. I'm Detective-Lieutenant Radigan, Philadelphia Police Department. And the woman you came in here to murder is Mrs. Janette Harmon."

Birdella blanched as "Jane" sprang off the bed—looking, for the first time, truly sick; sick but relieved. "I'm Edna May Murphy's sister. These are my children, Roddy and Jennifer." She nodded toward "Jungquist" and "Ruth Van Ness."

The young woman stepped forward and put her arm around her mother.

"I owe you an apology. I was so sure you were wrong about Aunt Edna being murdered."

Mrs. Harmon smiled. "You were a good sport to go along with my idea. All of you were." She turned an almost pitying look on Birdella. "I knew it was the only way to get at the truth. Trick you into showing your hand."

Birdella sank onto the bed with a grievous sigh and with a look that said plainly, What did I ever do to deserve this? "I never even knew the old gal had a sister."

"No," Mrs. Harmon said. "I'm sure you didn't. Edna never mentioned my name after she insisted on marrying that young fortune hunter—in spite of all my pleas. She was a good woman, but she was a fool."

So, like most Ideal Situations, Birdella's was fated to remain what it had always been: a dream.

A Left-Handed Profession

by Al Nussbaum

He was a big red-faced man with a nose that was too large and eyes that were too small, and I never heard a grown man whine so much. He sat in the bar, surrounded by flunkies, and didn't shut up for a moment. To hear him tell it, and no one in the lounge of the Buena Vista Casino heard much else that afternoon, he hadn't made a nickel's profit in years. Taxes had left him with nothing.

He might have convinced the Internal Revenue Service, but he didn't convince me. His English leather shoes, hand-tailored suit and wafer-thin wristwatch all said he was a liar. So did the large diamond he wore on the little finger of his right hand—the hand he gestured with—and the thick roll of currency he carried.

From where I sat with my back to the wall, I had a good view of the bar and the entrance. I watched Benny Krotz nervously make his way across the casino floor, past the crap tables, blackjack dealers and roulette wheels. He paused in the entrance for a moment, blinking his eyes rapidly to adjust them to the reduced illumination. When he spotted me, he came over and dropped lightly into the seat beside me. Benny was a gambler who believed in flying saucers and luck, but he'd never seen either one. A loser if I'd ever seen one, not that my white hair and conservative clothes made me look like a world-beater.

I nodded toward the bigmouth at the bar. "Is that the mark?" I asked.

Benny hesitated, afraid of giving away the only thing he had to sell. Finally he acknowledged, "Yeah, that's the guy. How'd ya make him so fast?" His expression was glum.

"I'd have to be deaf, blind and have a cold to miss him," I said quietly.

"A cold?"

"Even if I couldn't hear him or see him, his smell would give him away." I allowed myself a brief smile. "He smells like money."

Benny brightened. "He looks good to ya, huh?"

"He looks almost perfect. He's a liar who lives well, so he's probably dishonest and greedy. There's no better target for a con game. There's only one trouble."

"One trouble?" Benny echoed.

"Uh-huh—this town is crawling with hustlers. If I can spot that guy in less time than it takes to light a cigarette, others have done it too. He's probably been propositioned more times than the chorus line at Radio City Music Hall. And, considering the type of person he is, he's probably already fallen for more than one con game and is extra cautious now. That's right, isn't it?"

"Yeah," Benny admitted. "That's right. He's been burned."

"Badly?"

"Yeah, pretty bad. He's been taken in card games, crap games and a bunch o' con games, already."

I finished my drink and signaled for the waitress. When she had taken our order and left, I turned back to Benny. "What kind of con games?" I asked.

"All the usual—phony stock, underwater real estate, cheap stolen goods that turned out to be perfectly legitimate factory rejects. And Red Harris took him for twenty thousand about six months ago with a counterfeit money swindle. Red gave him fifty brand-new twenties, telling him they were samples of the stuff he had for sale. He let him try them out all over town, then sold him a wrapped-up telephone book and made a nineteen-grand profit."

I laughed and looked over to where the mark was sitting. "That must have hurt his pride," I said. "How about his wallet? What kind of shape is that in?"

"Good shape. Very good shape. That's Big Jim Thompson, the drilling contractor. He has about half a hundred rigs working throughout the Southwest, and he gets paid whether they hit anything or not."

"That's fine," I said, smiling again. "It would ruin my Robin Hood image to take money from a poor man."

The waitress brought our drinks and I paid for them while Benny fumbled politely in his empty pockets. Because my money clip was already out, I removed three $100 bills and passed them to Benny. "For your help," I said.

"You're satisfied with him?" Benny asked, snatching up the money. He couldn't conceal his surprise. "He's gonna be mighty cautious."

I shrugged. "I don't think that will be a problem. Can you introduce us?"

"Yeah, sure." Benny started to push his chair back. "What's your name? For the introduction?"

Benny had been recommended to me as a source of information. Since he was in the business of selling what he knew about people, I hadn't given him any more about me than he needed to know, which was nothing. I had been in the game too long to make that kind of mistake. Now I gave him a name. "William Henk," I said, but I didn't move to get up. "There's no hurry, Benny. Finish your drink, then we'll go over."

Benny could have had ten more drinks; it wouldn't have mattered. Big Jim Thompson was firmly ensconced at the bar. He was still holding court over his followers when we walked over to them a few minutes later, and he gave every impression of being there for hours to come. He glanced contemptuously at Benny, then he noticed me and his small eyes narrowed. "Mr. Thompson," Benny said, "my friend William Henk wants to meetcha."

Thompson swung around on his stool, but he didn't extend his hand, and I didn't offer mine. "Why?" he challenged.

"Because I've been hearing a lot about you," I said.

"What have you been hearing?"

"That you're a real sucker for a con game," I answered, and Benny looked as though someone had just kicked him in the stomach.

Thompson's face started to go from red to purple. "What business is it of yours?"

"I might have a deal for you."

"*Might* have?" Thompson snorted disdainfully.

"OK, *will* have. Tomorrow. Meet me here at this time and I'll tell you about it."

"What makes you think I'll be interested in any deal of yours?"

"It will give you a chance to get even for your losses. Maybe get a little ahead. You'd like that, right?"

"So why wait till tomorrow?"

I nodded pleasantly at all his friends. "The audience is too big, and I have someone waiting for me. There's no rush. This is no con game," I said, then turned on my heel and walked away. I could feel their eyes on me, but I didn't look back. I had sunk the hook into Thompson. Now I could reel him in—carefully.

I bought a stack of out-of-town newspapers, then drove back toward the hotel where I was staying. I made a lot of unnecessary turns to be sure I wasn't being followed and put the rented car in a lot a block away. I could hear the shower running when I opened the door of the suite, and my wife Margie's soft voice floated out to me. She was singing an old folk song, but she'd forgotten most of the words.

I slipped out of my suit coat, kicked off my shoes, and sprawled across the bed with the newspapers. I read all the crime news I can find. Doctors read medical journals; I study newspapers. Both of us are keeping abreast of the changes in our professions.

Margie came out of the bathroom wrapped in a yellow robe. Her long chestnut hair was freshly brushed and shiny. She sat on the edge of the bed and kissed me. "Anything new in the papers?" she asked.

I married Margie because she was beautiful and young, and made me feel young too. Later I noticed I had received a bonus—no one ever looked at me when we were together.

"Not much," I answered. "A couple of bank robberies in New York City—amateurs; a jewel robbery in Miami that has the police excited; and the Los Angeles cops are still hunting for the four men who held up the armored car three days ago."

"Do you think they'll catch them?"

"Probably. Men who have to make their livings with guns in their fists will never win any prize for brains," I said.

Margie stood up and started to unpack more of our clothes. I stopped her. "Don't bother," I said. "We won't be here as long as I figured. I've found a live one."

"Are you going to tell me about it?"

"When it's over. I'm still working it out in my head."

The next afternoon, Thompson was waiting for me in the lounge of the Buena Vista Casino when I arrived. He was alone and seemed smaller. He was one of those people who needs an audience before he can come alive.

"What've ya got to sell?" he asked, bypassing all small-talk preliminaries.

"Counterfeit," I answered, handing him a single bill.

Thompson stood up without another word and headed for the entrance. I followed him across the casino floor, and into the coffee shop. There were a couple of customers at the counter, but that was all. Thompson went to the last booth along the wall and sat down, waving away a waitress who started toward him. I took the seat opposite his and waited.

He pulled a ten-power jeweler's loupe out of his pocket, screwed it into his right eye, and examined the $50 bill I had given him. I knew he was studying the portrait of Grant, the scrollwork along the borders, and the sharpness of the points on the treasury seal—and he was finding everything perfect.

"You must think I'm a real fool," he said with a nasty smile. "This ain't counterfeit."

"You don't think so, huh?" I handed him another $50 bill. "What about this?"

He was a little faster this time, but his verdict was the same. "It's real."

"And this one?"

A look, a feel, a snap. "Good as gold."

"Nope." I shook my head. "Counterfeit."

He pointed a blunt finger at the center of my chest. "Listen, punk, I know genuine money when I see it. Whatever you're planning ain't gonna work, so forget it."

"You can be sure of one thing."

"What's that?"

I gave him a nasty smile. "I won't try to sell you a twenty-thousand-dollar telephone book."

His jaw tightened.

"Instead," I continued, "I'm going to give you the chance of a lifetime. Those bills *are* counterfeit. In fact, these samples have one major flaw that the rest of my stock doesn't have."

I took the three bills out of his hand and lined them up on the table between us. Then I added three more fifties to the row. "Unlike genuine currency," I told him, "all six of these bills have the same serial numbers."

Thompson's eyes jerked back to the bills, and he snatched up two of them. He held them up to the light and studied them, frowning. After that he compared two more and sat staring at the six identical Federal Reserve notes.

"Do you still think they're real?" I taunted.

"I've never seen anything like this," he said in an awed tone. "These bills are perfect."

"*Almost* perfect," I corrected. "But I'll deliver brand-new, absolutely perfect bills."

He started to scoop up the money from the table, but I put my hand over his. "Where do you think you're going with that?" I asked.

He gestured toward the gaming tables. "Out into the casino to test some of this."

"Not without paying for it first. I don't give free samples, mister. I don't have to. I've got the best queer there is, and I get fifty cents on the dollar for *every* dollar. That three hundred will cost you one-fifty."

"That's pretty steep for counterfeit, isn't it?"

"You said yourself, you've never seen anything like it. I've been in business for five years and not one bill has ever been questioned, let alone detected. It's not every day you get a chance to double your money."

Thompson gave me a hundred and fifty from the roll he carried, then took my six identical bills into the casino. I ordered a cup of coffee and a hamburger, and settled down to wait for him. I was drinking my second cup of coffee when he returned.

He looked a little stunned by his success. "Not one dealer so much as blinked an eye. I've had 'em look closer at good money," he said.

I didn't have to give him any more of my sales pitch. He was selling himself. I sat back and sipped my coffee.

He didn't keep me waiting long. "Tell ya what, I'll take twenty-five thousand worth."

I shook my head.

"That too much?" he asked.

"Too little. You've seen the last samples you ever will. From now on I sell nothing smaller than hundred-thousand-dollar lots."

He did some mental arithmetic. "That's fifty thousand to me, right?"

"No. The hundred thousand is what *you* pay. In exchange, I give you two hundred thousand in crisp, new tens, twenties and fifties. Each bill with a *different* serial number."

He didn't say anything right away. I gave him two full minutes to think about it, then slid out of the booth and stood up. "Hell, I thought you were big time," I said disdainfully, then started to walk away.

Thompson called me back, as I knew he would. He was as predictable as a fixed race. "OK," he said. "You've got a deal, but you better not be planning a rip-off."

"How can there be a rip-off? You're going to examine every bill before you pay me, and you can bring all the help you think you'll need. And I'm not worried about being hijacked by you because I'll tell some friends who it is I'll be doing business with. If anything happened to me, you wouldn't be hard to find."

"So we understand each other," he said. "OK, when can we complete the deal?"

"The sooner the better," I said. "The sooner the better."

Four hours later, Margie and I were on our way out of town with Thompson's hundred grand. We were in the rented car because I figured we'd better leave before there was any chance of Thompson getting wise to how I'd tricked him.

"You're really something," Margie said, hugging my arm while I drove. "When you bought the loot from the armored car robbery in Los Angeles, you paid ten cents on the dollar because all the money was new and the numbers had been recorded. You said it was so hot you'd be lucky to get fifteen to twenty cents on the dollar, and then only after you located the right buyer."

"That's what I thought until I met Thompson."

"Didn't he know the money was stolen?"

"No. He thought it was counterfeit. I showed him six perfect fifties, all with the same serial numbers." I told her what had happened in the coffee shop.

"Where did you get counterfeit money?" she demanded.

"I didn't. It was good. Part of the armored car loot, in fact."

"You must think I'm stupid," Margie said. "I know good money doesn't have the same serial numbers."

I stopped for a traffic light, then got the car rolling again after it changed. "It does if you take half a dozen consecutively numbered bills and erase the last digit."

Margie's mouth opened in surprise. "You can do that? You can erase the numbers?"

"Easier than you'd think, and without leaving a trace, either."

We rode in silence for a few minutes, then Margie said, "Why didn't you erase the first digit on all the bills? That way they'd all be good to spend and you'd have gotten one hundred cents on the dollar." She was smart as well as beautiful.

"Because the risk of detection was very slight with only six bills, but some smart teller would surely have noticed if I'd tried to change the numbers on every bill. Then it would have been you and I back there, trying to explain where we got the money, instead of Big Jim Thompson."

Second Spring

by Theodore Mathieson

Maud Gullick was only eighteen on the spring morning in 1932 when she bludgeoned her mother and father to death over their breakfast.

According to the police report, Maud had calmly gone down to her father's basement workshop—the Gullicks lived at the top of a set of three flats in the San Francisco Richmond District—had picked up one of her father's hammers, and carried it back up, concealed under her bathrobe. Entering the kitchen, she called the attention of her parents to a roofing operation going on across the street. She hit her father first at the base of the skull, then her mother in the left temple. One blow was sufficient for each, for Maud was a big girl, six feet one, and weighed almost two hundred pounds. Afterwards she called the police, but by the time they arrived, she had lost control of herself, and they could make little of her story. Later she refused to tell them anything.

Neighbors had given the police some information, but not enough to explain the murders. Old Man Gullick was in his fifties, a carpenter by trade, who'd been out of work most of the winter. He'd been married before, and Maud was the child of his first wife, now dead. The second Mrs. Gullick was ten or twelve years younger than Gullick, but didn't look it. A small, perpetually harried bird type, with a malicious tongue, she talked incessantly against her stepdaughter.

"Maud's as lazy and stubborn as a jackass," Mrs. Gullick used to say in the interims when she and her neighbors were on speaking terms. "Been tryin' to get her to go to business school after she graduates from high school, so she can get a decent job and support herself. It isn't as if she's goin' to attract the men, looking the way she does. But she won't listen. Just shrugs those big humpy shoulders of hers, and then goes on mooning over the movies and listening to those crazy records of hers."

Neighbors living directly under the Gullicks reported that they would hear screams and thumps now and then from overhead, but they could

87

never make out what the fuss was about. They'd seen Maud going off to school occasionally with suspicious welts across her cheek, and once with a blackened eye.

Maud had a black eye the day the police jailed her for the murders.

When Joe Barnes, my city editor, heard about the black eye, he shook his finger at me and said, "Every other paper in town is calling the Gullick kid an unnatural monster. Just to be different, Caxton, I'm assigning you to uncover a little justification for slugging her old man and old lady. You can't miss. You can always fall back on mental incompetence. By the look of her photograph, I'd say that might be your best bet. But see what you can pick up."

Barnes was right. Maud's photograph was just a pale image of the unprepossessing original which I visited on her second day in jail. Her face looked small, set on that tremendous hulk of body, and her pallid skin had a middle-aged, pouchy look. On the other hand, her hands and feet were small and feminine.

"Miss Gullick," I said politely, "I am a reporter from the *Express*. My editor sent me over to see if there isn't anything we can do to help you."

Maud looked at me sharply for a moment, then blinked as tears came to her eyes. I imagined the police and other reporters had given her a hard time; she didn't have much to charm them with.

"How do you mean—help?" she asked. "Why would you want to after what I've done?"

"Well, you must have had a very strong reason for doing what you did," I said. "Maybe if we knew what it was, and could tell the people, it would be easier for you later—at the trial."

"My father beat me. Often," she said after a pause.

"He gave you that black eye?"

"Yes."

"And is that why you—?"

She shook her head, started biting her nails, which were already bitten to the quick.

"I think it would really help you to tell the truth."

Again tears appeared in her eyes. "If the others had asked me like that, I would have told them."

I waited patiently, and finally it came.

"Poppa broke my Victrola. Dropped it on the floor and smashed it. And then he took my Buzzy Bidell records and—and he put them in the stove. Oh, it was terrible. They turned all bubbly and melty, and I just—I couldn't help—"

"It was after he put your Buzzy Bidell records in the fire that you went down to the workshop?"

"Yes, after that—and after the things he said about Buzzy!"

It took a moment to get to me. "You—like Buzzy Bidell?"

Maud's eyes which a moment before had been a drab and hopeless grey began to soften and glow, transforming her face from the middle-aged look to one of rapt youthfulness.

"Oh, yes, I think Buzzy's real keen. There's never been anybody like him. When he sings I just get beside myself. I've seen every movie he ever made, and I have—had—all his records. But the police lady says she's going to get me another victrola and some of Buzzy's brand new records—and, Mr. Reporter—could you take another picture of me for your paper?"

"I think it could be arranged. Why?"

"Well, I didn't like the ones they took when I first got here. I was upset, and well, maybe if you took another it would turn out better. I know I'm not pretty, but—who knows? *He* may even see it, and—"

"Who?"

"Why, Buzzy Bidell. After all, if my picture appears again in the paper, and he sees it, he might get interested in me, *and even come to see me.*"
In a sudden rush of conspiratorial enthusiasm, Maud put her hand under the pillow on her cot and brought out a small brown pencil tablet.

"I'm keeping a daily diary of everything that happens to me here," she said in a whisper. "When I think I've got enough to interest Buzzy, I'm going to send it to him. He might really get interested in me then. Just to *talk* to him would make me feel so much better about *everything.*"

"Could you let me—read your diary?"

"Oh, no—nobody but Buzzy will ever read this."

"I see." Then a thought struck me. "Have you ever kept a diary before, Miss Gullick?"

"Oh, yes. I've kept one for the past year. It's home in my bureau drawer. I didn't get a chance to take it with me."

A sergeant came shortly after that and showed me out. I think word had got around that Maud had spilled a good deal more to me than she had to the police, because on the way out I was detoured into Brown of homicide.

"What did you find out?" he asked.

"Exactly what you'll find out if you'll treat her nice." I said it several times in several different ways. Brown didn't like it, but he had to let me go.

The Gullick flat was on Tenth Avenue, just off Lake. You'd think the tenants in the downstairs flats would have seen enough going and coming in the last couple of days to last them for a while, but no; there were tremors at front door curtains of both flats as I went upstairs. I didn't have to be sneaky about it either; my editor, Barnes, had arranged to get me a key from the downtown realtors.

As I closed the door firmly behind me, making sure the lock was set, the first thing I smelled was stale bacon. From that fatal breakfast? The shades were drawn on the solidly conventional furnishings in the front room; I glanced in at the kitchen and saw that somebody had cleaned up. At least the dishes were off the table, and there were no stains around that I could see. Maybe hammer victims didn't bleed much.

It wasn't difficult to find Maud's room; it was the one with the walls covered with glossy photos of Buzzy Bidell, and pieces of sheet music of songs he'd made popular. Maud was obviously a jig-saw puzzle fan, too, because a shelf by her day bed was filled with them. I saw one labeled *Down Lover's Lane*, another *Moonlight on the Swanee*, a third *Buzzy Bidell at the Piano*. A pile of movie magazines lay under the bed, and near a window stood a tabouret whose dust traces told me it once held Maud's phonograph.

Maud's diary was in the bottom drawer of her bureau, as she said, under some well-worn nightwear. It was the size of a cookbook and half as thick, with red, simulated-leather binding generously covered with greasy smudges. Maud was clearly a messy eater.

I opened the book at random, and read:

"*February 2nd*. I just found out that Buzzy's birthday and mine are the same! April 22nd! Just think—somewhere I've read that astrologists consider people born on the same date as having a natural affinity for one another. As if I didn't know that already! I wish Buzzy knew it. I wish just that he knew I was alive."

I skipped a few pages and read:

"*March 1st*. The Junior Ball is tonight. Those high school boys are too green for me. I'll take a bath, go to bed early, read my magazines, and listen to my records . . .

90

"*March 15th*. Went to see Buzzy in *Love Me Tonight* at the Lyric. My God, he's *handsome!* There were times I just had to close my eyes because I couldn't stand the sweet pain of looking at him. There was a girl sitting next to me who started laughing right in the middle of one of Buzzy's songs, and I hit her in the ribs as hard as I could with my elbow. She yelled and the usher came, but I said I had the jerks. I said I had them often, so the girl moved, and I was glad. I can't stand these snotty people who pretend they don't like Buzzy Bidell.

"*March 22nd*. I just had the most wonderful idea! I learned from the last issue of SILVER SCREEN, that Buzzy collects novelty tie clips. I saw one at Bascom's last night. It's only $1.98 and it's a treble clef. I'll have engraved on the back of it—from Maud to Buzzy. I wonder how much they'll charge?

"*April 19th*. I sent the tie clip off tonight. I was so thrilled putting the package in the mailbox; it was just like slipping it into Buzzy's own hand! Of course I don't expect any answer. But wouldn't it be wonderful if he sent me a post card or a signed photograph?

"*April 30th*. Gladys has been nagging me all week about signing up for secretarial school after graduation. She said a lot of pukey things about my looks, but I know. She's just jealous because I'm younger than her. I just don't listen to her. (I know things she don't even guess about—about Buzzy and me and what *could* happen!) Gladys is even mean about Buzzy. Says she can't stand him, because she knows it makes me mad. Mad! My God, I could kill the people who don't know enough to like Buzzy. It's worse than saying they don't like *me—I just can't stand it*."

I'd read enough. I hid the book inside my overcoat under the arm, and pressing it close I went down the stairs past the twitching curtains and into the street.

The defense used that diary, and I think it saved Maud's life. That, and my articles based on it. Public opinion had been against her at first, because she was not as frank with the police or with her lawyer about her motive for killing her parents as she was with me. It wasn't that our birthdays coincided, either—mine is in June—but the fact that I always treated her gently and with a certain amount of respect as an individual. I don't think she ever had had much of that. I'm certain that nobody ever called her Miss Gullick before. She was used to insults and black eyes, of course; she had plenty of *those*.

91

But when Curry, her attorney, read selections from her diary at her sanity trial, she listened with tears running down her cheeks, and I could see the jury beginning to get thoughtful. After a protracted out-session, they recommended commitment, and Maud's future seemed settled.

I got a last interview with Maud while she was on her way to Napa, the state asylum. Crossing the ferry to Vallejo she sat between two plain-clothesmen, and I sat opposite, my knees almost touching hers. We sat upstairs in the middle of the boat, although Maud had wanted to sit up front, outside. Her guards weren't going to have her jumping overboard before they got her to the asylum. I'm sure now she didn't have the faintest intention of doing so.

"Don't look so glum, Maud," I said softly, patting her hand. "Life in Napa won't be so bad. It's not like prison, you know. It's a beautiful place, and you'll be allowed a good deal of liberty."

Maud glanced sadly through the ferry boat windows at the tawny, bare hills of Richmond and the Carquinez straits.

"It's fall now. Come spring again, I won't be free. I won't be free ever again."

From her expression I knew she was thinking of Buzzy Bidell. That girl didn't give up easily.

"Well, you've got the radio, and records," I said. "Your little world isn't shut away from you."

She suddenly burst into tears. It was a while before she quieted down and spoke again.

"He didn't send me a single word," she said finally. "Even though he must have known I did it only for him!"

Six months later, Maud Gullick walked out of Napa State Hospital and disappeared as completely as if she'd never been. For over twenty-five years no trace of her was found.

I was one of the first to hear of her again.

It was April, 1957. Now literary editor for the *Los Angeles Gazette*, I was taking a much needed rest at Las Vegas, and sitting one evening in the Nevada Room watching a frenetic floor show, I was approached by a waiter who bent over and whispered in my ear.

"There is a gentleman who would like a word with you," he said. "He would like to join you at your table."

"Who is he?" I asked.

"His name is Bidell, sir. Buzzy Bidell."

For a moment the name stirred memories dully, then suddenly remembrance exploded like a big one on the Fourth of July. "Tell him to come over," I said.

Bidell could only have been in his late forties, but he looked sixty, with lines of dissipation scoring his eyes and mouth. Even his voice sounded old and tired.

"Mr. Caxton," he said, sitting down at my invitation. "They told me you were here—my friends. You see, I work at a night club down the street, the *Adobe*. You must come and catch my show."

"If I have time, I certainly will," I said, and asked Bidell to join me in a drink. He seemed pathetically grateful and ordered a Scotch.

"You see," he said, "I've been—out of show business the past few years. My voice went back on me there for a while, but now I'm in great shape again." I knew he'd taken the cure several times, and I doubted if his voice was in great shape again. "I'm making quite a serious come-back, you know, Mr. Caxton," he went on. "Even have written a book. Van Fleet is publishing it. Expecting the galley proofs any time now—tells about my road back."

I saw the light.

"I always enjoy reading books on comebacks," I said truthfully. "I'll look forward with pleasure to reading yours, Mr. Bidell."

"Oh, that'll be real George! I certainly would appreciate a favorable reading. Make a big difference, you know, to my future." He made a facile, juvenile gesture with his hands, and tried to flush youth back into his raddled features with a boyish smile. The attempt was pitiful.

"The finest experience has been to find that they haven't forgotten me—all those hundreds of thousands of fans of a few years ago.

"I still get letters from them. Look." He dug his hand into his coat pocket and brought up a fistful of envelopes, some of them suspiciously yellowed around the edges.

"Twenty-five years," he said, "and they haven't forgotten me. And here—" drawing one letter from an inside pocket. It looked new. "Got this one just the other day. Let me read it to you. 'Dear Mr. Bidell: This is the first letter I have written to you in a long, long time. I cannot say that I've thought of you often, just now and then, in a sweet, distant way. But now I have been thinking of you more lately. I cannot tell why.

Perhaps it is because I heard you on the radio the other night and it brought back memories. Your voice still sounds wonderful to me. I have been buying all the reissues of your old records, too. Then I heard you were publishing a book about yourself. I certainly will be one of the first to read it. And I sometimes wonder if in this book you will ever mention the names of some of the girls who wrote to you years ago. I was one of them. I sent you birthday cards (your birthday is the same as mine!) and once I even sent you a birthday gift.

" 'But I think maybe I did more for you than *any* of the others; if you could only know about this, maybe you would put me in your book, as part of your life. But I cannot tell you what I did except to say—I did it only for you.

" 'Please, dear Mr. Bidell, dedicate one of your songs to me there in your club in Las Vegas some night. I won't hear it, I know, because you don't broadcast like you used to, but it'll make me happy just thinking about it.

" 'The kindest, best, and most loving wishes . . .' "

Bidell looked up, his eyes revealing the charge which reading the letter aloud had given him.

"How did she sign it?" I asked, trying to keep my voice casual.

"Maud Milham, Roswell, New Mexico."

"When was it written?"

"I got it about a month ago. It's not dated."

I left then, after promising Bidell I would review his autobiography. In my hotel room I walked up and down for a long while, feeling for the first time in years the solar plexal excitement which the uncovering of a big lead always gave me. To find the whereabouts of the long-missing Maud Gullick! What a story that would make! I had the better part of a week to myself; I had planned to go north to Salt Lake City, to visit a former newspaper buddy; but it would be just as easy to head for Roswell.

I went out then and started looking up bus schedules.

I determined later that it was around the time I caught the bus south to Kingman, Arizona, at eleven fifteen the next morning, that Maud Gullick or Milham, as she signed herself now, was entering Dr. Eberle's office in Roswell.

Eberle, a wizened dapper little man with a memory like a tape recorder, showed Maud into his office and sat down behind his desk. It was the first time he had seen her, and he told me he was impressed with her buxom, matronly size, the pallor of her skin and her petulant, self-pitying expression.

"What can I do for you, Mrs.—ah—" he glanced at the card the nurse had had her fill in—"Milham?"

Maud's voice was sullen. "My husband—he made me come. He's waiting downstairs. I—well, I haven't been acting myself, he says, for about five or six months, and he insisted that I see a doctor."

"I see," Dr. Eberle said briskly. "What seems to be the trouble?"

"I'm—restless, and can't seem to sit still. I cry a lot. That makes Buck mad and he—he—" She began to sniffle.

"Well, now, suppose we begin at the beginning. How long have you been married?"

"Seventeen years. Buck and I have gotten along very well, until lately."

"Any children?"

"Two. A boy and a girl."

"Ages?"

"The girl is thirteen, the boy sixteen."

"Do you all get on well together?"

"We always have. I guess I haven't been myself lately."

"What exactly do you do that annoys your husband?"

"He says I just don't seem to keep my mind on things. Like getting supper or—things like that. It's just that living by the clock doesn't seem important. I can't see that it is, doctor; so long as a person is happy—"

"Are you happy then?"

"If they'd just leave me alone, I would be."

"What do you think about when you let time slip through your fingers, so to speak?"

"Oh, I have a lot to think about!" Doctor Eberle noticed that as she spoke her expression cleared, her voice became younger and almost timid, like that of a girl. "I read my magazines—"

"What sort of magazines?"

"Motion picture magazines."

"What else?"

"I—listen to my records."

"What kind of records?"

"Well, I've got a big collection of reissues of Buzzy Bidell's records." Maud looked at the doctor hopefully, as if she expected him to respond.

"Bidell—Bidell—isn't he one of the old-style crooners?"

"He's not old-style!" Maud flared up, her eyes getting a wild look. "That's what Jack—my boy—is always saying. 'Mom and her crummy Bidell records!' " Her voice became sharp, vicious. "I slap him across the face for that, and then when Buck finds out about it, he hits *me*."

Dr. Eberle cleared his throat and looked thoughtfully down at the card. "Well, Mrs. Milham," he said at last, "what you're going through is not uncommon. How old are you?"

"Forty-three."

"There, you see. Some women pass through this stage younger, some later, but all of them pass through it sometime. It's a time of great physical change, and along with it there are often emotional symptoms. What actually happens is that you have a sort of second adolescence; a resurgence of the old interests that held you when you were eighteen or nineteen. I imagine that Buzzy Bidell, for instance, was a great favorite of yours around that age."

"Yes—he was."

"Some women who were interested in dancing in their teens, and who have been good, steady wives for a quarter of a century, suddenly want to become ballerinas; or authors, or painters. It takes many forms. Some want to start another family. But this stage, fortunately, is temporary, and you will pass through it. I will write out a prescription for you, and you must take it faithfully. Come back and see me in about two weeks, and tell me how you're getting on."

I figured the whole time chart out later. I was waiting to change buses in Kingman when Buck Milham took Maud home after a visit to the pharmacist and stood watching in the kitchen while she poured a glass of water and pretended to take one of the capsules the doctor had prescribed. Actually, she told me, she never took one of them. The only reason for her refusal, so far as I can see, was that *she didn't want to be cured of her daydream.*

"And now, for God's sake," Buck said after Maud apparently swallowed the capsule, "get that washing done this afternoon. You can't get in the back door, it's piled up so damned thick. Besides, I need some clean clothes, so my customers don't back away when I serve 'em. Do you hear? If that washing ain't done when I come home, I'll blacken your eye!"

Buck ran a bar in Roswell, and usually didn't open up until noon, so now he had his lunch of steak and french fries, which Maud cooked for him, and then he went to work. He usually had his suppers at the restaurant next to the bar, so he wouldn't get home until one or two the next morning.

First Maud went out to the back porch, where she looked drearily down at the dirty clothes and sighed. Then she piled the lunch dishes in the sink, and went upstairs to an attic storeroom which she had appropriated as a sort of extra bedroom for herself. There was an old cot close under the roof. Pictures cut from movie magazines were pasted against the bare board walls.

A portable record player with three speeds occupied the place of honor under a dormer window.

Maud put a Buzzy Bidell forty-five on the turntable, and as the Voice filled the attic she sat down at an old drop-leaf sewing machine which she used for a desk and started writing in a wireback tablet.

"Buck made me go to the doctor today," she wrote. "He's trying to get me to forget you again, Buzzy. Quiet is all I need, my dear, to imagine myself with you, but they will not let me have it. There are times when Marcia and Jack come screaming up here demanding to play their terrible records on my phonograph when they have one of their own, and Buck never stops them. He seems to enjoy seeing me miserable. I can keep the kids out when he's not here, because I'm strong enough. But I'm not stronger than Buck.

"But I have done something that will keep them all out. I had our neighbor next door, Mr. Custer, who does odd jobs, build me a strong door made of one-by-twelves, to put at the head of the stairs. He installed it yesterday, but I was clever enough not to ask him to put on the heavy bar to keep the others out. He thinks I just want it to keep the noise from coming up. He only charged me $7.50. I shall make the bar myself. So I can have the peace I want, dear Buzzy, and think of you as often as I wish . . ."

She turned off the record player, then, and went to work. She had her tools ready; the saw, the bit, the screwdriver, the hammer. She cut her bar from a two-by-four and bolted it to the door; to hold it firm when it was closed, she screwed a two-inch metal U-bar to the door frame. It took her a long time, because she was clumsy with the bit and the saw, and by the time she had finished and swept up the sawdust, she heard Marcia and Jack yelling in the back yard, on their way home from school. She heard the slam of the screen door and went downstairs at once. As usual, Jack, sullen and black-haired like his father, was the first to the bread and jam.

"I see you been layin' on your fat backside again," Jack said arrogantly, pointing to the washing. He always used expressions which he heard Buck use to her.

"Don't you talk like that, or I'll wash your mouth out with soap," Maud said.

"Oh, corn," Jack said, his cheeks stuffed with bread.

"Hi, Mom," Marcia said. She was a small, skinny blonde girl with her father's razor-sharp features. "I'll bet you *have* been listenin' to your ancient ol' dreamboat again!"

"How long is this gonna keep up?" Jack asked. "Pretty soon, we'll have to be gettin' our own supper. Dad might just as well throw you out in the middle of the street, for all the good you are around here!"

"Just leave me *alone!*" Maud shouted and fled into the front room. The children followed her, leaving a trail of stickiness on wall and door.

"Why don't you listen to a real singer," Jack said and turned on a popular rock-and-roll record on his portable phonograph.

"Stop, stop!" Maud cried and ran for the stairs.

The children followed her.

Buck broke tradition by coming home to supper, possibly to check on whether the washing had been done. When Maud saw him coming, she fled to the attic and Jack met his father at the front door with, "She didn't do the washing, Pop!"

Buck growled a swear word and tore up the stairs to the attic, only to thump his head hard in the dark against the closed wooden door. Then he began cursing in earnest.

"Shall I get the crowbar out in back, Pop?"

"Why in the hell didn't you tell me she had put a door in here!" Buck yelled at him.

"You didn't give me time."

"Get me the crowbar!"

With the two children watching in anticipation, Buck beat the bar against the door, and pried and pried until it splintered open. Maud was cowering on the cot. Buck grabbed her roughly by the shoulders and practically dragged her down the stairs and into the kitchen.

"Now you're going to do that damned washing while I sit here and watch!" he yelled. The kids were delighted. This was better than T.V.

Maud began loading the washer as if she were doing it in her sleep while Buck made a running commentary on what he was going to do to her if she didn't pay attention to business from now on; how he was losing money right this minute, having to hire a man to take his place down at the bar; how she must be crazy hanging a useless door in the house without telling anybody.

Jack and Marcia watched their mother's somnambulistic activity until they got bored, then Jack poked his sister slyly and pointed upstairs. The children went quietly up to the attic and for a while picked curiously into the things. Finally Jack uncovered his mother's collection of records.

"This'll help Pop out," Jack said. "If she doesn't have all these records to play, she won't waste so much time, and might start doin' a little work around the place again."

Marcia nodded eagerly as Jack spread a newspaper on the floor and started breaking the records up into little bits and dropping them on the paper. Marcia helped too, and when they were finished, Jack picked up the paper and carried it like a sack downstairs and into the kitchen.

"Look, Pop," Jack said. "Now maybe Mom won't spend so much time listenin' any more."

The boy threw the paper down with a clatter, and the shards of chitinous record poured out on the red linoleum.

"Good boy," Buck said, touseling his son's hair.

Maud stopped her washing then to look.

I got into Roswell around nine the next morning, and the first thing I did was look up Milham in the phone book. There was only one. I got into a cab that was waiting at the station and gave him the Milham address.

It was only two or three blocks from the center of town, a two-story green frame house set on a flat, brownish lawn bordered by locust trees. I told the cab to wait as I went up the walk.

In a moment now I would know whether I had found Maud Gullick.

I knocked on the door and nobody answered. Three times, no answer. I walked along the verandah and tried to look in the windows, but the shades were drawn. I went back to the door and turned the knob. The door was unlocked, and I pushed and went inside. For a moment I could see nothing, except that I stood in a kind of hall with a stairway.

There was somebody standing on the stairs.

"What in the hell do you want?"

A needle-faced character with a red face stood there in a beacon robe watching me.

"Is this the home of Maud Milham?"

"This is my home—Buck Milham. What do you want?"

"Does Maud live here too?"

"Yeah, she's my wife."

"I'm—a friend of hers."

He looked at me as if he were considering throwing me out, then walked across the hall and flung open a door.

"G'wan in and sit down," he said. Then in a big voice he yelled upstairs. "Maud! Maud!"

As I went into the living room, I saw two children come curiously along the hall, a girl and a boy.

"Friend, you say? Where did you know Maud?" Buck had followed me into the room and stood by the door.

"San Francisco."

"Yeah? She never told me she was in Frisco."

"These your children?" I asked, to change the subject.

"Yeah. Boy's Jack, girl's Marcia. I didn't get your name."

"Caxton. I'm a newspaperman."

"Oh, yeah?" Buck became a fraction more amiable. "I run a bar here in town, the Cactus, on Main Street. It's just a block from the bus station; a lot of newspaper guys drop in there. Oh, here, Maud. A friend to see you. Mr. Caxton."

I recognized Maud Gullick, all right. And she knew me the moment she saw me, because her face paled and she put her hand out against the door frame to support herself.

"Hello, Mr. Caxton," she said distantly.

"Hello, Maud," I said. "I'm surprised to see you married and with a family and all. How long have you been married?"

"Seventeen years."

All of a sudden a feeling came over me that I had no right coming here. The past was past. If Maud could go away quietly and get married and raise a family and live her own life for seventeen years, what right had I—

"You never told me you lived in Frisco," Buck said to his wife.

100

"I never liked to talk about that," she said almost primly.

"We knew each other only a short while," I said, rising. "I just happened to be alone in Roswell, and remembered—" I edged towards the door. "It's good to catch a glimpse of old acquaintances again, you know." Buck was eyeing me suspiciously.

"Maud lent me five bucks when I was down and out," I said, putting my hand in my pocket. "I thought after all these years, it's earned a little interest." I handed a ten-dollar bill to Maud. Buck's suspicion cleared; he could understand that.

"That's all I wanted, just to clear my conscience," I said. I wanted to get out of there, away where I could think. Maud was eating me up with her eyes.

"Goodbye, Mr. Milham—good luck, Maud. Nice children you've got there."

I got the front door open and looked back as Maud spoke.

"Mr. Caxton," she said. "They broke my door down."

"Did they?" I said and laughed uncomprehendingly. "Well, have your husband buy you a new one!"

Buck laughed and the children laughed this time, and I left. I was glad I'd had the cab waiting. I told the driver to take me back to the bus station.

Now that I had found Maud Gullick living, it seemed, so normally, I didn't want to inform the authorities; I just wanted to keep hands off. At the same time, I wanted more time to think about it.

I bought a ticket to Lincoln, up in the mountains. I'd always wanted to see the territory Billy the Kid had battled around in, and I thought a couple of nights away from Roswell, but not too far from it, would clear my mind and I'd know what to do.

I spent a day seeing the jail where they locked up the Kid; I saw the bullet holes in the wall where the Kid shot at the Warden. I visited the Mascalero Indian Reservation, and that night at the hotel I couldn't go to sleep. Her last words to me went round and round in my mind: "They broke my door down—they broke my door down." It was like a discord in a piece of music that sounded pretty good otherwise.

The next day I took a bus back to Roswell. I got the full blow as I came out into the afternoon sunlight and saw the newspaper in the stands: WOMAN KILLS HUSBAND, TWO CHILDREN. Their pictures were on the front page, and I had no trouble recognizing them. In a daze I went to the nearest bar. I couldn't understand why the place should be locked up until I looked up and saw the painted lettering on the door: The Cactus.

I went over into the plaza in front of the courthouse and sat down and read the paper with a mind that didn't take in much.

Only one fact I got quite clear. Maud had used a hammer again.

When I got hold of myself, I went over to the jail where they were keeping Maud. I showed my press card, but they wouldn't let me in. She was too hot. I wired my editor in L.A. and told him to do what he could, that I'd be sleeping for the next forty-eight hours on the police blotter, and if he swung it, I'd give him a story that would scoop every other paper in the country. Somehow he did it, and the next morning they let me in to see her for five minutes.

Five minutes were enough.

"It was you," she said. "You helped me do it. They broke my door down. There was no place for me to go. And then you came and reminded me. On the ferry boat, remember? You said the hospital wouldn't be bad, that I'd be quiet and free. And I was. And now I want to go back where I can be alone with Buzzy and they won't break my door down."

I had my story.

Bank Night

by Arthur Porges

Page Hampton was thinking very hard about the massive vault a few yards from his desk. Since he was president of Security-American Bank, this might seem quite normal, but his thoughts were hardly orthodox. He wasn't worrying, as other bank presidents might have, about the safety of the steel-and-concrete box; rather, he yearned to loot it.

Aside from the intriguing fact that it usually held half a million dollars or more in currency, Hampton had to get in because he was, in a sense, already there—into the bank's funds for well over $800,000. Only a much bigger loss, carefully staged, could cover his own peculations.

Compared to the underpaid tellers and cashiers, he had no excuse. His salary was quite high. But his expenses were even higher. As a widower possessed of good looks, prestige and a most attractive personality, he indulged a taste for glossy, expensive girls. Defying the usual "image" expected of a banker, he drove a Jaguar. His conservatism in financial matters related to banking made this deviation practicable. People inferred that all his recklessness went into the car, leaving none for bad loans.

A property-albatross in the form of a $65,000 house he had bought on the bluff overlooking Spanish Cove also played a part in forcing Hampton's hand. It was, to begin with, more house than he could afford, but to make matters worse, the cliff had been ripped apart (as is usual in southern California) with no regard for natural slopes or preservation of the vital watershed. As a result, the rains turned the subsoil to jelly and many of the area's magnificent structures, designed by top architects, were sliding inexorably toward the edge of the bluff.

Thanks to Jefferson Reed, a distinguished engineer and early settler there, the slippage had been halted. By assessing all the property owners, Reed had installed freezing coils at several key points—a trick learned from dam-builders—thus solidifying the loose earth and arresting the

103

water's shearing action. After the next wet season, more permanent measures would be taken, but for the present, the houses were safe, he had assured them.

This was a good long-range program. It had saved highly valuable property that would have brought peanuts on the open market a few weeks earlier, for who would have cared to own the finest home built by a master architect—even one with an incomparable view of the Pacific—when his equity was heading for the deep six?

On the other hand, the assessment had come at a bad time for Hampton, when he was already overextended financially. And his share of the electrical bill for the essential freezing coils was at least manslaughter, if not murder. All of which explains why he thought constantly about the vault and of the power of negative thinking.

Hampton had always been a schemer. He had finagled his way through a good college by outwitting the professors. Instead of studying the books, he had studied the teachers. It's an old trick, but it seldom fails when practiced by a sharp-eyed lad.

Having acquired a degree with a minimum of effort, Hampton then wangled his way into banking, making full use of his assets. His appearance was impeccable; his voice dripped warm honey; and his powers of perception were finely honed. No matter how his quarry zigzagged, Hampton swerved at the same angle, always agreeing with, and supporting the ego of, those who counted. Yet he did this in so manly and frank a manner that nobody ever thought him a yes-man or a toady. And so, at 43, he was president of a bank—and a criminal de facto, if not de jure.

Now, when a schemer like Hampton puts his wits to work on a problem, he usually solves it. But even the best operator doesn't often hit on a gimmick so clever that he can't quite believe others have overlooked it. When he conceived his foolproof plan, Hampton considered himself with a kind of awe: He could not only loot the vault, cover his embezzlement and clear almost half a million, but with any luck, he would not even be suspected. Better yet, no one would be suspected; it was highly probable, in fact, that no crime would be recorded officially anywhere.

There was one small problem still to be solved: he needed technical help—someone who knew about explosives. And that little obstacle vanished almost as soon as it appeared. Who else but Morrie? Morrison Ball, formerly a sergeant in a demolitions platoon, and now, still in the National Guard, which had an armory—containing explosives galore.

104

in Korea, the team of Hampton & Ball had done very well on the black market. If Hampton was a schemer, Ball was the perfect accomplice. A roughneck from Chicago's West Side, his estimate of the value of a human life was more in accord with Attila the Hun's than Albert Schweitzer's. And yet, oddly enough, Ball had a code of his own. Far from being bright, he was nonetheless fiercely loyal and did exactly as he was told, once he accepted a leader. When he was tagged in Korea and faced severe punishment, he refused to implicate Hampton, who, using his rank, pulled every wire he could to help clear his partner. Both got away clean, while some luckless natives and a few of the squarer GI's were credited with an operation far beyond their abilities.

To Ball, uncouth, illiterate, with the manners of a stockyard hog, the handsome, urbane, glib and ingenious Hampton was a demigod. And it was also true that the brains of the team was both good-natured and openhanded, in appreciation of his subordinate's useful qualities. Once back in the States, they had drifted apart, of course, but now, Hampton felt, it was time to revive the team for some business at the old stand.

At the little bar well off the beaten track, Hampton met his accomplice-to-be and laid the whole plan on the line.

"There's bound to be about $300,000 in there," he told Ball, mentally dividing the true amount by two-plus. A hundred grand was plenty for Morrie, Hampton thought. Probably the horses would get it all, anyway.

"Now," he went on, "I'm in and out of the vault every day. I could take the money any Friday evening and skip. But where to? These days they can extradite you from anyplace. Besides, I like this country. I don't care to spend a fortune somewhere along the Amazon, where all a guy can buy is bananas and the nearest doctor is 3,000 miles north, where it's all solid bugs, crocs, man-eating fish and headhunters! Not for me!"

"Yeah," Ball said with surprising shrewdness, his muddy blue eyes glittering. "And that's too simple for you, ain't it? You'd rather go around a few corners."

"Could be," Hampton grinned. "Anyhow, I've got a whale of a plan. Hell, they may not *ever* be sure anything was stolen. My idea is this: Suppose there was an explosion—a really big one. Blow that vault wide open. And a fire, too. With some of that stuff—what's it called—thermite?"

Ball nodded slowly. "Betcher life. Aluminum powder and iron oxide. When it goes off, you got melted iron"—he pronounced it "eye-run"—"and that will burn damn near anything."

"Good. Maybe napalm, too. That should burn anything the thermite misses."

"How you gonna work it?"

"Easy. You make up some bombs. Not too big; flattish, if possible. But maybe one big one for the main job—say, shoebox-size. There are a lot of shelves and pigeonholes in the vault that aren't touched for days at a time. I'll put bombs all over the place in such spots. The big one right near the currency boxes. Can it set off the others, or do they need timers?"

Morrie reflected for several moments, his brow furrowed. "Been a long time," he apologized. "I don't do that stuff in the Guard nowadays. Yeah," he assured Hampton. "I can use primacord or something that will go off when the big one does; then that'll start the others—as long as everything's only a few feet apart." He gave his partner a puzzled stare. "They'll know the stuff was inside. How you gonna explain that?"

"The deposit boxes are in a sort of anteroom. Anybody could put a bomb in one of them. I can get keys to the empties and really load that room. My idea is to have so many big explosions in and near the vault that nobody will be able to say just *where* the real blast came from. We've got to wreck the place, but good. As to a general explanation, I have a whole file of crank letters. You just can't imagine, Morrie, how many creeps get mad at a bank. We bounce a check that's overdrawn by six cents and then charge the sucker three bucks for giving us trouble! That would make Little Nell kick a blind man."

"You mean Little Nell, that big blonde from Jay Street? She'd belt a blind man just for bein' in her way, an'—"

"Forget it," Hampton interrupted, his lips twitching. "Point is, some nut could get even with the bank by loading his deposit box with an explosive. Maybe one box won't account for the damage, but as I said, we're going to do so good a job, nobody will know *what* happened. Besides, there are cashiers who go in and out. They aren't well-paid and I know at least two who are in hock up to their ears. If they knew how to get away with it, they'd beat me to the punch!"

"Well," Ball said, "you know I'm with you, regardless. Like old times, Page. And I can use some moolah. What's my cut?"

"Since it's my idea, I thought a third—one hundred grand—would be fair. How's it sound?"

"Wow-e-e-e-e!" Ball said softly. "Nothing chintzy about you, Page. I ain't arguin' one li'l bit!"

"Okay. Make up the bombs, but be damn careful. Choose an armory away from your own area. You can still pick locks, I suppose."

"You can say that again."

"After you get the stuff, remember: one shoebox-size, with a timer. An ordinary clock setup should do, but make it reliable. If the explosion doesn't come off, I'll have enough egg on my face for the biggest omelet in San Quentin. Eighteen to 24 hours should do it. I'll smuggle the packages into the vault during the week. Friday evening, before the guard and I lock it, I'll plant the one with the timer and set it. And when the big boom comes, I'll be away, out of reach, on a fishing trip for the whole weekend."

"When will you grab the dough?"

"At the last minute. I've been getting the guard used to running little errands for me just before closing. I'll send him for something and clean out the vault in the twenty minutes that he's gone. Then we lock up. If I'm right, and your bombs really blast the place, they'll think all the paper money was destroyed. I'll leave plenty of bonds in case they expect ashes, but with a thermite fire I should think ashes wouldn't mean much. Best of all," he chuckled, "I have access to the denominational number lists. I'll see that they disappear."

"Won't that look phony?"

"It's a small risk. I figure some of the offices will be messed up, too. Say—" he paused a moment. "I could guarantee that. Make me *two* timed bombs. I'll set one where it will ruin a lot of records *outside* the vault. That'll confuse matters even more. That should make it look like a nut with a grudge, all right."

"How many people gonna get clobbered?"

"None," Hampton replied coolly. "The bank will be deserted. So will the neighborhood—in case any bricks fly. That area's dark on a Saturday night. It's a business district. By the way," he added, "we can't touch the money for a while. I might be watched. I'll put it in a safe place I've got picked out. You'll have yours in about a week. But I won't spend a penny of mine for about a year—if I can hold out. Then I'll resign or something, and go east."

"Why should they watch you?" Ball demanded. "You said—"

"Ah," Hampton interrupted. "We're not dealing with a lot of suet-heads aged in brass, like in Seoul. The cops—and the Treasury boys and the insurance investigators—they're not stupid. When half a mil—er—all

107

that money disappears in a mysterious fire, they'll have nasty suspicions. But they won't be able to prove a dime ever left the vault—I hope—and after a while they may begin to believe the currency got destroyed incidentally when some crackpot blew up the Security-American. I'm counting on some flooding, too. There's a big waterpipe somewhere in the wall—leads to the fancy fountain in the lobby. So make the bombs, Morrie-boy, and leave the planning to me. Then we ride in a private car on the Gravy Train for life."

"How much time I got, you say?"

"Well, I'd like to blow the place the weekend of the 25th. Monday's a holiday. So the bank will be closed Friday night, Saturday, Sunday—and Monday. I'm going fishing, where there isn't even a phone. I'll come home Monday evening and when I hear the news, I'll be astounded. By then, they might begin to suspect I've skipped. My return should make them ashamed of doubting good old Page. That'll work in my favor—a bit of reverse psychology.

"They'll hesitate to suspect me again. But the cops will watch everybody. That's their business. Looking for a big spender. They won't find one in *my* neighborhood! Not yet. All clear?" he asked, looking Ball in the eye. "The explosion should come Saturday morning, between 7 and 10 A.M. I'll have to set the timer no later than 6:30 P.M. on Friday—we're open until 6, you know. So it'll be a bit over 12 hours."

"That'll take two good, small clocks, workin' together," Ball said. "One starts the other after 12 hours. It's the safest way, although under 12 hours would be a lot easier."

"But are they dependable? They *have* to work—or we're up the creek."

"They'll work. Don't worry about that," Ball assured him, a note of disdain in his gruff voice. "Kid stuff to an old pro like me."

The following days crawled by as if mortally wounded. As the critical weekend approached, the bombs passed from Ball to Hampton and were carefully placed in the vault, deposit boxes, at the backs of desks in the outer office and even on the tops of filing cabinets.

On Friday, everything went as planned, almost too smoothly to be reassuring. Such luck violated the age-old Murphy's Law: If anything can go wrong, it will.

At 6:12, with everyone gone but the guard and himself, Hampton sent the man out for cigarettes and, while he was gone, looted the vault of roughly $572,000. The number lists had been destroyed an hour earlier. They were incomplete to begin with, but why take chances?

The guard returned, accepted a generous gratuity from his openhanded employer and together they closed the vault. Inside its padded box, the first clock was ticking. Hampton, keyed up to concert pitch, thought he could hear it, but obviously the guard wasn't that alert. Like so many of his kind, he was ancient, slow and arthritic; in an emergency he would be more dangerous to customers and himself than to a holdup gang.

Having done all that was humanly possible to avoid detection, Hampton went fishing—far up Garrapata Creek, where the country was rough and communications lacking. There he sweated out a long weekend, relieving the boredom with visions of large bills and petite girls.

Naturally, he didn't leave the money lying around the house. Some days earlier he had prepared a good cache down on the beach, well above the high-tide mark. There under a huge rock, in a waterproof box buried deep in the sand, were 50-odd pounds of currency. And there they would stay for at least a year; maybe longer. Ball's share, however, had been turned over to him on Friday night, with a warning to spend it cautiously, just in case some smart cop connected them. Not that this was likely; the two men had seen little of each other since Korea and their few recent meetings had been in spots where they ran little risk of being observed.

The drive back on Monday evening, in heavy holiday traffic, seemed to last forever. Finally, Hampton came within sight of the winding, unimproved road that led to Spanish Cove. He got a terrible shock when he turned into the road leading to the residential part of the bluff: There were red lanterns in profusion, wooden stands with reflectors—and a horde of curious sightseers.

His house had vanished. Reed's was gone, too; and Harrison's; and the towering Truman place. Everywhere the raw earth, a network of gullies and dark cavities, was exposed.

As he stood there, bug-eyed, trying to make sense of it, a voice exploded behind him.

"That you, Page? What a mess, eh?"

He whirled. It was George Palgrave, whose own house, a sprawling ranch-type, was also among the missing.

"What happened?" Hampton managed to ask.

"You don't know? Say-y-y—that's right. You were away over the weekend." He brightened at this chance to break such big news—even if

109

bad—to a new audience. "We've had it, Page. The whole cliff's taken a tumble—slid like hot grease when the power stayed off for so long and Reed's freezing job broke up completely."

"B-but," Hampton stammered, "he told us over and over that the earth would stay frozen even if there was no power for 36 hours. Don't tell me you've been without longer?"

"I do tell you. That explosion at the bank—*your* bank. Say, you don't know about that, either—brother!"

"What about it?"

"It ruined the bank building, to begin with. But that wasn't our headache. You know the power station across the street? Well, the explosion—and it was a lulu—threw those generators right off their beds. People heard 'em whining like animals blocks away. That shut off the power—and you don't fix generators overnight. It's not like a break in the lines. Hey, where you going? Be careful!"

Heedless of life and limb, Hampton stumbled over craters and mounds to the edge of the cliff, where he looked down at the moon-bright surf. It no longer creamed over a beautiful beach. About half a million tons of rubble—one for each dollar—had entombed the stolen money.

But he was no crybaby. "Hell!" he told himself, "I'm clear on the embezzlement. I still have my job. The money at the bank will be replaced by Uncle Sam. The house was a white elephant, anyhow. And if I can't hit Morrie-boy for at least five grand, I've lost my touch."

He looked up at the stars, then at Palgrave, peering down at him anxiously.

"Where were you, anyway?" Palgrave asked.

"Supposed to be fishing," Hampton said. "Actually, it was business mixed with pleasure. Had a chance to make a pile—a real killing."

"What happened?"

He looked up at the stars, then fixed his eyes on his neighbor. "I tried too hard," he said coolly, "and blew it."

The Contagious Killer

by Bryce Walton

I chased more wild leads all through another hot July day and got back to the squadroom late and depressed. The case was going badly for me, but I had done all I knew how to do. The pressure was starting to build up.

The air conditioning was out again. The squadroom was sticky and smelled like a stale cigar. A few other boys stopped typing reports and mumbled embarrassed greetings. Someone even said "Hi," then hesitated before adding "Lieutenant," as if it were an uncertain afterthought. I hung my jacket over the back of my chair, rolled up soggy shirtsleeves and checked the memo spike on my desk. Nothing, as usual, but negative reports; and a note to call my wife. I didn't want to call my wife. My boy, Jamie, would forge into the act. He would ask, "Dad, how come you haven't solved the murders yet?"

I could tell him what I'd been telling the reporters for a week, that I expected a break in the case any minute now. But kids, especially Jamie, know you're lying as soon as you open your big mouth.

I called the Bureau of Criminal Identification to see if they had turned up any sex criminals we hadn't questioned yet. They had not. I called Miller to see if he'd finished another check-through of cab company trip sheets; always a chance some cabbie might remember some suspicious character in a vital pick-up or let-out area. Miller had nothing new. I called to see if the pictures sent to the girls' home towns, to firms they had worked for, to schools they had attended, had turned up anything. They had not. I called Morelli to see if any anonymous tips had come in worth investigating. None had. I called Hoppy to see if he'd turned up anything by dragging all the flophouses again. He had not.

Then I just sat there feeling that frightening sense of failure and helpless anger. The truth was, I had to admit, I had a "cold case." When women are killed on impulse by a psychopath, you have to get a strong lead on

111

a suspect within twenty-four hours, or it ices up and you may be years nabbing a killer; or you never do. The killer isn't usually acquainted with his victim. Probably he's never seen her before, has no personal connection with her other than some sudden sick compulsion. That eliminates all ordinary motives or leads, and there's no other way to connect this sort of murderer with the victims than through eyewitnesses and/or very obvious clues left by the killer. My killer hadn't left witnesses or clues. All he'd left lying around were the parts of his two dismembered victims, two young pretty girls who had come to the city to live a more exciting and glamorous life, but who had gone bad; the sort you see walking along the honky-tonk streets looking for adventure.

I felt an itch along the back of my neck, about where the axe would fall. It was my first big murder case since being made lieutenant, and it would likely be my last. Not that I'd get fired or downgraded. I'd be shoved down the hall to the clerical department as a typewriter jockey or a public relations stooge. No thanks, I wouldn't care for that.

The phone rang and I had the sinking feeling even before I picked up the receiver that it was the Chief.

"Get up here on the double, McKenna," he said.

The Chief's air conditioner worked just fine, but that office felt like an airless mousetrap to me. Our Chief is a heavy, intense and practical fellow who has few ideals and is very conscious of politics. He doesn't waste time or words and he didn't waste them now. He said, "Someone else is being put on your case, McKenna."

I felt numb, and for a minute I couldn't say anything. Then I said, "Well, all right, I'll see you around." I turned and started to walk out.

"Don't be stupid, McKenna. Just wait and listen a minute."

I turned. "It won't do any good. I've done all that anyone can do."

The Chief twisted his hands nervously. He blinked at me uneasily. "Just cool down a minute, McKenna, and listen. I know you've done all anyone can do; at least, all that any ordinary mortals around this precinct can do. But this is something special—a sort of weird, way-out thing. And I want you to listen. First, get this clearly, McKenna. Bringing this other guy in isn't my idea. It's the D.A. He's crazy for a quick arrest and conviction. It's his business, it's political. Our business is to do what we're told, and to remember that the D.A. is the mayor's nephew. Okay?"

"Okay," I said.

"Ever hear of an ex-cop name of Steve Blackburn?"

I shook my head.

"You were transferred to this precinct after Blackburn left," the Chief said. "But he was a lieutenant here too, in homicide. One day he found himself in charge of a butcher murder case, three women and a psycho. A case much like yours, McKenna."

He hesitated and gave me a funny squinting look. "In fact, according to Blackburn, it *is* the same case. He's convinced the D.A. that it's the same killer making a comeback."

I didn't care to say anything. I waited.

Finally the Chief went on. "This means a lot to Blackburn. His case was about a year and a half ago, and his killer got away. The case froze over. Blackburn was hit hard. Seems he was wrapped up in this case. It was like a fever. He couldn't think of anything else. Month after month he refused to do anything but hunt this psycho. For over a year he devoted all of his time to this obsession. That's what it got to be—an obsession. He says he learned everything about the killer. He studied pathological crime until it was running out of his ears. But the guy disappeared. He didn't kill again. Blackburn had learned so much about the psycho he had a trap laid for him, but the guy didn't kill again, so Blackburn lost him. Blackburn kept saying, 'If he'd only killed again I would have nabbed him.' Anyway, to tag a long story, Blackburn was so obsessed with this thing that when he lost it, he couldn't stand the gaff. He hit the bottle too much, and finally he had to leave the force. It was all an ugly business."

"Blackburn's being put in charge now?" I asked.

"No. The D.A. has brought him in as a special consultant," the Chief said. "After all, if it is the same killer, Blackburn's way ahead of us."

"But what if it isn't the same killer?" I said. "What if Blackburn is, like you say, obsessed? What if he just has to come back to try to prove something, make up for his failure?"

The Chief laced his fingers together and pretended he was having trouble pulling them apart. "Ours not to reason why, McKenna. The point is, officially you're still in charge. Blackburn's not on the force." The Chief took a deep breath. "Anyway, Blackburn is certain he's right. Know where he is now? He's cruising in a police car down on South Main where the killings occurred. He says the killer will strike again. Tonight!"

"Tonight," I said. My mouth suddenly felt dry.

"That's right," the Chief said. "You're to take a car down there. Meet Blackburn at the Third and Main parking lot at six-thirty."

The unmarked patrol car rolled into the parking lot at exactly six-thirty. I walked over. There was a hot haze of smog that stung my eyes. Blackburn had a dark lean face that looked out at me like a vulture's. He said in a quick nervous way, "You drive, McKenna. That's your name, isn't it?" I nodded and he slid away from under the wheel. "You drive now. I want to look and get the feel of it again." He turned and looked out the opened window of the cruiser. "It's like getting in the mood again, McKenna. You get the beat and feel of a killer, and this is his street. This is Joe's street. You know it is."

"Joe?" I said.

"About the only thing I didn't find out about him was his name," Blackburn said. "I call him Joe."

"Where to?" I asked.

"Just cruise slow. Up and down Main."

"How far up and down Main?" I asked. I turned out of the lot into the traffic.

"Between First and Eighth," Blackburn said. He wore a dark suit, a dark tie, and he had black thinning hair speckled with white. He was in his forties, but had a dried-out look and his skin was as tanned as leather. He kept his head out of the window most of the time and sniffed like a bloodhound.

"No hard feelings I hope," he said to me once.

I shrugged. "It doesn't matter."

"Sure, you resent me coming in, McKenna. Don't blame you, but I had to do it." His voice got low and tight. "But don't worry, you'll get the credit. All I want is Joe."

"That's the important thing," I said, with effort. "To get him—get him before he kills again."

"No," Blackburn said softly. "The most important thing is that you should never get filed away in the books as the guy who let a big one get away."

He paused. "I'm not here to prove anything, or get back at them. It's too late for that. All I want is to finish that job. I just want to get Joe. I want to finish it for good and go home."

"Where's home?" I asked.

"San Fernando. I have a little dairy ranch out there." He looked out the window as I cruised easily along the street, and the neon lights went on, and the all-night shooting galleries and hot dog stands and bars and

114

strip-shows and all-night movie houses lit up. "Don't worry, McKenna," he said. "Whatever we do, you say you did it. This is strictly personal with me."

After another block, he touched my arm. "This is going to be a rough night probably. You have any questions before it starts?"

I thought a while. "How do you know—I mean how can you be so sure it's the same guy?"

"What little they had about it in the papers added up," Blackburn said. "Then I dropped into the police lab and checked. All the other clues were the same, especially those police photos." Blackburn chuckled, but I couldn't say what kind of humor it was, if any. "The public likes gore, but the dirtiest sensational sheet in the country could never publish pictures like that."

"I guess not," I said, to continue the conversation. The memory of those cheap rooms where Joe had done his work was bad. I'd been broken in to all the sordid stuff by serving my time with the Black Maria squad, but those two murder rooms had been too raw for my taste. Even the memory of them made me queasy.

"Take the gin bottles," Blackburn said. "You found two empty gin bottles. Well, there always was. In my three cases there always were two empty gin bottles. It always took him about ten hours to do a job, and all the time he was locked in the room using his knife on them he would be taking nips of gin. In both of your cases there were two empty gin bottles, right?"

"Yes," I said.

"And didn't the autopsy show that in both your cases the entire operation covered about ten hours?"

"Give or take a few minutes," I said. Blackburn's eyes were brighter now, and his voice was edgy with excitement. It was a very warm night but I felt a chill go down my arms.

"Same brand too," Blackburn said. "King's?"

"That's right," I said. "King's Gin."

"I know him, you see, McKenna. And every one of his kills are the same. Every detail is the same. With these psychos, murder is a ritual. I've read about all there is on the subject. It's part of a cycle, a repetition syndrome, as the books say. Everything in the ritual must always be exactly the same. In some, the cycle is longer than others. But this pressure builds and builds, and finally they have to do it. A ritualistic

115

act, McKenna, and each Jane is what they call a live fetish. Each Jane is the same Jane to this Joe, always about the same age and looks. And everything Joe does just before the murder and during it is a strict repetition. That's how I know."

"But how can you know he'll kill again? Here, tonight?"

"He has to kill three of them," Blackburn said, "always three. I didn't know that before, you see. I set a trap and waited, but he'd already filled his quota and he didn't turn up again. But now I know there has to be three, and I know how many days apart the jobs are spaced. You've had two so far. There has to be a third. The time is tonight."

"You knew he would come back?" I said.

"Nobody could know that," Blackburn said, "but I knew he'd come back if he were able. Things can happen to a psycho. Sometimes they get better and don't need the ritual anymore. They have split personalities. They can be fairly respected guys in some community, maybe with a family. They get this psychotic pressure and they go off somewhere—usually to the same or a similar place—and get rid of the pressure. Then they go back home and are good members of the community until the urge seizes them again. It goes in a regular cycle, so I figured if he ever repeated again, it would be here." His voice had risen and now had the taut sound of a stretched wire. "I've waited and waited, McKenna, and I insisted that the D.A. let me have one more chance at butcher boy. I had to convince him. You think I'd miss this chance?"

"I don't think so," I answered.

"Pull in there behind the station wagon," he said. We got out and Blackburn took a deep breath as if he enjoyed the smell of South Main, the sour feverish smell of that wild street on a hot Saturday night. "Let's walk, McKenna."

We strolled past the dark doorways under cheap signs saying ROOMS $1.50 AND UP. About every other entrance went into a dim bar with juke music beating out over the street, and girls perched on bar stools looking out into the dusk like hungry owls.

We strolled on through a dizzy glare as more midway neon blazed on. We walked past the sparkling jukelights. Sirens whined. A screaming woman was dragged out of a doorway by two uniformed cops. A bearded man, barefoot, sat on a curb, laughing softly. The air was ripe with the smell of chili, pizza pies, and stale beer.

Then it turned damp and misty and a thin drizzle fell under the blinking

116

neon. Blackburn led me back down the west side of skid row, past the recreation palace and the girlie shows.

Once he stopped and stood looking up silently into the mist. I looked up and realized with a shiver that it was one of the cheap rooming dives where the second killing I was investigating had occurred. "You see, there's always the liquor store within a few doors, and within one block there's always the monster show." He pointed.

At the corner I saw the marquee of the horror movie, and I heard Blackburn say in an odd, tight voice, "Come on, McKenna. We have to get the mood of it. We only have a few hours."

We stood in front of the all-night, two-bit movie house which specialized in a triple horror bill. The teasers out front were life-sized cardboard cutouts of monsters, each holding in his arms a scantily clad woman whose mouth was painted a bright red, always open and fixed in a silent scream. The huge cutouts seemed to be leering and offering these screaming women to the pedestrians walking by, some of whom seemed to be secretly wishing they could accept the monsters' offers.

Blackburn said in almost a whisper as he stood close to me, "Take a good look, McKenna. You'll start to get the feel of it and of him—I mean Joe. See, the monsters and their Janes all look pretty much the same too, in a way, just like it is for Joe, and every movie is a ritual killing someone experiences vicariously."

"You sure have thought about it a lot," I said.

"For years," Blackburn admitted. "Is there much difference between Joe and the rest of us? A difference only in degree, McKenna. Every guy who enjoys this movie feels like our boy Joe, a little. It isn't so hard to see what this pressure is that builds up in Joe. You can feel it and so can I, and everybody else who will let himself do it. And that's how you catch guys like Joe. You have to identify with them as much as possible. I'm going to catch Joe because I've thought and studied, and I can *be* Joe. I mean, I know enough about what makes him tick—"

"I get the point," I said quickly.

"Good, that's fine. I'm glad you're getting it, because if we work this through to the finish, you've got to get in the mood."

"I'm getting into it now," I said.

A wino jostled us. Blackburn gave him a disgusted shove and he fell flat in the gutter.

We kept looking at the gorilla-man, wolf-man, and tattered mummy

117

handling those silently screaming women. Characters kept ambling along and stopping and looking, and some of them kept looking and moistening their lips. It occurred to me that any one of them might be Joe.

Blackburn had gotten change out of his pocket and was stepping toward the ticket-seller's booth. I grabbed his arm, and he turned around slowly and looked at me for a second as if he had never seen me before.

"What's up now?" I asked.

"We're going to see the show. This is where it starts."

"I saw these shows years back," I said.

"Not the way we're going to see them now, McKenna. This is the first step." He paused and rubbed the flat of his hand across his thin mouth. "You see, this is where Joe always goes—before he does it."

I had to take a deep breath. "How do you know that?"

"Ticket stubs. Didn't you find them, too, McKenna? In those rooms, there must have been ticket stubs, from this particular theater?"

I felt a drop of sweat run down the side of my face. "Yes, there were. But they couldn't mean anything. The ticket seller here, the usher and ticket taker admitted hundreds that afternoon. They couldn't recall anything, or anybody unusual. The tickets could have been anybody's. They just don't add up to anything, so I don't see how you can tell."

Blackburn gave me a thin smile. Under the neon in the dark mist, that smile looked like a twist of black wire. "Five murders, and in every room a ticket stub from a local horror movie is hardly coincidence, is it, McKenna? In fact, every one of those killings was in a room rented within a block of a house showing these creep pictures."

"So how do the creep pictures figure in it?" I asked.

"Gets Joe in the mood," Blackburn said softly. "You can see how that is, can't you? Forget everything else, the way I do, and try to think like Joe thinks. You sit in the dark and look at this and you're all alone, sort of secret-like in the dark, watching this stuff, and you identify with it and start getting stirred up. It's part of the ritual, sort of like those war dances the Indians used, to get themselves worked up and in the mood. Come on, let's go in, get in character."

He bought the tickets and we went into the lobby, which had a stale, suppressing smell of wine, stale smoke and beer, sweat; the smell of skid row bottled up on a wet summer night. We stood there and Blackburn was breathing quickly. He moved over toward the center aisle and looked down it. I heard growls and screams from the screen. Empty bottles rolled in the dark somewhere. A few guys were snoring, their heads propped up skillfully on their hands. Bums scrounged a nickel here and another nickel or two there, and came in here to get a little sleep. They knew enough, though, to keep their heads from wobbling so the usher and the cops wouldn't notice and give them a whack and kick them back out into the wet night.

"It's about the fifth row from the front, in the center," Blackburn said. "Those seats are empty. That's where Joe sits."

"You couldn't know that," I said, "what row and seat he sits in."

"Just about," Blackburn said. "I worked it out very carefully with an optometrist—several of them in fact. I know how tall he is too, and his build and the color of his hair. I've run lab tests on all that, strands of his hair, his skin, which we find under the fingernails of the Janes, and this all adds up to—"

"But how can you tell where he would sit in a movie?"

"One of the Janes broke his glasses, McKenna. We found part of the broken lenses. Couldn't trace the manufacturer, but we went over the lenses and figured out the exact degree of astigmatism. You can figure just about exactly where he sits. But the important thing is the mood, McKenna, the feel of it."

An usher with slumped shoulders, pimples, and a greasy uniform jacket came up and said, "You got to keep your voices down."

Blackburn looked at him like he was something pinned to a board. "Get out of here, boy," he said. The usher blinked and said it again. I showed him my wallet with my identity as a police lieutenant, and my badge. The usher backed off and Blackburn gave him a push. "Get lost."

Blackburn looked at his watch, then at the screen. "I've checked the show times. Joe usually starts working on the Janes about two a.m. He goes right up to the room from the movie. He's already got the Jane up there, drunk, or already too hurt to get away. He watches the horror pix, gets himself worked up to just the right pitch, then walks straight out of here to the room and goes to work with his shark-killing knife. That's an odd one, isn't it? The shark-killing knife. I never figured out where he picked up one."

"How do you know it's a shark knife?" I asked.

"We figured the length, breadth, thickness of the blade, also the sharpness. Also I got an isotopic analysis of the steel from particles in the bone. It's a shark knife, all right. Let's sit down."

119

Another movie started. My eyes ached, from straining at the screen and from the smoke-filled air. The smell was bad, too. I kept imagining I was inhaling about ten million germs a second. Six horror movies had gone by. And it was hot in there, but I kept getting chills up and down my arms.

I wasn't discriminating by this time. The monsters all looked alike, and the women being dragged away to a hideous fate, their clothes mostly ripped off, screaming and screaming, all looked alike to me, and their screams sounded the same, all phony and unconvincing. But the shadowy faces around me were absorbed in it. They sat there, their eyes wide and sort of glazed in the reflecting light from the screen.

"I figure this is about it, maybe another twenty minutes or so. It's nearly one-thirty. That means Joe's big hypo scene has to be coming up in about twenty minutes. Just keep a straight face and wait. I'll give you the sign. I'll squeeze your arm."

"Then what do we do? If we grab him, what about the woman?"

"What does that mean?" Blackburn asked.

"I mean," I said, "that according to your theory, Joe's already got the woman up in the room. He's already done some work on her, or tied her up. She has to be waiting when he leaves the movie here, all worked up and in the mood for it. So what if he gets shot, or gets away, or just won't tell us where the woman is?"

Blackburn stared at me, his face pale in the light from the screen. I don't think he'd considered the woman at all until then. "Oh yes, sure. Well, I'll give you the sign, and when he goes out of here we'll tail him."

I nodded. We waited. Then Joe came in.

Blackburn squeezed my arm, and I rolled my eyes a little and my headache went away. Joe stood at the end of the row on the aisle, and he wasn't anyone you would single out to be much different than the rest of us. I couldn't tell the color of his hair, nor see that he was wearing glasses until he turned his face toward me, but somehow I had the feeling I would have known anyway that it was Joe. Maybe I was in the mood by then. I'd seen enough monster stuff to last me a lifetime. I had the beat, the feel of it.

I watched Joe out of the corner of my eye as he moved in and sat down just to my right. Only one seat separated us. He leaned back and braced his knees against the back of the seat in front of him. He sighed. Later—I don't know how much later but it was the longest period of my life—he leaned tensely forward. He put his hands on the seat in front of him and his head moved. It kept moving back and forth, and I saw the light shining on his glasses.

Blackburn had timed it within a few minutes when Joe would get up and leave the theater. We followed him. He went into a liquor store. He bought, I knew, two fifths of King's Gin, and came out twisting the sack and hurrying through the mist. A raincoat flipped, and thinning hair and glasses glinted in the drizzle.

We followed him to a dark entranceway under a sign that said ROOMS $1.50 AND UP. He hesitated, then ducked in there. I had a raw edgy feeling and a nasty taste in my mouth as Blackburn opened the door and looked up the stairs. I could hear his sharp quick breathing. When he turned and grinned at me his eyes had a shine like dark glass.

"We're wasting time," I said.

"We have to give him a little time too," Blackburn whispered. His eyes glittered with excitement.

"Listen," I said, "there's a girl up there. God knows what's happening. We've got to get up there."

"We've got time," Blackburn said. "First the drinking, the gin, remember. He has to work up to it."

"We've got him now," I said. "Let's go up!"

"Easy," Blackburn said. "You want to break the mood?"

"What's the matter with you?" I asked. "Who cares now about mood?"

The night man at the fleabag's closet-sized lobby told us the man we described as Joe had rented 307. I followed Blackburn up there. He was moving fast, then he started taking his time again, going up the stairs like he was suddenly tired.

The third floor hall was like a yellow cave. It smelled of stale grease and disinfectant and cockroach powder. Blackburn stopped and bent down and stuck his ear carefully against the door of 307.

I heard glass clinking in there. I heard a grunt and a sigh, and something like a moan in there. I could feel the sweat running down my face. I released the spring clip of the holster under my jacket and got my .38 out into the open. I touched Blackburn on the shoulder. He didn't move.

"Let's go in," I said, very low.

He didn't look at me. His body was rigid. He didn't seem to be breathing. He had his ear tight to the door and he was staring.

I heard other sounds then. Something in my stomach seemed to turn completely over. "Let's go in now," I whispered. He held up one hand for me to be quiet. He didn't look up at me. I heard those sounds again. I dug my fingers into Blackburn's arm. It was supposed to be his show. But what was he doing just listening to it?

"Blackburn?" I said.

He didn't move. He just squatted there, listening, and I heard a quick excited wheeze in his breath.

"I'm going in," I said.

His hand came around and touched my wrist. It was cold. It shivered a little. He whispered, and his eyes were pleading. "McKenna, wait! Give him a few more minutes. You can see how it is—I mean after all this time—you have . . ."

I saw how it was all right. I felt a moment of real horror. I saw how it was in his eyes—that glint of excitement.

"He's going to kill her," I said.

He gripped my arm and his mouth turned hard. "What does it matter?" he whispered. "Know what I mean, McKenna? You know? I mean, listen, some little chippie who will end up on a slab anyway, what does it matter now? Think about it, you'll see. You just don't feel it enough to know."

I felt his cheekbone slide under my swinging fist. Then I hit the door with my shoulder. I hit it again. I could feel Blackburn's hands dragging at me, and I kicked him in the face to get him off me before I got a shark knife in my belly.

The girl was too drunk to care much about whatever had happened so far. Joe looked at me through his thick-lensed glasses in a weird way, as if I had interrupted a study period in a dormitory. Then he came at me with his ten-inch hunting knife. I shot him.

When I went back out to go downstairs to call, Blackburn was on his knees. He was looking into the room and saying over and over, "Joe, Joe"—as if he had lost his brother.

The Man Who Came Back
by Edward D. Hoch

New York is a sweatbox in August, and Paul Conrad often wondered why the city didn't simply shut down for the month as Paris did. This August seemed especially bad, with daily temperatures above ninety, and it was no wonder that he thought often of his sister with her cottage on Fire Island. He thought of her, and then went back to his drawing board to work on the winter ad campaigns.

He'd been working nights all month, if only because the office was air-conditioned. After work there was nothing awaiting him but a hot and lonely bachelor's apartment, with a bar or a movie as the only likely alternatives. He was between girls at the moment, much to his sister's displeasure. She felt that any man of 31 should be bringing up a family. Helen, two years younger and already on her second husband, had three children from her first marriage, with another on the way.

This night, alone in the agency art department, he was hunched over his drawing board when the telephone rang.

"Paul Conrad?"

"Speaking."

"Paul, I took a chance on catching you there, when nobody answered at the apartment."

"Who's this?" The voice was familiar, and yet some barrier of his mind kept him from identifying it.

"Ralph," the voice answered.

Ralph. He sat down hard, clutching the telephone as if it might suddenly fly away. "Ralph Jennings?" he whispered, though now he recognized the voice and knew the impossible was true. "You're *alive!*"

"I have to see you, Paul. Tonight."

"Where are you?"

"The Manhattan Manor Motel. It's over on the west side, near the river."

"I'll find it. Are you using your own name?"

"Sure." He hesitated a moment on the other end of the line and then added, "Paul . . . don't tell Helen. Not yet."

"Don't worry, I won't."

He hung up and sat staring at the phone for several minutes. Ralph Jennings, his sister's first husband, had returned from a watery grave after five years. The only trouble was, Helen now had another husband.

No, he wouldn't tell Helen.

The motel room was neat and modern, an impersonal room, but Paul Conrad barely noticed it as he faced the man he'd never expected to see again.

"What happened?" he asked, though he wanted to ask why. *Why did you disappear, why did you come back now, why did you call me? Why?*

"I fell off the boat, just like the newspapers said, but I didn't drown."

"I can see that," Paul said.

Ralph Jennings smiled. He'd always been quick with a smile, always the charming young man with the bright future. Helen hadn't been able to resist him. "I made it to shore somehow, but I was dazed and didn't remember clearly. It took me a couple of days before I was myself, and by that time Finley had told everybody I'd drowned. I didn't know what to do."

"So you did nothing."

Jennings averted his eyes. "Well, I guess so."

"What have you been doing for five years?"

"Sailing, mostly. I've been working on a cruise ship out of Miami. I always liked the sea, you know. We make several runs each year between the various Caribbean ports, and to Bermuda. I only get to New York in the summer."

He was talking too fast, telling too much, and yet not enough. "What do you want me to do, Ralph? Helen's remarried, you know."

"I know. I saw it in the papers last winter. You probably won't believe this, but every year when I got to New York I'd say to myself maybe this summer I'll call her. This year, with the remarriage and all, I figured I should. But the shock might hit her pretty hard—that's why I called you first."

"Weren't you ever curious about your three children?"

"Sure Sure I was curious." His eyes were pleading, but somehow to

124

Paul the pleading wasn't quite sincere enough. "You must think I'm some sort of a monster."

"You disappeared and let Helen think you were dead. You left your three children without a father."

Jennings ran a hand through his dark hair. "They had the insurance."

"Which will now have to be paid back."

"I don't know, Paul. I don't know what I was thinking of! So I was wrong! What can I do about it now?"

"Helen's pregnant, you know."

"I didn't know. How could I? Who is this guy, Paul?"

"Jack Winegood. He makes a pretty fair living as news director on one of the smaller New York radio stations. A good enough living so they can afford a cottage on Fire Island."

"Is that where she is now?"

Paul nodded. "Do you really want her to know you're still alive?"

"Of course! We've got to get this thing worked out."

Paul sighed and stood up. "I'll go talk to her, see how she's feeling. The police might take a dim view of your defrauding the insurance company, you know."

"*I* didn't get the money. And she was acting innocently. She didn't know I was alive."

"How long will you be in town?"

"The ship sails the first of next week, but I'll stay longer if necessary."

"It's too late to see her tonight," Paul decided. "I'll take off from work tomorrow and go see her in the morning. Stay close to your phone around noon."

"Right." He held out his hand. "And thanks, Paul."

"Don't thank me. You're in big trouble, as if you didn't know it."

The street was still hot, but he didn't really notice. On the way back to the apartment he stopped for a couple of stiff drinks.

In the morning he drove out to Long Island's south shore and took one of the summer ferries over to Fire Island. The day was clear and a breeze off the ocean was just strong enough to make the heat bearable. He strolled along the boardwalk until he reached his sister's cottage, then went out through the sand to where he saw them at the water's edge. Helen was there with the three children and another woman, enjoying a morning swim in the salty surf.

As he approached, Helen stood up to greet him. "Playing hooky from

125

work? This is only Friday, isn't it?" The white one-piece bathing suit was flat against her stomach, with no sign as yet of her pregnancy. At 29, she still looked like a college girl, and acted like one sometimes, too.

"How are you, Sis? Just thought I'd take a run out to see you."

"Great! Do you remember Sharon O'Connell? She was a bridesmaid at my first wedding."

Yes, he remembered Sharon O'Connell: tall and graceful and eternally sad, a serious girl in a world that needed one. He shook hands with her, noted the absence of a wedding ring on her left hand, and wondered what she'd been doing with herself. "I didn't recognize you at first. How've you been, Sharon?"

"Fine. Just fine, Paul. It's been a long time."

"You working in New York?"

She nodded, studying him through heavy eye makeup that seemed out of place on the morning beach. "I still do a little modeling, though both the years and the pounds are catching up with me. I went to a party here last night and ran into Helen. She invited me to spend the night, since Jack was working."

He turned to his sister. "Jack's in town?"

Helen nodded. "Covering the U.N. thing. He hopes to get out for the weekend."

"I wonder if Sharon would excuse us for a few moments, Helen. There's something I want to talk to you about. A family sort of thing."

Sharon rose to her feet on cue and grabbed the children's grasping hands. "Sure, you two go ahead. I'll take the kids for a run down the beach."

Paul watched her go, the long tanned legs kicking up sand as she ran. He was remembering that she'd once dated Ralph Jennings, a long time ago when they'd all been younger.

"Now, what's all the mystery?" Helen wanted to know.

"I'm afraid I've got a bit of surprising news for you. Last night—" He was interrupted by the ringing of the telephone in the cottage. Helen ran to answer it and he slipped out of his sport jacket, relaxing on the sand. Far off down the beach, Sharon and the children splashed noisily along the surf.

Helen came back after a few moments, her face pale even through the suntan. "That was Jack," she said.

"What's the matter?" His heart pounded with sudden apprehension.

126

"He said . . . he said Ralph was alive. He said Ralph was alive until this morning, but that somebody had murdered him."

Ralph Jennings had died in the motel room where Paul had met him. He'd been shot in the forehead at close range, with a small-caliber pistol that made little noise. It appeared that he'd just opened the door to admit his murderer when he was shot. Another guest had discovered his body near the half-open door around eight a.m., and Jack Winegood had been covering the story for his station when Ralph's identity was determined.

Paul left Helen at the cottage with Sharon and the children, and caught the next ferry to the mainland. An hour later he was with Jack Winegood in his office.

"How's Helen taking it, Paul?" the big man asked. Jack was not a great deal unlike Ralph Jennings, though he'd always lacked Ralph's twinkle of charm. He was a businessman, and his business was the news.

"She's stunned, of course." Paul told Winegood about Ralph's phone call, and their meeting of the previous night at the motel.

Helen's husband nodded as he listened. "The police will want to talk with you. That may have been the last time he was seen alive."

Paul had already considered the possibility, and he didn't like it. To his knowledge, on the previous evening he was the only one who knew that Ralph Jennings was still alive—and certainly that was one of the prerequisites for the killer: to know Ralph Jennings was alive. "You'd better get out there with Helen," he told Winegood. "I'll see the police."

He didn't, however, go directly to the police. They would only tie him up with hours of questioning or worse. There was somebody he wanted to talk with first.

Oat Finley had been a neighborhood character when Paul and Helen were growing up on the New Jersey coast. He'd come back from the war to open a boat charter service that allowed him plenty of time to sit on the dock and smoke his pipe. There had been those who spoke of an old war injury, of Oat being not quite right, but he'd always been friendly enough to Paul and his sister.

When Helen married Ralph Jennings, a strange sort of friendship had developed between Jennings and Oat. Before long, Jennings had bought a share of the failing charter-boat business, and he spent many nights and weekends on the water with Oat. It had been on one of those trips, five years ago, that he'd fallen overboard in the dark, and Oat Finley had reported him dead.

Paul hadn't seen Oat recently, but he knew where to find the man. The charter-boat service was still in operation, though now it had been moved to Staten Island, where its main customers were weekend fishermen who traveled out into the Atlantic with a collection of exotic lures and a couple of cases of beer.

It was midafternoon when Paul walked down the sagging wooden ramp to the deck of the *Brighter II* and called out to Oat Finley, "How are you, Oat? Remember me?"

Though Oat couldn't have been more than forty, he had a slow way about him that constantly brought forth guesses regarding his age, placing it anywhere over fifty. His hair was already gray, and the weather-beaten lines of his face seemed almost like old leather when he turned to smile at Paul.

"Conrad, aren't you? Helen's brother."

"That's right. Haven't seen you in a number of years now, Oat."

"Been that long?" Oat bit on his pipe. "What can I do for you? Give you a good price if you want to rent the boat."

Paul sat down on a canvas deck chair opposite him. "I came about Ralph Jennings, Oat."

"Ralph Jennings?"

"He's dead."

The wrinkled eyelids closed for a moment, then opened to meet his gaze.

"Ralph Jennings has been dead for five years," he said finally.

Paul shook his head. "No, Oat. Only for about ten or eleven hours."

The expression of friendly indifference didn't change. "He drowned."

"You thought he drowned, but he swam to shore. He's been alive all these years, working on a cruise ship. Last evening he called me and told me about it. Then sometime during the night he was murdered."

"What do you want from me?"

"I thought Ralph might have phoned you yesterday, too."

"He didn't. To me, he's been dead for five years, ever since that night on the boat. I don't know about anything else."

"Just what happened that night? Where were you bound?"

"I told all that when it happened. One of our boats, the *Brighter* it was, had developed engine trouble. We'd worked on it most of the day and took it out for a run to see if we'd gotten the kinks out. It was still making a funny noise, and Ralph leaned over the engine to try and spot

128

the trouble. Just then we hit a swell and he went over the side. I swung the boat around, but in the darkness I couldn't find him."

"All right," Paul said. "And you haven't heard anything from him since?"

"What would I hear from a dead man?"

It was useless to explain any more. Paul thanked him and climbed back to the dock, feeling the sweat beginning to roll down the small of his back. He had visited Oat Finley and learned nothing at all. Now there was nobody left but the police.

Paul returned to the city and told his story to a calm and well-dressed detective who asked questions in a quiet voice and wrote everything down. They even gave him a cup of coffee, and when he left the station house it was with a relieved feeling that the worst was over.

"Hello, there," a voice spoke from the shadows as he was opening his car door.

"What?" He turned and saw Sharon O'Connell leaning against the car next to his. "Well! This is unexpected."

"I always do the unexpected," she answered with a smile. "I spotted your car and decided to wait."

He wanted to ask how she knew what his car looked like, but instead he said, "Let's get a cup of coffee, then."

"I could use a drink a lot better, if you're buying."

"Sure."

She drove her own car, following him to a nearby bar that was reasonably quiet for a Friday night. Over two tall, frosty glasses he studied her carefully cool image and asked, "All right. You wanted to talk to me. What about?"

"Now that's a romantic opening!"

"My brother-in-law was murdered this morning. I'm not feeling romantic. You shouldn't, either, if memory serves. Didn't you date Ralph at one time?"

"My good man, that was a lifetime ago! He married your sister nearly ten years back. I went with him in college."

"Still—"

"Still, nothing! Besides, I didn't come here to talk about me. It's about your sister."

"Helen? What—?" Suddenly he was afraid of what was coming. He signaled the waiter for two more drinks.

129

"I told you I spent the night at Fire Island with her, but that's not strictly true. I met her at this party and came back to the cottage with her, but then she asked me to look after the children and she went out again. She was gone for three hours, Paul."

"Did you tell this to the police?"

"Of course not. Do you think . . . Paul, would that have been time enough for her to drive into Manhattan and back?"

He thought about it and nodded. "Just barely. Are you implying that Helen drove into town and killed Ralph Jennings?"

"Of course not! I'm just telling you because that's what the police might think if they get wind of this. Helen is a friend of mine, and I think she needs help. I think you're the only one who can reach her right now."

"What about her husband?"

"Oh, sure! I'm going to go to Jack Winegood and tell him his wife was away from home for three hours in the middle of the night! While he was working! How do you think that would sound?"

"Better than murder, I suppose. You know, another man might be her only alibi if this thing gets out."

"How's it going to get out?"

He played with his glass, forming moist circles on the table. "Things have a way of getting around. If there's another man, he might talk. And if she took the ferry, several people must have seen her."

Sharon leaned back in her chair. "So now you can worry about it, too."

"Did she get a phone call while you were with her last night?"

"No. Not after we got back to the cottage. This all seemed to have been set up before."

He knew he'd have to face Helen with his knowledge. They'd never had secrets from one another, not all through childhood when they confided their innermost thoughts while hanging upside down from the big elm in Grandmother's yard. "All right," he said finally. "Thanks, I think."

"Is there anything I can do to help, Paul?"

"I guess not. Except . . . Well, you knew Ralph pretty well at one time."

"So did you."

"I know, but not the same way. Sometimes I wonder if I really knew him at all." He paused, not knowing how to put it into words. "Sharon, did he ever give you any hint that he might have been involved in something not exactly honest?"

130

"What do you mean?" Her eyes sharpened with something like apprehension.

"He'd been hiding for five years. Why? Was he hiding from Helen, or something else? If it was from Helen, why would he have come back this summer? Not just because he suddenly heard about her marriage. Examine the thing logically, Sharon. The news of her marriage brought him out into the open, therefore it couldn't have been hatred or dislike of my sister that kept him away."

"Maybe he reappeared just to make more trouble for her."

"Then why did he call me first, to ease the shock? Why didn't he just barge in on her—or better still, call her husband?"

Sharon O'Connell lit a cigarette. "Maybe he did call Jack. He was in town last night, remember. Jack could have killed him."

Paul tried to examine his current brother-in-law objectively. Yes, he could imagine Jack Winegood committing murder; but would he have shot Ralph Jennings, a man he'd never met, as soon as Ralph opened the door of his room? "I doubt it," he told Sharon.

"Then it gets back to Helen, doesn't it? There's no one else he would have called."

"I'll talk to her," Paul said. "Tomorrow."

"I'm driving back to Fire Island tonight, if you want to come along."

"Sure," he decided suddenly. "Helen and Jack have a guest room. I'll stay with them overnight."

The ride out was uneventful, and he began to regret having left his own car in town. Now he'd be stranded out there till Jack drove in sometime the following day, and he didn't know just when that might be.

"Looks like rain," Sharon said on the ferry, glancing up at the stars as they gradually faded from view behind a curtain of clouds.

"Summer storm. In another month we'll be having hurricanes."

"You're a dreamer, Paul. You always were. Only most of your dreams are nightmares." She gazed out at the rippling waters. "Why don't you get married and settle down?"

"Is that a proposal, or are you just filling in for Helen with the kid-sister bit?"

"Neither one. I like you, that's all."

"You liked Ralph, too," he reminded her, awaiting her reaction.

"Sure I did. I liked a lot of guys back in those days."

"What was it about Ralph? Why didn't you two ever hit it off?"

She turned her eyes toward him, just for an instant. "Maybe Helen came along. That's what you wanted me to say, wasn't it?"

"No."

"Maybe I left those kids alone last night, and took the ferry in myself. Maybe I killed him, because he'd come back to Helen again. That's what you're thinking, isn't it?"

"No."

"Damn you, Paul Conrad! You never change, do you?"

"How should I change? Should I go away and disappear for five years, like Ralph did? Should I jump over the side right now?"

They were mostly silent for the rest of the trip across, and Sharon left him before he reached his sister's cottage. It was night on Fire Island, but it was a Friday night, and there were parties in progress in some of the cottages. He found Helen and Jack alone on their porch with tall glasses clinking of ice cubes, and he settled into a chair opposite them.

"Can you put me up for the night?" he asked Helen. "I'll ride in with Jack tomorrow."

"Sure. How'd you get out here?"

"Sharon drove me. I ran into her at the police station."

"Anything new?" Helen asked.

"Jack probably knows as much as I do."

Jack Winegood shifted in his wicker chair. "The police think it might have been a sneak thief who thought the room was empty and panicked when he found Jennings there."

"Sure. Guys come back from the dead every day to get killed by hotel thieves."

Winegood shrugged. "Stranger things have happened."

"Jack, get Paul a drink, will you? We've been sitting here talking and he doesn't even have a glass."

Winegood mumbled something and disappeared into the cottage. It was the chance for which Paul had been waiting. He stared into the darkness at the glowing tip of his sister's cigarette. "Sharon says you were away from here last night."

"What? Oh, I guess I went up to the store for something."

"Are you in trouble, Helen?" he asked, wishing he could see her face more clearly.

"Why should I be?"

132

"You'd have been in trouble if Ralph had lived. You'd have had one husband more than allowed."

"So I'd have hired myself a good lawyer."

"Helen . . . I don't think I ever asked you this before. Did you still love Ralph when he disappeared?"

"He was the father of my children."

"But did you still love him?"

The screen door slammed and Jack Winegood reappeared with Paul's drink. "Hope you felt like gin, boy. The Scotch is all gone."

"Fine." He wondered how much of the conversation Helen's husband had heard, but he didn't particularly care.

"You'd better get some sleep if you're driving in with me tomorrow. I have to be at the station by nine."

"I'll be ready."

He sipped his drink, tasting the burning coolness of the gin going down. When Helen and Jack went in to bed, he decided to stay up a while longer, and strolled down the beach with his glass, feeling the warmth of the sand as it sifted into his shoes. There was a moon now, and the threat of a storm had passed. He remembered Sharon, and headed for the cottage where she was staying, but there was a party going on there. A girl who might have been Sharon was laughingly fighting off a shadowy young man on the front steps.

Paul felt old and tired and went back to his bed.

By noon on Saturday he was back at the police station, seeking out the young detective who'd questioned him. The man's name was Rivers, and he remembered Paul with a casual greeting. He was still well dressed, but this time he didn't offer Paul any coffee.

"You've remembered something else, Mr. Conrad?" he asked pleasantly.

"Not exactly. I just had an idea that might help you."

"Oh? What's that?"

"Well, if Ralph's killer wasn't just a sneak thief—if it was someone who *knew* Ralph was still alive and back in New York—then Ralph must have phoned him as he did me. Hotels and motels keep a record of calls made by guests, don't they?"

The detective smiled slightly. "They usually record the total number of local calls made, and the individual telephone numbers in the case of long-distance calls."

133

"Then you can check—"

"We have checked, Mr. Conrad."

"Well?"

"Ralph Jennings placed only one call from his room, and that would have been the local call to you. It looks as if you were the only person who knew he was still alive."

After that, Paul had one more angle to try—the nagging suspicion that something other than Helen had kept Ralph in hiding during the past five years. Something else, and that something else just might have been an illicit undertaking of some sort. He'd always been suspicious of the amount of time Jennings spent on the boat with Oat Finley.

He found Jack Winegood at the station, checking the news ticker for the latest out of Washington. "I was wondering if you could help me, Jack. You've got an in with the police."

His brother-in-law blinked and put down the yellow sheets of news bulletins. "What do you want?"

"Can you find out if a man named Oat Finley has a police record? Either here or in New Jersey?"

"Finley? Wasn't he on that boat with Jennings five years ago?"

"That's right. He lives out on Staten Island now."

"You're trying to solve this murder all by yourself, aren't you? Mind telling me why?"

"I'd rather not, Jack."

Winegood studied him a moment longer. "Look, I didn't want to mention it in the car coming in this morning . . . I guess maybe you and I haven't been the closest of friends, but I heard part of your conversation with Helen last night. I know you're doing this for her, and I appreciate it."

"Then you'll check on Oat Finley?"

"Wait in my office. If he has a record in New York City, I can get the information over the telephone. New Jersey will be tougher."

Paul went into the office where he'd met with Winegood just twenty-four hours earlier, when both of them were still shocked by the news of Ralph's reappearance and murder. He dropped into one of the sticky leather armchairs and lit a cigarette, prepared for a lengthy wait while Winegood was busy on the phone. The office was a reflection of the man, drab and ordinary, with occasional flashes of interest in the form of framed and autographed pictures. A former mayor, a current senator—the newsmakers. On his desk was a paperweight in the shape of a microphone.

Winegood returned in ten minutes. "That was a good guess," he said. "Oat Finley's been arrested twice. The first time was eight years ago, on suspicion of running contraband Scotch whisky into the country from a ship ten miles offshore. The charges were finally dismissed, because of some problem with the evidence—illegal search and seizure. Two years ago, Federal agents grabbed him on a similar charge—this time selling whisky without a tax stamp on it. He was convicted, but received a suspended sentence for a first offense."

"Interesting."

"Here's something even more interesting. Did you know it was Finley who identified Jennings' body yesterday morning? A card in Jennings' wallet listed him as next of kin."

"I'll be damned!" Paul moved to the edge of the chair, feeling the rush of excitement through his veins. It was a long shot, but it had paid off. "I talked to him yesterday and he never mentioned it. In fact, he pretended to know nothing about Jennings surviving the boat accident."

"He knew, all right."

"I guess he did." Suddenly the pieces were dropping into place for Paul. "When I talked with Ralph, he mentioned that he was dazed after the accident. The water wouldn't have done that, but a hit on the head might have. I think Ralph was in on Oat's smuggling activities. He must have known about them, with all the time he spent on the boat with Oat Finley. Something happened that night five years ago, and Oat tried to kill him. Ralph was scared and decided to play dead, until he heard about Helen's remarriage to you. Then he decided to return and straighten things out—and Oat killed him again."

"Where is this guy?" Winegood asked.

"Staten Island. I'm going out there."

"So am I, Paul."

"I think I can handle him."

Jack Winegood smiled. "I'm still a newsman, and this is the best story I've had all summer. I'm sticking with it."

They left together, and headed through Brooklyn toward the bridge to Staten Island.

Oat Finley's boat was there, bobbing gently against the dock, but he was nowhere in sight. Paul squinted into the sun and finally settled on a bald little man who ran a hot-dog stand at one end of the pier.

135

"How's the fishing, Pop?"

"Good, I guess. Don't fish much myself."

"We wanted to rent a boat. Oat Finley's boat."

"That one out there, with the big mast. Nice one, but he don't rent it much."

"You seen him around today?"

"Not in the last hour or two."

"Where does he live, when he's not on the boat?"

"Got an apartment with a nephew of his, up on the hill. That red brick building."

"The nephew been around today?"

The bald man shook his head. "He usually works the boat with Oat, but I ain't seen him in a couple of days."

Paul climbed the hill, with Winegood behind, thinking as he always did that Staten Island was a place apart. Even the bridge, stretching across the harbor entrance like some steel umbilical, had fed the island only with greater numbers, but not yet with the peculiar turmoil that was the real New York.

"Wait outside," Paul told Winegood when they reached the apartment building. "He might try to get away."

"All right."

Paul went up the steps carefully, wishing he had some weapon, then remembering that this was Oat Finley—old Oat, the neighborhood character. No one to fear, even if he were a murderer.

"Oat!" He knocked softly on the door, then louder. "Oat!"

The door was unlocked. Oat had never been one for locking doors. He stepped in, ready for anything except what he saw.

Oat Finley was seated in a chair facing the door, staring at him with three eyes. The third eye was a bullet hole, and old Oat wasn't needing any of them to see.

Downstairs, Paul found Jack Winegood still waiting. "He's dead, murdered. Not too long ago."

The blood drained from Winegood's face, and he seemed to sway.

Paul steadied him. "I know how you feel. If Oat Finley was guilty, that meant Helen was innocent. Now we're back where we started, only worse."

"She's my wife, Paul."

"And she's my sister. I think . . ." He was staring back down the hill

136

at the shoreline, watching one of the crafts pull slowly away from the dock. He couldn't be mistaken. It was Oat Finley's *Brighter II*. "Jack! Stay here and call the police!" he shouted, already running down the hill.

"Where are you—?"

Paul couldn't hear any more. He was running with the momentum of a downhill race, his eyes never leaving the sleek white hull as it moved slowly, but with gaining speed, through the choppy waters of the Lower Bay. It might have been heading for Fire Island, or for a thousand other points on the opposite shore.

"Quick!" Panting, gasping for breath. "What's the fastest boat I can rent here?"

"Well, mister, I've got a speedboat over there that's pretty fast."

"Can you catch the *Brighter II*?"

"Oat Finley's barge? Any day in the week!"

"Here's ten bucks if you catch it right now."

"You're on, mister."

The man knew his craft, sent it kicking through the crests as if driven by a fury. Within five minutes they were gaining, closing the gap with the *Brighter II*.

"He thinks it's a race," the man told Paul. "He's speeding up."

"Catch him!"

"I saw it go out, but that's not Oat on board."

"I know," Paul said. He no longer had to ask who it was.

"Clouding up. Looks like a storm to the east."

Spray in his face, salty to his tongue, Paul didn't bother to answer. They were overtaking the *Brighter II* again, and this time they would catch her.

"When you're close enough, I'm going to jump for it," Paul told the man.

"Damn fool stunt! Give me my ten bucks first!"

He handed the man his money, then stood upright, grasping the sticky windshield. "Get a little closer."

"You'll kill yourself, mister."

Paul waited another instant, until he felt he could almost touch the sleek silvery side of the other craft. Then he launched himself into space, clawing for a handhold. One foot hit the water, and he thought he'd be grabbed under, but then he was pulling himself over the railing, rolling into the stern of the craft.

137

He got shakily to his feet and clawed his way forward to the tiny cabin. He knew there'd be a gun, and when he saw it pointed at him he felt no fear.

"Hello, Ralph," he said above the roar of the engines. "Back from the dead a second time?"

Ralph Jennings didn't lower the gun. He kept his left hand on the wheel, but his eyes and the pistol were both on Paul. "You had to come after me, didn't you?"

"Helen's in trouble, Ralph. They're going to think she did it."

The eyes were hard and cold above the gun. "They'll know soon enough it wasn't me that got killed. I only needed to confuse things until I could get to that rat Finley and catch him off guard."

"I know about all that, Ralph."

"How, Paul? How'd you know?"

"I didn't tumble for a long time, not till just a few minutes ago, in fact, when I saw the way you were handling this boat. But I should have. Of course I didn't see the body, and neither did Helen. Winegood might have seen it while he was reporting the killing, but he'd never met you. And this morning I learned that Oat Finley had identified the body! That really set me to thinking. I'd already figured out how you and Finley were running whisky ashore from ships and selling it tax-free back in the old days. Your story about being dazed after the accident made me think that it wasn't an accident at all, but a case of thieves falling out. Finley tried to kill you, and you decided to go into hiding rather than call the police and get yourself deeper into trouble."

The craft hit a swell, and Ralph had to steady himself. "Keep talking."

"So this summer, finally, you came back. Helen had remarried, and I guess you realized you weren't being fair to her. You phoned me, and then you phoned Oat Finley, because you knew he'd find out you'd returned. You were more clever with those phone calls than you realized. The police check showed you'd only made one local call from your room. This baffled me, till I realized that there wouldn't have been a Staten Island phone book in your room. You could have called Information, but instead I suppose you went down to the lobby, looked up the number, and called Oat from there."

"You're smart, Paul. Wasting your time in the art business."

"Oat Finley knew you were going to have to tell everything about your disappearance, including his attempt to kill you and his illegal smuggling business. He was already on a suspended sentence, and he knew it would mean prison for him. You figured he'd try to kill you again Thursday night, but what you didn't figure was that instead of coming himself he'd send his nephew—who'd taken over as his criminous partner after you disappeared."

"You're guessing now."

"Not at all! You were ready for something, killed the nephew, and switched identification with him, to confuse things till you could kill Finley and be safe from him. But in switching wallets you must have missed a card he carried listing Oat Finley as his next of kin. When I heard that the police called Finley to identify the body, I should have known right away it wasn't you. You wouldn't be listing your would-be murderer as next of kin. Apparently this card didn't have the nephew's own name on it, because the police only needed Finley's word to be convinced the body was yours. Of course, the truth would come out quickly enough if they checked the fingerprints or showed the body to Helen, but you needed only a few hours. Finley gave you more time than you expected, because he saw an advantage to himself in identifying the dead man as you—he could kill you later and throw your body in the ocean, and the police would never untangle the thing. He must have figured his nephew wouldn't be missed. He could always make up a story to cover his absence."

Ralph suddenly swerved the boat, scanning the harbor area with a quick eye. "Talk faster, Paul. I'm getting impatient."

"You got to Finley this morning, before he could find you, and killed him. When I found his body, the pieces began to fit together. The first dead man was a kin of Finley's, and a nephew was missing. If the dead man was the nephew, I figured you'd killed them both—otherwise, why go into hiding again right after reappearing? When I was chasing the boat just now, I could see it was in the hands of someone who knew it. That made it you for sure. Now tell me where you're going."

"Away. Just away."

"You think you can? Even if the police don't go checking fingerprints, some newspaper's bound to print your picture from five years ago. The cops will know quickly enough that it's not your body, that you set up the scene in the motel room to look like you were shot opening the door. They've probably got a pickup out for you already."

"Then Helen won't have to worry." He stared down at the gun in his hand, as if seeing it for the first time. "I thought Oat was just running untaxed whisky, and I helped him with it. Then one night I discovered there was heroin in the cases, too. I wanted out, and that's when he tried to kill me. That's why he sent the nephew to kill me, too. I don't feel guilty about killing either of them."

The craft hit another harbor swell, throwing Ralph off balance. Paul went at him, trying for the gun, but he wasn't fast enough. There was a single shot and Ralph Jennings crumpled into the corner. By the time Paul tore his shirt away, Ralph's blood was on them both. He tried to speak, and then died in Paul's arms as the *Brighter II* cruised unmanned in widening circles.

Paul looked down at his sister, playing in the sand with her youngest child. "Do you want to tell me where you were that night, Helen?" he asked her quietly.

"I've told Jack, and he's the only one who needs to know. It was just a messy little Fire Island affair, and it's over now."

"I'm glad. Jack's a pretty decent guy."

She nodded. "Maybe this summer hasn't been so bad after all."

Paul kicked at the sand with his bare foot. Down the beach he could see Sharon O'Connell walking toward them. "Maybe not," he agreed.

Bad Actor

by Gary Brandner

Young would-be actors filled the waiting room of the Bowmar Talent School. They paced the carpet or perched on the chairs, sizing up the competition. I walked through the crowd to the reception desk and gave the girl my phony name.

"I'm Alan Dickens. I'd like to enroll in an acting course."

The girl smiled without really looking at me and answered in a voice like a recorded message. "Fill out an application and leave it in this basket. You will be called for an interview."

I took a blank form from a stack on her desk and went over to a table where a couple of beach-boy types were struggling with their spelling. In this room full of eager kids I felt about a hundred years old.

I had felt much younger the day before when I rang the doorbell at Frank Legrand's house in San Gabriel, where the suburban greenery was a refreshing change from my dull office.

Legrand himself answered the door. A narrow-shouldered man in his mid-forties, he wore a dark business suit and a worried expression.

"Thank you for coming out, Dukane," he said. "I—I've never done business with a private detective before."

"Not many people have," I told him.

After inviting me in, he got on with the business. "As I told you on the phone, I want you to investigate this Bowmar Talent School."

"You said your wife and daughter were involved," I prompted.

"Yes. A month ago Tina, that's my daughter, acted a small part in her high school play. A couple of nights later a man from this Bowmar outfit came to the house and said he'd seen Tina's performance, and wanted to enroll her at the talent school. I was against it, but Tina got all excited and Esther, my wife, said it couldn't hurt to go down and talk to them. So the next day she and Tina drove into Hollywood, and *both* signed up for acting lessons. The cost seemed way out of line to me, and it sounded

141

like those people had made some questionable promises about putting Esther and Tina into the movies."

"If you think there's fraud involved you ought to get the police in on it." I lit a cigarette and looked around for an ashtray.

Legrand jumped up and said, "Here, let me get you something." He left the room for a minute and came back with a china saucer. "You can use this. When Esther and I quit smoking she threw out all the ashtrays in the house so we wouldn't be tempted."

I took the saucer from him and dropped my burnt match into it.

He said, "I don't really have anything to go to the police with—just a feeling. Anyway, I don't care about prosecuting these people. The important thing to me is my wife and daughter. I don't want them to get their hopes built up and then be hurt."

Legrand's eyes strayed to a pair of silver-framed photographs on the mantel. One was a dark-haired woman with dramatic eyes. The other was a pretty teen-ager with a face unmarked by emotion or intelligence.

"What makes you suspect that the school isn't on the level?" I asked, tapping ashes into the saucer.

After a moment Legrand said, "Dukane, I love my wife and daughter. There is nothing I wouldn't do for them. But I know them both very well, and believe me, they are *not*, and never will be, actresses."

I had accepted a retainer then and gone home to prepare for my entry into show business.

Now I waited in the lobby of the Bowmar Talent School while the receptionist worked her way down through the completed forms to mine. Then I almost blew the cue by not reacting when she called my new name. When the girl repeated it, I came to and hurried up to the desk.

"Miss Kirby will talk to you," she said, indicating a tall female seemingly made of styrofoam and vinyl.

I followed Miss Kirby through a short hallway with several doors opening off it, and into a small office with walls the color of cantaloupe. She sat down and I took a chair facing her.

"Well, Alan," she said, scanning my application form, "so you want to become an actor, I see."

"I hope so," I said bashfully.

Miss Kirby leaned toward me, and the shadow of a frown marked her plastic features. "I hope you won't take offense, but you *are* just a tiny bit, er, mature to be starting out on an acting career."

My face stretched into what I hoped was a boyish grin. "I suppose I am starting a little late, but I just decided last month to have a fling at it. If it doesn't work out, I can always go back to the bank."

"Bank?" Miss Kirby's interest picked up.

"My father owns a bank back home in Seattle. I'll have to take it over eventually, but in the meantime I'd like to try what I've always wanted to do—acting. Unless you think it would be a waste of time."

Her tiny frown erased itself. "You know, Alan, now that I look at you more closely, I think you're just the type the studios are looking for these days. There are plenty of handsome juveniles around, but rugged leading men are hard to find. Yes, you're definitely the Burt Lancaster–Kirk Douglas type."

I lowered my eyes modestly.

"Come along now and we'll get some pictures of you."

"You want pictures of me?"

"Right. To send around to the studios and agencies. You want to get your face known in the business as soon as possible."

"Oh, sure," I agreed.

Miss Kirby led me across the hall and into a room where a man with orange hair and a big nose sat gloomily smoking a cigarette behind a desk. Photographic equipment cluttered the room, which smelled faintly of developer.

"This is Lou Markey," Miss Kirby said as she left me. "He'll take good care of you."

"Have a seat," Markey said, studying me without enthusiasm.

I put on an eager look and returned his gaze. There was something familiar about the bright little eyes, the comical nose, and the orange hair of the photographer. He used the glowing stub of his cigarette to light another, then jammed the butt into an overflowing ashtray. He offered the pack to me, but I saw they were triple-filter menthols and declined.

"Your nose is going to give us trouble," Markey said.

"It's been broken a couple of times," I admitted.

"They can straighten it, I suppose, but it won't help us now with the photos."

"Sorry," I said.

Markey sighed wearily. "Don't worry. I can light you so it doesn't look too bad, and later I can hit it with an airbrush."

"That's good," I said, feeling foolishly relieved.

He stood up and walked around the desk. "Let's get you over here by the curtain first."

When I saw the up-and-down bouncing motion of his walk I knew why he was familiar.

I said, "Are you *Beano* Markey, by any chance?"

He smiled for the first time. "Thanks for the present tense. Most people ask if I used to be Beano Markey."

"It was the early fifties, wasn't it, when you made your movies?"

"That's when it was. I must have been in two dozen low-budget teen-age epics. I was the comical kid who always lost his pants at the prom."

"Do you do any acting now?"

"Not since my voice changed. Of course, the critics said I didn't do much acting then either, the ones who bothered to review those pictures. And they were right. I never could fake reactions that I didn't feel, so I was always playing myself—the comical, clumsy high school kid."

Markey sat me down in front of a dark curtain, told me to turn this way and that, look up, look down, while he snapped away with a small, expensive-looking camera and kept up a low-key conversation.

"You seem like a fairly intelligent guy," he said at one point. "Why do you want to be an actor?"

The question surprised me. "I don't know, I guess it seemed like it would be fun and exciting."

"Yeah, exciting," Markey said in a flat voice. "Let me tell you something—"

Whatever he was going to tell me was interrupted when the door burst open and a young man with a thousand-watt smile bounced in.

"Hello there," he said, "you must be Alan Dickens. I'm Rex Bowman, president of Bowmar. How are you coming, Lou?"

"I just got started," Markey grumbled.

"You can finish up later," Bowman said airily. Then he turned to me. "Miss Kirby has been telling me about you, Alan. Let's walk on down to my office and we'll lay out a program for you."

He hustled me out of the photographer's room and into a large office walled with pictures of show business celebrities. A mountain of a man with blond curls was just leaving as we entered. Bowman took a seat behind an acre of desk and pushed a legal form across the polished surface toward me.

"That's our standard contract," Bowman said. He lit a long greenish cigar and blew the smoke toward the ceiling where an air conditioner sucked it out.

I ran my eyes down the paragraphs of fine print and saw that the contract implied much, but promised little.

"What's this 'career assistance'?" I asked, pointing to a line near the bottom.

"We make every effort to launch our graduates into successful careers in movies and television," Bowman said smoothly. "And I don't mind telling you that my personal contacts in the industry are a big help in landing that first part."

"What contacts are those?" I asked, as innocently as I could.

He chuckled indulgently. "The names probably wouldn't mean anything to you, but I'm in constant touch with the men who run things in Hollywood from behind the scenes." He walked quickly to a pair of filing cabinets and slid out one of the top drawers. He dipped into a row of manila folders and drew out several 8-by-10 glossy photographs. "Now, these are a few of my graduates whom you're probably seeing a lot of on the screen these days."

The attractive young folks might or might not have looked like somebody on television. All the stars under thirty seemed to come equipped with the Standard Face.

Bowman stuffed the pictures back into the file drawer. "That will give you an idea of the help I give my people to get them in front of the camera."

It gave me no such idea, but I nodded and said nothing. So far, though Rex Bowman appeared pretty fast on his feet, he didn't seem to be breaking any laws.

He took a look at his jeweled wristwatch. "If you want to sign the contract, you can start right in with classes this morning."

"Fine," I said, "I'm anxious to get started. But if it's all right, I'd like to take the contract home tonight and read it over."

Bowman's eyes narrowed a millimeter. "Ordinarily we don't let a student into one of our classes without a contract. You can understand that."

"Well—" I began.

He dazzled me with a smile. "But I'll make an exception in your case. That's how positive I am that we are going to have a long and profitable association."

"I appreciate that," I said.

Bowman touched a button on his desk and the plastic Miss Kirby floated into the office.

"It's almost time for the morning break," he said, "but Miss Kirby will take you in to catch the last few minutes of theatrical speech class."

In the classroom some twenty students sat on floor cushions listening to a young man who was mumbling something unintelligible. I spotted Esther Legrand and her daughter Tina near the front of the group. Both wore flared jeans and tie-dyed shirts. Esther had a loop of beads around her neck, and Tina wore a hammered silver ankh. The kid looked pretty good, the mother would have looked better if she dressed her age. I carried a cushion up front and sat next to them.

For several minutes I listened to the mumbler without understanding a dozen words. To start a conversation with Esther Legrand, I said, "There's a guy who really needs speech lessons."

She gave me an icy look. "That," she said, "is our instructor."

With that conversation out of the way I returned my attention to Mushmouth. Just before I dozed off he must have adjourned the class because my fellow students began standing up and chattering among themselves.

I turned to try again with Esther Legrand, and found her staring back at the doorway where her daughter was in animated conversation with Rex Bowman. He looked over and gave us the big smile and started in our direction. Tina frowned as he walked away from her.

Bowman said, "Glad to see you're getting involved, Alan. It will be about twenty minutes until the next class. You're welcome to sit in."

"Thanks, I'd like to."

"Most of us go up the street to a coffee shop for the break. Would you like to come along?"

"No, thanks," I said. "I'll stay here and look around."

"We'll see you later, then."

When Bowman and the students had trooped out I wandered back into the office part of the building, trying to look inconspicuous. The lobby was still full of aspiring stars. Through the open door of the photography studio I could see Lou Markey arguing with a chubby blonde about which was her good side.

As soon as I had a chance I slipped into Rex Bowman's office. His desk was clean except for the ashtray filled with cigar stubs. I moved to the filing cabinets and started pulling out drawers. Other than the one he had opened for my benefit, they were empty.

A bookcase gave me nothing until I came to a file folder wedged in at the end. The papers inside concerned the financial aspects of Bowmar. I hadn't read very far when I heard the voices of the returning students.

I was heading back toward the classroom when Bowman came in. He answered my smile with an odd look, but said nothing.

According to a schedule pinned on the door, the next class was going to teach us how to walk. I wasn't too surprised to see that the instructor was my friend Mumbles from Theatrical Speech. Before I had a chance to learn much about walking, the bruiser I'd seen leaving Bowman's office came to the door and waggled a finger at me. I walked back to see what he wanted.

"Mr. Bowman has a special class he wants you to take a look at," the big man said.

He led me down the hall toward the back of the building and held the door open while I walked into another room. At that instant I sensed that something was wrong—half a second too late.

The sap hit me high on the back of the neck, in just the right spot and with just enough force. Curly was an artist.

I landed hard on my hands and knees, and tried to shake the buzzing lights out of my head. The room was small and bare with nothing to look at except the blond giant standing spraddle-legged in front of me.

He said, "Mr. Bowman thinks you ought to have a special class in minding your own business."

As I tried to push myself up, he leaned forward and tapped the point of my shoulder with the sap. My right arm went dead and I kissed the floor.

Curly was enjoying himself. He grinned and laid the sap along the side of my jaw. Pain clanged through my head like a fire gong.

"This class is just for private snoopers, Mr. Dickens-Dukane." He leaned over to let me have one in the kidney.

Curly stopped talking then and just moved around me picking his spots. My head had never cleared from the effects of the first blow, and every time I tried to get into some kind of fighting position he would hit me with the sap, just hard enough to put me down again.

After a while Curly tired of the game. Or maybe I wasn't showing enough life anymore to make it interesting.

The last thing I remember was the big blond face saying, "Nightie-night, snooper. Don't come back." He swung the sap at my temple and the lights went out, suddenly and completely.

I awoke to a sound like the surf. Then the sound grew louder and I got a whiff of diesel exhaust. I opened my eyes to see I was parked on a dead-end street next to the Hollywood Freeway. My head and body felt like I'd rolled down a mountain, but nothing seemed to be broken and there were few visible bruises. My wallet and watch were still with me, but the Bowmar contract was gone from my pocket.

As I reached for the ignition I saw that my registration slip had been rotated from the underside of the steering post where I kept it. Bowman must have got suspicious and sent the muscle man out to check my car.

I kicked the engine to life and drove painfully home to my apartment. From there I called a friend on the staff of *The Hollywood Reporter*. She did some checking for me and learned that nobody of importance in the entertainment industry had ever heard of Rex Bowman. He had been a member of the Screen Actors' Guild a few years back, but was dropped for nonpayment of dues.

With a glass of medicinal brandy within reach, I eased my aching frame into a hot tub to soak and think. It was questionable whether Bowman was breaking any laws at his talent school, but at least I had enough information to cause him some trouble with the state licensing board. Also, I had a personal grievance now. Tonight I would pay him a visit and persuade him to let the Legrand ladies down easy, and then we would discuss my bruises.

Rex Bowman's house, I found, was small by Bel Air standards, which means it had something less than twenty rooms. It was after ten o'clock and the streets were empty when I pulled to the curb behind a gray sedan.

I climbed out of my car and started up the walk. When I was halfway to the house the front door opened and a woman ran out. When she saw me the woman stopped, looking around as though for an escape route.

"Hello, Mrs. Legrand," I said.

She went past me with a rush, swinging at my head with something on the end of a silvery chain. I made no move to stop her. She ran awkwardly across the lawn to the sedan, jumped in, and drove off with a shriek of rubber. As I continued up the walk to the open door of Bowman's house I had a feeling I wouldn't like what I found inside.

I didn't.

Rex Bowman sat in the center of a furry white sofa, his head sagging forward as though he were examining the bullet hole in his bare chest where the silk robe gapped open. One hand rested on the back of the sofa while the other lay in his lap with a burnt-out cigar between the fingers.

In front of the sofa was a glass-topped coffee table bearing a heavy ceramic lighter, a clean ashtray, and today's edition of *Daily Variety*. A molded plastic chair was pulled up to face Bowman across the low table.

I went to the telephone and dialed Legrand's number. I told him he'd better get hold of a lawyer and get him out there tonight. Then I called the police.

When Sergeants Connor and Gaines from Homicide arrived I told them as much as I knew, including how I ran into Esther Legrand on her way out. They let me come along when they left for Legrand's house in San Gabriel.

Legrand's lawyer was there when we arrived. He stood protectively behind Esther's chair, advising her whether or not to answer the detectives' questions. Tina, who had been summoned home from a party in Beverly Hills, sulked on the couch next to her father.

Esther Legrand admitted being at Bowman's house, but she refused to say why. Her story was that she found the man dead on the sofa, then ran out the door and panicked when she saw me.

Legrand, in something like shock, said he had no idea his wife had gone to Bowman's place. She had told him she was going to a club meeting, and he spent the evening alone watching television.

While Sergeant Connor questioned the family, Gaines went out to check the gray sedan. In a little while he came in and called his partner aside for a conference. Gaines handed something to Connor, who came over and dangled it before Esther. It was the silver ankh I'd seen Tina wearing earlier.

"Do you recognize this, Mrs. Legrand?" Connor asked.

Esther turned to the attorney, who shook his head negatively.

The detective turned to me. "How about it, Dukane, is this what Mrs. Legrand swung at you when you met her coming out of the house?"

"It could have been," I said.

Connor returned to Esther. "It was found tucked under the driver's seat of your car."

"I don't know anything about it," she said in a monotone.

Tina spoke up then from the couch. "Oh, Mother, it's no use. They'll find out sooner or later." To Connor she said, "It's mine. I was at Rex Bowman's house tonight. I slipped away from the party and went there—it's only a five-minute drive. We were . . . in the bedroom when somebody came to the front door. Rex didn't want us to be found together, so he told me to go out the back way. While he slipped on a robe to answer the door, I gathered up my clothes and ran out. I must have dropped the ankh."

"Did you see who was at the door?" Connor asked.

"No."

"It wasn't me," Esther put in. She brushed aside the protests of her lawyer and went on. "Rex and I were . . . " here she forced herself to look at her husband, "having an affair. When I found out he was seeing Tina too, I went over to have it out with him. When I found Rex dead and Tina's ankh lying on the floor, I was afraid she had killed him. I picked up the ankh and ran out. I still had it in my hand when Dukane saw me."

Sitting motionless on the couch, Frank Legrand looked like he'd just taken a shot between the eyes with a poleax.

While the Legrand family talked themselves into deeper trouble, I got out of there. I wasn't helping anybody, and there were some unformed ideas in the back of my head that I wanted to pull up front and examine.

It was the middle of the morning, and I was on my third pot of coffee and the last of my cigarettes when I figured it out. All I had to do was prove it, and I thought I knew how.

I drove out to the Bowmar Talent School. The death of the boss hadn't slowed the operation. I found the lobby as full of applicants as the day before. I walked past the reception desk to the office area. Through her open door I saw the plastic Miss Kirby in worried conversation with the mumbling speech teacher. As I continued along the hall, the big blond sap expert rounded a corner in front of me. He put on a weak grin and stuck out his hand. "Hey, no hard feelings, Dukane. Okay?"

I hit him twice in the belly before he could tense his muscles. The big man's mouth flopped open and he turned the color of raw modeling clay. I stepped back and planted my feet for leverage, then let him have my best shot on the hinge of the jaw. His face jerked out of shape and he hit the floor like a felled oak.

"No hard feelings," I said.

Lou Markey looked up from behind the desk when I walked into Bowman's office. His hair was uncombed and his cheeks were sprinkled with orange stubble. The ever-present cigarette smoldered in his hand. It took him a moment to place my face.

"Oh, hello, Dickens. Were you looking for someone?"

"My name isn't Dickens," I said. "It's Dukane. I'm a private investigator."

"Are you here about Rex Bowman?" he asked.

"You know what happened last night?"

"I heard it on the radio early this morning," he said. "I thought I'd better come in and start getting our papers straightened out. There's a lot to be done."

"Does that include changing the name back to the Markey School of Acting?"

"How did you know that?"

"I ran across it in some of Bowman's papers. It looks like he kind of took over your operation."

Markey shrugged. "Rex knew how to make money, I didn't. The new name, Bowmar, was supposed to be a combination of his and mine, but most people thought it just came from Bowman."

"What was he going to do next, phase you out completely?"

Markey's forgotten cigarette singed his fingers and he jumped to light another. "It doesn't make any difference now, does it? As the surviving partner I'll take over the school."

When he had his lungs full of smoke I snapped, "Give me the gun, Markey."

"What gun?"

The words popped out immediately, but Markey's eyes flickered down and to his right.

I got to the desk drawer before he moved, and lifted out the .32 automatic that lay inside. Markey sagged back in the chair and aged ten years before my eyes.

"I didn't go there planning to kill Rex," he said. "But I couldn't let him push me out of my own school the way he planned. I hated what he turned it into, anyway. Sure, he made money, but all the lies he told the kids who came to us. I told him it was wrong to lead them on like that, but Rex wouldn't listen to me. He wouldn't give an inch." He blew his nose, then looked up at me. "Where did I slip up, Dukane? How did you tumble?"

"It was the way you left things in Bowman's livingroom after you shot him. Something was wrong, but I didn't pin it until this morning. Bowman was smoking a cigar when he was shot—it went out in his hand. Yet the big ashtray in front of him was empty. Wiped clean. It had to be the killer who cleaned it—not to get rid of Bowman's ashes, but his own. Neither Esther nor Tina Legrand is a smoker. Frank Legrand either, for that matter. But you light one after the other, a distinctive cigarette that would point straight to you."

He stared down at the desk top for a long time, then looked up with the ghost of the crooked smile that belonged to Beano Markey, the comical kid in the high school movies. He said, "You didn't really know I had the gun here, did you?"

"No," I admitted, "but I figured you came straight here, not even going home to shave."

"And you tricked me."

"I just counted on your honesty. You told me you never could fake reactions."

"The critics were right," Markey said. "I'm a bad actor."

Pigeon in an Iron Lung

by Talmage Powell

I lay in the iron lung listening for some sound of her. The lung chuffed softly with that steady rhythm that meant breath and life for me.

The door of the room opened and I saw her in the tilted, curved mirror that was attached to the lung over my face. She stood motionless for a moment, lithe, tanned, tall, beautiful in white shorts and halter, a yachting cap cocked to one side on her close-cut blonde hair.

I caught the dark thing in her face and eyes. It was there only a moment. Then she was crossing the room, smiling, as only she could smile, with her full red lips and perfect white teeth.

"How do you feel, darling?" she asked. She had a soft, liquid southern accent that made you think of lazy water in the depths of a hot, mysterious bayou.

"Fine," I said. "Going out?"

"I thought I would go sailing with Arnold."

"Arnold again?" I said with a laugh.

She kissed the tip of her forefinger and pressed it to my lips. "Don't fret, Dave. I have little enough to do here."

"I won't fret, Cindy. I'm just a trifle narrow-minded."

For a moment, it was almost naked in her face. Her distaste of anything sick and helpless. Her boredom. Her realization that she could do anything she pleased and that I couldn't do a damn thing about it.

I felt tired and drained. I closed my eyes. "Will you be back for dinner?"

"I think so."

I was hungry for companionship, for talk. I hated myself, but I said, "Why not bring Arnold?"

"You mean that, Dave?"

"Certainly. If he's your friend, why shouldn't he be mine?"

"I'll see if it can be arranged," she said. She turned and went out.

I lay there thinking about my wife, about us. The road I'd travelled had started in the slums of Chicago. A tough kid with a lot of ambition and money hunger. And a yen to be respectable. I had fought my way to the top of a labor organization and put a couple of politicians in my back pocket. I had a sharp instinct for putting money in the right investments. As a consequence, I had made a mint. It wasn't enough. I had hit Florida at the beginning of the post war housing boom. The money had doubled, tripled, quadrupled. State senators asked my opinion on pending legislation that would affect real estate. I even had my own lawyer in the capital.

No doubt about it, I was at last respectable.

But it was not quite enough.

Cindy had been the house guest of a wealthy Miami Beach developer when I'd met her. She came from an old southern family that could trace its lineage back to revolutionary times. The pages of southern history were dotted with the names of her forebears. But time had decayed the glory of her family and dissipated its money. Cindy was the end of the line.

She spent her time drifting from Miami to Charleston to Bar Harbor. From friend to friend. She was beautiful and decorative and that social background still brought her in contact with people eager to have her as a guest.

She accepted their gifts and favors as a matter of course. Just as she accepted my proposal to marry her. She looked up at me with her lazy green eyes. "Even if I don't love you, Dave?"

"You're what I've been looking for," I said. "I think we'll make a team. I'll reach you in time."

Her eyes had flashed briefly. "Are you sure anyone will ever reach me, Dave? I warn you, I like myself. I like myself very much."

"I don't exactly hate myself, Cindy. I'm glad we understand each other."

For a wedding present, I gave her the long, sweeping house on Indian Shores Beach. It overlooked a thousand feet of private beach, a boat dock where a cruiser bobbed at anchor, and the limitless stretches of the Gulf of Mexico.

The first few months were O.K. by me. The terrace and long living room, that gave you the feeling you were living out of doors, was the scene of gay parties where smart people moved and talked.

We danced, swam, fished from the cruiser. Cindy never talked a great deal and the remoteness never completely left her green eyes. One night on the cruiser deck when I was kissing her, I raised my head to find her staring abstractedly at the distant stars.

Then one morning I woke with fever and nausea. I was in my physical prime. But a few days later, I couldn't move. The polio virus had done what the slums had never been able to do. It had put Dave Ramey on his back.

Lying there, with the lung sucking life into me, I tried to clear my mind of its train of thought. I wanted to quit thinking of the way in which Cindy had changed her life after my illness. But I couldn't stop thinking.

Now there was Arnold Barrett. He was the sort, dark and tall, that some women would call a dreamboat. He and Cindy had met a week ago. He lived in a cottage down the beach. They were seeing each other constantly, and a foreboding of disaster grew stronger in me each day. Arnold had nothing, except his good looks. While Cindy had a helpless hulk of a husband who was kept alive by mechanical means.

"Miss Collins!"

The short, stout, middle-aged woman who was my private nurse came in from the adjoining room. "Yes, Mr. Ramey?"

"I'd like to go out on the terrace, please."

She turned the lung on its big rubber casters and rolled me out on the long, screened terrace.

"Turn me so I can see the water, Miss Collins."

She turned the lung and adjusted the mirror. "Anything else, Mr. Ramey?"

"No, that'll be all."

"Yes, sir. By the way, Mr. Ramey, Mrs. Ramey said I might have the evening off."

"Oh?"

"Yes. She said she would be here with you. Of course, if you prefer—"

"No," I said. "That's all right, Miss Collins."

"Thank you, sir."

She settled on a chaise longue at the far side of the terrace, picked up a book, and started reading.

I lay on my back, looking into the mirror. Its curvature gave me a broad view. The Gulf was beautiful today, green as an emerald. A light breeze, right for pleasant sailing, rippled little mare's tails across the water.

I saw the rented sailboat as it hove into view. Arnold was at the helm and Cindy was forward. Distance made them smaller than doll creatures in the mirror. But imagination could magnify them. Could bring to life the lazy ripple of water against the boat. The stir of the semi-tropical breeze with its tang of salt and its heat. The image of her standing on the prow, a tall, golden figurehead. Especially desirable, because she lingered just beyond reach.

Lips parted, she gazed into the reaches of open sky and water. Undoubtedly thinking of the sickening wreck who had once been her husband, but who now was nothing more than an obstacle between her and freedom.

The signs were there. I had observed them for days now. But I had to know. I had to make sure. I must be positive that the sickness of my body was not now becoming a sickness of the mind as well.

Arnold tried to tack, lost headway. The sails flapped. She went back to help him, moving along the boat with feline grace.

The boat got underway and moved beyond the view line of the mirror.

"Miss Collins."

"Yes, Mr. Ramey?"

"Bring me a phone, please."

The nurse got up, with a rustle of her crisp nylon uniform. She left the terrace and returned with a phone. She plugged it in, set its special cradle on the small platform beside my head, and put the phone on the cradle. By turning my head, I had the phone in position.

She dialed a delicatessen for me and I ordered a dinner to be delivered that night. Roast chicken, oyster dressing, a good selection of relishes and wine. Miss Collins took the phone away and I slept.

When I awoke, I knew I had been having a nightmare. I couldn't remember the dream, but its effects lingered. I was sweating, my mind upset with the turbulence of anxiety.

It was late afternoon and Miss Collins still sat near me, reading. I became calmer and asked her for a cigarette.

I had finished the cigarette when I heard their voices. Cindy's and Arnold's. He was laughing at something she had said. He had a big, deep, easy laugh. It fitted his dark good looks. It caressed a woman with the right shade of intimacy.

They came onto the terrace, warmed by the sun, healthy, alive. They came walking into the soft chug-chug of the lung and Arnold wasn't laughing.

"Hello, Dave."

"How was the sail, Arnold?"

"Oh, fine. Your missus—she really knows boats."

"She knows a lot about a lot of things, Arnold."

Cindy glanced at me. "Yes, don't I, darling?"

I gave her a smile. "I understand you told Collins she could take the evening off."

For an instant, it was there between them. She returned my smile coolly. Arnold let his head swing around, his gaze search the Gulf's expanse.

"You don't mind, do you, Dave?" Cindy said.

"Of course not. You're familiar with the workings of the lung. It won't be the first time Collins has had a few hours to herself."

"That's right. She's only been off twice in the past two weeks, hasn't she? She really deserves it."

"Why not let her go on now?" I asked. "I've already arranged to have dinner sent from Max's. Arnold will stay, of course."

They couldn't keep from flicking a brief glance at each other. I was playing into their hands and I could sense that it was working even better than Cindy'd hoped.

"Well, I was supposed to—" Arnold began. Then he reached a decision. "I'd enjoy staying, Dave."

"Good. Why don't you mix a drink while Collins gets ready to go? Then you could drop her at the bus stop, if she's planning to spend the evening in town."

"Where else would I plan an evening?" Miss Collins said.

She left the terrace. Arnold made drinks. Cindy brought mine to me, put the bent glass straw between my lips. I took a sip. Arnold mixed a very good martini.

Miss Collins was ready to go in a few minutes. I heard the car leaving the driveway. My car. Arnold driving it. What was he thinking as he drove? That it was a nice handling job?

Cindy was on her third drink. I watched her in the mirror.

"I hope it will be painless," I said.

"Painless?"

"The killing," I said.

She moved around until she was standing just to one side and over me, looking down into my face. There was no emotion in her eyes. But in the

157

soft gold column of her throat a tiny pulse beat. Another pulse showed in the soft hollow of tanned flesh below the white halter.

"What are you talking about, Dave?" she said softly.

"All my life I've dealt with people, Cindy. I know them pretty well. You don't have to draw me a map. It was O.K. for awhile, wasn't it?"

She stood for a long time without speaking. The surf murmured in the near distance and the lung beat softly. Like a heart that would never stop. I knew she was listening to it.

"Yes, Dave, it was fine when you were on your feet."

"But everything is different now."

"You're more dead than alive," she said without inflection. "I've wondered—knowing you—don't you want to die?"

"No, Cindy. And that shows how little you really know me. Life in the lung isn't too bad. With assistance I read, play cards. I do a certain amount of business by telephone. I watch television—secondhand from the mirror. I enjoy the breeze on the terrace here and I like the feeling that I started with nothing and built this house. What man has more, Cindy?"

"Except a wife, Dave."

"I've never had you."

"Yes, you did. For awhile. As much of me as I was able to give."

"Now I have none of you."

"That's the hard, cold fact of life, Dave. You have to accept these things."

"Without shame, remorse, guilt, any feeling?"

She shrugged. "You started this conversation. What are those things?"

"You wouldn't know, would you, Cindy?"

"I didn't want to talk about it, remember."

"But I do. Now there is Arnold. There is freedom, just over the horizon, and barrels of money. Nothing at all in your way, except a man more dead than alive. Did you plan it for tonight?"

"Do you really want to know?" she said. A faint glow had come to her eyes. She looked more alive now than she had in days.

"I guess not. How will it happen? A little accident, a cotter pin or some little something going wrong with the lung?"

"No one could ever blame me, Dave."

"They might suspect."

"Who cares? Suspecting and proving are two different things."

"I might tell someone what you're planning."

158

"But there's no one here but us, darling."

"There's the phone."

"And who's to plug it in for you? I'm afraid, Dave, there's another hard, cold fact you'll have to face up to. There's nothing you can do. You can't move; you can't even breathe without that thing doing it for you. You're helpless, Dave, completely at my mercy."

"I see," I said. "One thing I insist on—that the killing be painless."

"I'm really sorry, Dave, that you had to come down with this thing. I liked you—as a whole man. I saw your courage when this thing struck. Now I see how deep that courage really is."

She drained her glass, looked at me over the rim of it and smiled. "I'll always remember how brave you were, darling."

She fed me that evening, sitting close to me, arranging my after dinner coffee so I could sip it with a straw. Arnold was silent during most of the meal.

When dinner was over, I caught his eye. "This has been pretty drab, I'm afraid. Why don't you two go for a swim?"

"Well, I—" Arnold said.

"I insist," I said. "Turn on the television for me and enjoy yourselves. Later, we'll have drinks."

"Why not?" Cindy said. "It's still early. I feel like rolling in the surf. I want to feel the pull and tug of the tide. Come on, Arnold. Dave will be right here when we get back."

"That's a certain bet," I said. "Arnold, you can borrow a pair of my trunks. Cindy'll get them for you."

I heard them leave the room. Alone now. The lung and I. The metal casing that served for a body. The cell that made me helpless.

I pictured them walking into the surf together. Arnold big and handsome and she lithe and slim. The plunge into the water. His laughter. The roll of their bodies as they swam together in the moonlight. I wouldn't think beyond their swimming together.

An hour passed.

I heard the door open and close. Arnold entered the room alone. He walked over and turned down the sound on the television set.

"It's all over, Dave. It'll look like an accident. They'll find her body with the early change of tide tomorrow. I checked the currents the way you instructed."

"You were always a good strong-arm man, Arnold."

159

"Thanks," he said. "Just like old times in Chicago, eh, Dave?"

"Just like old times. I'm glad you came down when you got my call. The money'll reach you by special messenger after you get back to Chi, Arnold, and the whole thing dies down. Fifty grand for it."

"Fair enough," Arnold said. "Now I think I'll have a drink."

He turned toward the liquor cabinet across the room. He was an efficient man in his job. I knew he had made it as painless for her as possible. I was glad she hadn't suffered. I had insisted the killing be as painless as Arnold could make it. Only a brute would have wanted her to suffer needlessly.

ALFRED
Hitchcock
PHOTOQUIZ

by Peter Christian

Alfred Hitchcock throughout
his long career invested such
visual mastery in the mystery
film that his style and wit and
look are invariably recognizable,
memorable. This distinctive
quality, glowingly individual,
shines in all his films, an
unmistakable
trademark. In the pages
which follow we present
a portfolio of Hitchcock
motion pictures—nearly
all his major films, in
chronological order— as
a tribute to the zest and
the art which were
Hitchcock's alone. And
to make this parade of
Hitchcockian people
even more interesting,
each still photograph
includes a quiz question
for you to answer about
the world of his films. You will
find the answers on pages 191
and 192. If you don't wish to learn
too much of the plot of a
Hitchcock movie you may not yet
have seen, simply skip that
question.

1. An early star for Hitchcock was Herbert Marshall, who in *Murder* plays a famous actor who, after serving on a jury which convicts a girl of murder, becomes convinced of her innocence and sets about to find the real killer. The film is remarkable in many ways, but is notable particularly in that Hitch here tackled something he would later rarely do. *What is it?*

2. Leslie Banks, on the right, is being menaced by a threatening Peter Lorre in *The Man Who Knew Too Much*, first filmed by Hitchcock in 1934. In the title role, Banks knows that a political assassination is being planned, but the villains believe him powerless to stop it *because of what reason?*

3. Robert Donat and Madeleine Carroll here look deceptively cheery in a scene from *The Thirty-Nine Steps*, a screen masterpiece Hitchcock fashioned from the John Buchan thriller. In his version The 39 Steps is a name for an organization of spies; in the new British adaptation, due to be released here this year, they mean a stairway going up to Big Ben. *What are they in the Buchan novel?*

4. John Gielgud is the British spy Ashenden, drawn from
Somerset Maugham's espionage stories, in *Secret Agent*. Hitchcock's approach to the dangerous work of spies is here un-
glamorous and Gielgud's agent is ordinary and unheroic.
Indeed, only the villain is dashing and handsome. *Name him.*

5. Sylvia Sidney here looks quite pensive. The film is *Sabotage*, from Joseph Conrad's novel, *The Secret Agent* (no relation to the Gielgud film on the previous page), and she is plotting revenge on her anarchist husband—Oscar Homolka—who has just inadvertently caused the death of her younger brother. *How does the boy die?*

7. "Jolly good luck to them" are the parting words benign villain Paul Lukas utters at the climax to *The Lady Vanishes,* as the train containing the hero and heroine makes its escape to freedom. *Who and what is the title character who causes all the trouble—the lady who vanishes?*

☞ 6. An innocent-appearing children's birthday party is one of the scenes in *Young and Innocent.* Nova Pilbeam, right, is using the party as a cover to hide a young man accused of murdering his girl friend; she's sure he didn't. *Can you name the rather well known British mystery novel on which this film is based?*

8. *Rebecca* was the first film Hitchcock directed in America, and an international success. In it a nameless heroine marries a brooding widower and is taken to his vast estate, Manderley, filled with ghostly reminders of his dead first wife, Rebecca. Here—at a costume ball—she is doing something quite unforgivable. *What is it?*

9. Europe is on the brink of World War II, and a brash young American reporter on the trail of spies and assassins finds it all high adventure. In *Foreign Correspondent* an elder statesman has just been savagely murdered, and Joel McCrea (center, holding raincoat) has called the police to this Dutch windmill because he has noticed something decidedly amiss. *What has he spotted?*

11. Hitchcock had a fondness for showing his heroines wearing glasses. It is established the very first time we see the fragile Joan Fontaine of *Suspicion* that she needs glasses in order to read. Here she is reaching for our very favorite reading: the mystery shelf. *Why?*

10. In 1941 Hitch embarked on his only attempt at comedy, *Mr. and Mrs. Smith.* Although light and frothy, it was not a success. Audiences wanted him to stick to murder. And as murder could not intrude in a comedy, *what is the ghastly problem facing this couple (Carole Lombard and Robert Montgomery)?*

12. Both dog and fugitive are suspicious of a noise outside. The film is *Saboteur,* in which a handcuffed Robert Cummings—falsely accused of wartime sabotage—makes his way from this western cabin cross-country to New York City. *True or false: Is this the film where at the climax he hangs from the torch of the Statue of Liberty?*

13. Teresa Wright cringes from her beloved Uncle Charlie (Joseph Cotten); she has begun to suspect he is the notorious lonely-hearts killer the police are seeking. This is one of Hitchcock's personal favorite films. *Name both the tune associated with the film and the famous author who collaborated on the screenplay.*

15. The new doctor (Gregory Peck) at the private sanitarium exhibits some very strange behavior in the operating room. The eerie qualities of *Spellbound* are enhanced by the contributions of a distinguished artist and composer. *Name them both.* ☞

172

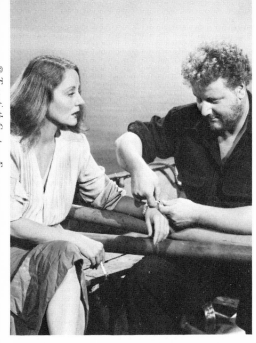

14. A bedraggled Tallulah Bankhead allows U-boat officer Walter Slezak to use her diamond bracelet as fish bait in a scene from *Lifeboat*, a film set entirely on a raft in the churning Atlantic. The Nazi has taken command of the motley crew of survivors aboard the lifeboat, dispirited because of lack of food and water. *What is the source of the Nazi's superiority?*

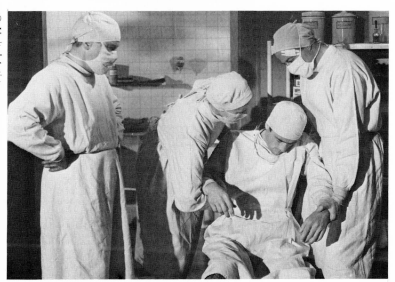

16. Ingrid Bergman and Cary Grant are the lovers of *Notorious*, an elegant, sensual spy story. They are rummaging through the well stocked wine cellar of Claude Rains, and are not searching for the proper vintage. *For what are they looking—perhaps Hitchcock's most famous MacGuffin (that object, of no real use in the story itself, which nonetheless propels the plot)?*

17. Gregory Peck in *The Paradine Case* is a British barrister determined to defend a beautiful, mysterious woman from the charge of murdering her blind husband. In the process, he falls in love with her—she is played by Alida Valli—even though he learns her husband's stable-groom had been her lover. *Can you name the dashing French actor who plays the groom?*

19. *Under Capricorn* was one of Hitchcock's rare costume films. Rarer yet, it was a non-mystery—although its central figures (Joseph Cotten, Ingrid Bergman, and Michael Wilding) were very troubled. *Where is the setting of this colonial drama?* ☞

18. The setting is a New York loft party, with sunset gradually darkening the skyline outside. James Stewart is a professor who gradually realizes his two young hosts, students of his, have just murdered a fellow student for the thrill of it. The film is *Rope*, from the play by Patrick Hamilton, who originally set it in England. Hamilton wrote another famed psychological thriller with a British setting. *Can you name it?*

26. In *The Trouble with Harry* Hitchcock said he "took melodrama out of the pitch-black night and brought it out into the sunshine." The Vermont sunshine, to be precise. Shirley MacLaine and John Forsythe are Vermonters involved in a light, macabre comedy, as here they view a corpse nestled in the greenery. *Just what is the trouble with Harry?*

27. *The Man Who Knew Too Much* was the only film Hitch ever remade, and it was an elaborate remake. We all know about the climax at Albert Hall, where James Stewart and Doris Day must prevent an assassination. This is the beginning of the film, wherein a knifing at an Arab market reveals to two American tourists that the assassination will take place. *Who is the French actor who plays the agent who has just been killed?*

28. *The Wrong Man* is Henry Fonda, a musician wrongly accused of a series of robberies actually committed by a look-alike. This true story was filmed by Hitch in documentary style. Here the man is with his wife (Vera Miles) discussing his seemingly hopeless case with a New York attorney, Frank O'Connor. *Who is the actor playing the real-life lawyer?*

29. A detective whose fear of heights has prevented him from stopping the suicide of a friend's wife believes in *Vertigo* that the woman has returned from the dead. A bizarre and compelling film starring James Stewart and Kim Novak, *it was filmed in what American city—a city whose sense of history and the past added greatly to the mood of the story?* And perhaps you can answer this question as well: *What is the name of the suspense film based on another book written by the authors of the novel which suggested* Vertigo?

30. Cary Grant and Eva Marie Saint might well develop vertigo too in this climactic scene from *North by Northwest*, a delightful cross-country chase film, in which spies pursue Grant, thinking him an agent who in fact does not exist. *What was Hitchcock's first notion of a title for this film?*

31. *Psycho* is surely the most famous suspense film ever made, and the book on which it was based, by Robert Bloch, is justifiably celebrated. *However, who wrote the screenplay—a man who then went on to help create an hour-long anthology television series devoted to the bizarre?*

33. Tippi Hedren shrinks from Sean Connery; as *Marnie* she is a compulsive thief with whom a rich man falls in love—in an interesting and very complicated film. *Can you name the scenic stretch of American highway down which the two drive and talk during the film?* ☞

32. Rod Taylor carries Tippi Hedren down from the attic as Jessica Tandy looks on. The girl has just been savagely attacked by our feathered friends in *The Birds*. Aside from *Daphne du Maurier (who wrote the story on which the film was based), Evan Hunter (who wrote the screenplay), bird-trainers, and hundreds of birds large and small, what revered cinema craftsman contributed greatly to the look of this film?*

35. *Topaz* is the code-name of a Communist spy group in-filtrating the highest level of French security; here Dany Robin (right), as the wife of a French secret agent, and daughter Claude Jade wait anxiously outside a sports stadium as the husband—Frederick Stafford—confronts the man he believes leading the ring. *Before Topaz, with what had Stafford made a name for himself in European movies?*

34. In *Torn Curtain*, a noted American physicist (played by Paul Newman) pretends to defect to East Germany in order to bring back out with him a secret formula. Julie Andrews tags along. In the film Newman must commit an act he finds quite repugnant. *What is it?*

36. Critics called *Frenzy* Hitchcock's return to the top of his form. Here Jon Finch buys a newspaper, knowing that by some awful twist of fate the necktie strangler the police are seeking is *him. One of the delightful secondary characters in this film is Chief Inspector Hunt's wife (Vivien Merchant)—what is her specialty?*

37. Barbara Harris and Bruce Dern are dazed as they walk away from an accident in *Family Plot:* their car has careened down a mountain road. (As well, they have become involved in a kidnapping scheme.) Considering their respective professions, both these two should have avoided this crash. *What are their professions?*

Bonus Question

38. At the start of each episode of his television show, Alfred Hitchcock stepped into a line-drawing of his profile which seemed to be composed mainly of half circles. *What creative artist drew the cheeky caricature that across the decades has become such a Hitchcock trademark?*

190

ALFRED
Hitchcock
PHOTOQUIZ
The Answers

1. The whodunit form. Hitchcock often said he preferred stories of suspense to filming whodunits.
2. They have kidnapped his daughter to insure his silence.
3. Steps leading up a deserted beach on a British seacoast.
4. Robert Young.
5. The boy is sent with a parcel carrying a bomb. He does not know the contents of the parcel, and when the bus he is riding is delayed the bomb blows up.
6. Josephine Tey's *A Shilling for Candles*.
7. Miss Froy, a kindly middle-aged governess (Dame May Whitty).
8. She is wearing Rebecca's dress.
9. The blades of the windmill have been turning in the wrong direction.
10. Because of a bureaucratic error, they are not legally married.
11. She suspects her ne'er-do-well husband (Cary Grant) is adding murder to his schemes.
12. False. The man dangling from Liberty's torch is the villain, Norman Lloyd, whom Cummings then tries to save.
13. The *Merry Widow Waltz*. Thornton Wilder.
14. He has a secret supply of water; the others discover this when they notice he is the only one who perspires.
15. Salvador Dalí (who designed the abstract dream sequence) and Miklos Rosza.
16. Samples of a uranium substance have been hidden in the wine bottles.
17. Louis Jourdan.
18. *Angel Street*—which was filmed as *Gaslight*.
19. Australia.
20. Alastair Sim.
21. Raymond Chandler.
22. Quebec City.

23. The ringing of the phone is to bring Grace Kelly into the outer room, where the murderer is waiting to strangle her. It was shot in the 3-D process, though not released that way.
24. Raymond Burr—three years before *Perry Mason.*
25. Jessie Royce Landis.
26. That he is dead.
27. Daniel Gelin.
28. Anthony Quayle.
29. San Francisco. *Diabolique.*
30. As the climax took place on Mount Rushmore, Hitchcock toyed with calling it *The Man on Lincoln's Nose.*
31. Joseph Stefano, who wisely did not change much of Bloch's structure. He later was connected with *The Outer Limits.*
32. Ub Iwerks of the Disney Studio, who helped create Mickey Mouse and Flip the Frog, as well as the soaring flocks of *The Birds.*
33. The Pennsylvania Turnpike (they even stop at a Howard Johnson's).
34. He must help kill an enemy—and discovers it's very hard to do.
35. Stafford played a James Bond-type hero in a series of flamboyant spy films popular in Europe.
36. The preparing of ghastly, inedible "gourmet" dinners.
37. Bruce Dern is a taxi-driver and Barbara Harris is a psychic.
38. Alfred Hitchcock himself—of course.

If You Scored...

30-38: You're the fan who knew too much.
10-29: Dial M for More Hitchcock.
0-9: You're for the birds.

King of the World

by John Lutz

"**D**id you inform him of his rights?"

"Sure," the detective sergeant said to his lieutenant, "but I don't know if he even heard me. He just sits there like that."

"An ambulance is on the way with a police doctor," the lieutenant said. "We have to be very careful with this one." He looked down at the motionless man. "What did you get out of his pockets?"

The sergeant leaned toward a small night stand and picked up a black leather wallet and some keys. He was a grossly overweight man who breathed heavily, possibly asthmatically, and he moved as if his back hurt. "His name's Harry Beckman, thirty-six years old, seems to be single, some kind of confidential investigator from Chicago who specializes in finding missing persons. These keys are to a rented sedan parked out front."

"Search the car?" he was asked.

"Yeah, nothing." The sergeant handed the keys and wallet to the lieutenant and, breathing deeply, stared down at the dark-haired man sitting cross-legged on the floor. "I guess he's in some kind of shock," he said. "I almost went into shock myself when I walked in here. Do you suppose the doctor can pull him out of it?"

The lieutenant's face was calm but his hands were moist and nervous, clenching and unclenching. "We've got to get him to talk somehow," he said. "He's the only one who knows. The only one."

Money had always been Beckman's problem. He'd never had enough when he was a kid, never had enough when he was a cop and now, after establishing his own business and earning a sporadic but adequate income, he still felt as though he didn't have enough. The deep ache of never having enough money starts in childhood and never really leaves some men.

So, Beckman was glad to get the job Ida Goulart offered him over the phone. He made an appointment to see her at her home that afternoon, a mediocre address on Gavin Street.

The second-floor Gavin Street apartment was no surprise to Beckman. The furnishings were of low-average price, in a wide range of taste, just what the outside of the apartment building indicated. Ida Goulart wasn't much of a surprise either. On the phone her voice had given the impression of a rather dull sort of woman, confused by an unexpected slap of fate; and when she answered Beckman's ring, that's how she appeared to him, a plain-faced brunette with a chunky figure and a bewildered expression in her dark eyes.

With a hasty smile she motioned for him to come in, and sat facing him on the low sofa, leaning forward stiff-backed as if she really would rather be standing.

Beckman settled into his chair and crossed his legs comfortably. "You said over the phone that your husband had disappeared."

Ida Goulart nodded. "Two weeks ago yesterday—a Tuesday night."

"Have you heard from him at all?"

She swallowed hard and shook her head.

"You've called the police, haven't you?" Beckman prodded.

"Yes, that's the first thing I did when I saw the next morning that Bill was still gone. So far the police haven't found any trace of him. That's why I called you. You found the husband of a friend of mine once, a girl named Marie Boyd."

"I remember." Beckman recalled a weeping, lean-faced girl. "Why don't you tell me the circumstances, Mrs. Goulart? Tell me how he left."

The bewildered expression lighted her eyes. "That's the thing about it . . . there's hardly anything to tell. I was in the kitchen fixing us a snack while Bill was watching the ten o'clock news on television. When I came back into the living room his chair was empty. I heard footsteps on the hall stairs, and I looked out the front window and saw him get into a taxi. Then . . . he was gone."

"Could he have phoned for the taxi before, perhaps when you were out of the room?"

"I suppose he could have, but he didn't say anything—not a word—about leaving," she told him.

"Were you and Bill getting along all right before he left?" Beckman asked.

"I . . . think we were. Only for the past month or so Bill had been

194

acting . . . well, distant, I guess you'd say. I'd find him just sitting at times, apparently thinking about something, and when I'd talk to him he'd act as if he hadn't even heard me. But we didn't have any arguments, nothing like that."

"Where was your husband employed?"

"At Mercer and King Supply Company. He managed the accounting department. And he seemed to like his work . . . he seemed to like his life."

"But we do know that he left of his own volition," Beckman said. "The question is why, and why hasn't he returned?" He fixed direct green eyes on Ida Goulart. "I'd like a photograph of your husband, and a list of his charge accounts. And do you own a car?"

"Yes," Ida Goulart said, rising from the sofa, "it's still parked downstairs. I don't know why Bill didn't take it."

Beckman waited while she left the room and returned with a snapshot of a thin, blond-haired man posed before a fireplace. Ida Goulart told Beckman that her husband was five feet, ten inches tall, had blue eyes and a semi-circular scar on his right cheekbone. Then she handed him a slip of paper with the names of some department stores and oil companies written on it, along with corresponding charge account numbers.

Beckman got Ida Goulart to talk some more about her husband, and he got the impression of a somewhat nervous man with an average-paying job and few close friends. Goulart had become an accountant three years after his discharge from the Navy, and two years after his marriage. Their doctor had informed the newlyweds that Ida could never have children, but that hadn't seemed to upset William Goulart too much, and it was seldom mentioned.

"I'll do everything I can," Beckman said, after accepting Ida Goulart's retainer check, "and I'll give you regular progress reports as I go along." As he was leaving he turned at the door. "If the police tell you anything, you call my office and let me know."

Ida Goulart nodded and managed her hasty smile as he went out.

When Beckman got back to his office he began his routine. He had a watch put on all Goulart's charge accounts so that if the missing man used a charge card, Beckman's office and the police would be notified. Then Beckman called a contact on the police force and asked what they knew about the Goulart case. They knew practically nothing. The only information they could add to what Beckman already knew was that they'd

195

checked the cab companies and found that Goulart had been taken to the intersection of Forest and Vector Streets, where he'd paid the cabbie and got out to stand there until the cab turned the corner. That dimmed one of Beckman's theories. Also, the police seemed bored with the case; in big cities men got disgusted and left their wives every day.

Beckman talked to Goulart's co-workers, his neighbors, and friends of his wife. None of them could help, and all of them had been surprised by Bill Goulart's sudden disappearance. He contacted Goulart's bank and found that he'd cashed two thousand dollars worth of government bonds the day before he vanished.

Then Beckman decided to play on a hunch that had been growing in the back of his mind. Probably, since he hadn't surfaced by now, Goulart had left the city, and the most likely way for a man with two thousand dollars in his pocket to do that was to fly. From the Goulart apartment to the airport was approximately a twenty-minute drive. The intersection of Forest and Vector, a desolate, open space, was on the most direct route from the Goulart apartment to the airport, almost at the halfway point. Bill Goulart had left home during the ten o'clock news commercial, at exactly ten-fifteen. He probably would have reached Forest and Vector at about ten twenty-five. Beckman began the monotonous task of contacting all the cab companies and asking them to check their records for a fare picked up at the Forest and Vector intersection at about ten-thirty the Tuesday night that Goulart had left his wife and home.

By noon the next day he'd found the information he needed. A Suburban cab had picked up a man at the intersection at ten thirty-two that night and taken him to the airport; and when the cabbie looked at Goulart's photograph he remembered vaguely that his fare had been of the same general appearance. William Goulart was taking great care to cover his trail. There was no doubt the man wanted to disappear completely.

What it meant was that Goulart would have reached the airport at about ten forty-five. Probably the flight he went there to take had departed around eleven o'clock that evening. The word 'probably' was cropping up too often for comfort in Beckman's chain of logic, but he picked up the telephone and called the airport.

Three commercial flights had laid over, then departed that Tuesday night between ten-forty-five and eleven-fifteen: one to Miami, one to New York and one to Saint Louis. Beckman managed to get a passenger list for all three, with lines under the names of the passengers who boarded the planes at the airport. In all, there were over a hundred underlined names; forty-six of them male, one undetermined. Beckman was sure one of the forty-seven names was William Goulart's alias.

Beckman spent the next two days with the telephone and the city directory. Most of the names he found listed in the directory, and telephone calls to each of the bearers of those names revealed to him that such a person underlined on the passenger list did indeed exist and had taken the Tuesday flight.

Finally he was left with twenty-seven male names, people who had been visiting or on business in the city and lived out of town. Beckman checked the Miami, Saint Louis and New York directories and eliminated twelve more names. The Saint Louis flight continued on to New Orleans, and with that city's phone directory Beckman eliminated six more of the underlined names.

Nine names left. Beckman sat back in his desk chair and studied them.

Four of the names were unusual, names it was possible but unlikely Goulart would have picked for an alias. Beckman drew a circle around each of these names and concentrated on the other five. Three had flown to New York, two to Saint Louis. Probably Goulart was in one of those two cities, but that information wasn't a great deal of help.

There was one last play left.

Beckman picked up the phone and called Ida Goulart. He read the five names to her over the telephone to see if any of them struck a note in her memory.

None of them did.

Then Beckman read the circled names on the chance that one of them would provoke a reaction.

One did: Ivan Katky.

"I've heard his name," Ida Goulart said in a sure, firm voice, "though not in a long, long time. I think he was a friend of Bill's years ago on the West Coast. They met at a lounge Bill used to go to before we were married. Why do you ask? Does he know something about Bill's disappearance?" she asked anxiously.

"I doubt it, Mrs. Goulart. I'll let you know if anything comes of the lead."

Beckman didn't even replace the receiver in its cradle. He depressed the button with his finger to get a dial tone, then called the airport for a reservation on the next flight to Saint Louis.

As his plane circled in its holding pattern over Saint Louis, Beckman sat looking out the rounded window at the backward flashing wisps of cloud. His professional instinct told him he'd discovered the thread that would lead him to the center of the case. If everything worked out, that thread would grow thicker, less tenuous, easier to follow, until finally it led to William Goulart and the reason for his disappearance.

Goulart was more clever than most in choosing his alias. Often a fleeing man will use an alias with the same initials as his own name; convenient if any of his possessions happen to be monogrammed, and also quicker to ring a bell if he is paged or addressed by a new acquaintance. Goulart had used an alias that was just as convenient, but harder to trace: the name of an old friend from a distant past. If he heard the name spoken by a hotel desk clerk or someone he just met, it would register immediately and there would be no telltale vacant stare for a fraction of a second.

As the big jet airliner touched down, Beckman could only hope that Goulart hadn't decided to change his alias. If he had, that would be the end of the trail. Another possibility was that Beckman was pursuing a real Ivan Katky, possibly even Goulart's old friend. Coincidence though that would be, Beckman was prepared for it. He had run up against coincidence too often in the past not to be prepared.

Beckman collected his luggage, then rented a compact sedan and drove it to a large motel by the airport, where he registered. He didn't bother to unpack but immediately got out the Saint Louis telephone directory and began dialing hotels and motels.

He dialed over thirty of them before he got the response he was seeking.

The deskman at the Three Pines Motel in south Saint Louis County told Beckman that there was an Ivan Katky registered there, in room twenty-one. He asked Beckman if he wanted to be put through to Mr. Katky, but Beckman told him he'd just wondered if Mr. Katky had arrived yet, thanked him and hung up.

Within ten minutes Beckman was checked out and driving the rented compact toward the Three Pines Motel.

Two hours later Beckman knew he'd accomplished his mission. He sat in a webbed lounge chair near the Three Pines Motel swimming pool and watched William Goulart take dives off the low board. Goulart was a smaller man than he'd appeared to be in his photograph, smaller, leaner and more nervous. He was concentrating earnestly, waiting his turn on the board behind three teen-age girls, trying to make each dive into the sparkling blue water more perfect than the last.

Beckman was considering going to his room to place a long-distance phone call to Ida Goulart in Chicago, and was in fact rising from his chair to do so, when the man with the yellow sunglasses arrived.

Beckman sat back down.

The man had walked to the side of the pool and stood with his hands on his hips, a middle-aged fat man with sloping shoulders, wearing unflattering skintight red swimming trunks. When Goulart saw the man, he immediately swam toward him and lifted himself out of the water onto the edge of the pool. The fat man squatted down beside Goulart and they began to talk very seriously.

There was something about the way they were talking that arrested Beckman's attention. Their faces were grave, their bodies tense in the hot, late afternoon sun.

When they parted, Beckman followed the heavy man to see in what room he was registered. He waited, watched, and within an hour the fat man left, now wearing a neat blue business suit, and met William Goulart in the motel lounge. While they were occupied over drinks, Beckman decided to let himself into the fat man's room.

He was in and out in ten minutes.

It hadn't taken him long to discover the simple facts he was after. The man's name was Arthur Morganthau, and he was a banker from Minneapolis. He was also carrying three unloaded revolvers in his luggage, beneath his folded undershorts.

When Beckman got back to his own room he called the desk and found that there was no Arthur Morganthau registered at the motel. A second phone call netted Beckman another interesting fact. Five days ago in Minneapolis Arthur Morganthau had been reported as a missing person.

Beckman then called his office and had Carol, his secretary, run a check on any possible tie-in between Goulart and Arthur Morganthau.

Later that evening Carol's return call told Beckman that there had indeed been a time when the two men's lives had touched. Goulart and Arthur Morganthau had been in the Navy together twenty years ago. They had been involved in and almost court-martialed over a black market scandal in Korea. For security reasons, however, the case had been hushed up, the charges dropped, and along with a third man who'd been involved, Goulart and Morganthau were—officially, at least—absolved of guilt.

Beckman went to the motel dining room and thought about it over a supper of ravioli and garlic bread.

The third man, for the third gun, arrived that same evening. Lounging casually at the vantage point he'd chosen in the bar, where he could keep an eye on the motel lobby, Beckman saw him come in, a graying, handsome man with a small, darker moustache that was trimmed to exact symmetry. He was tall and well-built, but with a developing middle-age paunch even his immaculately tailored suit couldn't quite conceal. As with every new guest, Beckman got up and nonchalantly followed the man to his room.

Ten minutes later he followed the well-dressed man, now accompanied by Goulart and Morganthau, back to the bar. Beckman left them then and used the same procedure he'd used earlier to search the man's room and determine his real identity. Nevin—Roger Nevin; the name made Beckman smile as he let himself out of the room. Roger Nevin was the barely-mentioned third man in the twenty-year-old Navy black market episode.

Beckman sighed as he entered his own room and sat on the edge of the bed to use the telephone.

It didn't surprise him to find that Roger Nevin had disappeared seven days before in Los Angeles. He'd been thoughtful enough to leave his wife a terse, almost rude note, so the police wouldn't investigate the possibility of foul play.

The electric alarm clock on the night stand by Beckman's bed read nine o'clock. There wasn't much need to watch the three men now; since Nevin had just checked in, it was a sure bet they would spend at least the night in the motel. As he lay back on the soft bed, Beckman laced his hands behind his head and stared at the mottled pattern of light and shadow on the ceiling.

Three old friends from a hazy past, walking out on their lives and meeting again in secret . . . Had they met at all in the past two decades? They'd had to, of course, but how often? They lived in different cities in different parts of the country. Apparently, there was nothing to link them except . . . their youthful dishonesty. A man would have to probe deeply, more deeply than the police would, to discover that long-ago link. What did it mean? Why were they arming themselves?

Beckman had a feeling about it, an instinct; and he was intelligent enough to trust his instinct. There was something here that fascinated him, drew him, puzzled him.

His mind was tired, groping restlessly, coming up with nothing. Beckman reached over and set the alarm for seven the next morning, then stood and undressed to his undershorts. He knew the sensible thing to do now was to sleep, and within five minutes he was doing just that, oblivious to the vibrating hum of the air-conditioner.

The next day the three men checked out, at different times. Goulart was the last to leave, and Beckman waited patiently and followed him. Morganthau and Nevin had left in cabs, but Goulart was driving a light green sedan that Beckman hadn't seen before.

Goulart drove out Chippewa Avenue, then turned onto a four-lane highway that led toward the green sedan well under the speed limit, and Beckman, following in the rented compact, had to stay four cars back to remain inconspicuous.

Now Goulart's route began to wind as he took an off-ramp from the highway and turned right. Beckman stayed a comfortable distance behind him as the green sedan traveled a few blocks, made another right, then a left onto a narrow, untraveled side street where Goulart pulled to the curb to park in the shade of a large tree. Beckman passed him, drove around the block and parked some distance behind him.

Goulart didn't get out of the car.

Beckman sat patiently, and through the rear windows and the windshields of the two cars that separated them he saw Goulart glance twice at his watch.

Five minutes passed. Nothing happened. Again prodded by instinct, Beckman reached inside his suit coat and lightly touched the butt of the automatic in his shoulder holster.

Then, abruptly, Goulart simply started the sedan and drove off. Carefully, eyes fixed unwaveringly on the green car, Beckman followed.

Three blocks, a left turn, then a right, then a right into an alley; Beckman slowed as he approached the mouth of the alley, letting the car inch forward, leaving room for a quick decision and a quick turn into the alley as he peered down it—but he didn't turn.

The green sedan was stopped near the back door of a large brick building. As Beckman watched, Morganthau and Nevin, dressed in their neat dark business suits and each carrying two large suitcases, emerged through the doorway and unhurriedly climbed into the sedan.

Beckman knew Goulart wasn't going to back out to the street, so he sped up and began to drive around the block to latch onto them at the other end of the alley.

When he made a right turn and passed the First Mercantile Bank sign a cold excitement flashed through Beckman. He made another right, saw the green sedan moving ahead in time with the traffic, and switched lanes to draw closer to it. After a few blocks a police car sped past them, going in the opposite direction, red light flashing and siren screaming. In the distance more sirens sounded.

Beckman moved up to within two cars of the green sedan and looked at the three men it contained. They appeared to be just what they were, three sedate, middle-aged businessmen. Another patrol car roared past with screaming siren. The moderate speed of the green sedan remained steady, the three men didn't even glance to the side.

Five minutes later Beckman followed them into a large shopping-center parking lot. They left the green sedan halfway down one of the rows, neatly parked between the yellow lines, then on foot the men cut across three rows of gleaming parked cars and got into a tan hardtop.

They left the lot by the opposite exit, still followed by Beckman.

By now the news was on the radio. The First Mercantile Bank had been robbed by two well-dressed men armed with revolvers, who had escaped with an undetermined amount. The men had worn stocking masks over their faces and the robbery had been very brisk and businesslike.

No doubt it had been businesslike, Beckman mused, admiring the unhurried coolness of the escape he had witnessed. The three fugitives had blended into their surroundings with the camouflage of normalcy to protect them.

Beckman followed the tan sedan for another ten minutes, then parked across the street as it entered the underground parking lot of a large apartment building. The building was old and in a neighborhood of similar buildings—tall, stained brick and brownstone—each containing well over fifty separate units. They weren't the sort of buildings that sported doormen or parking attendants.

Quickly Beckman got out of his car and jogged across the street. He entered the lobby of the apartment building and walked toward the other end and the elevator doors. The indicator arrow for the elevator on the

202

left had just begun to move from the 'B' when he pressed the up button.

None of the three men appeared startled or guilty as the metal doors slid open and Beckman stepped into the elevator. He nonchalantly pressed the already glowing button for the fifth floor.

The air in the rising elevator was hot, close. William Goulart was holding one of the large leather suitcases now. Morganthau had two suitcases and Nevin was holding the remaining one before him casually, with the fingers of both hands laced about the handle. None of the men gave any sign of recognizing Beckman from the motel, or of thinking it too much of a coincidence that he was taking the elevator to the same floor as themselves. The elevator doors opened onto a long hall with worn gray carpeting. A television was playing the evening news too loudly somewhere and faint smells of cooking lingered in the hall. Beckman waited politely and was the last off the elevator.

As he walked behind them down the long hall he could sense the change that was coming over them, the three businessmen-bank robbers with their first qualms, their first frightening suspicion that things weren't going as planned in their big gamble. None of them turned or glanced back, but Beckman saw their paces falter slightly, their backs stiffen. A rashlike flush crept above the collar of Nevin's shirt. They were still waiting, holding their breaths, hoping that Beckman would stop walking and enter one of the units off to the side.

Their paces slowed, became unsteady, and Beckman knew they'd reached the apartment that one of them had rented under his alias.

Beckman was thinking of hunger and humiliation, of his childhood on Bolton Street, as he drew his automatic from its shoulder holster. "I don't mind if I do come in," he said.

Now all three of them turned and stared at Beckman. He could see the fear and puzzlement beneath the expressions they tried to wear. Goulart's slender hand was quaking, though his eyes were unblinking.

"You wouldn't want one of the other tenants to step out of his door and see the gun, would you?" Beckman asked.

It was the aging, handsome Nevin who sighed. "No," he said, "let's go in, Mr.—"

"No need for introductions, Mr. Nevin."

Nevin's eyes narrowed at the sound of his real name and he turned away from Beckman, almost as if he'd been insulted, and fitted the key into the apartment lock.

203

"After you, Mr. Goulart, Mr. Morganthau," Beckman said.

Inside the apartment, small and furnished badly with overstuffed chairs and a sofa, Beckman had the three men take seats opposite him while he sat in the room's one hard, low-backed wooden chair near the alcove that was the kitchen.

"Who are you?" Goulart asked in a voice brittle with fear.

"A man who knows enough already, but a man who wants some more answers."

Nevin asked, "Would it be useless for us to say we don't know what you're talking about, Mr.—"

"Absolutely," Beckman interrupted. "Now I want you to tell me: why?" He thought of the revolvers the men were carrying. They had been empty when he'd seen them in Morganthau's suitcase, and no ammunition had been packed. Beckman was willing to bet they were still unloaded. These men weren't fools, but they weren't hard and tough-minded either, ready to grab and make a stand. Beckman was, and he knew that was his strength.

"Why what?" Morganthau spoke for the first time, his eyes widening in his flabby face.

"Three old buddies, middle-aged crooks," Beckman said reflectively, "not strong-arm types at all. Then suddenly they run out on their wives, their occupations, everything, to pull a bank job. How much could you get? What if it were a hundred thousand? That's a little over thirty each. How could it be worth it?"

"You're right, sir, it wouldn't be worth it if it were a hundred thousand," Morganthau said calmly, and now the eyes seemed very small and shrewd in the beefy face.

Goulart looked at Morganthau too quickly.

"I believe Mr. Whoever-he-is knows," Morganthau said in a level voice. "We might as well face the fact that we're going to have to come to terms with him."

There was a long, charged silence.

"Agreed," Nevin said firmly.

Goulart nodded curtly.

"All right," Beckman said, settling back and holding the automatic easily. "Why?"

"It all started with a love affair," Morganthau said, acting as spokesman

204

for the group. He motioned toward Nevin with a plump hand. "Mr. Nevin here has always been a classic ladies' man, and two years ago he was involved in an illicit romance with the wife of a certain bank vice-president." Morganthau chuckled. "Mr. Nevin tells me she was quite an affectionate creature—completely and unabashedly devoted to him behind her husband's back."

"I'll take your word for Nevin's finesse," Beckman said, "only I don't see what it has to do with armed robbery."

"No doubt you've reached the conclusion the woman's husband is a vice-president of the bank we've just robbed," Morganthau said with a fat, crooked smile.

"I have reached that conclusion," Beckman said, "and the conclusion that you had something on him."

"Exactly," Morganthau said, as if pleased with Beckman's mental agility.

"Then you had inside help."

"Oh, no." Morganthau raised his eyebrows. "You misunderstand. We did everything quite alone."

"The big thing I don't understand," Beckman said, "is how you figured that after splitting the money three ways the whole thing would be worth chucking your past lives and identities."

"I can see where that would puzzle you," Morganthau said, "and I'm getting to that, if you'll demonstrate some patience. You see, the devoted adulteress informed Mr. Nevin, in a moment of romantic weakness, that her husband was an embezzler. She even went so far as to show Mr. Nevin a secret set of books her husband kept. Mr. Nevin, a professional financial adviser, saw immediately that the woman's husband had embezzled almost half a million dollars from one of the largest banking corporations in the city."

"And that's what you had on him," Beckman said, moving the automatic barrel to take in the three men.

"Correct," Morganthau said with a nod. "The enterprising Mr. Nevin took photographs of the books without the woman's knowledge. He then contacted me because he knew I was a minor official in a banking concern and might know how best to use the information. Together we began to plan, came to the conclusion we needed a third trustworthy partner, and called on our old friend and accomplice, Mr. Goulart. I won't bore you with the details of the actual robbery plan. Suffice it to say that no one is better qualified to rob a bank than a banker. You described us as three businessmen, sir, and that was accurate. We went about the robbery in a brisk, businesslike fashion, and we got cooperation because the people at First Mercantile knew we meant business."

"Okay," Beckman said, and a cold hardness had edged into his voice, "now all you have to tell me is why."

Goulart and Nevin both stared at Morganthau. The fat man gave them each a reassuring glance and continued. "We are not unintelligent, sir, and we knew, as you know, that shedding our former identities for less than a certain sum of money would be foolish and unrewarding. Why, even several hundred thousand dollars split three ways amounts to little enough under those circumstances. So we used the information we had to best advantage. We sent photostatic copies of the vice-president's secret ledger books to First Mercantile. Of course the man was dismissed immediately and as quietly as possible and, as usual in such cases, charges were not brought, on the condition the unspent portion of the money be returned. We then informed First Mercantile that on Friday, August the tenth, tomorrow, we would send our information to several newspapers. Just what effect do you think that would have on a banking institution like First Mercantile?"

Beckman started to answer but was cut off as Morganthau continued by answering his own question.

"Why, when the news was made public, clients by the hundreds would be lined up to make withdrawals. Who'd know how much money was actually embezzled? Who'd know how good the insurance on their savings actually was? How many would stay on the safe side and immediately withdraw their money? Enough, sir, more than enough. And they would want their withdrawals in cash." Morganthau smiled widely. "I see you begin to understand our well-conceived plan."

Beckman looked at the heavyset man in admiration. "You arranged a situation where the bank would be stocked with cash before you hit it!"

Morganthau's grin had faded to a slightly self-satisfied smile. "In preparation for the news that would break and the ensuing run on their bank, the officials of First Mercantile had to have on hand, aside from their usual sum, an enormous amount of cash. We would remain anonymous for the rest of our lives, sir, but we planned to be well-compensated. For reasons of reputation, First Mercantile probably will never admit to a theft of this magnitude, and publicly the exact amount of cash may never

206

be mentioned. But these four suitcases contain over three million dollars in cold cash."

Beckman felt a tremor move through his body at the sound of the amount. He knew that all three of the men were staring at him intently, but still his eyes darted for a moment to the four suitcases. "We come now to the terms of our deal, sir," Morganthau said smoothly, striking where the confusion and softness should have been created.

Beckman hardly heard him. His mind was racing, turning, leaping ahead of itself. When he looked at the three men his face was pale and determined, his eyes shallow and cold. He saw the deeply buried glint of hopelessness and fear come into Morganthau's eyes.

"We both know you're not in any position to deal," Beckman said softly.

They did know, all three of them, that he was right, that he alone held the whip hand.

They were businessmen, not gunmen, and they saw the hardness and uncompromising decision in Beckman's eyes, so they obeyed.

In ten minutes he had the three of them bound tightly with their ties and shoelaces. It would take them a good half hour to struggle free. The four suitcases were almost too large to handle, but by carrying two under his arms Beckman knew he could take them downstairs in one trip.

"What are *we* supposed to do now?" Goulart asked in an enraged rasp, as Beckman inched open the door to the hall and lifted the suitcases. Nevin was sitting uncomfortably with handsome head bowed, and Morganthau was staring up at Beckman with philosophical sadness. He smiled vaguely, and Beckman wondered why.

"Count yourselves lucky you're not dead," Beckman said, "and do the only thing you can do. Go back to your other lives."

He was trembling as he closed the door behind him and walked to the elevator with the heavy suitcases.

Three million dollars, Beckman repeated to himself as he loaded the suitcases into the trunk of his car and drove away. He found his lips shaping the words. "Three million dollars!" The three would-be thieves had the right idea: the only safe way to enjoy that kind of money was to give up your real identity. But who cared, with three million dollars? With that kind of money a man could be a king, the anonymous king of the world.

Beckman drove west for hour after hour, until finally it came to him like a revelation that he was exhausted. He pulled into a small motel and registered, all the time thinking of the money in the trunk of the car, the new and glorious life. Three million dollars . . . three million . . .

Alone in his motel room, he locked the door and stacked the suitcases on the floor. The delicious secrecy of the thing made him grin and fold his arms across his stomach. He had never actually *seen* that much money. Few men had actually seen such a sight. He drew a deep, loud breath and reached for the shiny spring latch on the top suitcase.

Beckman's mind went back to when he was five years old, opening a present, something somebody had given him, something or nothing . . . The latch clicked.

There it was—green—some of it crisp, some worn; green and with a faint perfumed scent, banded in neat stacks. Beckman giggled, reached into the suitcase and drew the green, green paper out by great handfuls. He had read about the exquisite pleasure of fantastically wealthy people, sitting, burying themselves in mounds of money that was all theirs . . . their own! *The king is in his countinghouse* . . .

Beckman laughed loudly and opened the second suitcase, the third, the fourth! His hands groped, scooped, faster and faster, pulling the green bills out in batches, hurling them about the room. Then he let himself slump onto the floor, sitting cross-legged amid the fantastic piles of sweet green paper. He began to weep. His hands caressed the crinkling bills, drew them to him, kneaded them until his fingers ached, and then he sat quietly.

He was still sitting that way the next morning when the maid came to clean, when she stood staring, screamed a low, breathless scream and backed out, when the manager came down from the motel office and stopped wide-eyed in the doorway, then ran for a telephone. Beckman still hadn't moved when the police arrived.

Nice Shooting

by A. E. Eddenden

When you first approach the Provincial Rest Home, you have the feeling you're visiting rich friends in the country—until you see the heavy mesh screens on each window. The receptionist, in her starched white uniform, pleasantly asks you which inmate you wish to see; or rather, which guest. She is surrounded by the usual waiting-room array of objects—magazines, uncomfortable chairs, ashtrays, plastic flowers—except for one item.

On the wall near the door, a magnificent trophy rests on a specially built shelf. It has a central, fluted column, flanked by miniature, bronze golf clubs and laurel leaves, which supports a small, bronze, plus-foured golfer frozen at the top of his follow-through. At the base of the trophy is a plaque inscribed elegantly with the words: BECKWITH MEMORIAL MATCH PLAY TOURNAMENT. The space under the heading: WINNER, is provokingly blank.

It was wet and drizzly—cool for this time of year—but that didn't affect the last round of the Beckwith Memorial Match Play Tournament. The two finalists were sitting in their electric cart on the first tee. They had played this type of head-to-head competition over the last twenty-five years, always with the same result. Everett Jameson had never beaten Barney Swatz.

It didn't seem fair to Everett, or to most of the other seniors, either. The two were close in handicap but Everett was a sweet, classic swinger compared to Barney. It was Barney's mouth that won most tournaments. He was a smooth talker, a needler, a master gamesman.

In the quiet of the locker rooms, when lesser men had gone home to their families, and the old guard was relaxing in the mellow surroundings of the nineteenth hole, the Barney Swatz stories were told again and again. He was a man to be reckoned with on the links, but Everett knew it. This was a new day, a new tournament, and he was determined to win it.

Everett won the toss. He teed up his ball and drove, straight and true, into the heart of the first fairway, about two hundred yards, with approximately six feet of draw.

"Not bad for a young fella, Ev," Barney said.

Everett was younger than Barney, five months to be exact, but it didn't really matter. They were both in their mid-sixties.

Barney waggled for a full minute, made three or four practice swings and finally, when you least expected it, took his unorthodox cut at the ball.

It was a good shot. A little left to right but ten yards farther than Everett's.

"Damn!" Barney said. "Hit the top half." The match was on.

One of Barney's strong points was his inept appearance when he held a golf club. His swing was enough to send a true student of the game back to the library. Because of his short, rotund body, with matching arms, he had to swing around his large stomach, and the strange compensations he had to make in order to strike the ball squarely gave him the look of a spinning hippopotamus.

His clothes didn't help, either. A baggy, faded shirt, one or two buttons always missing, khaki shorts, a little too long, diamond knee socks that sank lower and lower with each hole he played, eventually disappearing on the eighteenth inside heavy, spiked boots; and on his blushing, hairless head, he wore a spotless, white pith helmet. When Barney played a new member, his costume, in the side-bet action, was worth an unofficial two strokes; but Everett knew this also. By the time they'd reached the eighth tee, Barney was down one.

"Ev, old buddy," Barney said, "if I was smart, I'd give you the match right now. We could go in and tell the guys and drink to your victory." He rummaged around noisily in his bag. "How about a little smash now? I brought some with me."

All this rambling, distracting monologue started with Everett's approach to his teed ball and ended with the crack of another well-hit shot down the fairway. Everett smiled to himself—he was confident of winning. So far, he had withstood all the old tricks that had lost him matches with his crafty competitor in past years. All the remarks about his picture swing, his tasteful clothing, his thin frame and balding head had not affected his concentration on playing to win.

However, on the par three fourteenth, Barney's remarks, now harsher

210

and cruder than ever, were beginning to poke holes in the thin veneer of Everett's good spirits. He was four up with five to play.

"C'mon, Ev," Barney said, "hurry up and hit the ball. I'm getting cold."

Everett stood up to the ball.

"Whatever you do," Barney said, "don't shank it."

Everett hit a crisp four iron on a perfect line to the green. It landed about five feet to the right of the pin, took a short hop, stopped and backed up three feet—a dream shot.

Barney said nothing. He threw his ball onto the hairy tee and, after the usual gyrations, hit a textbook shank. It squirted off to the right in a hideous, low arc and landed in the bushes that lined the edge of the short fairway. From there, he took two to reach the bunker in front of the green. He blasted out and two-putted for a six.

Everett, unable to contain his excitement, stepped up to his putt and yipped it past the hole by ten yards. He then composed himself and got down in three more blows for a five.

Everett was ecstatic. The trophy was his. He had finally downed the great Barney Swatz, most formidable match player in the club, on the fourteenth! Wait till the guys heard. He turned for the customary handshake but Barney was already sitting in the electric cart.

"You're pretty quiet, Barney," Everett said, trying to ignore a small, worrying stab of self-doubt.

"I know you wanted to win . . ." Barney paused.

"What do you mean, wanted to? I won."

"And I know you wanted to win fairly."

"What are you talking about?"

"Your clubs, Ev. I counted your clubs."

"Eh?"

"You've got fifteen. One over the limit."

Everett was stunned. He walked over to his bag and counted the clubs—once, twice, and a third time. Fifteen. "I don't understand . . ."

"If it was just a fun game, Ev . . ." Barney said. "But this is different. In a tournament, the PGA is quite explicit. Automatic disqualification."

"But I only *have* fourteen clubs," Everett pleaded. "Someone must've . . . maybe at the pro shop . . ."

"Ev," Barney shrugged, "I don't make the rules. C'mon, get in."

Everett climbed into the golf cart in a state of shock. They drove to the next tee.

"Might as well play in," Barney said. "Give you a chance to pull yourself together. Hell, Ev, it's only a trophy."

Barney hit what he called a real twitcher, straight down the fairway—his best of the day—while Everett sat glumly in the cart.

"C'mon, Ev, you're up."

Everett roused himself and shuffled over to the tee where he sniped a sickening duck hook well off line.

When they found his ball, it was at the base of a small bush with several branches blocking his swing.

"I've had about enough for today," Everett said. "I think I'll pick up."

"Nonsense," Barney said. "Hit the ball. It'll make you feel better. Here, I'll give you a hand."

Barney took off his ridiculous hat and knelt down to hold the interfering branches out of Everett's way. His head was about ten inches from the ball.

Everett automatically pulled a club from his bag. It felt odd—unfamiliar. He examined it—an old, scratched, rusty, one iron. The fifteenth club. It wasn't his, but something tugged at his memory.

"C'mon, Ev," Barney shouted from his awkward position. "I'm getting a cramp."

Everett, still puzzled, lined up his shot. At the start of his forward press, a series of clear, bright pictures, like an orderly slide presentation, flashed through his head: the same old one iron in the trunk of Barney's car; the one iron in Barney's grip, chipping practice balls on someone's front lawn; the one iron as a walking stick for Barney's evening strolls; and the last slide—not from memory but conjecture—Barney stuffing the one iron into Everett's bag just before the match; his insurance for winning the tournament.

"Are you going to hit the ball or aren't you?"

Everett's take-away was as smooth as ever. His downswing, a little faster than usual, caught Barney squarely on the temple with a noise that sounded surprisingly like a well-hit ball. Barney Swatz made no sound as he rolled over onto his back, gave one last, unnatural shudder and stared with unseeing eyes at the dull, overcast skies. He had played his last tournament. He was no longer a man to be reckoned with on the links or, for that matter, anywhere.

Everett experienced a strange, inward peace. He kicked his ball over the inert form of his quiet companion to a preferred lie and hit a frozen rope of a shot to the center of the green. "Not a bad club at all, Barn," he said, smiling.

The next five minutes were spent getting Barney into the cart, and it was no easy job. Everett finally wedged Barney in, crossed his legs in a macabre but nonchalant attitude, and jammed the pith helmet back onto his head at a jaunty angle. They proceeded down the fairway, with Everett scanning the horizon. All was clear.

Everett holed out for a bird—not charging himself for moving the ball over Barney—and played the next two holes in par figures. As he hit his approach shot to the eighteenth green, a plan was taking shape in the back of his mind. He wasn't quite sure of it yet, but it had something to do with the big hill behind the clubhouse. If he could make it to there with nobody seeing him, he could turn the cart over at a spot he had in mind. He could jump out—maybe say Barney was driving—and then the cart would roll down the steep hill, through the hardy sumacs and, with a little luck, Barney would end up in the rock garden with the alyssum and portulaca.

At the eighteenth green Everett holed out in two. "One under for the last four," he said to Barney. "Not a bad finish."

He steered the small, quiet cart up the slight rise in front of the clubhouse, bumped onto the asphalt driveway and headed for the top of the hill.

There were no spectators.

Then the front doors of the clubhouse burst open. Seven or eight of the old reliables, drinks spilling, some with spikes on, others in stocking feet, ran on varicosed legs toward their two friends. Shouts of "Who won?" and "Who gets the cup?" and "Who buys the drinks?" came from the crowd of over-sixty rowdies. They surrounded the cart and smiled expectantly.

Everett stood up. He noticed that one of the boys was carrying the real cause of all the commotion, the trophy. "I won," he said, "on the fourteenth. Five and four." He held out his arms.

"Way to shoot, Ev!"

"Good boy!"

They handed him the trophy.

"You finally did it."

"Nice shooting."

A red-faced, puffing senior approached Barney. "What happened, Barney? You're awful quiet." He prodded him playfully in the stomach. That was all it took.

Slowly at first, then with increasing speed, the lifeless form of Barney Swatz, fierce competitor, crashed to the driveway. He lay still, stomach up, arms and legs stiffly outstretched like a child making angels in the snow. After a silent eternity, Everett stepped down from the cart and, clutching his trophy, walked through the circle of his stunned comrades toward the showers.

On a reasonably clement day, if you drive the winding, back roads ten miles out of town, you can see Everett playing golf. It's a pleasant nine-hole course attached to the Provincial Rest Home. He plays alone now—if you don't count the white-coated, muscular caddy—and holds the course record.

Everett seems happy, particularly on his daily trip through the lobby. They show him his trophy and he smiles. The doctors agree that he'll never leave. They say he'll have to spend the rest of his days at the Home, playing golf if he wishes. It's a shame, really, but a just and fitting end for one who took a life; and not all that bad for an old golfer.

Too Solid Mildred

by Jack Ritchie

I approached the desk clerk. "Do you have a spare key to room 4168?"

"You've lost yours, sir?"

"No. My wife has the key. But she's either gone out or she's inside asleep. I suppose I could wake her by pounding on the door, but she's a heavy sleeper and I'd prefer not to create a scene in the process."

He checked the register. "Room 4168? James Dodson?"

I nodded. "Mr. and Mrs. James Dodson."

He pursed his lips for a moment. "The register lists only a James Dodson."

I peered at the inverted name for a moment and then shrugged. Apparently I had registered myself only; possibly wishful thinking.

Mildred and I had arrived here at two-thirty in the morning. We had intended to get in much earlier, but I'd had trouble with the car, trouble which still hadn't been properly diagnosed by a succession of crossroad mechanics.

After registering we had gone up to our room, accompanied by the bellboy with our luggage. Before retiring I had set my traveling alarm for seven.

When the alarm rang, I had left Mildred to her sleep, and driven the car in search of a garage. I had found one some eight blocks from the hotel and left the car there. On the walk back, I had stopped at a restaurant for breakfast.

All in all, I had been gone for an hour or possibly an hour and a half. When I reached our room, Mildred had not answered my tentative knocks.

The desk clerk handed me a key and I took the elevator back up to the fourth floor. I inserted the key into the lock and opened the door.

Mildred was not in bed. The door to the bathroom was ajar and I could see that she was not in there either.

I shrugged. Probably she had gone out for breakfast, though usually she was a late sleeper.

I sat down. The day outside had begun hot and muggy and it would not improve, but the room was comfortably cool. Frankly, I would have preferred to spend the day up here—the room was quiet and relaxing—but Mildred would drag me about the oceanside in search of what she deemed a vacation.

There was a knock at the door. It was the maid to change the sheets and tidy up the room.

Mildred had spent the night on the twin bed nearer the window, but now I noticed that it appeared to be neatly made up, as though it hadn't been slept in at all. My bed, on the other hand, was considerably rumpled.

The maid finished my bed and appeared about to skip Mildred's.

"My wife slept there last night," I said.

The maid glanced at me for a moment, shrugged, then pulled back the blankets. From where I sat, it seemed that the sheets were still crisp and ironed. The maid sighed, but changed them.

She began dusting things here and there, then got down on her hands and knees to peer under the beds.

"What are you looking for?" I asked.

"The other ash tray. There are supposed to be two in this type room. One on each bedside table. But one's missing."

I helped her look, but we did not find the other ash tray.

She regarded me obliquely. "Sometimes the guests accidentally pack an ash tray in their luggage when they leave."

I stared at her coldly. "I am not leaving. Besides, I steal only towels and soap."

When she was done and gone, I took off my jacket and opened the closet to hang it up. My clothes still hung there in a neat row, but Mildred's things were gone.

I frowned. I had seen her unpack her suitcases before she turned in and she had hung up her things. I was positive of that, and she had left her empty suitcases beside her bed.

Her suitcases were gone too.

Strange. I opened the bureau drawers. My shirts and underwear were there and in order, but the other drawers were empty.

I moved to the bathroom. My toothbrush in its plastic case and a small tube of toothpaste lay on the basin counter, but only *my* toothbrush.

Mildred's was missing. Yet she had brushed her teeth before retiring. She made a ritual out of it.

I searched the room more thoroughly. There was not a trace of Mildred's things, not even the hotel key. It was almost as though she had never been in this room at all.

I sat down again. It was all most peculiar. If she had merely gone out for breakfast, surely she wouldn't have taken along bag and baggage.

I smiled at a pleasant thought. Suppose Mildred had decided to leave me. I sighed. Mere fantasy, I was afraid.

There was really nothing to do but wait a bit. No sense in running about creating noise. There was some logical explanation to this and Mildred would return soon and clear up everything.

I turned on the television set and became absorbed in a program on coopering in early colonial America. That was followed by a segment on the collecting of antique glass beer bottles, whole and fragmented. Even The Busy Knitter proved fascinating. At home, Mildred's daytime television viewing was reserved exclusively for serials and game shows.

At the onset of Sesame Street, I turned off the set. I rather wished I'd brought some books along. However, spending a vacation with Mildred does not leave allowance for anything as intelligent as reading.

I went to the window and looked down at the street. There they were, the people moving and sweating in the sun, dragging whining sunburned children from place to place, desperately telling themselves they were having a glorious time. Why the devil didn't people have sense enough to spend their vacations in their own comfortable air-conditioned homes, surrounded by the conveniences of modern life?

Actually, Mildred had left our home a week before I did. She had spent that time with her sister in Pennsylvania and then taken the local bus to Harrisburg. I had picked her up at the bus depot and we had continued on to the coast.

I sat down in the easy chair again. Why had I married Mildred in the first place? We really had nothing in common, even now. All the money was still firmly in her name. By marrying Mildred, I had achieved security, though not serenity and prosperity.

Had Mildred gone down to breakfast and met with some accident? Surely I would be notified, wouldn't I? In time. She had plenty of identification on her, including the tagged hotel key.

I frowned. There was that baggage to consider. That indicated a certain

217

design. She had left *with* her luggage. It was not simply a matter of stepping out to breakfast.

My eyes went to the second twin bed again.

Suppose, just *suppose*, that Mildred had actually run off with another man. How could she possibly have attracted him? She was six years older than the day I had married her and time had lent no improvement to her beauty, nature, or tongue. Besides, I rather felt that if there were another man, I would know about him. I am not entirely unobservant.

At noon I went downstairs to the hotel restaurant for lunch and then stepped outside of the building, intending to take a walk. I stopped in my tracks. The temperature was at least in the mid-nineties with a commensurate high humidity. It was insane to venture out in such a hostile atmosphere, and yet the streets were teeming with perspiring flesh and bad tempers.

I stepped back into the hotel, picked up some paperbacks at the stand in the lobby, and went back up to the coolness of my room. I telephoned room service, ordered a bottle of brandy sent up, and spent the afternoon reading and sipping brandy. By six, Mildred still had not returned.

Was it actually possible that she had run away with someone? Surely not with any of our socio-economic peers—but possibly some ambitious chauffeur?

I chuckled. We had no chauffeur. Just a cook, who lived out, and a housekeeper who lived in and was really quite sullen about her status.

I stared at Mildred's bed again. Why should she have made up her bed before leaving? Did she even know *how?* As far as I could remember, she had never made a bed in our entire married life.

I sipped more brandy.

The Prescotts had a chauffeur, a ratty-looking little man; and the Dormans, though their chauffeur was really a college student hired for the summer to transport the Dorman children to tennis lessons and such nonsense.

If not a chauffeur, why not a gardener? We had no gardener either. The Acme AAA Landscaping and Lawn Service people sent over two men once a week during the summer and adequately cared for our half an acre. Could it be one of them?

I resisted the impulse to giggle. If not a chauffeur or gardener, why not a gamekeeper? There ought to be some of those around somewhere.

By eight o'clock I felt quite happy, fuzzy, and sleepy. I yawned and lay down on the bed. When I woke, it was nearly 11:30. Mildred still had not come back.

I sat up slowly. I could still feel the effects of the brandy, though not as pleasantly as before. I am really not a drinking man—perhaps three or four times a year on festive occasions is enough for me. I took some aspirin.

If Mildred had run away with someone, would she have left without her money? Of course not. Mildred was quite sensible about money. She would never abandon it, I felt certain, despite any passion involved.

Had she been liquidating her assets behind my back? I shook my head. No. That was not possible. Liquidating one's assets is not done by a snap of one's fingers. It takes time. Too, I was aware of the placement of every penny of her money and none of it had been moved.

Yet Mildred was missing—bag and baggage.

I went back to the brandy. When a wife disappears without a word, people, especially the police, have a tendency to suspect the worst—possibly foul play—and the husband is invariably the chief suspect, especially if he were somewhat tardy in reporting his wife's disappearance.

I would have to report Mildred's disappearance here and now, this moment.

I put on my jacket, took a bit more brandy to steady me, and took the elevator to the main floor.

It was nearly midnight and the desk clerks appeared to be changing shifts. I recognized one of them as the man who had been at the desk when Mildred and I arrived.

I spoke to him. "Pardon me, but how does one go about reporting a missing wife? Which authorities do I notify and such?"

Both desk clerks appeared immediately interested, and Hames—I learned his name later—spoke. "Mr. James Dodson?" he asked.

I felt somewhat flattered that he remembered my name, especially my first. I had no idea I made such a strong impression on strangers.

Hames smiled. "You said something about a wife?"

"Yes. I haven't seen her since seven this morning when I went out to see about some car repairs. I thought she might have gone shopping or something of the sort, but she still hasn't come back and frankly, I'm beginning to get just a little worried."

Hames back-turned a few pages of the register. "Ah, yes. James Dodson. That is the only name we have here. No wife."

219

I smiled. "I don't care what the register says. I came here with a wife and she's missing."

Hames appeared apologetic. "I'm sorry, sir. But I distinctly remember that when you registered, you were alone. Absolutely alone."

I blinked.

So did the clerk going off duty. His name subsequently proved to be Mulligan. He was a small, sharp-featured man who rather reminded me of the Prescotts' chauffeur.

I tried a laugh. "When I registered, I had a wife with me. One is hardly likely to forget something like that, is one?" I said.

Hames agreed. "No, sir. However, you were alone." He turned to a group of bellboys, all ears, lounging close by, and beckoned imperiously.

One of them detached himself immediately and trotted to the desk. I now recognized him as the same man who had carried our bags up to our room. "This man," Hames said, indicating me, "says he registered here with his wife. If I remember correctly, you took his bags up?"

The bellboy nodded eagerly. "Yes, sir. But it was just him, sir. He was alone. He didn't have any wife with him or any other woman either."

I stared at him. "She is a tall, large-boned, unforgettable woman who wore a monstrous red hat."

"I'm sorry, sir," the bellboy said, "but you were alone."

I am not one to doubt my sanity, my intelligence, or my eyes. My wife had been with me when I registered. Hames had been at the desk. Come to think of it, Hames and the bellboy had been the only people about at that hour of the morning.

Yet now the two of them lied. Why?

Mulligan edged into the conversation with a sharp-toothed smile. "Not that I wish to alarm you, sir, but have you tried calling hospitals? Did she carry identification with her?"

"She has plenty of identification. I think I would have been notified by now if anything had happened to her."

Mulligan nodded. "I think we'd better call in the police, sir. Among other things, they could search the hotel from top to bottom."

Hames glared at him. "This is *my* shift. You have been officially relieved for the last five minutes. If the police are to be called, *I* will make that decision."

Why should Hames and the bellboy lie? My mind suddenly leaped to the ultimate. Was this more than just a disappearance? Was foul play

220

indeed involved? Was Mildred dead? Murdered? Were Hames and the bellboy deeply involved in the death? If they were, undoubtedly they had arranged some sort of self-protection or alibi—and this was it?

I found myself faintly perspiring.

Would that leave *me* vulnerable? In a murder situation it hardly seemed wise for me to have been the last person to have seen Mildred alive. The police tend to fasten on situations like that.

Wouldn't it be more intelligent if I said that Mildred had *failed* to meet me at that bus station in Harrisburg? I'd had trouble with the car and been late. I had assumed that she had gotten tired of waiting for me and had continued on by other means. That would mean her sister was the last one to see Mildred alive. Let *her* do the explaining and the sweating. After all, she was into Mildred's will by at least a third.

What, after all, was really the point in my insisting that I had come here with Mildred? Hames and the bellboy were here to contradict me—for their own reasons—and they outnumbered me, two to one.

If I scratched their backs, so to speak, they would scratch mine.

I smiled vacuously and hiccupped. "To be absolutely honest, I don't really remember registering at *all* last night." I grinned, and exhaled essence of brandy about me. "I remember waking up this morning, but that's about it. Did somebody have to help me up to my room?"

Hames quickly appropriated that. "You were just a bit under the weather, I'm afraid, sir." He indicated the bellboy. "Eddie had to help you up. You went to sleep as soon as he put you down on the bed."

I hiccupped again. "What I really need is a little old drink and I've got that in my room." I moved back toward the elevators, managing to stagger a bit.

I found Mulligan guiding me by the elbow. "I'll see you to your room, sir. But I still think that you ought to notify the police."

"Nonsense," I snapped. "I have these hallucinations about my wife all the time."

"Are you positive it was a hallucination, sir?"

"Positive. Mildred never wears red hats. Can't stand the color. Whenever I see her wearing a red hat, I know I'm hallucinating."

"But you didn't seem to think that you had been hallucinating when you approached the desk."

"Sometimes it takes me longer than usual to realize I've been hallucinating."

221

Mulligan accompanied me up in the elevator. "Have you and your wife been traveling in India or the Far East lately? When you last saw your wife, did she appear a bit ill? Did she show any traces of the bubonic plague?"

I stared at him.

He had sharp yellow-black eyes. "Suppose she contracted a plague, though not necessarily bubonic. It would be bad for the hotel's image, not to mention a threat to the entire region's tourist trade. Suppose Hames tried to cover it up? He spirited away the corpse and pretended that nothing had happened, even to the extent of maintaining that your wife had never been here in the first place. I wouldn't put anything past Hames and his brother."

"His brother?"

"Yes. The bellboy. Eddie. He's an ex-convict, you know. Breaking and entering."

At the door of my room, Mulligan peered intently at the number plate. "What are you looking for?" I asked.

"I thought it just possible that the number plate on this door might have been switched. But I see that there is dust here that couldn't have accumulated in just one night. Are you certain this is the same *floor* Eddie took you to last night?"

"I have never lost a floor in my life." I unlocked the door and left Mulligan outside.

I now dismissed entirely the idea that Mildred had run away. Something had happened to her, and the Hames brothers were deeply involved.

Eddie was an ex-convict; breaking and entering.

I had left this room at approximately seven A.M. Mildred had been stirring when I left. Had she gone back to sleep or had she decided to go out for breakfast?

Had Eddie seen both of us leave this room? Had he let himself in and begun rummaging among our things?

Since Mildred's breakfast usually consists of a cup of coffee, she had returned too soon, had walked in on Eddie, caught him in the act. There had been a struggle. He had struck her with something. The missing ash tray? Those things always seem to be around when you need them—and Mildred had died.

Eddie had gone to his brother and told him what had happened. They had decided that if the body were found, Eddie, being the hotel's only ex-convict, would be immediately suspected. They had decided not only to get rid of the body, but to make it appear that Mildred had never been here at all.

But wouldn't that still leave a rather sticky situation for them? I would insist that I had come here with Mildred and they would insist that I hadn't. The police would undoubtedly be called in to referee.

Wouldn't it have been much better for Hames and his brother if they had just maintained that they *saw* Mildred walk out of the hotel, with or without baggage?

I poured brandy and tried to think. A half hour later, there was a knock at my door.

It was Mulligan, rubbing his hands. "I managed to sneak a look at the register. Page 79 is missing."

"I fail to see any significance in that."

Mulligan giggled slightly. "I think I see it all. When you came here with your wife, you registered as Mr. & Mrs. James Dodson on the top line of a new page. Page 79, to be exact. But later, Hames, for his own nefarious reasons, tore out that page and copied your name, and the names of guests who registered subsequently to you, on page 81."

"What happened to page 80?"

"Well, page 79 is on one side of the sheet and page 80 on the other."

"How clever of you hotel people. But I did not come here with my wife. Nor did I register the both of us. I registered only myself. I now *distinctly* remember that as I was signing in—in my fumbling condition—I accidentally tore the page nearly in half. So Hames removed it entirely from the register and I signed the next page."

Mulligan stared at me, a revolting half-smile on his face. "If you weren't involved with the Hames brothers before, you appear to be now." His eyes seemed to glitter. "I don't know the reason for all of this, but I will find out. I know how to put two and two together."

I had the sinking feeling that he did, and would. I shut the door in his face and went back to the brandy.

What about Mildred's body? Not to mention her luggage. Can one blithely cart a body out of a hotel at eight or so in the morning without running the high risk of being seen? No. The most obvious thing to do would be to store it in another room until it could be picked up at a more convenient time. Possibly in the early hours of this very morning? Where would this room be? Close by, certainly, and the closer, the better.

Inspired by my rationale, I stepped into the corridor. I moved cautiously to the door immediately to the right of mine. Slowly I turned the knob. The door was unlocked and I eased it open a crack.

The room was quite occupied by two people of the opposite sexes. That much was readily apparent and they were both very alive, active, and preoccupied.

I quickly closed the door. Why the devil didn't people have the decency to lock their doors when they were doing things like that?

Obviously I couldn't continue going up and down the corridor trying doors. There was no telling what I might stumble into.

My eyes went to an unnumbered door squarely at the end of the corridor. The service closet? Would Mildred's body be in there? Not very likely, but it would be a perfect place for me to hide and watch, in the event that someone chose to retrieve Mildred's body from wherever it was stored.

I fetched the bottle of brandy from my room and made myself as comfortable as possible among the mops, pails, and detergents in the service closet, leaving the door slightly ajar. I waited, sipping brandy. At 2:30 I restrained the considerable impulse to break into song, namely "Abdul Abulbul Ameer."

By three o'clock I had finished the bottle and was contemplating a return to my room, when I heard the high squeak of wheels and Eddie hove into view, pushing a hand truck on which reposed a large steamer trunk. He trundled it farther down the corridor to a door, opened it, and disappeared inside.

I waited ten minutes, fifteen, twenty. What was taking him so long?

Finally the door opened again and Eddie appeared, wheeling the hand truck with its steamer trunk, on top of which reposed Mildred's two suitcases.

I opened the service room door and stepped out, lurching just slightly. "Ah, ha! Do you deny for a moment that a corpse resides in that trunk?"

Eddie whitened and then sighed. "I don't deny it, but I got to talk to my brother. He does the thinking for both of us."

"Very well," I said stiffly. "You may use the phone in my room."

Eddie wheeled his cargo into my room and used the phone. He wiped his forehead. "My brother will be right up."

I folded my arms. "You murdered my wife because she caught you red-handed trying to ransack our room."

224

Eddie looked hurt. "I wasn't ransacking. Just looking. I been going straight for seven years now and I got a wife and three kids. I don't steal anymore, but I still got the hobby."

"Hobby?"

"I go through people's stuff and figure how much I *could* steal if I wanted to. But it's all on paper. Last year I could've cleared over forty grand, but I never took a thing."

"But my wife caught you and she *thought* you were stealing?"

He nodded glumly. "She came at me swinging this purse, and I ducked. Her heel caught on something and she fell. Her head hit the ash tray on the night table and broke it right in two. The ash tray, I mean. Didn't do her head much good either. But it was a swift death, sir. She felt no pain, I assure you."

"Why didn't you just leave the premises? Why go through all this hocus-pocus?"

"Fingerprints," Eddie said. "Even if the police thought it was an accident, they'd still go through the routine of covering the room for fingerprints. Just in case. And I left mine all over the place. So how would I explain that to them? Me, an ex-con. I didn't wear no gloves because I wasn't going to steal anything, so why bother? I left fingerprints in places that I couldn't even remember, so there was no point in even trying to wipe them off. I told my brother what happened and we decided that the only thing to do was get rid of the body so that nobody would even think murder."

"But why take the luggage too?"

"Because when she fell she got blood on the suitcases. She didn't bleed much. Just on the suitcases, one of which was open, and a blanket that was draped on the floor. So we had to get rid of all that. And we knew that when the police investigated your missing wife and found that her *empty* suitcases were gone too, they'd do a lot of probing because people just don't disappear with empty suitcases. That meant we had to pack up all the rest of her things too. We decided that it would be best just to pretend that she had never been here in the first place and it would be our word against yours."

"Wouldn't it have been simpler if you and your brother had simply said that you *saw* her leave the hotel? With the baggage?"

"We thought of that too, but somebody would have had to carry her baggage downstairs, and the doorman would have had to call a cab. And

225

the concession stands were open and them people got sharp eyes. A lot of people would have had to remember seeing her go. Like you said, she was big-boned and such and hard to overlook."

"What were you going to do with my wife's body?"

"My brother's got this piece of land up north with an old dry well. We thought we'd dump her down there and just fill it to the top with dirt. Nobody would ever know one damn thing about it."

There was a knock at the door and I let Hames into the room.

He glanced quickly about the room, at the trunk, and then at his brother. "What have you told him?"

Eddie cleared his throat. "Practically nothing."

Hames rubbed his hands. "Let me see. What do we have here? You, Mr. Dodson, called the desk. You requested that a steamer trunk be sent up to your room. Eddie brought it up. You told him to return in twenty minutes. He did. You told him to take the trunk downstairs to the basement where you would arrange to have it picked up later. Eddie noticed bloodstains on the suitcases."

Here Hames turned over the suitcases, revealing dark blotches. "And considering all of this hanky-panky business about a missing wife, he immediately suspected something amiss and called me. And here I am. Shall we open the trunk or shall I leave that to the police?"

"Now just one damn minute," I said, righteously outraged. "You aren't going to pin this on me."

Hames smiled. "Why not? It is our word against yours. We are *two* and you are *one*."

I countered. "Eddie's fingerprints are all over this room and probably also on the *inside* of that trunk. How will you explain *that* to the police?"

Hames pondered for a moment. "Very well, then, sir. If Eddie and I must go to prison, we will take you with us. We will maintain that you *hired* us to murder your wife."

Eddie regarded him with admiration. "That's right. If we got to go down, we take everybody with us."

Obviously they were prepared to drag me into this mess too. What, after all, did they have to lose? As a matter of fact, they might have a lot to gain if they cooperated with the police and testified against me.

Hames broke the impasse with a smile. "On the other hand, sir, why should mature men such as we go to the police at all? A lot of trouble for all *three* of us could be avoided if . . ." He shrugged.

226

I sighed—a sticky business. Hames did seem to have a point there.

"And what about Eddie's children?" Hames said. "Without his guidance and counseling in future years they will probably become delinquents."

Eddie wiped at one eye.

The last touch had hardly been necessary. I stared at them coldly. "So be it. Take the body and dispose of it. What is done cannot be undone."

Eddie prepared to leave with his cargo. "I'll unload the trunk in the station wagon and then bring it back up for your wife's body, Mr. Dodson."

I stared at him. "My wife's body isn't in the trunk?"

"No, sir," Eddie said. "I was just about to put her into the trunk when Mulligan jumped out of the closet. I guess he put two and two together, like he always claimed he could, and he was waiting for me. What he had in mind wasn't the police. It was blackmail. For all three of us." Eddie coughed slightly. "I guess I broke another ash tray. Mulligan's in the trunk."

Hames sighed. "I suppose I'll have to arrange a reason for Mulligan's disappearance. A shortage in the hotel's accounts should cover it."

When they left, I gave Eddie five dollars. Ordinarily, I do not subscribe to overtipping, but there are exceptions.

Then I hiccupped genuinely and went to bed.

Free Advice, Incorporated

by Michael Brett

Charlton McArdie took his first step toward becoming a millionaire as the result of a woman who dialed a wrong telephone number.

The way it happened, Charlton and myself, I'm James Hamilton, were trying to muster strength to leave the office and go home—not that we'd done anything to make us tired, but you can get tired doing nothing. We were the eastern sales representatives for Cool-Cool, a new midwestern air-conditioning firm, and it was the coldest, dampest summer in twenty years. Most of the few shoppers purchased name brands. Those who had bought Cool-Cool called back to complain about breakdowns, excessive noise, overheating, short circuiting and exploding sets. A fan blowing across a chunk of ice would have been more efficient than a Cool-Cool air-conditioner.

Charlton and I had already decided to sever connections with the firm when our contracts terminated at the end of the month. However, since we were on straight salary, we came to the office every day and put in our time.

Frankly, the prospect of being without a job worried me more than it did Charlton. I've got a wife and a small house. Charlton, on the other hand, is single and lives in a fleabag hotel over on Forty-third Street. He keeps talking about how he's going to get a duplex apartment and a fancy girl friend someday.

Charlton does a lot of daydreaming.

He also spends his time doing newspaper crossword puzzles and commenting disparagingly on the columnists who give advice to the lovelorn, on health, on finance, on not getting old—on just about everything.

His attacks were usually preceded by an explosive horse-laugh which shattered the silence in the office. Then he'd say, "Now look at this. You'd never believe that people can be so naive. Here's a college girl, writes to this Miss Common Sense. She's a college girl who believes in free love. Sex is an important part of marriage and she wants to be the perfect wife when the time comes. So Miss Common Sense tells her, 'Insofar as sex is concerned, practice does not necessarily make perfect.' That's just common sense. Now she didn't need Miss Common Sense to tell her that. Isn't that so?"

So I said, "Sure."

"And take this one here, for instance," said Charlton. "Here's a gal who writes that her husband is overweight and how can she make him lose weight. So Miss Common Sense gives her a diet to follow and tells her to broil his food instead of frying it. Then she says, 'Send for my booklet, How To Keep Hubby From Becoming Tubby.'

"Here's another one. Somebody writes in and wants to know if it's all right to neck. So Miss Common Sense says, 'I will be glad to help you with your problem. Send fifty cents in coin and a self-addressed envelope for my booklet, How to Cool It.' Did you hear anything as silly as all this business about people writing in and asking for advice?"

He walked over to the window.

"Now look down there. There's thousands of people and the one thing you can be sure of, each and every one of them needs advice. Don't you think so, Hamilton?"

I was a little tired of the way he kept attacking the newspaper columnists, so I said, "You're probably right, Charlton. Why don't you go into the advice business? With your attitude, you'd probably make a fortune."

"You're telling me," said Charlton, and he gave out a loud guffaw.

Of course I had no idea that he was going to take me seriously when the telephone rang just then, or I might not have said it.

Charlton got it and said, "Hello." Then he listened for a minute and said, "One moment, Mrs. Abernathy." He covered the mouthpiece and said, "You know what? This is a wrong number. I'm talking to some dame who thinks she's talking to her psychiatrist, a guy named Dr. Kazoola." He winked. "You told me to go into the advice business. O.K., I'm going to give her some." He uncovered the mouthpiece.

"Mrs. Abernathy, now what can we do for you, dear?" He listened, nodding sympathetically and repeating bits of what she was saying so I could follow the conversation. "I see, the pills haven't worked. You still haven't been able to sleep . . . Well, that's bad . . . Ummm . . . Your life is confused . . . I do understand . . . I want you to remember one thing. There is absolutely everything in life but a clear answer . . . Yes, of course I sympathize with you over your husband's peculiar behavior, but many men think they're Hollywood idols. People are people, Mrs. Abernathy. When it comes to people there aren't any cut and dried answers . . . I agree, the situation with your husband is deplorable."

I laughed and said, "Cut it out, Charlton."

He ignored me and went on. "What I want you to do, Mrs. Abernathy, is place yourself completely in my hands. You may not approve or agree with what I'm about to say, but that's beside the point. Remember, it's for your good, no matter how unorthodox it may sound to you. Actually, what it is is a famous Far East method which is based upon the theory of taking strength from within. A form of mysticism. To make it work, you have to accept the treatment without question. Through it you'll be able to gain insight into your own character. The first act of insight is to completely throw away all of the accepted methods of psychiatric treatment. Now, Mrs. Abernathy, when I say go, I want you to take the telephone receiver and move it in a circle around your head, all the while chanting, *ah-zo, ah-zo.*" He coughed. "I know it must sound ridiculous, but please believe me, it has a definite function. Now *go!*"

Then he covered the mouthpiece again, looked at me and said, "Hamilton, she's doing it. She's waving the telephone around in the air."

I said, "What's with you, Charlton? You nuts, or something?"

"Not me. She's the one, waving that telephone around and chanting. All I'm doing is proving something. You told me to give advice, right?"

"Charlton, you're crazy. I was kidding."

"You think *I'm* crazy? *She's* waving a telephone."

"She's crazy too."

He glanced at his watch. "The way I figure it, in about three minutes her arm is going to get tired and then I'm going to give her another routine. The point I'm trying to make is that people will listen and believe almost anything as long as they think the advice they're getting is from a competent source."

He moved his hand off the mouthpiece and spoke to Mrs. Abernathy again. "All right, Mrs. Abernathy, you can stop the ah-zo. Now what I want you to do is walk around the block in sneakers." He paused, listening. "Yes, house slippers will do. When you've done that, I want you to take a hot bath, then I want you to drink eight ounces of Scotch and go right to bed. I guarantee that you'll sleep." A pause. "All right, since you don't

230

drink, you can make it four ounces. You'll sleep wonderfully . . . Yes, tomorrow I want you to call me. Thank you very much, Mrs. Abernathy."

He hung up and looked at me thoughtfully.

"Do you know the last thing she said? She said, 'Thank you, Doctor. I'll send you a check.' How do you like that?"

I had to laugh. "Wonderful. She's going to send this Dr. Kazoola, whoever he is, a check for nothing, and tonight the poor woman is going to run around the block and fall into bed potted. You ought to be ashamed of yourself, Charlton."

"Ashamed nothing." He crossed the room mumbling to himself and came back again. "Mrs. Abernathy gave me an idea. How to get *rich*. We can both get rich. Think of what happened. I gave a woman advice over the telephone and she's going to send her doctor a check. Now what does this mean? Do you have any ideas?"

"It means she's paying for services rendered. So what?"

"That's true, but what's important is that she's sending him a check for advice."

"Listen, Charlton, I'm beginning to get a headache. What are you driving at?"

"I'm going into the business of giving advice. I've given it lots of thought and the potential is great."

"That's good. In what field do you intend to specialize, law, medicine, finance? What?"

He sat down behind his desk and closed his eyes. With his eyes closed he said, "Medicine and law are out. The Bar Association and the Medical Association would crack down on me. Finance would be O.K., though. I'll be a *stock market analyst*."

I thought he was losing his mind. "Charlton, we've been here for too long, business has been bad for too long."

He opened his eyes. "That's right. Time for a change. I'm tired of not doing business, of being in hock, of worrying where next month's rent is coming from, of not being able to buy a new car. I'm going to give people advice and they're going to pay me for it."

"Yeah, I'd like to see it. Tell me something, what qualifies you as a stock analyst?"

"Your trouble is that you're negative. I'm a financial expert because I say I am. I've been reading about some guy, the leading exponent of transcendental meditation. It's a theory which says that people can do

231

anything if they really think about it and tell themselves they can. It's like self-hypnosis. O.K., I tell myself that I'm a stock expert and I am. It's as simple as that."

"That's fine. Why don't you announce that you're a brain surgeon—are you something merely because you say you are? Be sensible."

"I didn't say anything about being a brain surgeon, did I? All I want to do is give people financial advice. Think of the possibilities. Do you know anyone who doesn't need advice on one matter or another? Everybody wants advice. There are people who don't make a move without consulting their horoscopes, and if the signs aren't favorable they won't get out of bed, much less leave their homes. What does it mean? They're following advice. And what about the millions of dollars spent with public relations firms, promotional attorneys, financial advisors, crystal ball gazers, mediums, psychics, goonies, and loonies? Name it and you've got it—there's somebody to give advice."

I could see that I wasn't getting anywhere. "Granted, but why should people come to you? Who knows you? What makes you qualified?"

"Nothing. I have no qualifications, but the one thing I can do is give advice, and the way I'm going to advertise it we'll make a million dollars. The advice I give will be free."

I thought he was demented. "Free advice—you'll go broke."

"Wrong. We'll clean up. They'll just think the advice is free. Let me explain my plan. Let's assume a man buys a certain stock. O.K., then what happens?"

"It goes up or it goes down. He makes or he loses money."

"Very good. You're getting the idea. There are two things that can happen, and right off the bat as far as you're concerned, the odds you're working with are fifty-fifty. Now suppose you predict a winner. The guy who's got it is going to send you a small donation for putting him onto a good thing. Or suppose you tell a stockholder to sell off or to purchase additional stock. Without knowing anything about the stock, you're bound to come up with the right advice merely through the laws of chance and probability."

"That's all fine and good. Now what about the guy who follows your advice and comes up a loser?"

"You can't worry about him. There's a hundred guys selling books on how to beat the market. More guys go broke following the tips in those books than you can count. Let's face it. If the guys who were writing those books really had a surefire way of predicting the market, they wouldn't be writing books in the first place. They'd be wheeler-dealer speculators."

"What about collections? What makes you think that a guy, even if he makes money on your advice, is going to send you money?"

"The honor system," he said.

"That isn't business."

"Exactly. But if I were going to follow the rules of business, this gimmick wouldn't work." He looked at me. "Hamilton, all it costs us is the price of an advertisement and we're in business. What do you say?"

I doubted that anything would come of it, but I said yes anyway. We went to work on the ad immediately. He took it to a newspaper and I went home. I didn't say anything to my wife about it.

We'd taken a good sized ad, a square, heavily outlined. FREE ADVICE, INCORPORATED. STOCK ANALYSTS; a phone number and address. I kept thinking that I'd simply thrown away my share of the advertisement's cost. I also thought about the idea catching on. The prospect was bewildering. I couldn't sleep.

After breakfast, I rushed off to the office. Charlton was already there. "Any calls?" I said.

He whooped with laughter. "It's eight o'clock. Give people time to read it."

At nine the phone rang. It was a man threatening to sue unless we took back a Cool-Cool air conditioner he had purchased a month ago.

At eleven, when I was beginning to think that the advertisement was a washout, the phone rang. It was the first reply to our ad. Charlton took it and said, "Free Advice, Incorporated. Yes, ma'am, there's no charge for this. This is a public service function. We need your name and phone number for our files. We'll give you a reference number. We are not responsible for any information that we dispense. This is a non-profit organization. However, if you feel that our advice has benefited you in any way, your donation allowing us to continue will be appreciated."

He wrote down the information and then said, "All right, ma'am, what can we do for you?" He listened, interrupting from time to time. I could follow the drift of the conversation. "All right, you've got a thousand shares of Santa Maria Railroad stock. It's gone up five points during the past month and you want to know whether to sell. My advice to you is, sell and take your profits . . . No ma'am, it's against our policy to reveal

the information we use. However, I will say this, Santa Maria is negotiating two hundred million dollars in new loans from banks and insurance
companies to refinance millions of dollars in outstanding debts. My advice
is to sell. Your number, incidentally, is B 28." He hung up.

I was stunned. "Is that true about Santa Maria Railroad?"

"How do I know?" he said. "It could be. Railroads are always negotiating
loans. It really doesn't matter. The main thing is that I've told her something." He wrote B 28 next to her name and the advice he had given her.

I took the next call. It was from a man named Summerfield. After I'd
taken down the necessary information and had assigned him a number
and had gone through the policy spiel, he told me that he had five hundred
shares of Northern Tractor, which he planned to sell, and then he was
going to invest the money in a Florida land development company.

"What's the name of the company, Mr. Summerfield?" I asked.

"Flamingo Land Development Company."

"Flamingo Land Development Company?" I shouted. "Forget it."

"What is it?" he asked excitedly. "Do you know something?"

"Sell off the Northern Tractor, deposit the money in a bank, and then
call me at the end of the month. Ask for Mr. Hamilton," I said, and ended
our conversation.

Charlton looked at me incredulously. "What do you know about the
Flamingo Land Development Company?"

"About as much as you know about Santa Maria Railroad," I said. "That
isn't important, though. What counts is that Mr. Summerfield *thinks* I
know something about it. That land could be under water."

"It certainly could," said Charlton. "It probably is."

There were fifty-four calls the first day. The second day brought an
even heavier response to the ad. We became more scientific. In giving
advice on a specific stock, we advised fifty percent of those who called
to sell and the other half to buy additional stock. We kept records. We
watched the progress of our stock tips for a month. In that period the last
number we assigned was B 5028. We had advised five thousand people.
Charlton was right. Money began to roll in from the winners who were
eagerly seeking new ways to make additional monies. We had a good
thing going. Those who had followed our advice and made big money
were generous in their donations. To them we were heroes. We forgot
completely about the others who had followed our advice and lost. To
them we were bums.

234

Some good had come from our advice.

We had advised prospective purchasers of an oil company stock to buy as much as they could. Drilling for oil, the company had hit a vast underground source of natural gas and the stock had skyrocketed. The stockholders had become wealthy.

The woman Charlton had advised to sell off her Santa Maria stock called, angrily. The stock had gone up ten points.

"Don't worry about it," Charlton told her. "I have inside information that the bottom is going to fall out."

The man I'd warned about Flamingo Land Development Company called. I'd saved his life's savings. It was an out-and-out land swindle. "I'm sending you a hundred dollars, so you can continue with your good work," he said.

At the end of two months we were making big money. Charlton moved out of his room into a six-room duplex, got a fancy girl friend and bought her minks and diamonds. And all around us people were becoming wealthy. We began to study the market and the more we studied it the less we knew.

Charlton kept going through the records, talking to himself. "Look at this B 336. Here's a guy I made a millionaire. He didn't know what to do and I was the guy who tipped him off. It's absurd, Hamilton. We're making people into millionaires and not doing it for ourselves. I knew this stock was going to rise. The trouble with us is that we're not smart enough to follow our own advice."

"What about the people who listened to us and lost their shirts?"

"What about them?" Charlton shouted. "You're being negative again. Try to look at the good we've done for the rest."

I could already see what he had in mind.

At the end of the week he told me that he knew of a stock selling at four and a half dollars that was going to go to fifty.

"How do you know?" I said.

"How do I know? I know, that's all."

I really believed he did, but I didn't want any part of it anyway. "What do we need it for, Charlton?" I said. "We're doing all right, the way things are going."

"I'm going into it with every cent I have," Charlton said. "It's going to hit and it's going to make me a millionaire."

"I'll sit back and watch," I said.

"Suit yourself, but I want to tell you something. This is something that happens once in a lifetime." He laughed. "The difference between us, Hamilton, is that a guy like you doesn't really have imagination. Two years from now you'll be back selling air conditioners."

I went home and thought about it. I didn't sleep all night. Six months ago I had nothing, and today I had fifty thousand dollars in the bank. One thing was sure, no matter how scatterbrained his schemes had sounded, I hadn't lost anything by listening to him.

In the morning I withdrew my money from the bank without telling my wife, and Charlton and I bought fifty thousand dollars' worth of the new issue apiece.

That was on Monday. By Friday my investment was worth ten thousand and by the following Monday the stock had gone off the board. It had all been a swindle. Charlton was going to ask his girl friend to return the mink coat and some of the diamonds he'd bought her, but she'd heard about what had happened and had gone somewhere.

My wife left me.

Charlton went slightly mad. He came in on Wednesday and pointed a gun at me and said it was all my fault. If I hadn't invested with him he never would have gone in all by himself. "Look what you made me do," he said. "I'm going to kill you."

"Let's talk it over," I said. "Now put the gun down. Look, let's not lose our heads. We still have a good thing going for us. We made money. We can do it again."

"I don't know how," Charlton said doubtfully.

"Think positive, Charlton. We can do it."

He burst into unexpected laughter and put the gun down. "I must be losing my mind. What was I thinking of? Sure we can do it again."

We were both laughing so hard by then that we didn't see the little man who stepped into the office.

"Are you Free Advice, Incorporated?" he asked.

"That's us," said Charlton exuberantly.

"You told me to sell off my oil shares. I had three thousand shares at a dollar. Do you know what the price is now? Ninety-four dollars. You ruined me."

When he drew a gun and started firing, I took cover behind a desk. I could hear Charlton fall, and the gunman running away.

236

I got up, walked over to where Charlton lay dead, and unthinkingly picked up the gun that his murderer had used.

When people came running, that was the way they found me, with the gun in my hand.

Explaining it to the police was very difficult. They didn't believe there was a little man with a gun. They found Charlton's gun on the desk and they came up with the theory that Charlton and I had an argument and that I'd killed him.

When I asked permission to check through my records—we were up to B7800—on the chance that I might learn the identity of the man we'd misadvised, they sent me to a police psychiatrist, who had an overbearing manner until I described the scheme Charlton and I had used to found Free Advice, Inc. He thought I was crazy.

I believe he would have committed me to a mental institution if Charlton's killer hadn't come forward then and surrendered to the police.

I was released. As I was leaving the psychiatrist's office, he said, "I'm lucky. If I had known about Free Advice, Incorporated, I might have been tempted to call you. I own three hundred shares of something called Western Pump. What do you know about Western Pump?"

I'd never heard of Western Pump, but, I thought, why should I tell him that? "Buy as much as you can get," I said. "That one is going to go to the moon. It has great potential."

He leaned forward eagerly. "Do you really think so?"

I nodded and went out, wisely.

Payoff Time
by Clark Howard

The phone rang at three o'clock in the afternoon, just as Joe Collins was getting ready to go to work. His wife Doris answered it. She listened quietly for a moment, then looked at him and said curiously, "It's long distance."

Joe frowned. His lips parted slightly and his eyes clouded with instant worry. There was only one person in the world who would be calling him long-distance. He swallowed tightly and crossed the room to take the phone.

"Hello . . . I'm fine, sir. How are you? . . . No, sir, I haven't forgotten . . . I'll be glad to do whatever I can to help you . . . Yes, sir, I can meet him there . . . Yes, I know where it is . . . No, tomorrow at one is fine . . . Yes, sir. I'm still married and settled down . . . Doris. Her name is Doris. She's fine, sir . . . Two grandsons? You must be very proud of them, sir. Please tell Al I said hello . . . Yes, sir, six years is a long time . . . Yes, sir, it's been nice talking to you, too. Good-bye."

Joe carefully hung up the receiver, as if it were some fragile thing that might break. He slumped into the nearest chair, suddenly feeling very weak. "Was that who I think it was?" Doris asked excitedly.

Joe nodded. "Yeah."

"Well, what did he *want?*" she asked impatiently. She hovered over him like a vulture over carrion.

"What do you think he wanted? He wants me to repay the debt I owe him."

"How?"

"I don't know yet. I have to meet a man tomorrow afternoon. I'll find out then."

Doris knelt before him and put her hands on his knees. Her eyes were alive with ambition. "This could be your ticket into the organization, into the big time!"

238

"I've already told you, Doris, I don't want to be in the organization. I had a chance for all that six years ago. I didn't want it then and I don't want it now."

Doris jerked away from him, her full body rising to loom over him. Her expression darkened.

"What the hell, Joe," she spat. "Do you want to be a lousy blackjack dealer for the rest of your life?"

"No, but I don't want to be a syndicate hoodlum either."

"Well, what then?" she challenged. "What do you intend to do with yourself between now and the time you're an old man?"

Joe shrugged. "I like casino work. I could get to be a pit boss or a shift boss someday."

"Someday!" she shrieked, her voice an accusation. "And what do we do until someday, Joe? Keep going from week to week like we are now? Keep living in this lousy little apartment and driving that six-year-old junk you call a car?" Her face became a rigid, demanding mask. "I want more than that, Joe. A lot more."

Joe rose and walked to the mirror to put on his necktie. "Better find yourself a new husband then," he told her flatly. "That's about the best I can do for you." He looked at her in the mirror. "Why don't you go to see a lawyer, Doris? Let's stop eating at each other. Get a divorce."

"Oh, no," she said, shaking her head unequivocally. "Not on your life. We're married and we're going to stay married. And if *you* try seeing a lawyer, I'll go to the Gaming Commission and tell them about your prison record. They'd be very interested in how the syndicate pulled strings to get a casino work card in Las Vegas for an ex-con." In quick, nervous movements, Doris put a cigarette between her lips and lighted it. "We're going to stay married, Joe. And you're going to make something of yourself. If you don't, I'm going to drive you to an early grave nagging you about it."

Driving down the Las Vegas Strip toward the club, Joe shook his head in silent amazement that so many things could become so fouled up in such a short time. Just a month ago everything had been fine in his marriage, his job, and for his future. A month ago Doris had not been nagging him about getting ahead in the world. She had finally stopped trying to get him to be something he wasn't, and seemed content just to live a day at a time and enjoy life as it came to them. On his job he was

239

being watched as a potential candidate for the next pit boss job, which was to open up in a couple of weeks. He was one of two or three dealers being considered, and he was sure he had the inside track. He had felt good just thinking about it. If he made pit boss at his age, he would be a shift boss by the time he was forty; then he'd be making *real* money—and making it honestly, too. He was so pleased with himself that he had kept it a secret from Doris. He wanted to surprise her when it actually happened.

A month ago, he mused. A month ago everything was fine. Then one night on his supper break he had wandered across the street to the Four Queens and met Jackie. She was a change girl in the slot arcade; blonde, tightly built, perky, with a face like a high school girl even though she was well into her twenties, and as different from the sultry, sexy Doris as daylight from darkness.

A waitress he knew in the coffee shop introduced them when he was having a sandwich and Jackie sat down beside him for her coffee break.

"Sure, I've seen you around," Jackie said. "You work at the Clover Club, don't you?"

"Yeah. How'd you know?"

"I go in there with my boy friend once in a while," she said. "He works roulette out at Caesars, but he likes to gamble downtown."

"He works roulette and he *gambles?*" Joe had asked incredulously.

She nodded. "Yeah, I know. Casino help should have better sense than to play against the house. It's dumb. But then, he's dumb."

"If he's dumb, how come you see him?" Joe asked.

Jackie's eyes met his. "Maybe I won't if somebody better comes along."

That had started it. They began meeting every night on his supper break. Within a week he was going home with her for an hour or two after work, telling Doris he was working overtime. On his days off, he began making excuses to get out of the house so he could go see her. It was crazy but he couldn't help himself; he had to see her.

Stealing time with Jackie began costing him points at work. He was returning late from supper, taking too long on his breaks because he was going across the street to see her. He was making mistakes at the table; little mistakes, but he was in a business that required total accuracy. The shift boss spoke to him the two times he got caught, and Joe promised to watch himself, but a couple of weeks later the pit boss job was given to someone else.

There probably wouldn't be another such job open for a year, he thought bitterly as he pulled onto the club parking lot, found a space, and parked. For a few minutes he just sat there, staring out through the windshield at nothing. He had thought things were about as bad as they could get, but the telephone call a little while ago had proved him wrong. He had always known that the day would come when he would have to repay Mr. Markov for getting him paroled. He just hadn't expected the phone call at that particular time, when everything else was going wrong.

Joe's involvement with Mr. Markov had begun eight years earlier, when Joe was in the third year of a six-to-ten sentence in Illinois for a stickup that went sour.

At Stateville Penitentiary he had celled with Al Markov, Mr. Markov's son. Al had gotten himself involved with a seventeen-year-old girl and was doing a flat five for statutory rape. The two had become close prison buddies, and two years later, when Al had been paroled, he had prevailed upon his father, an influential syndicate executive, to help Joe get a parole also and bring him into the organization. The elder Markov did as his son requested, and a year later Joe walked out of Stateville.

Al Markov and his father were both more than slightly surprised a few days later when Joe told them he did not want to come into the syndicate. "I appreciate what you've done for me," he said as he sat self-consciously in Mr. Markov's plush Chicago office. "Your friendship means a lot to me, Al, and I respect your father very highly. That's why I have to be completely honest with both of you. I've had enough of living outside the law. I've been a crook of one kind or another since I was six. Now I'm tired of it and I want to get away from it. If I took a job in the syndicate, I'd be doing you both a disservice, because my heart wouldn't be in it. I'd hate what I was doing, I'd probably do poor work, and sooner or later I might get careless and make a mistake that would hurt you. That's the last thing in the world I'd want to do." Joe had looked across the desk at Mr. Markov, who was studying him thoughtfully. "With my record, I never would've made parole on my own. You saved me some long years on the inside, sir. I'll do whatever you want me to do to pay you back for that. But I don't want to be a syndicate man."

The elder Markov had risen from his chair and turned to face a wide expanse of glass that looked down on Michigan Avenue, Grant Park, and the lake beyond. He folded his hands behind his back and stood like that for a full two minutes, his lips pursed in deep thought. Finally he turned

241

back and nodded brusquely. "OK, Joe," he said quietly. "You don't have to come into the organization. I wouldn't strong-arm you."

Joe had expelled his first comfortable breath of the meeting. "Thank you, Mr. Markov," he said gratefully. "I owe you."

Markov had gestured broadly as if dismissing the debt, but he knew, just as Joe knew, that it was still owed.

"So what do you plan to do with yourself?" Markov asked.

Joe shrugged. "Get a job. Live quietly."

"What kind of job you want?"

"I don't know. Any kind that won't put me back in the joint."

"Tell you what," Markov said, "I got a friend owns a place in Vegas. He's always looking for good, reliable blackjack dealers. Let me send you out to him. He'll put you through dealers' school and give you a good job. And you won't have to worry about going to jail; it's all nice and legal in Nevada. What do you say?"

"Sure," Joe said, delighted. "That sounds great. I appreciate this, Mr. Markov. Maybe I can do something for you someday."

Markov had smiled pleasantly. "Maybe you can, Joe. Maybe you can."

Now, after six years, there was no more maybe to it. Markov had called him. He was to meet a contact tomorrow. The books had been audited. Payoff time had arrived and he had to accept it.

Sighing, Joe got out of the car and locked it. When he walked into the casino, he saw the new pit boss give him a dirty look. Joe glanced at his watch. He had sat in the car too long. Now he was five minutes late for work . . . again.

On his supper break that night, he sat in a corner booth with Jackie and told her all about it.

"What exactly does this Mr. Markov want you to do for him?" she asked.

Joe shook his head. "I don't know. It could be anything. I'll find out tomorrow when I meet the contact."

"There's no way you can get out of it?"

"None," Joe said emphatically. "Just like there's no way I can get out of being married to Doris. If I try to divorce her, she's threatened to tip the Gaming Commission about my prison record."

"What would happen then?"

"They'd lift my work card. Then they'd probably start an investigation into how I got it in the first place. I'd have to answer a lot of questions. They'd call in the people I work for. It could get very hairy, believe me."

Jackie was quiet for a long moment, then she took his hand across the table and said, "There's another way, Joe."

"How?"

"Split."

Joe frowned. "Split?"

"That's right. You and me together, Joe. Leave it all behind. Your wife, this Mr. Markov, everything. Just get in your car and go. Tonight."

Joe squeezed her hand and smiled a brief, sad smile. "I wish it was that easy, honey. But it isn't. See, a guy like me can't just drop out of sight like an ordinary guy could. First of all, I've done time. That means in most cities I can't stay seventy-two hours without registering as an ex-felon. If I don't register and I get caught, I go to jail for it. Second, there's the syndicate to consider. They have people all over. No matter what city we settled in, sooner or later a syndicate man would spot me and word would get back to Markov where I was."

"What would he do?"

"I don't know," Joe said honestly. He shivered slightly. "And I don't want to find out."

Jackie's eyes widened in fear. "He wouldn't kill you?" she whispered tensely.

"No. But he might have someone break my elbows. Or my ankles. Or rupture my eardrums. That's easy to do, you know. One guy holds you while another one hits both your ears at the same time with his open palms. Four or five blows like that and you're deaf. I once saw a guy get it that way on the yard at Stateville."

Jackie shivered this time. "I guess you'd better do what Mr. Markov wants you to," she said solemnly.

"I guess," Joe agreed.

The meeting with Markov's contact took place the next day in Swenson's Ice Cream Parlor in the lower level arcade of the MGM Grand Hotel. When Joe arrived at one o'clock, the contact was already there, sitting at a table for two, eating a hot fudge sundae. Joe spotted him by the paperback copy of *The Godfather* that Markov had said would be lying on the table. Markov liked little touches like that.

Joe pulled out a chair and sat down opposite the contact. He was an

243

ordinary-looking man who could have been a tourist from Iowa. Around a mouthful of hot fudge he said, "You Collins?"

Joe nodded.

The contact held out his hand.

"Call me Benny. You want a sundae? Soda?"

Joe shook his head. "Just had lunch."

"OK," Benny said affably. "Let's get down to business, then." He glanced around inconspicuously. No one was sitting near them, but he lowered his voice anyway. "What's gonna be going down here is a hit," he said.

Joe's stomach shriveled into a tight knot. His mouth went dry. A hit. The very worst thing that it could be.

Benny saw the discomfiture in his expression and smiled. "Relax," he said easily. "You aren't going to be doing it. We've got a professional for that. He'll be coming in from L.A. on a morning flight, and flying out for Chicago a few hours later. He'll only be in Vegas long enough to make the hit, then right back out again. That's why we need your help. You're going to be our finger man. We need you to set the guy up."

Joe swallowed dryly. He felt a little better, but not much. He was still going to be a hell of a lot closer to a killing than he wanted to be. "Who's the target?" he asked.

Benny leaned across the table another inch. "Guy named Robert Sampson. Used to be an FBI agent about ten or eleven years ago. He's a lawyer now. Got offices in the Merchant's Bank Building."

"What'd he do to be set for a hit?" Joe asked.

Benny shrugged. "Who knows? Like I said, the guy used to be an FBI man. He probably stepped on somebody's toes a long time ago, and the toes are still sore. Anyhow, that doesn't concern you and me, right? What we've got to do is work out a plan for you to finger him. Right?"

"Right," Joe reluctantly agreed.

Instinctively, the two men leaned closer together across the table.

Doris was lying on the couch, drinking beer from a can, watching an afternoon movie on television, when Joe got back to the apartment. He turned off the set and slumped down in a chair facing her.

"It's a hit," he said.

Doris stared at him with wide eyes. "You?" she said. "You're going to do it?"

244

"No. There'll be a pro to do it. My job is to set him up." He paused, biting his lip, then added pointedly, "I'll need some help."

"Me?" Doris said, surprised. Then she thought about it a moment and shrugged. "Sure, honey. Sure, I'll help you." She put down the can of beer and came over to sit at his feet. "Did the contact say they might be interested in having you come into the syndicate if this goes well?"

Joe shook his head. "No. He was just a contact. He wouldn't have anything to do with that."

"But Mr. Markov would," Doris said enthusiastically. "I'll bet anything that after it's over he calls you again. Maybe just to say he's glad everything went well."

"It hasn't gone well yet," Joe reminded her.

"It will," she said firmly, as if she alone controlled destiny. "And when it does, he'll call. And when he calls, Joe, you'll have a perfect opportunity to ask him for a job." Doris gripped his knees. "Just think, Joe! Real money for a change. A plush Chicago apartment; maybe in one of them places with a doorman. And a new car to drive. For the first time in our lives, we could really *live!*"

Joe rested his head against the back of the chair and stared at the line where the wall met the ceiling. There was a jagged, twelve-inch crack at the edge of the ceiling, and a corner of the wallpaper had started peeling down. Joe grunted quietly. "Maybe you're right, Doris," he said. "Maybe it is time to start a new life. The old one doesn't seem to be getting me anywhere." He looked at her steadily. "Do you really think you've got the guts to help me? It would mean handling a gun . . ."

"If it'll get us out of this rut we're in, I'll pull the trigger myself," Doris said coldly.

Looking at her, at the hard pitch of her eyes, Joe could easily believe it. "OK," he said finally. "OK, we'll do it. We'll shoot the works."

Doris reached up and threw her arms around his neck. She entwined her fingers in his hair, nibbled on his earlobe, and then began whispering her secret things to him.

All the while she was doing it, Joe kept thinking about Jackie.

When the setup of Robert Sampson was finally worked out, Joe sat down with Doris and went over the plan.

"Sampson has his law offices in the Merchant's Bank Building. The building provides parking for its tenants in an underground garage.

There's an elevator from the garage up to the lobby and the other floors in the building. There's also stairs leading up to the street level just inside the building entrance.

"Now, this is how we'll work it. Sampson leaves his office around a quarter of twelve every day to go to lunch. He takes the elevator down to the garage, gets in his car, and drives out to the Tropicana Country Club where most of the lawyers and judges eat. Tomorrow when he comes down to his car, you'll be standing in back of the car next to his, rummaging in your purse as if you can't find something. Sampson will look at you, and naturally you'll glance up at him, but only very briefly, as if his being there doesn't mean a thing to you. Just go on back to rummaging through your purse while he goes over to his car. As soon as he gets behind the wheel and closes the door, you walk over to the passenger side and take the gun from your purse. If the passenger door is unlocked, open it and get in; if it's locked, cover him with the gun and make him open it."

"What if he won't?" Doris asked.

"He will," Joe assured her. "He's an ex-FBI man; he knows what a bullet would do to him at that short range through a piece of safety glass. See, the slug would be partially flattened out by the glass; when it finally hit him, it'd be like grenade shrapnel—all ragged steel. Sampson will know that. He'll open the door. OK?"

Doris nodded and lighted a cigarette with that jerky motion of hers. Despite her outward braggadocio, Joe knew that she was nervous about the whole thing. He sought to reassure her.

"You have to trust me in these things, honey." He smiled. "Just think about that fancy Chicago apartment. We'll get us a canopied bed with a mirrored top. You've always wanted one of those. You'll be able to have everything you've always wanted. OK?"

"OK, Joe," she said, nervously exhaling smoke.

"The rest of it is very simple. You just keep the gun on him, have him drive up the ramp, out of the garage, and turn north on Fourth Street. I'll be waiting right on the corner. Have him pull to the curb and I'll get in the back seat. Then we drive to the freeway four blocks farther down and head out to the western city limits. We go out to the end of Charleston Boulevard, and that's it. There'll be another car there with one man in it. We don't know him, he doesn't know us. We make Sampson get out of the car and we leave him there. Then we casually drive to one of the big shopping centers, park his car, wipe off our prints, and leave it there."

246

He sat back and looked at her. "It's a very simple setup."

"There's just one thing I'm curious about, Joe," she said, her eyes on him unblinkingly.

"Yeah, what's that?"

"Why me? Why am I the one to lay for Sampson in the garage? Why not you?"

"It's like I explained," Joe said. "Sampson used to be a federal agent. He's had the best law-enforcement training in the world. He's got cop instincts. He'd never fall for a guy being in that garage near his car. He'd be alert the second he stepped off the elevator. But a woman—and a good-looking woman, at that—will throw him completely off guard. Especially if you wear one of your tight sweaters. He'll be so busy getting his eyes full that he won't think of anything else."

"What would you do if you didn't have me to help you, Joe?" she asked.

He shrugged his shoulders. "Probably have to set it up another way that wasn't as safe. Look, Doris, if you want out, just say so. I'm beginning to like the idea of asking Mr. Markov to let me in the organization. I don't want to blow it because you're suspicious."

"Who said I was suspicious? I'm not suspicious. I'm just careful, Joe. And curious. You've got to admit that after six years of refusing even to consider going into the syndicate, you've done a pretty quick turnaround."

Joe self-consciously looked down at the table. "There's something you don't know," he admitted. "I was up for a pit boss job at the club. But they gave it to somebody else."

Doris touched his hand. "Gee, honey, I'm sorry. I know you worked hard for that job." She got up and sat on his lap. "But don't worry about it. Next to what we'll have when you go to work for Mr. Markov, that pit boss job will look like peanuts. We'll pull this Sampson thing off so smooth that he'll *have* to give you a syndicate job. When is it, anyway? When do we do it?"

"Tomorrow," Joe said. "We do it tomorrow."

The following day, Joe and Doris drove downtown and parked in a city garage two blocks from the Merchant's Bank Building. They walked up Fourth Street, looking like any other Southern Nevada couple coming into the Las Vegas financial district to conduct their banking business—except that the gun in the purse that Doris had on her arm was a little heavy, and the gun under Joe's belt beneath his sport coat

247

made him feel a little funny walking. Joe had not packed a piece in a long time, not since the stickup that went sour back in Illinois eleven years earlier. He had thought he would never have to carry a gun again but, like a lot of things, that hadn't worked out either.

"You were gone so long this morning I was starting to get nervous," Doris said.

"The guy I got the guns from was late." Joe looked at his watch: it was 11:39. "Let's walk a little faster," he said.

They crossed Bridger and stopped just short of the big quadruple-doored entrance to the bank building.

"OK," Joe said tightly. "Just walk inside, go past the elevators, and down the stairs to the garage. Remember, Sampson's car is the ninth one on the left. A white Continental. He should be coming down in three or four minutes." He squeezed her arm. "I'll be waiting right over there on the corner."

Doris swallowed, clutched her purse a little tighter, and walked toward the building entrance.

Joe wet his lips, looked around briefly, and strolled to the corner. He stepped into a doorway and lighted a cigarette. Smoking in short, tense puffs, he checked his watch every half minute, and the rest of the time kept his eyes riveted on the ramp leading from the underground garage.

He had been standing there for five minutes and ten seconds when the explosion ripped from under the building and almost at once a gush of rolling black smoke poured out of the garage ramp door.

An hour later he was in Jackie's apartment having a badly needed drink. Jackie had the radio on and there had already been two bulletins about the explosion that had blown up local attorney Robert Sampson's automobile, killing Sampson and an unidentified female companion. Firemen at the scene indicated that a powerful plastic explosive had been used; so powerful that, combined with the gasoline in Sampson's car, it had destroyed the vehicles parked on each side of it. Coroner's investigators had already expressed doubt that enough of the woman's body was left to identify her. Police were checking all female employees of the building to determine if anyone was missing. Mrs. Sampson had issued a statement to the effect that she had no idea who the woman was.

"Are you sure there's no way they can trace the man who put the explosive in the car?" Jackie asked after listening to the second bulletin.

248

Joe shook his head emphatically. "None. The guy's a pro—probably been doing this kind of thing for years. There's no way they can trace him because he doesn't leave any clues. Everything is blown up."

"You're sure nobody saw you with him?"

"Positive. He came in on the nine o'clock flight from L.A. carrying a briefcase with his stuff in it. He took a cab to the Fremont Hotel, got out, went in the front door and out the side, and walked to the bank building. I met him in the garage at ten and showed him Sampson's car. I watched the street stairs and the elevator indicator while he took the stuff out of his briefcase and put it under the hood. The guy was a real pro; it only took him a couple of minutes. Then we went back up the stairs and separated. He had an eleven o'clock plane to Chicago to catch. I went back home with the two guns I had stashed in the trunk and told Doris I'd just bought them from a guy I know. Which reminds me," he said, pulling the .38 from his belt, "I want to get rid of this on my way to work."

"They can't trace the gun Doris was carrying, can they?" Jackie asked.

"Not to me," Joe said positively. "They're both foreign-made; I bought them from a guy who brings small arms in from Mexico. They're not even registered in this country."

Joe stepped into the kitchenette and put the gun in a convenient drawer. He returned to the couch, sat back, and took Jackie in his arms. "We're all set, honey. In a few days I'll tell my landlady that Doris had to go back East to take care of her sick mother. In a couple of weeks I'll say her mother died and I'm moving back so Doris and I can live with her old man. Then I'll come over here and move in with you."

"This place isn't really big enough for two," Jackie said. "Maybe we should look for a larger apartment." Her head was on his shoulder and she was talking against his neck.

"Sure," Joe said. "We'll get a little bigger place if you want to."

Jackie breathed a sigh of relief. "I'm so happy you'll be taking care of me now, Joe," she said. "You don't know how glad I'll be to quit that stupid change-girl job."

Joe frowned. He hadn't really thought about her quitting work. They could use the extra money. Of course, it probably wouldn't make that much difference as long as they lived modestly.

"When can we start picking out furniture for our new apartment, Joe?" she asked. "I can't wait to start decorating."

"Well, I—I don't know," he said. "I hadn't really given it much thought . . ."

Jackie sat up and faced him. "You know, Joe, the way you planned this whole thing was really terrific. I mean taking the plan they had and working your own plan into it like that. You've got real brains, Joe. If you ask me, you're wasting your time being a blackjack dealer. I don't see why you *don't* ask Mr. Markov for a job. Working for him, you could really make big money!"

Looking at her, Joe had the odd feeling that he was still listening to Doris. He glanced into the kitchenette, at the drawer where he'd put the gun.

Maybe he wouldn't get rid of it on the way to work after all. Maybe he'd keep it for a while.

The Way the World Spins

by Bill Pronzini

It was very cold as I stood at the edge of a small, grassy slope in Golden Gate Park, my hands pressed deep into the pockets of my topcoat, and looked out over the flat shallow water of Lloyd Lake. On the far bank, to the right of where the lake turned into the mouth of a tiny green valley, a narrow waterfall bubbled over a rock stairway. Eucalyptus trees grew among the gray rocks there, and the smell of them was redolent on the quiet, chill air.

Ducks, like small, white toys, floated on the surface of the lake. Farther down the slope, and ringing the lake at intervals, were great bushes of chrysanthemum, explosions in white and tipped in pink. At the base of the slope, below me, stood the tall marble and stone Portal of Residence of A. N. Towne, Vice President and General Manager of Southern Pacific Railroad, a relic of the conflagration of April 18, 1906. It was one of several historic "Portals of the Past" that marked this section of the park.

Overhead, the sun had come through the early-morning fog. Reflections of light danced on the surface of the lake now, turning it from gray to a translucent blue. It was all very peaceful, almost pastoral, in its serenity. San Francisco is a nice city, sometimes.

I heard the sound of a siren and looked toward John F. Kennedy Drive and the gently rolling lawns beyond. A white city ambulance came into view and pulled off the Drive in front of the lake. Two men got out, took a stretcher from inside the ambulance and carried it up onto the path. A uniformed patrolman came forward to meet them, motioning. I watched them talking for a moment, and then the two men started up the spongy slope to where I stood.

I turned then, looking toward the small knot of men at the foot of a fanning, stilted cypress tree. They had covered the body of Christine Vance with a sheet, and it lay before them, white and cold on the damp ground. I was glad they had covered her. It did not seem right that she

251

should be lying there uncovered, even in death, on such a cold morning.

The two men from the ambulance crested the slope. One man wiped a hand across his forehead. "Damn stretcher is heavy."

"Think of it going down," the other man said.

They began walking toward the knot of men. As they approached, one of the men detached himself from the group, came over and stood beside me, looking out over the lake. After a moment I turned, too. We stood in silence.

The man, whose name was Eberhardt, was a detective lieutenant with the San Francisco Police. He took a pipe from his pocket, tamped tobacco into it and put it into his mouth, but he did not light it.

"Well?" he said without looking at me.

"I'm sorry," I said.

"You don't know her?"

"No."

"She had your card in her purse," Eberhardt said.

"Yes, that's what you said."

"Were you working on something for her?"

"I'm between clients."

"Maybe she talked to you, then."

"I don't know her, Eb," I said. "I told you that."

"Why would she have your card?"

"She may have been planning to see me at some time."

"But she never did?"

"No."

"You hand out a lot of cards?"

"Not many."

"How do you suppose she got one?"

"I couldn't say."

"All right."

We stood looking at the lake, not speaking. After a while I said, "I'd tell you anything if I knew it. You know that."

"Sure."

"Can I go now?"

"You going down to your office?"

"Yeah."

"Maybe I'll drop by later."

"If you like."

252

Eberhardt turned and went back to the group of men. They were just lifting the body of Christine Vance onto the stretcher, and I could see that one slim, white hand had fallen from beneath the sheet. About twenty-three years old, and somebody had shot her dead.

I went down the slope, slowly, to keep my feet from slipping on the soft, mossy bank, then followed the path around the edge of the lake to the drive and went to my car. I sat there for a moment, and felt very cold. I put the heater on and started the car, waiting until the engine warmed up before I pulled away. Even with the heater on high, I could not seem to get warm.

My office smelled of dust and stale cigarette smoke. I opened the window, letting in the traffic noise from two floors below, and sat down at my desk. The dregs of a cup of coffee and the waxed wrapping from a sandwich littered my blotter. Living alone for a long time does that to you. I put the cup in my bottom desk drawer and threw the wrapping in the wastebasket.

Still a little cold, I looked out of the open window. Pneumonia or suffocation—it was six of one and a half dozen of the other. I lit a cigarette, coughed, and put it out again. You could add lung cancer, too.

Sitting there, I thought about how it was to grow old. Nothing surprises you, or even shocks you anymore, not even death. You begin to look at it with a kind of detached objectivity, a disembodied eye. You don't feel it inside, the way you did when you were a young man. It is a sad milestone when a man no longer feels awe in the presence of death.

After a time I went to the hot plate on top of the metal file cabinet. I lifted the lid on the coffeepot there and looked inside. It was about half full, and there didn't seem to be any of the greenish substance that collects around the edges sometimes. I plugged in the cord and went over and sat down again. The clock on the wall read a quarter of ten.

I picked up the phone and called my answering service. "Any messages?" I asked the girl.

"A Mr. Gerald Demeroy called," she said.

"Did Mr. Demeroy say what he wanted?"

"Only that he wished you to return his call. He said it was urgent."

"What's the number?"

She gave it to me and I wrote it down on my desk pad. The coffee was bubbling on the hot plate. I got up again and poured some into a fresh cup. I looked in my desk for some sugar, couldn't find any, so I sat down

253

and looked at the number on my pad. All right, Mr. Demeroy. I dialed the number. A young, feminine voice answered. "Hello?"

"Mr. Demeroy, please."

"May I ask who is calling?"

I gave my name.

There was a brief pause, and then the voice said, "Oh," and there was another pause. Then, "Just a moment."

I drank some of the black coffee, waiting. A pigeon flew by outside the window, squawking the way pigeons do. On the street below, a bus clanked past, polluting the air with its exhaust; voices rose, floating; the sounds of a city.

A man's voice came on the line and identified itself as Gerald Demeroy. "I was wondering," he said, "could you come out to see me?"

"Possibly," I answered. "What is it you want?"

"You find people, do you not?"

They get that kind of snappy talk from the television. "Well," I said, "that would depend."

"I'd rather not discuss it over the phone. Do you suppose you could come out?"

I did not feel like leaving the office but there was nothing for me to do here.

"Yes," I said, "I think I can. What's your address?"

He gave me a number, then asked, "Do you know where that is?"

"In Sea Cliff."

"Yes. What time may I expect you?"

"Right away," I said. "Good-bye, Mr. Demeroy."

"Good-bye."

I sat looking at the dead line. Sea Cliff was a synonym for money. Well, I could figure what it was. His wife had run off, or his daughter; if it was the wife, she would be trying to recapture a fading youth with some Adonis on a beach in Acapulco; if it was the daughter, she would be shacking up with some bearded artist in Carmel Valley. It's an old, sad story. You would think they'd get onto it but they never do.

Still, I needed something to do. I did not want to think about the young girl named Christine Vance who had been lying in Golden Gate Park with a bullet in her head and my card in her purse.

I called my answering service and told them I would be out for a while. Then I put on my coat and went down the hall to the office of a man named Novinski, who was a very able CPA. For some unknown reason, he likes to work with his door open, looking into the hallway. I asked him if he would mind keeping an eye out for anyone who might come around for me, and he said he would be delighted to. It was sort of a game between us. I had been asking him the same question, and he had been giving me the same answer for a much longer time than either of us cared to remember.

Sea Cliff sits high on a bluff overlooking the entrance to San Francisco Bay. It is quiet and discreet and aloof, and it is said that you can measure a man's success in San Francisco by the size and location of the home he buys there.

If this is true, Gerald Demeroy was a very successful man.

I parked my car on the street and sat there for a moment, looking at the house. I felt uncomfortable. I seemed always to feel that way in Sea Cliff, the same feeling a man might have if he found himself at a formal party dressed in slacks and a sport shirt.

I left the car and walked up the brick stairs and along the brick path to the door. Behind the house I could see the gray and white waters of the Pacific Ocean.

At the door, I pressed a small pearl button and chimes, muted and rolling, sounded inside. I stood waiting, holding my hat in my hands.

The door opened finally, and a tall, thin girl, perhaps twenty or twenty-one, looked out. She had blonde hair that was cut short into what we used to call an Italian bob, and her wide eyes were green and oddly flecked with yellow. She was wearing gray slacks and a white blouse, and her manner was nervous, fidgety, like a caged squirrel.

I gave my name and said, "Mr. Demeroy is expecting me."

"Yes," she said. "Well, come in."

Inside, the hallway was very dark. The girl led me down it and through an archway into the living room. The floor was tiled in lieu of carpeting, and my heels clicked loudly. It made me self-conscious, and I leaned forward, walking on the balls of my feet.

The girl stopped before a large, bulky sofa. "I'll tell my father you're here," she said.

"Thank you."

The girl went out. I sat on the sofa with my hat on my knees and looked at the room. The Spanish effect seemed overdone. The furniture was old and heavy and ponderous. An imposing scrolled desk, an electric typewriter on top of it, stood on one side of the room. There was no sound, not even the ticking of a clock. My feeling of discomfort increased. I wanted a cigarette, but there were no ash trays that I could see.

I sat there about five minutes, and then a man in a dark, conservatively-cut business suit came through the archway from the hall. He walked across to me, carrying himself in the approved British manner—the brittle posture of breeding—and extended a well-manicured hand.

I got to my feet and took the hand. There was strength in his grip. "How do you do?" he said. "I'm Gerald Demeroy."

"How do you do?" I said, and felt foolish saying it.

He was about forty-five, a handsome man with a smooth, tanned, aesthetic face and an impressive head of bluish-silver hair. His eyes were gray, steady, and contained a tangible power; I couldn't read them at all. He was trim, athletic, with no sign of a thickening at the middle the way there is with some men when they approach middle age; tennis, I decided, and an hour or two a day in the pool.

"Please sit down," Demeroy said, and I sat down again. "Would you care for a drink?" I refused. Drinking in the morning depresses me, but of course I did not tell him that.

"I believe I'll have one, if you don't mind."

I said nothing. It was his house.

He went to a small serving tray near the patio archway, poured some amber liquid into a glass, lifted it and put his head back and tossed it off like a longshoreman. He set the glass down carefully, pivoted and then stopped, facing the hall archway. The tall, thin girl who had let me in was standing there. Demeroy impaled her with his gray eyes. "Haven't you something to do, Bianca?"

She brought a thin hand up and touched her chin. Then she turned quickly and hurried off down the hallway.

Demeroy came over to the sofa and sat opposite me. "My daughter," he said. "An inquisitive girl. She wants to be a writer someday."

I nodded. "You mentioned something on the phone about finding someone, Mr. Demeroy," I said. It sounded awkward, but I didn't know how else to start.

"Yes," he said. "My son."

"Your son?"

"Yes, my son Jeff. He's been missing for two days now. I'm frankly rather worried."

256

Well, you can't have them all figured. I cleared my throat. "Have you contacted the police?"

"No," he said. "I'm sure you can understand my reasons for not doing so."

I understood, all right. The people of Sea Cliff judiciously avoid any contact with the police. The merest hint of a scandal lowers their rating in the Social Register; discretion, in Sea Cliff, is an absolute.

I said, "Do you have any idea where your son might be?"

"None at all. He left for school Monday morning—he's a law student at the university, you see—and he hasn't returned. I have contacted several of his friends, but none of them seems to know where he's gone."

"Maybe he went off on a lark," I said. "Hitchhiking down south. They do that sometimes."

"Jeff is a very conscientious young man," Demeroy said. "He is not given to . . . larks, as you call them. If he had been planning to make some sort of trip, he would most certainly have informed me beforehand. That's his picture there on the table behind you." Demeroy raised a hand in an affected, somewhat theatrical gesture.

I turned politely and looked at the picture. The boy was blond and well-groomed, with nice, even features. He looked the way you would expect a boy from Sea Cliff to look.

I brought my eyes back to Demeroy and smiled and nodded, and wished I were back in my office.

Demeroy said, "He and my daughter are all that I have now. My wife died three years ago, and it's rather difficult to be both a father and mother to growing children."

I fussed with my hat. "Look, Mr. Demeroy," I said, "I'd like to help you find your son. But I don't know the first thing I could do."

His gray eyes studied me.

"You've talked to the boy's friends," I said. "I'm afraid that would be about all I could do, too. I could go to the university, and speak with his teachers and nose around, but that seems rather pointless in view of what you've told me. By the time I learned anything, the boy would, in all likelihood, have returned home. I'm sure the reason for his being gone the past two days is an innocuous one."

Demeroy's face was stoic. "Am I to take that to mean you won't help me?"

"No, sir, not at all. I'm simply trying to be honest with you."

"I see," Demeroy said. "But in your considered opinion, I'm making a mountain out of a molehill at the present time."

"When a member of your family is 'missing,' there's always cause for worry, Mr. Demeroy," I said. "However, two days is a very short period for a college student—even a conscientious one—to be away from home."

"You would suggest, then, that I wait before taking action?"

"I'm not trying to suggest anything, Mr. Demeroy. I'm only offering an opinion. If you sincerely feel there's some cause for alarm—that your son may be in some kind of trouble, or has met with an accident of some kind—then by all means you should do whatever you feel necessary to have him located."

Demeroy stood abruptly. I got to my feet, too, and we stood looking at each other. I still could not read his eyes. After a time he said, "Perhaps I have been overly concerned. A typical parental reaction."

I couldn't think of anything to say to that.

"May I call on you again if Jeff does not return home, or if I have not heard from him within a more reasonable period of time?"

"Certainly."

Demeroy took a wallet from the pocket of his suit coat, extracted several bills and extended them to me. "You've been helpful," he said, "and most kind."

"That isn't necessary, Mr. Demeroy."

He ignored my words, pressing the bills into my palm, then showed me to the door. I thanked him and we shook hands and said good-bye. In my car, I looked at the bills: fifty dollars. I put them in my wallet. Fifty dollars—I could have got five times that, maybe more. I could have . . . Then I stopped thinking like that, because it never gets you anywhere. What I'd told Demeroy had been the truth. When it comes to lying for profit, you either can or you can't, and that's all there is to it.

Eberhardt came around to my office at two-thirty.

I was sleeping, sitting up in my desk chair. The sound of the door opening startled me, and I was half out of my chair before I realized what it was. Eberhardt came inside and shut the door. He walked across to the only other chair and sat down tiredly.

"You're getting old," he said. "Sleeping in the afternoon like that."

"Sure."

"Have you got any coffee?"

I had put some on when I returned from Gerald Demeroy's. There had been no telephone messages, and Novinski informed me that no one had come calling. So I had put the coffee on, drunk a little of it, and smoked, and thought, and then I had fallen asleep.

I poured some coffee into a relatively clean cup and took it to Eberhardt. "I don't have any cream or sugar."

"You never do," he said. He tasted the coffee. "This is lousy."

"Uh huh."

He drank from the cup. "New development on this Christine Vance thing. I heard it around noon from the coroner's office."

I waited.

"She was pregnant," Eberhardt said. "Three months."

I took in a breath, let it out slowly. "They never learn, do they?"

"It seems not."

"Did you find out anything about my card being in her purse?"

"As a matter of fact, yes," Eberhardt said. "It seems Christine had been getting some kind of crank letters in the mail. You know the kind. She was pretty upset about them, I gather, and was planning to see a detective."

"Me."

Eberhardt inclined his head. "You," he said. "I guess she never got to it, somehow. Anyway, it pretty much puts you out of it."

"Maybe," I said. "How did you learn all this?"

"We did some checking around," Eberhardt said. "Friends of the dead girl, you know. She lived with a kid named Lainey Madden. Both of them are students over at UC, in Berkeley. We got it from her."

"You think there's some connection between these crank letters and Christine's death?"

"Possibly," Eberhardt said, "but the way it looks now, Christine's boy friend is it."

"She had a steady one, then?"

"Uh-huh. Engaged to be married, in fact."

I lit a cigarette, nodding thoughtfully.

Eberhardt went on, "Naturally we wanted to talk to this boy friend. We called his home a little while ago. It seems he's missing. His father says he's been missing for two days, now."

I sat up very straight on my chair. "Missing?" I said. "For two days?"

"That's right. Nobody knows where the kid went. He and Christine had a fight, according to the Madden girl. The boy took off right after that."

I moistened my lips slowly. "What's this boy's name, Eb?"

"Demeroy," Eberhardt answered. "Jeff Demeroy."

A few minutes later, after he had gone, I sat at my desk and looked through the window at the gray sky. The pale sun had vanished now, and a thick, rolling fog moved in from the west. The smell of it was already thick in the air.

Jeff Demeroy . . . I had told Eberhardt about talking to Gerald Demeroy earlier this morning, and he was very interested. Mr. Demeroy had not mentioned to him that he had called me about his son, but before we could discuss the point at length, a call had come through for Eberhardt—something urgent, I gathered, though he didn't offer to tell me what it was—and he had left hurriedly, saying he would see me later.

I kept thinking, sitting there alone in my office, about that card in Christine Vance's purse, and about the crank letters Eberhardt had said she received. He didn't seem to think there was any tie-in, but I had the feeling there was, somehow, in some way.

After a time, I leafed through the city telephone directory and found a listing for Lainey Madden on Broderick, out near the Presidio. I wasn't sure why exactly, but there seemed to be some reason why I should talk to her.

The house where Lainey Madden now lived alone was what I think is called a Queen Anne Victorian. It was old and tired and a bit frowzy, but standing with its turrets and gables still held proudly erect. It had, at one time, been somebody's fine home—until time and the scavengers came along—and then it had been subdivided into small apartments. On the row of mailboxes in the foyer I found *C. Vance—L. Madden* listed for an apartment on the second floor, rear, number 203.

I went inside and climbed old and musty-smelling stairs. There was a little brass plate on the door of 203 with a white card that said the same as the mailbox. I knocked.

I heard the pad of bare feet and then the door opened and a girl looked out. "Can I help you?" she asked.

"Are you Lainey Madden?"

"Yes?" she said, looking at me questioningly. She was a very pretty girl, with long, straight black hair and great sad eyes, colt brown, and a

260

small, round little mouth. She wore no makeup, and the sad eyes were red-flecked. She was dressed in one of those shapeless, printed dresses the girls wear when they aren't expecting any company.

I told her who I was, and asked her if I might speak to her about Christine Vance.

"Are you trying to find out who killed her?" she asked.

"Not officially, no," I said. "But there was a card of mine found in her purse."

"Yes, the police asked me about it when they were here," she said. "I told them she had it because of the letters."

"Yes," I said.

It seemed awkward to be talking to her from the hallway, and I shuffled my feet slightly. She seemed to sense it too.

"Won't you come in?"

"Thank you."

I stepped inside and she closed the door. We were in a small but comfortable front room. "Sit down," Lainey said.

I found a place on one of the chairs by the window, moving aside a school book on Anthropology. Lainey sat on the couch, drawing her knees up under her.

"I'm really very sorry to bother you at a time like this," I said.

"It's all right. I've finished my crying now."

It was easy to see that she and Christine Vance had been very close, and that she was making an effort to bear up under the shock of her friend's death. I said gently, "About these letters, Lainey."

"Yes?"

"Can you tell me what they said?"

"A lot of terrible things. Oh, I don't mean obscenities; just crazy things. Threats, mostly."

"What sort of threats?"

"Telling Chris she had better get out of town right away or something terrible would happen to her. Things like that."

"What happened to the letters?"

"I think Chris gave them to Jeff."

"Jeff Demeroy?"

"Yes."

"Do you know what he did with them?"

She shook her head slowly. "No," she said. "But he must still have them, because they were going to give them to the detective—to you—if they kept coming in the mail."

"Do you know how Christine happened to get my card?"

"I think from Jeff," Lainey said. "A friend of his in school had a stack of them. He collects business cards."

"I see," I said. I felt very old and tired sitting there. "Can you tell me something about Christine?"

"She was a wonderful person," Lainey said without hesitation. "Just the finest person." Her great sad eyes blinked. "She was quiet, kind of shy, really, and sort of, well, unassuming."

"Unassuming?"

"She trusted everybody, do you know what I mean? She had faith in people. I guess she had too much faith," Lainey said, sensing my thoughts.

I went on to something else. "The police seem to think Jeff Demeroy had something to do with her death."

"That's ridiculous. Jeff wouldn't hurt Chris."

"Do you know him well?"

"Pretty well," Lainey said. "I dated him for a while. That was how he met Chris. I introduced them."

"They were engaged, is that right?"

She nodded. "They were going to be married here in December."

"There was something about a fight," I said.

"Not a fight, really," Lainey said. "Just a kind of argument. It had to do with Jeff's family."

"His family?"

"His father, and his sister, Bianca. They were against the marriage. It was the same old thing, you know? She wasn't good enough for him, and like that."

"They argued about it?"

"Yes. Chris was afraid Jeff's father was going to get between them. God knows, he tried hard enough. Jeff listens to his father, you see, and he was considering postponing the wedding for while."

I was silent for a time. "Did you know Christine was pregnant?"

Lainey averted her eyes. She stared straight ahead for a moment, and then looked back to me. "Yes," she said.

"Did Jeff know?"

"No."

"Are you sure?"

262

"I know Chris didn't tell him. I was the only one she told."

"Why did Jeff go away, then?"

"Because he wanted to think things over, he said."

"Christine told you that?"

"Yes. She came home crying the night they had the argument and said Jeff was going away to think about what he was going to do. She was pretty miserable. She was sure he'd go along with his father, and she'd lose him."

"She could have told him about the baby."

"Sure," Lainey said, "and trap him into marriage. She didn't want that. What kind of marriage is that?"

You hear a lot about the kids these days, but not the kids like Lainey Madden. I said, "Can you tell me about last night?"

"Chris got a call about seven," Lainey said. "I was taking a shower, so I didn't hear the conversation or anything. Later on, about nine, Chris told me she was going out."

"Did she say where?"

"No," Lainey answered, "but I kind of thought it was to meet Jeff."

"Oh?"

"Well, she seemed sort of excited. I asked her what it was about, but she just smiled and said she'd tell me when she got back. Only . . ."

She seemed about to cry, but then her face set and her small, round mouth tightened. Suddenly, I wanted to get out of there; you can look at grief only so long. I said, "Do you have any idea where Jeff might have gone to think things over?"

"No, I . . ." Lainey broke off, frowning slightly. Then she said, "Well . . ."

"Yes?"

"They have this cabin down near Big Sur," she said. "The Demeroys, I mean. It could be that Jeff went there."

"Did you tell this to the police?"

"No, I don't think so. I was . . . upset when they came. I wasn't thinking clearly."

"I understand," I said. "Where is this cabin, do you know?"

"Trident Road, I think," Lainey said. "A name like that. I remember Jeff saying once that he went there sometimes when he wanted to be alone or to do some studying for exams."

I nodded, chewing something around in my mind. Neither of us spoke for a moment, and then Lainey said, "I think it must have been some crazy person."

"Pardon?"

"Whoever killed Chris. Nobody who knew her could do a thing like that. Maybe it was the crazy person who wrote those letters."

"Yes," I said slowly. "Maybe it was." I got to my feet. "Well, I guess that's about all. I want to thank you for your time, Lainey."

"It's all right," she said. "I hope I gave you some help."

"I think you did."

She walked me to the door. "The funeral will be day after tomorrow," she said. "Will you come?"

It was an odd question. I said, "Yes, I'll come."

She nodded, a faint, sad smile on her small mouth. "I want a lot of people to come," she said. "Chris liked people."

A chill touched my neck. "Good-bye, Lainey. Take care."

"Sure," she said.

I went downstairs and outside. There was a telephone booth in a parking lot down the street. I walked there, put a dime in the slot and dialed the Hall of Justice. I asked for Eberhardt.

It took them a while to get him on the line. It was stuffy in the phone booth, and I could smell faintly lilac perfume. When Eberhardt came on, I told him, "I've just been talking to Lainey Madden, Eb."

"Yeah?"

"There was something she didn't tell you this morning," I said. "About where the Demeroy kid might be."

"Big Sur," Eberhardt said. "Family owns a cabin there."

I opened the door of the booth to let in some air. "How did you find out?"

"He told us."

"Jeff Demeroy?"

"That's right," Eberhardt said. "He walked in here a little over an hour ago; that's what that call in your office was about. He said he heard about what happened on the radio, and came right up."

"Are you holding him?"

"Sure we're holding him. What did you think?"

"Is it all right if I come down?"

"What for?"

"I'd like to talk to him, if I can."

264

I listened to his quiet breathing for a time. Then he said, "I guess you can. Come on down."

It was hot in Eberhardt's office.

He was coatless and appeared to be very tired. His eyes were criss-crossed in red.

I sat in a chair in front of his desk. "What did Jeff Demeroy tell you?" I asked.

Eberhardt shrugged. "That he didn't kill her."

"Is that all?"

"He said he went down to Big Sur to do some thinking," Eberhardt said. "About Christine Vance and him. Been down there since Monday, thinking. But all by himself. No alibi."

"Are you going on the assumption he killed her?"

"Maybe," Eberhardt said noncommittally.

"He didn't know about the girl being pregnant, you know."

"That's what he said. We kept it out of the papers and off the radio and hit him with it when he came in. He was shocked to beat hell, but he could have been putting on."

"He wasn't putting on," I said. "Have you called his father yet?"

He nodded. "He's with the boy now."

"Did you ask him why he didn't mention talking to me this morning?"

"He said he didn't think it was important."

"Uh huh," I said.

Eberhardt was looking at me critically. "Have you got something?" he wanted to know. "You act like you have."

"I think so, Eb."

"Give," he said.

"I'd like to ask Jeff Demeroy a couple of questions first."

He continued to study me. Then he stood, said, "All right, let's go, then."

Jeff Demeroy was taller than I had imagined him from the photograph. His blond hair was damp with perspiration, and he didn't look so well-groomed now. He sat in a wooden chair, his hands clenched tightly on his knees; he appeared to be very nervous. It might have been because he was a murder suspect, or it might have been prolonged shock at the news of his fiancee's death.

Gerald Demeroy was seated beside his son, a protective arm around

265

the boy's shoulders. On the way down, I had asked Eberhardt to let me talk to Jeff without his father being present, and he had consented. He asked Mr. Demeroy to leave us alone for a few moments; Demeroy didn't like it, but there wasn't much he could do except comply.

When he'd left with one of the officers there, Eberhardt introduced me to Jeff Demeroy. If my name meant anything to him then, his face didn't show it. We sat across the table from him.

"I'm just going to ask you a coupl? of questions," I said. "You don't mind answering them, do you?"

"No, no," he said. "Go ahead."

"The police found one of my cards in Christine's purse."

His eyes showed recognition. "You're that detective."

"Yes."

"It was on the radio about the card."

"You gave it to her, is that right?"

"Yes. I got it from one of my friends at school."

"How many cards did you get from this friend, Jeff?"

"Two," he said dully. "Why?"

"You kept the other one, didn't you?"

"Yes, I kept it."

"Where is it now?"

"In my room at home, I guess."

"And the threatening letters Christine got in the mail," I said, "what did you do with them?"

"They're there, too."

"Where, exactly?"

He wet his lips. "In one of my bureau drawers."

"One last thing, Jeff," I said. "Did you recognize the handwriting on those letters?"

"They weren't handwritten," he answered. "They were typed."

"All right, Jeff," I said. I paused. "And . . . I'm sorry."

He nodded, putting his head in his hands. He thought I was offering my sympathy for the death of Christine Vance.

He was only half right.

Back in Eberhardt's office, Eb asked, "What was all that about down there?"

"Don't you see it yet?"

"Maybe I do," he said. Eberhardt is a very smart man, but not one to rush into things. I have known him a long time, long enough to tell whether or not he is satisfied with a case. He wasn't satisfied with this one. He knew, just as I did, that Jeff Demeroy was innocent.

He began to fill his pipe. "Let's hear what you've got to say."

"All right. To begin with, there are two keys to this whole thing. The first is my business card—not the one in Christine's purse, Eb; the one in Jeff Demeroy's room. As soon as the boy told me there *was* a second card, then it all fell into place; there was only one way it could be."

"Meaning?"

"Meaning," I said, "that it explains why Gerald Demeroy called me this morning. The coincidence of his telephoning *me*, especially on the morning after his son's fiancee was murdered, is too much to take."

"Your name's in the book, just like all the rest," Eberhardt said, making argument. "Besides, when you saw him he didn't know the girl was dead."

"Didn't he?"

"You're doing the talking."

"He knew Christine was dead, all right. Either he, or his daughter, Bianca, had found both the letters and my second business card in Jeff's room. That's why he called and had me come out to his house, and why he pointed out his son's picture to me there. He had to find out if I *knew* Jeff, if Jeff had been in to see me about the letters Christine was getting in the mail, if I had been working for Jeff and in the process discovered the sender of those letters."

Eberhardt didn't say anything. I was pretty sure it was all clear to him now, too.

I went on, "The thing that put me onto him was his professing not to have any idea where Jeff had gone off to. Lainey Madden told me about the cabin the Demeroys have near Big Sur, and that Jeff went there sometimes to study and to be alone. Demeroy would surely have known this; it would have been one of the first places he would check if he thought his son to be missing."

Eberhardt's pipe went out. He scowled at it and put it in the ash tray on his desk. "Let's hear about the second key," he said.

"The letters themselves, Eb. They have to be directly connected with Christine's murder. Again, a coincidence would be too much to take."

"What you're saying," Eberhardt said, "is that whoever wrote those letters to Christine Vance was the one who killed her."

"What else, Eb? Anyone who would write crank letters, threatening letters, has to be unbalanced in some way. And probably capable of murder."

"Gerald Demeroy?"

"Demeroy is as sane as you or I," I said. "He's a strong man, a willful man, an influential man; do you think he'd resort to writing crank letters?"

"Then who wrote them?"

"Isn't it obvious? Demeroy was protecting someone by getting me out to his house this morning—but that someone wasn't Jeff. There's only one other person it could be."

"His daughter," Eberhardt said.

"Yeah," I said. "His daughter."

We were silent for a time. Then Eberhardt got slowly on his feet. "I think I'll go down and have a talk with Mr. Demeroy. You coming?"

"No," I said. "I've had enough of this whole thing."

He didn't answer, but he put a hand on my shoulder to let me know he understood. Then he went out and I sat there in his office for a while, smoking, before I decided it was time to leave.

I got the full story from Eberhardt later on that night in my apartment.

Gerald Demeroy had remained adamant to the last, refusing to admit anything, but Eberhardt had called for a matron and they'd gone out to his house in Sea Cliff and confronted Bianca. She'd broken down under questioning and admitted that she had murdered Christine Vance. Shortly after that she had become hysterical, and they'd had to get an ambulance to take her away. Eberhardt had got the details from Gerald Demeroy later, at the hospital.

Bianca had hated Christine Vance, hated her beyond all reason. She couldn't stand the thought of her brother marrying Christine, living away from her; she saw Christine—in her emotionally unstable mind—as some kind of evil force about to split apart her previously close-knit family. She'd written the letters to try to frighten Christine away, but when they hadn't accomplished their purpose, she had decided there was only one alternative, only one way to remove this threat.

She'd taken her father's gun—she knew he kept it in his desk in the study—and then she'd called Christine. She'd told her that she and her father had decided to consent to the marriage, and wanted to see her. Christine was naturally overjoyed, and had agreed to meet Bianca that evening. Since Christine had been a trusting girl, she had attached no ominous significance to Golden Gate Park as a meeting place.

268

Later, when Bianca returned home after killing Christine, she had broken down and confessed to her father what she'd done. Gerald Demeroy had responded then as most fathers would under similar circumstance; he had attempted to protect his daughter. He had got rid of the murder gun, throwing it over the cliff into the ocean, and had burned the incriminating letters—which Bianca found, along with my card, in searching through Jeff's room. Then, today, he had called me for the exact purpose I had postulated to Eberhardt.

The police found, in the fireplace at the Demeroy home, a scrap of one of the letters that had not burned completely. They checked the scrap against the typewriter I had seen in the living room, and the script matched exactly. That made it conclusive.

When Eberhardt had finished, I went into my kitchen and got two mugs and filled them half-and-half with coffee and brandy. I took them out and gave one to Eberhardt.

"It's a shame the way the world spins sometimes," he said.

"Yeah," I said. "A damned shame."

We drank from our mugs, and neither of us spoke much after that, thinking our own thoughts.

The Real Criminal

by James M. Gilmore

Except for the rare psychopath who kills for the pure pleasure of killing, and the equally rare professional killer who does it for money, murderers usually aren't the cold-blooded monsters they're cracked up to be.

Most of them are nice, normal, average folk, people like you and me, who ordinarily couldn't swat a fly or run over a cat without feeling a little squeamish.

You find that hard to believe? Look up the facts in any good book on criminology. You'll discover statistics prove the chances of a murderer ever committing a second murder are something like a million-to-one. Why? Because in many cases the victim was, in fact, the real criminal.

Take the case of George Winnard, or "Good old George" as his friends called him, before they heard he shot and killed Ray Barber.

George was everything you'd expect a good-old-George type to be; a ruddy, plump, good-natured man in his late thirties, always ready with a joke and an immense grin. He was absolutely faithful to his lovely, if somewhat flighty, wife, Ruth. His faithfulness, however, didn't stop him from playfully patting secretaries or making harmless passes at waitresses. He was the perfect father to his three sons. At least, he put up with their shaggy dog of undetermined origin, seven rabbits, and three pet turtles. He went to church every Sunday, ushered every fourth Sunday, and never, never fell asleep during the sermon. He worked half again as hard as most real estate salesmen, was a member of the Chamber of Commerce, the Kiwanis, and the Booster's Club. George was truly a big man, a man of stature, a man of heart.

Why then, you may ask, was he arrested for Ray Barber's murder?

It probably wouldn't have happened at all if George's boss, Mr. Walter P. Grimes, *the* Grimes of Grimes, Hackett and Pederson, hadn't called him into his office that sunny, warm Friday afternoon in May, a lazy spring day.

Mr. Grimes sat back in his big, leather chair, put the tips of his arthritic fingers together, looked across his huge walnut desk at George and asked, "What do you think of Ray Barber?"

George grinned his immense grin and shrugged, "He's a good salesman. . . ."

"But not the best?"

"I didn't say that."

"That's the trouble with you, George," Mr. Grimes said with a fatherly smile. "You can't see anything bad in anyone." The smile disappeared as he shuffled through some papers on his desk. "I just checked the salesmen's status reports. Berber hasn't made a sale or brought in a new listing in over a month."

"Everyone hits a slump."

Mr. Grimes shook his head. "It's more than a slump. I've had several complaints about him."

"Complaints?"

"From women prospects," Mr. Grimes said with a deep frown. "Seems he can't keep his hands off them. Now, George, you know we can't have things like that going on at Grimes, Hackett and Pederson. We're the most respectable real estate firm on the north side."

George nodded. "I'll talk to him," he said.

"Fire him. Now. Today."

"Fire Ray Barber? Me?"

"Yes, you. You're my office manager, aren't you?"

"But—"

"No buts. Fire him! He's crazy. I want him out of here for good by five o'clock. We're running a real estate office, not a home for maniacs!"

"But he's not—"

"Fire him!" Mr. Grimes shouted, pounding his desk.

"Yes, sir," George said, getting up to leave. "How much severance pay should I give him?"

"Not one red cent!"

It took George almost an hour to work up enough courage to call Ray Barber into his office.

Ray was a small, thin man with a small, thin moustache who had an annoying combination of tics and nervous quirks that gave him a look of constant agitation. He was the kind of a man you couldn't look in the eye for more than a few seconds without becoming nervous yourself.

After he sat down, George looked at the ceiling and, to sort of break the ice, said, "Nice day out, isn't it?"

The muscles of Ray's left cheek suddenly contracted and he pulled on his right ear lobe. Then his eyes narrowed. "Are you trying to say I should be out drumming up business? That I'm loafing?"

George grinned, a smaller than usual grin, and said, "Heck, no. I just think it's a nice day, that's all." He took two cigars out of his vest pocket and handed one across his desk to Ray.

He took it, nervously fumbled with the wrapper, and said, "Okay. It's a nice day." He put the cigar in his mouth and lit it. Then he blew out a puff of blue smoke and rolled the cigar between his fingers. "You're going to raise Cain with me for not making any sales lately, aren't you?" He made an annoying sucking noise through his teeth. "I saw you in there with Grimes. What'd you tell him about me?"

"Honestly, Ray, I didn't—"

"Don't give me any of that. What are you trying to do, get me canned?" His head jerked to one side. "Well, you try that, Georgie boy, and I'll get you."

"Now, wait a minute! I didn't have anything to do with this. It was all Mr. Grimes' idea."

"What was Grimes' idea?" Ray asked, drumming his fingers on the desk.

George decided he had better get it over with as quickly as possible. He took a deep breath and said, "You're fired."

The color drained from Ray's face. "So you finally got Grimes to do it—"

"I didn't."

"Who did then?"

"Do you want the truth?"

"Truth?" Ray laughed, a nervous, high-pitched laugh. "You don't know the meaning of the word. You've been lying about me for months, telling everyone I'm crazy. That's why I can't make any sales. Because you tell lies about me."

George was shocked. "Ray, believe me, I never—"

"No. You'd never do anything like that, would you? You're good old George, the all-American boy scout. Everyone likes and trusts you. That's how you get them. They trust you, and you lie about them. You stab them in the back with gossip. Well, I'm on to you, George. Maybe you

272

can fool all the other suckers, but you can't fool me. You're the kind of a man that should be destroyed. You should be stamped on like a bug! And I'll do it, George. I'll do it if it's the last thing I ever do!"

George was shocked. He rose to his feet and asked, "Are you through?"

Ray seemed to calm down. "For the time being."

"Then I suggest you clean out your desk. Mr. Grimes wants you out of here by five o'clock."

Ray stood up. The muscles in his left cheek suddenly contracted again. "Okay. But you'll be hearing from me."

"I hope not."

"You will be," he said, taking a puff from the cigar. He tipped his hand toward George in a mock salute. "See you."

A week later, at the Booster Club luncheon, it began.

George was standing at the bar, sipping a bourbon and water, when Al Wright, another Grimes, Hackett and Pederson salesman, sidled up to him.

"What did you have against Ray Barber?" he asked.

"Me? Nothing," George said with a grin. "Mr. Grimes asked me to fire him and I did. That's all there is to it."

"That's not the way Ray tells it."

"No?"

Al lowered his voice. "Maybe I shouldn't tell you this, but he's been calling everyone in the office on the telephone. He claims you're off your rocker."

George laughed uneasily. "Me, nuts?"

"He says you fired him because you've got some kind of phobia about guys who wear moustaches."

"He's the nutty one. Why, my own father wore a moustache all his life."

Al smiled and asked, "How did you get along with your father?"

George shrugged. "Well, you know how it is—"

"Did you hate him?"

"Are you kidding?"

"No. I mean, maybe that's why you've got this phobia about moustaches."

George stared at him for a moment, then he said, "You're the nut."

Al laughed and gave him a jab in the ribs with his elbow. "That's right, George, everyone's nuts but you."

"Look. I told you I fired Ray because Mr. Grimes asked me to. That's all there is to it."

"Sure, sure," Al said. "I know. You'd really have to be crazy to fire a guy because you didn't like his moustache. Come on. Let's go in and eat."

The man who sat across the table from George and Al had a moustache just like Ray's. No matter how hard he tried, George couldn't keep his eyes off it. The man must have felt his eyes on him because, just before dessert was served, he asked, "Is there anything wrong with my moustache?"

George could feel the redness working up the back of his neck. "No, why?"

"You've been staring at it all through lunch. I thought it might be full of soup or something."

Al looked at George, and then looked at the man across the table. "He's got a phobia about moustaches."

"I told you, I haven't got a phobia about moustaches!"

"Then why were you staring at his moustache all through lunch?"

"I don't know. I was just staring at it, that's all." George wiped his mouth with his napkin and got up from his chair. "I'm sorry," he said, "I've got to get back to the office." It was a lie, of course, but anything was better than getting into a crazy argument with Al over a stupid moustache.

When George got back to the office, he found a small package wrapped in brown paper on his desk. He opened it and discovered it contained a false moustache. He looked for a card. There wasn't any. Then he checked the brown paper to see if there were a return address. The only thing he found was his name scrawled in a handwriting he didn't recognize. Anyone could have put it on his desk. He buzzed for his secretary. When she came in, he asked, "Do you know who put this package on my desk?"

"No, it was there when I got back from lunch."

"Well, get it out of here."

"What was in it?"

"A false moustache."

He wasn't quite sure, but he thought she had a strange smirk on her face as she picked it up. Ray must have called her too.

Late that afternoon, a couple from Detroit came in and asked to see a four-bedroom colonial. George had the floor duty at the time. He looked at the multiple listing and discovered there were five. They wanted to see them all. Since they had to fly back to Detroit the next morning, George was out with them until almost ten-thirty. When he finally arrived home he was tired and hungry and not in the mood for jokes. But one was waiting for him.

As his wife, Ruth, served him warmed-over supper, she said, "You had the strangest phone call tonight."

"From who?"

"Whom," she corrected him.

"All right, dammit, from *whom?*"

"Ray Barber."

George almost choked. "What did that nut want?"

"He said to tell you he would never shave off his moustache. Why would he ever say a thing like that?"

"He thinks I fired him because I didn't like his moustache."

"Oh, George, you shouldn't have."

He looked at her blankly. "Shouldn't have done what?"

"Fired him because you didn't like his moustache."

"Look," he said, pointing at her with his fork, "I didn't say I fired him because I didn't like his moustache. I said, he *thinks* I did."

"Now, George, I know how you hate moustaches."

"What ever gave you a stupid idea like that?"

She smiled at him coyly. "Remember that New Year's Eve party we went to eleven years ago at the Fischers'?" She sighed. "And remember that tall, dark, handsome bachelor with the perfectly lovely moustache who kept flirting with me all night?"

"He was a short, skinny pipsqueak. And that stupid moustache of his made him look like Hitler!"

"Why, George, you're still jealous!" she squealed.

"Jealous!" he roared. "Not on your life!"

"Then why did you tell him you'd punch him in the nose if he didn't shave off his moustache?"

"Because I was drunk, that's why."

"You were jealous."

George's shoulders sagged. "All right. I was jealous. I hate all men with moustaches. I fired Ray Barber because I hated his stupid moustache. Are you satisfied now?"

"You shouldn't have," she clucked as she cleared away the dishes.

Everyone in George's dreams that night had a moustache.

Saturdays are always busy at a real estate office, so it wasn't unusual that George didn't notice the picture of his family that stood on his desk until just before closing. In fact, it wouldn't have been unusual if he hadn't noticed it at all, it had become such a fixture in his office. The only reason he did was that he was filling out an earnest money contract and he needed more room on his desk. He picked up the picture to move it and was dumbstruck. Every member of his family had grown a moustache! Then he looked again, closer, and found someone had drawn the moustaches on the glass over the picture with grease pencil. He buzzed his secretary.

"Miss Quinn, this has gone far enough!" he exclaimed the second she walked into his office.

Somewhat taken aback, she said, "I don't understand, Mr. Winnard."

"Look at this portrait of my family," he said, holding the picture within four inches of her face.

Her eyes opened wide and she giggled. "Why, they all have moustaches! Did you draw them?"

"No, I didn't draw them."

"Then who did?"

"That's what I was going to ask you."

"Don't look at me like that, Mr. Winnard. I didn't do it. I know all about your phobia—"

"I don't have a phobia about moustaches!" he yelled, slamming the picture down on his desk so hard the glass shattered.

"Mr. *Winnard!*" she shrieked, and she ran from his office in tears.

He sat down at his desk, and, as calmly as he could, tried to gather his thoughts. Suddenly, it all became perfectly clear. That crazy Ray Barber was trying to drive him crazy! Well, it wouldn't work. No, sir, it wouldn't work. He dialed Ray's number on the telephone.

Ray answered after the second ring.

"Ray," George said, slowly, trying to control the quaver in his voice, "if you tell one more person I fired you because I have a phobia about moustaches, I'll kill you. Do you understand? I'll beat your brains out with my own hands."

"Is that you, George?" Ray asked, calmly.

"Yes."

"George Winnard?"

"You know it's me. Now, do you understand what I just told you?"

"Of course, you said you'd kill me if I told anyone you fired me because you hated my moustache."

"I mean it, Ray, cut it out."

"Why don't you like my moustache, George?"

"Because I'm jealous, that's why!" George yelled into the receiver. Then he slammed it down.

That night, the Winnards gave a small, intimate dinner party for Mr. Grimes and his wife, Belle. It was the first time in almost six months that they had been to dinner, and George had been very careful with the guest list. It included a few select—if not close—friends, the kind that never drink or talk too much. Ruth had prepared a prime rib roast, laid out her best china and silver on her best lace tablecloth, and had even had Mr. Sandin, the somewhat effeminate but exclusive florist, arrange the centerpiece.

The party started out slowly, as all dinner parties do, but after two rounds of martinis and a few of George's choicest mixed-company jokes, the guests began to warm up. Mr. Grimes told the men about the state of the real estate business, while Belle deplored the deplorable household help situation to the women. By the time dinner was served, it was beginning to look as if it would be a successful party. It probably would have been, too, if the doorbell hadn't rung while George was carving the prime ribs.

You can imagine his surprise when he opened the door and discovered two policemen standing on the front steps.

"Are you Mr. George Winnard?" one of them asked.

"Yes, of course," he answered nervously. Ever since he had been a little boy, just talking to a policeman had made him nervous. "Why? Is anything wrong?"

"Sorry, sir, the Captain said to bring you down to headquarters," the other one said in a low monotone.

"Now?" George asked. "Look, I'm having a dinner party. Whatever it is, can't it wait until tomorrow?"

"Sorry, sir, the Captain said now."

"What is it, dear?" Ruth called from the dining room.

"Nothing," George called back. "Just two police officers." Then he

277

lowered his voice to a whisper. "I can't go now, don't you understand? My *boss* is here. How would it look if I were dragged out of the house by two policemen right in the middle of the prime ribs?"

"You should have thought about that before you did what you did," the first policeman said.

"But what *did* I do?"

"The Captain didn't say. He just said to bring you in for questioning."

Ruth came to the door. "What's this all about, dear? Are they selling tickets to the Policemen's Ball?"

"Sorry, ma'am," the second officer said, taking off his cap. "We have to take your husband down to headquarters for questioning."

"Whatever for?" she asked.

"They won't tell me," George said.

"Well, then I wouldn't go."

"But, ma'am, he has to," the first policeman said, taking George by the arm.

"O.K.," George said, pulling his arm free. "I'll go with you. Just don't make a scene."

"But what'll I tell the guests? What'll I ever tell Mr. and Mrs. Grimes?" Ruth gasped.

"Tell them anything," George said, resignedly, as he started down the front steps with the two policemen. When they reached the bottom, he turned and looked back at her. "Just don't tell them *why* I'm being taken to headquarters."

"But why are you?" she asked, on the verge of tears.

He gave a helpless shrug. "I don't know."

"Well, I just don't know how I'll ever explain it," she said, and she ran into the house.

Captain Watowski was a short, stocky, hairy man. He reminded George of a secret police interrogator he had seen in a movie once, except he hadn't worn a bushy, red moustache like Captain Watowski's.

"What's this all about?" George demanded.

Captain Watowski pointed to a chair and said, "Sit down, Mr. Winnard."

George did as he was told.

Captain Watowski lit a cigarette, then sat down on the edge of a table that had a tape recorder on it. He sat there smoking and staring at George for a few minutes. Then he snuffed out the cigarette in a coffee can cover that doubled as an ash tray. He reached over and punched the "play" button on the tape machine. At first, George didn't recognize his own voice. Then, suddenly, he realized it was a recording of the conversation he'd had with Ray Barber on the telephone that afternoon.

When the tape was over, Captain Watowski punched the rewind button and said, "Tell me, Mr. Winnard, was that your voice?"

George shifted uneasily in his chair. "Yes, of course, but I didn't mean it the way it sounded."

"How did you mean it?"

"It was just a figure of speech. I mean, I didn't mean it when I said I'd kill him."

"Just what did you mean, Mr. Winnard?"

George thought for a moment. "Well, I meant I'd *kill* him." He stopped and thought again. "No, that's not what I meant." He grinned his most expansive grin.

"I'm glad you think it's funny, Mr. Winnard." Captain Watowski lit another cigarette. "But let me warn you right now, I wouldn't make a habit of threatening people's lives if I were you. It could get you into a great deal of trouble, Mr. Winnard."

"I don't make a habit of it," George said, lamely.

Captain Watowski ignored him. "Unfortunately, I can't do anything but warn you this time. The recording was made illegally by Mr. Barber, without your knowledge. But illegal or not, I don't want you ever to threaten his life again. Do we understand each other, Mr. Winnard?"

"Yes," George answered in a low whisper.

"Good," Captain Watowski said, taking a deep drag from his cigarette. He sat and stared at George again until he had smoked the cigarette down to the filter. Then he deposited it in the coffee can cover. "You may go now, Mr. Winnard."

"You mean, that's all?"

"That's all."

George stood up and started to the door.

"Just a minute, Mr. Winnard."

"What?"

"How do you like my moustache?"

"It's beautiful."

Captain Watowski smiled. "I'm glad you like it."

The fury began to build up inside George as soon as he was outside the police station. Somehow, Captain Watowski's moustache had had the same effect on him as a red flag waved before a bull. He lowered his head and charged blindly down the street in search of the nearest bar. He had to have a drink to calm him down, to bolster his demolished pride, to help him think.

Unfortunately, the two double shots of bourbon he gulped down at the Clover Leaf Bar did none of the three. His rational thinking process came to almost a complete halt. The only thing he could see through the blindness of his rage was a moustache. A thin moustache, Ray Barber's moustache. Barber's moustache. Barber . . . shave . . . razor! George laughed to himself. Why hadn't he thought of that before? He threw five dollars down on the bar and headed for the door. He had to find a drugstore.

Twenty minutes later he found himself standing in the hallway outside Ray Barber's apartment, a shiny, new straight-edge razor in his hand. He knocked on the apartment door. "I know you're in there, Barber!" he shouted. "Open up! I've got a present for you!"

The door opened and there was Ray Barber, the thin moustache on his upper lip, a .38 revolver in his hand. "Why, hello, George," he said, pleasantly. "I've been waiting for you."

"You know what this is?" George asked, holding up his new razor. "It's a straight-edge razor, that's what it is. And you know what I'm going to do with it? I'm going to shave off that stupid moustache of yours, that's what I'm going to do!"

Ray's mouth twitched into a smile and he pushed the gun under George's nose. "You know what this is, George? It's a .38 Smith and Wesson."

George looked at the gun under his nose and blinked stupidly, trying to focus his eyes on it.

"And do you know what I'm going to do with it?" Ray went on. "I'm going to destroy you, George."

George was suddenly jolted to his senses. "Are you crazy?" he asked.

"No, you are," Ray said with snigger. "Everyone knows you have a phobia about moustaches." He lowered the gun and pushed it into George's stomach. "Now, please, won't you come in?"

"What are you going to do?" George asked, dumbly, as he walked into Ray's apartment.

"Why, I just told you," Ray said, closing the door behind them. His left cheek twitched. "But first I must call the police." He picked up the phone, tucked the receiver under his chin and dialed the number with one hand while he held the gun on George with the other. "Captain Watowski, please." There was a short wait, then he said, "This is Ray Barber. I'm afraid your little talk with George Winnard didn't do any good. He's here now. I think he was going to kill me with a straight-edge razor." There was a short pause. "No, I have a gun on him right now. You'll be right over? Good. We'll be waiting for you." He put the phone down. "You know, George, I could kill you right now—"

"You *are* crazy."

Ray shook his head. "No, you are. Don't you realize that by now? You were crazy to fire me. I could have been the best salesman Grimes, Hacket, and Pederson ever had. But you lied about me. And why did you lie about me? Because you're crazy, George. You'd have to be crazy to lie about me." He laughed and his head jerked to one side.

"You planned this whole, crazy thing," George said, helplessly.

"Of course," Ray said. "I couldn't be crazy and plan such a masterpiece, could I?" He made a sucking noise through his teeth. "Everyone knows about your moustache phobia, even the police. And you threatened to kill me. The police know that, too. They even gave me a permit to carry this gun, as protection."

"And now you're going to kill me?"

"Destroy you," Ray corrected. "Completely."

George blanched and his whole body began to shake uncontrollably. "You can't kill me. I have a wife and three children," he whined.

"Don't be melodramatic."

George fell to his knees. "Please don't kill me," he sobbed. "I'll talk to Mr. Grimes. I'll do anything. But please don't shoot me."

For a moment, the only sound besides George's sobbing was the wail of an approaching police siren. Then Ray said, "I didn't say I was going to shoot *you*."

George stopped sobbing and looked up at him. "You're not going to shoot me?" he asked, hopefully.

Ray laughed. "No. I'm going to *destroy* you!" His mouth twitched again, and he suddenly turned the gun into his own stomach and pulled the trigger. The deafening blast knocked him backward off his feet. He groaned and slowly sat up. "Here, George, catch!" he gasped, throwing the gun at him.

George made an instinctive one-handed catch. "You crazy fool!" he exclaimed, springing to his feet. He rushed over to Ray and looked down at him writhing on the floor. "You poor, crazy fool!"

"I'm not crazy," Ray said in a hoarse, labored whisper. "Shooting you would have been too easy. Now you'll suffer for months. People will lie about you, the way you lied about me. And then they'll kill you, George, they'll kill you." He coughed, and then lay still.

There was only one thing left for George to do. He opened the straight-edge razor and shaved off Ray's moustache.

And that's the way the police found him, standing over Ray's body, the murder gun in one hand, a straight-edge razor in the other.

Of course, George was charged with murder and would have been found guilty, too, if he hadn't been adjudged insane.

You see, everyone knew he had this phobia about moustaches. . .

Bang! You're Dead!

by Margaret B. Maron

Amelia Turner, still trim and petite at fifty, capped the bottle of pale-pink enamel which she'd been applying to her nails and shivered deliciously as the heroine on the TV screen walked down a dark alley where her father's murderer lurked. Background music, apprehensive and staccato, tensed Amelia's nerves unbearably. Forgetful of wet polish, she pressed a thumbnail to her teeth and willed the girl to turn and run. Too late! A dark hulk lunged out at her. The girl screamed, shots rang out, spotlights flared and the murderer sprawled on the pavement to gurgle a dying confession as the heroine collapsed on the young detective's shoulder. Triumphant music; fade-out; commercial.

Amelia released the breath she'd been holding, flicked off the television and began repairing her damaged thumbnail. With the television silent, all the small familiar noises of the old house crept back: the grandfather clock on the landing; the clicks and sighs as the furnace cooled in the cellar; the gentle scratch of a tree limb brushing an upstairs window; the creaking plank between the kitchen and dining room . . .

Amelia froze. That plank never creaked by itself; only when someone stepped on it. The kitchen door! As if in televised instant replay, Amelia saw herself taking her dinner scraps out to the garbage pail earlier *and leaving the back door unlocked when she returned!* Silently, she raged at her carelessness and her terror mounted when the plank creaked again, released from the intruder's weight.

Newspaper headlines detailing unmentionable crimes flashed through her mind, and the telephone seemed miles away as she forced her trembling legs to carry her across the room. As she reached for the receiver, the dining room door was flung open and a harsh voice snarled, "Touch that phone and you're dead!"

Whirling to face her assailant, Amelia was struck by laughter. "Oh, Amelia." The woman standing there giggled. "If only you could see your

283

face!" But when Amelia, pale and trembling, sank down on the telephone bench, the woman's giggles changed to remorse.

"Oh gee, honey, I really scared you, didn't I? Gee, I'm sorry, but you've got to be more careful about locking up. Think of that woman over in Ripton last week who had someone walk in her open front door and murder her right there in her own vestibule." Chattering nonstop, the woman bustled into the dining room and returned with a small glass of sherry for Amelia.

Clara Demarest was also in her early fifties, but fighting every month of it. Where Amelia was soft white curls and delicate pastel dresses, Clara was blue rinse and vivid pantsuits which overemphasized her hips. "I only meant to show you how easy it is for someone to break into a big barn of a house like this," Clara said righteously as Amelia's color returned. "I could have been a murderer—or worse!"

"That's the first time in months I forgot to lock the door," Amelia protested.

"Once is all it takes," Clara said darkly, and her eyebrows knit in a facial expression so like Henry's that Amelia's heart turned over. Clara's brother had been dead ten long years and they really hadn't looked alike, yet any memory of Henry's dear, earnest face could still evoke that aching sense of loss.

To cover it, Amelia busied herself with assuring Clara that she was all right now. Mechanically, she went through the motions of hospitality, but her thoughts still strayed to Henry and those lost days of innocence.

Theirs had been a leisurely, old-fashioned courtship; a love discovered and blossoming in middle age when both had outgrown the painful shyness of youth. She had been too much under her father's autocratic thumb to encourage a lover, even if one had existed in their small town with eyes to see the untouched emotions concealed beneath the guise of a dutiful spinster daughter.

Henry, too, had suffered from self-consciousness as a youth and had hidden himself in the bank's Estates and Trusts Department, where his years of careful attention to detail were eventually rewarded by a vice-presidency. At the death of Amelia's father, it was Henry who had guided her through the minor intricacies of the old man's estate. If she called at the bank too frequently at first for his advice on this or that investment, he never made her feel unwelcome. Soon it had been *he* calling *her*, and without any pretext of banking or estate matters.

"I think I *will* have a glass of sherry," Clara said, and her words brought Amelia back to the present, since Clara seldom accepted spirits of any kind. "One lush in the family's enough," she often told Amelia with coarse irony.

Amelia supposed it was better to laugh than cry about Henry's weakness; and, to do her credit, Clara never made the remark to anyone else, yet Amelia couldn't help wincing whenever she said it. If Henry had to be dead, then let his faults rest in peace, too. Remember only the good.

And he had been good, Amelia thought, as she brought Clara sherry and watched her plump fingers lift the glass daintily. Even Clara, who couldn't resist occasional innuendoes about Henry's alcoholism, remembered her brother's generosity with gratitude: the way he'd stood by her when her husband died, leaving her penniless and on the edge of a nervous breakdown; how Henry had arranged for her recovery at a decent rest home and later brought her to share his own house.

Over the years, Clara had told Amelia all the details, but at the time, Amelia had sensed Henry's embarrassment over his sister's misfortunes and she had asked no questions. Henry had been grateful for her tact, and Amelia remembered the hopefulness with which he had introduced her to Clara. He had so wanted them to become good friends.

Were they good friends? Amelia wondered now, watching Clara finish her sherry with unwonted relish. Certainly Clara was all that remained to her of Henry. Only with her could Amelia openly remember what might have been, even though Clara had treated their romance with amused contempt at the time.

"Poor thing. You were so naive," Clara always said. When she dwelt too long on Henry's drinking, Amelia almost hated her; but then Clara would remember how Henry had saved her from widowed penury and both would mourn his loss.

Now Clara set down her glass and hoisted herself from the chair, saying cheerfully, "Well, I'd better be getting behind locked doors myself while the night's still young."

Amelia returned her smile.

"You sound as if the streets were crawling with muggers, Clara. We don't have many crimes here."

"One's all it takes," Clara said meaningfully as she paused in the doorway. "Now, you be sure and lock this door after me, you hear? And don't forget the back door, either."

285

"Oh, Clara, stop it," Amelia said, suddenly tired of the older woman's patronizing airs. "You always think the worst."

"Better a live coward than a dead fool," Clara snapped; but then she turned and said earnestly, "I'm sorry, honey. I don't mean to treat you like a child, but you're my only friend in this one-horse town and you're so trusting—there I go *again*, for Pete's sake!" Once more her eyebrows furrowed like Henry's. "All I mean is that I'd hate for anything to happen to you."

Impulsively, Amelia clasped her hand and squeezed it warmly. "I'll lock up," she promised.

Putting on the night latch after Clara had driven away, Amelia thought again of her words. Perhaps she was an innocent, naive, trusting fool. She *did* take people too much at their words. Hadn't she believed Father when he told her it was best to devote her life to him? And hadn't she taken Henry at face value? Assumed his lavish use of after-shave lotion and breath mints were signs of personal fastidiousness and not for masking alcoholic fumes? Hadn't she believed him the many times he'd broken their dates, claiming another bronchial attack?

"Drunk as a lord, usually," Clara had told her after his death. "Not that he didn't have a weak chest, too—it runs in our family, you know," and Clara would touch her own buxom chest.

At least that much had been true about him. If his chest had been stronger, perhaps he wouldn't have died. Poor Henry! Always so respectable. Amelia was sure no one in town suspected that he had drunk, nor why he'd been out that raw night ten years ago in the freezing rain. Never once had anyone slanted their eyes at her and made her feel that the shameful story was buzzing around behind her back.

Over and over, Amelia wished that even she didn't know. Of course, that was impossible. Clara was the type who simply had to unburden herself to someone. "Out of whiskey, he was," Clara had wept afterwards. "You never saw him when he was drinking, Amelia. He was completely different then. I got him up to his room and thought he'd passed out; but when I checked on him later, he was gone. If only I hadn't hidden the car keys! He tried to walk—on a night like that, with his weak chest—to buy another bottle, but he passed out at the end of our driveway, soaked to the bone and half-frozen. I got so drenched helping him back up the drive it's a wonder I didn't die, too."

286

Clara escaped with only a light chest cold, but Henry had developed bronchial pneumonia and had died two days later, under an oxygen tent in the town's hospital.

Amelia moved through the empty rooms, straightening up and clicking off lamps as she went. In the kitchen, she recklessly threw open the back door and stared into the night. She'd never before feared the dark, but now she shivered, closed the door and rammed the bolt home, feeling vulnerable and exposed. Clara was right: times had changed and, after all, she was a woman alone with no one to protect her. Of course, the Higgins boy from across the street was on the police force now and he patrolled their street at least twice a night, but how could he prevent someone from sneaking across the dark yards and breaking a cellar window? She propped a chair under the cellar doorknob and decided to buy a hasp for it tomorrow—and perhaps she could locate Father's old pistol. She remembered seeing it and a box of cartridges last spring when she cleaned the attic.

Suddenly, Amelia was furious with Clara. Blast the woman for arousing fears which had never existed before. She deserved a good shaking!

Thus, it was with the idea of paying her back that Amelia hid in the shrubbery under Clara's window the next night. She'd parked her car down the street and crept in through the back gate. Stealthily, she tried the doors, but all were firmly locked. Through a slit in the curtains she saw Clara idly leafing through a magazine, with a glass of iced tea on the table beside her.

There was a guilty sense of power in secretly watching someone, and Amelia was fascinated at first. Eventually, though, she became annoyed at Clara's equanimity and the smug, unworried manner in which she sipped her drink and turned the pages. She'd come to frighten Clara, somehow to make her admit that she, too, was as much a potential victim as Amelia. But how? The doors were locked and Amelia did not feel equal to climbing through windows.

Should she just knock on the door and take her by surprise? No, Clara always looked before opening up. Inspired, Amelia suddenly remembered Clara's bitter complaints about a neighborhood dog which kept tipping over her garbage pails. She even kept a supply of small rocks on a shelf by the back door with which to chase it. Quietly, Amelia found a long-handled rake; then, hiding in the bushes, she gave a strong shove to the rake and one of the garbage pails clattered to the ground.

Almost immediately, a dim light clicked on beside the door. She crouched lower in the bushes as Clara peered through the window. With the rake handle, she nudged a tin can and sent it rattling along the walk.

Goaded, Clara flung open the door and walked threateningly down the steps. "Git!" she cried and strode past Amelia to fling a handful of rocks in the direction of the noise.

Stepping out from her hiding place into the light, Amelia triumphantly called, "Surprise, Clara! You've just been mugged!" She laughed at the expression on Clara's face. "There's no point in locking your doors if you can be tricked into coming out so easily," she teased, as Clara stood there looking first stunned, then angry. "You're not going to be mad, are you?" Amelia asked uncertainly. "After all, turnabout's fair play and you started it." She stretched out her hand, but Clara waved her back.

"Get away from me!" she gasped. "Coming here, spying on me, turning over my garbage!"

"Not spying," Amelia protested. "No more than you did to me." Hurt, she righted the pail and began picking up the debris.

"Oh, stop it!" Clara ordered sharply. "Just leave it alone! I'll clean it up tomorrow. Serves me right for being so dumb." Avoiding Amelia's bewildered face, Clara brushed by her heavily and went up the steps. "Good night, Amelia."

Feeling like a chastened fool, Amelia turned and fled. In the darkness, she didn't see the tin can lying on the path, and as it slipped away under her foot, her ankle took a sickening twist. By the time she'd reached the car, it throbbed unbearably. Painfully, she managed to drive as far as Dr. Sorkin's house.

The old man had given up most of his practice the year before, but he still maintained his old-fashioned office at home and would treat the minor ailments of such long-time patients as Amelia. Soon her ankle was comfortably taped and Dr. Sorkin brought her a glass of rosé while they waited for the pain injection he'd given her to take effect.

In retirement, the old doctor had grown garrulous and Amelia had always been a favorite of his, so he was happily prepared to turn her mishap into a sociable visit. "Turned your ankle coming down Clara Demarest's path, eh? How *is* Clara these days?"

Much later, as she let herself into the house, Amelia could hear the phone ringing endlessly. Without haste, she carefully closed and bolted the door before answering it.

"Amelia? Thank goodness! I was just about to call the police and have that Higgins boy go looking for you! Where *were* you?" Clara's voice sounded hoarse over the wire.

"I turned my ankle when I left your house," Amelia explained coolly, "and I stayed to talk with Dr. Sorkin after he took care of it."

"That old windbag! No wonder it took you so long to get home. Listen, Amelia, I just wanted to tell you—that is—well, gee, I'm awfully sorry I was such a lousy sport tonight. I mean, you really got my goat the way you suckered me outside; and on top of everything, I'm coming down with another rotten chest cold. I really wasn't myself tonight, but I shouldn't have yelled at you like that. You got me fair and square."

Amelia allowed her voice to soften. "That's all right, Clara. I'm not angry."

At the end of the week, when Amelia's ankle was on the mend and Clara had decided she didn't have a chest cold after all, Amelia invited her over for lunch.

It was a beautiful fall day and they ate on the back terrace under spreading trees which had just begun to change color. Clara seemed quite recovered from her chagrin of the other night and only laughed when Amelia teased her about being fooled so easily.

"You have to admit you played dirty, though," Clara defended herself. "A real intruder wouldn't have known about the dog."

"Nonsense," Amelia said. "I should think it an obvious trick. Everybody's had a dog knock over a garbage pail occasionally, and with that much noise anyone would think it *was* a dog. No one expects a burglar to raise an uproar. It was perfectly legitimate and it proves that in your own way, you're just as much of an innocent as you always accuse me of being!"

Clara pursed her lips but she refused to take umbrage, even when Amelia kept needling her.

As the afternoon drew to a close, a cool breeze sprang up and the two women began clearing things away. "I'll stick the chairs in the cellar for you," Clara volunteered, as Amelia wheeled the serving cart into the house.

"Oh, thanks," Amelia called, "and would you lock the door for me when you've finished?"

"Sure thing," Clara said as she disappeared down the shrubbery-hidden steps with the wicker chairs.

As soon as Clara had driven away, Amelia went around to the cellar door. As expected, the lock was open; Clara still thought she was a trusting fool. "Surprise, surprise!" Amelia thought wryly.

At full dark, she switched on all the downstairs lights and drew the curtains too tightly for anyone to see through. Leaving the radio playing softly, she then went upstairs and sat motionlessly by a back window in a dark bedroom. It was almost ten before her patience was rewarded and she'd had time to relive the conversation in Dr. Sorkin's office over and over, beginning with his words, "How *is* Clara these days? Going a little easier on the whiskey than she used to, I hope?"

At that, the distortions which Amelia had somehow sensed all these years suddenly gave a half-turn and everything fell into sharp perspective. She really hadn't needed to question nor even hear the rest of the old Doctor's meanderings. It was as if she'd known all along. ". . . a real saint, that Henry. Taking her in when her husband got fed up with her d.t.'s and kicked her out . . . Waste of money drying her out in that sanatorium. At least when Henry caught pneumonia from pulling her in out of a sleet storm, his death shook her up enough to make her stay home when she's drinking." Amelia had hardly heard him. She'd been remembering the "iced tea" in Clara's hand earlier that evening and her overly-angry reaction to Amelia's trick. Had there been any liquor bottles in Clara's overturned garbage pail?

Now Amelia waited until she saw Clara's blocky shape merge with the darkness of the cellar steps. Moving noiselessly, she slipped from the bedroom and down the stairs.

Strange that Clara had always jeered her for being too trusting and naive. Of all the lies which she, Amelia, had ever believed, Clara's were the most heinous. Not only had Clara caused the death of the only person she'd ever loved, she had also cheated Amelia out of the comfort of his memory—forced her to believe that Henry's love had been shallow and flawed.

Long-frozen passions had been thawing in her veins all week, but she was calm as she crossed the kitchen and opened the cellar door. On the stairway below, Clara blinked as sudden light hit her eyes; but nevertheless, she gaily pointed her finger at Amelia and chortled, "Bang! You're dead!"

"No, Clara," Amelia said as she aimed Father's pistol, *"you* are."

The Hard Sell

by William Dolan

"**B**uy a murdered man's car?" Sam Bates' revulsion at the suggestion was oddly balanced by the magnetism the car held for him because he had known its former owner. He hesitated, polarized between the red station wagon and another parked alongside it in the used car lot. The cars were identical except that the second was blue and lacked the garish black racing stripe which ran the length of its red stablemate.

"The red wagon is yours for $300 less than I'll take for the blue baby, and it's a better car." Joe Parkman, owner and sole salesman of Hensonville's only used car lot, sensed Sam's fascination for the late Charlie Walsh's car. "I'll level with you, Sam," he went on, looking earnestly at his prospect as he warmed to his sales pitch, "the car's been hard to sell. Everybody in town knows it was Charlie Walsh's car and nobody'll buy it. They all come to look, but nobody wants it. They're all fools, because it's in top condition. Now I've had it too long and it's got to go."

Sam Bates circled the red car while Parkman talked, then slid his slim six-foot length behind the wheel.

"Fits you good, Sam," Parkman interposed before expertly resuming the identical spiel he had practiced for the past month on anyone showing serious interest in the car. "A couple days ago I decided to give a break to the first one of my regular old customers who came by and showed interest. If I got to take a licking I don't want it from no stranger. And here you are and there the car is. Sam, you're in luck."

Sam didn't have much money, but the price was good, no question of it. Although Sam had known Charlie Walsh, he hadn't liked him. Charlie, the flashy type, had been meticulous with his cars—clothes, cars, blondes, everything—a big ladies' man. He was a bachelor like Sam Bates, who tried to be something of a ladies' man himself but never had possessed Charlie's ability to score. Then two months ago Charlie had been found in the little Midwestern town's park slumped over the wheel of his red car, with red blood staining his new red tie. He'd been shot between the eyes by person or persons unknown. There had been a big splash in the local paper, and tired-looking detectives from out of town had tirelessly gone about Hensonville asking embarrassing questions, but after a time people seemed to lose interest, and conversation in the local saloons returned to normal subjects such as crops and women. Now here was Charlie Walsh's car for sale at Joe Parkman's used car lot.

Was a $300 reduction enough discount for the faint bloodstain still on the front seat despite Parkman's skill in the chemistry of used car preparation? Sam wondered, felt revulsion a second time, then thought sadly once again of his financial inadequacy. Sam, thirty-three years old, had a minor government job, secure enough, but short on pay even for a bachelor.

"Knock off another hundred and it's a deal," Sam said impulsively, unaware, until he spoke, of his intent to make an offer.

Once he had spoken, he became faintly aware of other reasons for wanting the car, ones that he only partly acknowledged even to himself. They concerned his dislike for Charlie Walsh, which had been more intense than he liked to admit. Charlie's death hadn't satisfied Sam's feeling. Now Charlie's car seemed to offer a chance for Sam to continue the rivalry in which Charlie had always dominated.

The rivalry had been over women and had begun when Charlie and Sam dated several of the same girls. In a town the size of Hensonville it was almost inevitable for two long-time bachelors, both girl-conscious. Twice they had competed actively for the same girl's favor, with Charlie coming off the victor each time. The last girl had been Helen Pringle, whom Sam had thought of marrying but for whom Charlie had had no such noble intention. Helen had hurriedly left town, and Helen's father, burly Ed Pringle, was known to have visited the flat over the grocery store in which Charlie Walsh had lived. Pringle had carried his bull whip inside, but he had come out again without having used it. Charlie had been a good talker.

Sam had accosted Charlie and told him what he thought of Charlie's treatment of Helen. Charlie had listened sneeringly for a few moments before throwing the hard right hand out of nowhere that had left Sam sitting dazedly on the pavement. When Sam had risen it was only to be knocked down again. It hadn't been much of a fight.

Several months had passed after the fight before Charlie was murdered,

292

but Sam still had been one of the prime suspects. He had the motive, the police knew, but so did Ed Pringle and several other people in the area. A heel like Charlie manages to make plenty of enemies. He was heavily in debt to the bank, and was thought to have suffered large gambling losses to a racketeer who ran dice and card games in the city fifty miles from Hensonville.

Having seen Charlie's red car all the while it sat on Joe Parkman's lot, Sam had not approached it as a prospective buyer until today. Then, when he had kicked the tires the way any used car shopper does, he had felt a sense of mastery over Charlie Walsh. Unable to beat Charlie in life, he felt that somehow he could do it in death by controlling Charlie's possession. Sam kicked the tires a second time, harder. As he made his offer to buy the car his memories churned together—the humiliation of losing Helen to Charlie; the fight and the added humiliation of losing; Charlie's murder and still more humiliation while he was held at police headquarters as a murder suspect. Then came the thought of how he had felt when kicking the tires. Sam quizzically awaited the used car dealer's reaction to his offer.

Joe Parkman showed only a minimum of professional hesitation before accepting. The car was an unpleasant symbol of violence that he wanted gone. Before Sam had time to change his mind the papers were signed, Sam's license plates affixed front and rear, and the red station wagon with the black stripe moved hesitantly from the used car lot, its owner already feeling that somehow he had made a serious error.

Hensonville had only two bars. Sam drove the short distance from Parkman's lot to the first of them and drew up to the curb. He needed a drink. He also needed to make his purchase known, to sound out public opinion.

Comment was not long in coming. Another car pulled up to the curb and Ben Thorpe, pudgy cashier of the town bank, emerged. Sam stepped out of his car with his back toward Ben, but when he turned around, Ben's face turned gray and his jaw slacked.

"I thought you were Charlie Walsh, back from the grave!" Ben said.

Until that moment no one had ever commented on the physical resemblance of Sam Bates to the murdered Charlie Walsh, but now Sam felt the validity of the observation. In height and build he and Charlie could have been twins. The similarity even extended to the thick brown hair that Sam never succeeded in keeping combed for long. There it ended, physically. Sam's taste ran to the same loud clothes that Charlie had favored, though. Seen from the rear, emerging from Charlie Walsh's car, Sam Bates looked like a ghost.

With a self-conscious effort Sam passed off Ben Thorpe's remark lightly. "Got a real good buy," he said. "I'm not loaded like you bankers, you know. Besides," he leered with an attempt at humor, "I thought this buggy might make me a hit with the girls the way Charlie Walsh was."

"You won't get any local dame within fifty feet of that car," replied Ben. "Charlie Walsh got the last action in that wagon that this town will see." Ben's comment was casual, but his voice was strained. It was as though Sam's appearance with Charlie Walsh's car had suddenly thrown into focus a previously hazy picture. His identity with the murdered man was taking a turn which Sam had sensed but not foreseen.

"Have a drink on the First National," said Ben, changing the subject to relieve the tension as he and Sam entered the bar. "I'm here on official business for the boss and I never like to miss a chance to drink during working hours."

"I thought Mr. Grimes handled the outside work himself," said Sam, unconsciously using the formal "Mr." that everyone in Hensonville invariably applied in naming Frederick Grimes, president and practically the owner of the town's First National Bank. Hensonville was generally an informal town where everyone knew everyone else, but the town banker, its two doctors, and its four clergymen always were deferred to when named by its citizenry. Mr. Grimes was nearing fifty, tall and somewhat portly, known as "an imposing figure of a man." He was all the more imposing by virtue of being the town's only millionaire.

"Mr. Grimes has gone to visit his wife," Ben said.

Jane Grimes, some years younger than her husband, had gone East to care for her aged and ill father some four months ago, almost two months before Charlie Walsh was murdered. Mr. Grimes, who could afford it, frequently flew East to visit her, but Jane Grimes had not returned to Hensonville. She was afraid of airplanes, and the distance was too far for easy return by train or car.

Inside the bar Ben Thorpe ordered drinks for himself "and the new owner of Charlie Walsh's car." Comment on the purchase by the bartender and the two men at the bar was slight but unfavorable. The bartender, an affable man who deferred to his patrons, allowed to hearing that Joe Parkman had it priced way low.

Finding the atmosphere of the bar unfriendly, Sam soon left. As he self-consciously approached his new car he saw Tess Bowman, the postmaster's middle-aged and mouthy wife, staring tight-lipped at him across the dusty street. Sam defiantly took out his handkerchief and polished an imaginary spot off the fender before entering the car and starting it. He raced the engine loudly in neutral before driving off at a deliberately slower than normal speed.

"With Tess Bowman and the bartender at work there won't be anyone in town tomorrow who doesn't know I bought Charlie Walsh's car," Sam mused, his new feeling of defensiveness growing stronger within him. "Small-town hicks," he said to himself as he reached open country and trod hard on the gas pedal. The car ran beautifully. Not a rattle in it, not a scratch on the finish, and the interior was perfect except for one small brown stain on the front seat. Sam's right hand dropped to the stain and patted it.

When he entered the office the next morning, Sam felt a new distance from the eight other government workers whose hostile backs gave him a wordlessly negative greeting as he entered. By mid-morning the feeling was confirmed. There were three unmarried young women in the office, two of whom had shown signs of interest in bachelor Sam. One of the two he had dated occasionally. Today even the single girls avoided him. To be certain, he asked the girl he had dated to go out with him that Saturday. She flushed, hesitated, and stammered something about a previous date. In the afternoon Sam, who was a man of impulse, suddenly found himself asking the other two girls to go out. Both refused. The girl who had shown interest in him, but whom he had never dated, hurried from her desk to the ladies' room in tears moments after raising her somewhat plain face to his and saying simply, "I couldn't." The last of the trio, who had other amorous attachments, was more forceful. "To hell with you, Clyde," she said, and turned back to her typewriter, her faster and louder than normal clacking of the keys spelling out a message which Sam understood perfectly. Ben Thorpe had been right. The romantic qualities of Charlie Walsh's station wagon did not transfer to its new owner along with title to the car.

Shortly before quitting time Bob Hawkins, the boss, called Sam into his private office and closed the door. Hawkins was perhaps ten years older than Sam, a small man, rather officious. "Sam, you made a mistake buying that car," he began without prelude. "I know the price was right in dollars, but it still was a bad buy in this town. Everybody's talking about it," he went on somewhat lamely. "If I were you I'd get rid of it fast."

Sam had never liked Bob Hawkins. Sam's advancement in his job had been minimal, for which he blamed Hawkins. He did not take Hawkins' advice well, especially coming as it did after his rejection by the girls. "I don't like that truck you drive either, Bob," Sam said, referring to Hawkins' flashy convertible.

"Just trying to give you a friendly tip, Sam," Hawkins said in a tone of mild annoyance. "The big difference between your car and mine isn't one of make or model. Has it occurred to you that people in this town are going to start all over again to say you had something to do with Charlie Walsh's murder?"

There it was. Sam had to face it now. Before, he had only let it peek at him around the corners of his mind. He had thought hard of something else, such as his genuine need for a new car and what a good buy it really was. Before, when he had been a murder suspect along with all the others, Sam had felt a brief excitement. It had been a nightmare, of course, the whole business with Charlie Walsh, but the limelight of recognition by the town had also been thrilling. Even when suspicion moved away from him as the police chased other false leads, there had come the brief afterglow when the citizenry, one by one, had sought him out, shaken his hand and told him they knew all along that he was innocent.

Then the flame had grown quite cold. Sam had ceased to be of interest, but now that he owned Charlie's car things were back where they had been before. In the moment of his indignant reaction to his boss's question Sam felt something akin to a glow of pleasure.

"The idiots!" he exclaimed after a long moment. "The stupid small-town idiots!"

"That's precisely it, Sam," Hawkins said. "This is a small town. It recently had its first murder that anyone can remember, and that murder is unsolved. People were just beginning to forget it and now you've got them started again. Since you're the focal point of the conversation, it occurs to them to pin the murder on you. At lunch I heard the old rumor that you killed Charlie because he was beating your time with a girl."

"When the city detectives were in town they checked me out along with everybody else," Sam said heatedly. "They even gave me a lie-detector test. I passed."

"When a lie-detector test indicates guilt, everyone believes the test," Hawkins said. "When it indicates innocence, they say that lie-detector tests are inconclusive. Just the fact that you took a lie-detector test makes you fair game."

"Well they can all go straight to the devil as far as I'm concerned," Sam said. "I'm damned if I'll knuckle under to a scuzzy bunch of hick-town gossips." He hushed the voice inside him which still whispered his additional reason, his lust for the thrill of living dangerously that identification with Charlie Walsh gave.

"Your funeral, Sam," Hawkins replied as Sam walked through his office door to the outer room where town public opinion in microcosm awaited him, embodied in the self-consciously silent forms of his co-workers.

Years before Sam had lived in another small town where a false rumor arose about a rather odd neighbor of his that the man was a drug addict. The man, when the rumor got back to him, planted the path from the sidewalk to his front door thickly with poppies, their bright orange petals calculated to suggest opium to the scandal-mongers. Sam had enjoyed the man's triumph when the gossip stopped as the small minds were intellectually unable to cope with the wordless rebuff.

In the same spirit of defiance Sam next day entered a hardware store and asked to see some .38 caliber revolvers. Such a weapon had eliminated Charlie Walsh as his romantic competitor. The furrows deepened in the bald head of Jack Welley, the storekeeper, as he waved Sam toward his gun display. Welley's hand shook slightly when he handed Sam the gun. Sam flipped the gun open expertly, squinted knowingly into the chamber and said, "Sold."

A permit had to be obtained and the local police thereby informed of his purchase.

The paunchy desk sergeant said nothing until Sam placed his permit in his wallet and turned to leave the station, then, "How do you like your new car?" he asked.

"Fine," replied Sam. "Best car I ever owned. I expect to keep it for years."

"It used to be a real good girl catcher," said the policeman.

Sam led the sergeant on. "I figured maybe some of Charlie Walsh's good luck would rub off on me," he said. "The gun is to make sure I don't have his bad luck too." Sam returned his wallet to his hip pocket and carefully fastened the button before leaving.

Two days later the city detectives visited Sam at the house where he roomed. Ruth Caldwell, his landlady, called him from the foot of the stairs. "Visitors, Mr. Bates," she shrilled, her aged voice cracking nervously.

Sam had roomed with Ruth Caldwell for three years and never been called anything by her but Sam. Now her formality emphasized his new status in town as leading murder suspect. The gun purchase hadn't worked for Sam the way the poppies had for his former neighbor. Nobody appreciated what Sam considered the humor of its purchase two months after the murder. "Cover-up," they said. "Running scared," somebody commented. "He's a psychopathic nut who *wants* to get caught," said another. "It won't be long now before they arrest him for it," said the voice of the town, echoing back to Sam from the office, the diner, the bar. Nobody else had really said anything to him, except Mr. Grimes, the bank president, in refusing to accept the time sales contract that Sam had signed to finance his car.

"Joe Parkman should have sold that car out of town," Mr. Grimes had said when Sam called at his office to learn why his credit was no good. Mr. Grimes' lips had pursed as he looked at Sam with evident distaste. "If Parkman hadn't been so greedy he'd have wholesaled it at the auto auction in the city like he was supposed to do when he got it from Charlie Walsh's estate. I won't have anything to do with it, and if you've got any brains, young fellow, you'll get rid of it fast.

"I'll help you out there, Sam," Mr. Grimes had continued in a more kindly tone. "I'll get Joe Parkman to tear up the contract and take the car back. He sees his mistake now and he'll do it, all right."

Of course Sam had rejected the banker's offer, forcing Joe Parkman to handle the financing of the car personally. Sam's view of the situation was that he was engaged in open war against bigotry and he had no intention of knuckling under.

"Maybe it's because I haven't got a lot to lose," he told himself. "They can't fire me from my government job, and I don't have a family to worry about. Besides, if I give in now I'll look like a damned fool and I'll lose my self-respect as well."

So Sam went calmly down the stairs of his landlady's house and answered the policemen's questions in her sterile living room while she waited in the kitchen with her ear to the swinging door.

"No need for fancy electronic bugging devices in this town," said Sam loudly to the detectives as he saw the door to the kitchen move slightly. "All the people have big ears."

"Maybe we'd better finish this downtown," said one of the detectives. "Downtown" doubtless was a term that meant traveling a considerable distance in the city. In Hensonville it meant four blocks. The detectives had walked from the police station to Ruth Caldwell's. Now they accepted Sam's offer of a ride in his new red station wagon. At the police station they opened the file on their previous interrogation of Sam and proceeded to ask the same questions. They were even more thorough this time. They also repeated the lie-detector test.

Three hours passed before they looked at each other, shrugged, and told Sam that he could go.

Despite the late hour several people were lounging about the street near the police station when Sam left. He noticed others parked in cars nearby, their curiosity thinly concealed by the closed doors of their automobiles. The wolves weren't howling for blood yet, but they had the scent. Sam followed his now-standard practice of racing his engine loudly in neutral before driving off slowly. "Idiots," he muttered bitterly to himself.

His landlady met him in the narrow front hall as he entered the house, her husky son standing behind her. He lived a few blocks away with his wife and family. His mother obviously had called him over for a special purpose.

"I'd like you to leave my house, Mr. Bates," she said without prelude.

"Tonight," added her son menacingly.

Sam opened his mouth to argue, hesitated, then changed his mind. "I'm paid up until the first of the month," he said mildly when he finally spoke. "I'll want some money back before I leave."

Ruth Caldwell sniffed in what she intended to be her most contemptuous manner, but she produced the worn black handbag that to Sam had long been her emblem of office as landlady. Now it also became to him her badge of outraged middle-class respectability. She counted out the proper amount. Sam took it wordlessly and mounted the stairs to his room with the deliberate slowness of movement that had become characteristic of him.

Packing was simple. A few trips between bedroom and car and Sam's belongings were stowed. As he drove away from the house he wondered where he was going. At best, there were few places for a bachelor to stay in Hensonville. At worst—Sam's present situation—he could think of none. Private homes like his ex-landlady's would be closed to him. He wouldn't risk humiliation by trying any of them. The same thing applied to the one or two regular rooming houses in town. That left the two hotels.

Sam chose the lesser of the two.

Lew Brody, night clerk at the Hensonville Inn, carefully returned the paperback book he had been reading to the revolving wire bookstand, careful not to crease the cover as he did so. Then he looked up expectantly to the man with the suitcase coming through the hotel door, but appeared disturbed when he saw that the man was Sam Bates.

"I'll take a room for a few days, Lew," said Sam. "Make it one with a front view, please." The rear of the old hotel butted against railroad yards which tended to be noisy as well as dirty.

Lew Brody looked over his glasses and beyond the top of Sam's head. "I'm sorry, Sam, but without a reservation we can't let you have a room." Brody spoke evenly and with a trace of formality, as though he had rehearsed his words for the occasion.

Sam had feared rejection and did not yield without argument. He had frequently shot pool with Lew Brody in the hotel's decaying billiard room, coming by evenings when both he and Brody had time to kill. Brody wasn't a friend really, but he was more than just an acquaintance.

"Cut the nonsense, Lew," Sam said. "I know as well as you do that there's dust on most of the doorknobs in this big brick monstrosity. You told me yourself the bank only keeps it open for a tax loss."

"All right, I'll give it to you straight, Sam," Brody said, straightening his thin shoulders inside his threadbare suit and looking squarely into Sam's eyes. "Mr. Grimes, who *is* the bank, had Ben Thorpe call yesterday to tell me not to rent to you."

"Yesterday!" Sam was amazed. "I didn't have trouble with my landlady until tonight! How could they know yesterday that I'd be coming here for a room?"

"Apparently your landlady thought of putting you out as soon as you bought your new car," Brody replied, "and she told half of Hensonville. Shouldn't be surprised if there's a hex on you all over town. It looks to me as if you're going to have to sleep in your car, Sam. Good thing it's a station wagon," he added dryly.

Brody was reaching for his paperback novel as Sam walked thoughtfully back to his car.

"Sleep in it?" It was nearly one o'clock and Sam had no better idea.

He drove to the town park, which was large for the size of the town, thickly wooded with several narrow winding roads radiating from the pond in the center that the townspeople dignified by calling "the lake." Like parks everywhere this one was a favorite of young lovers. Evening traffic had fallen way off, though, since Charlie Walsh had been found dead in his car on one of the side roads.

Sam saw only one other car along the road he chose, but went well past it before easing over to a wide spot on the shoulder and cutting the engine. He piled the front seat with his worldly goods before letting down the rear seat to from a roomy deck area, then removed part of his clothing and pulled his winter topcoat over him as a blanket. He left the two front windows partly open, tiredly wondering how long it would be before insects would force him to close them.

Sam knew nothing more until he was awakened by sunlight well after dawn. Two flies were contending for possession of the end of his nose. He scratched several fresh mosquito bites, flexed away some of the stiffness in his back, and reflected that it hadn't been too bad a night. "But the coming nights will be better," he said to himself, thinking of the purchases necessary to minimal comfort in his portable bedroom. He had no intention of giving up. It was summer. There were no restrictions against camping out in the park. Boy Scout groups often did. There was a bathhouse down by the lake. Sam went there now to shave before going to work.

On his lunch hour Sam purchased a foam mattress to fit the rear of his station wagon, a sleeping bag, and mosquito netting to cover the windows of his rear doors so they could be left open. He also bought a telescoping rod that fitted behind the front seat on which he neatly arranged his clothes on coathangers. Sam decided against a portable stove and ice chest. He would continue to eat out.

Sam had not spent his third night in the park before everyone in town knew he slept there. When he noticed he was drawing the curious to drive past his parking spot, he calmly closed the magazine he had been reading in the long light of the summer evening and drove to a movie. That night he slept at a new location in the park, and each night thereafter he moved his bedroom. Soon people stopped treating his sleeping arrangement as a zoological display, and Sam began to feel that his housing problem was solved as long as the weather held. He hoped something would happen before winter.

Something did.

Sam had been sleeping in his car nearly a month and was beginning to worry about the sharp night air of approaching fall. The hostility of the town continued exactly as it had begun. There had been no violence, no open accusations. Sam had quietly been ostracized, and a kind of armed truce existed between him and the citizens of Hensonville. The town waited for its opportunity to pounce collectively upon Sam and publicly name him murderer. "Wait," they said. "It won't be long now."

Sam was in the car in the park one night about ten o'clock, listening to his transistor radio. He was unhappy with his situation. The recognition he had sought and received had all turned negative. Even the police worked hard at ignoring him. He would quit his job and leave town before he'd sell the car, he decided.

The oncoming car's headlights flashed full on Sam's car. Its brakes squealed slightly as the slow-moving vehicle stopped suddenly, then backed up and parked by Sam. A slender feminine figure leaped hurriedly from the car, ran to Sam's auto, then stopped and peered about the interior before speaking breathlessly.

"Oh, Charlie, darling, I was afraid you'd be here with someone else—another woman."

Sam sat rigid, speechless. The approach of the woman had surprised him. When she called him Charlie he was astonished. Everyone within a radius of fifty miles knew that Charlie was dead. Sam decided it must be a joke and true to his impulsive nature found himself going along with it. "Hi, doll," he said softly, as Charlie Walsh often had addressed women.

The slim figure pulled open the door on the passenger's side and threw herself into Sam's arms. The warm body pressed against him and Sam felt an avid mouth on his neck, his cheek, and finally coming to rest under his ear. *Some joke*, he thought as she held him tightly. When she spoke again he knew who she was.

"Charlie, I had to come back. I know what we promised, and I tried. Really, I tried! But five months was all I could take, Charlie." Her lips sought his hungrily. After a moment she mildly accused, "You've changed."

Sam thought of Charlie's reputation as a lover and by way of reply kissed her again. He had heard enough to make him want to hear more.

302

The woman was Jane Grimes, wife of Hensonville's banker, Frederick Grimes!

Jane Grimes had never been involved in scandal, and she had left town two months before the murder. But what of her husband? Nobody had so much as considered the possibility. Now Sam Bates did. Frederick Grimes was near fifty and he had a young wife. Charlie Walsh had been a big operator, and he and Jane Grimes obviously had been lovers. Now, Jane Grimes had been deceived by a combination of circumstances—the superficial resemblance of Sam Bates to Charlie Walsh, Sam's possession of Charlie's red car, the park which must have been their trysting place, and darkness.

Sam caressed the back of Jane Grimes' neck, holding her head on his shoulder so she would not turn and see his face. "Tell me about it, doll," he whispered into her ear.

Jane sobbed and clutched Sam as she spoke, almost frenziedly articulating the thoughts that had wordlessly churned inside her for months. "He flew out to see me every week. He was looking for an Eastern bank to invest in, but he was terribly slow about it. He was in no hurry to leave Hensonville himself, but he made me promise not to come back or even to write to anyone here. I was so frightened of what he might do after he caught us. You know how angry he was, darling. I . . ."

Jane drew her head back and looked into Sam's eyes. Calmer now, she saw the man who was there where previously she had seen the man she wanted to see. Recoiling from Sam, she pushed her slim shoulders back against the door.

"Charlie Walsh is dead, Mrs. Grimes," Sam said softly, sensing that his best tactic was to offset the shock of her recognition of him with a greater one.

He saw her eyes go wide, their whites reflecting what little light there was in the murky car. She seemed frozen in place.

"I'm Sam Bates, Mrs. Grimes. I bought Charlie's car after he was murdered." Sam realized by her gasp that the word "murdered" piled additional shock upon that caused by the harsh enough "dead" which he had used previously.

Sam looked away as she began to cry softly, then reached for her hand and held it gently. Finally she spoke.

"He promised not to do anything if I left town and never came back." Her voice was steady but her tone was lifeless. She stared through the windshield of the red car and seemed to be talking to herself more than to Sam. "He always was good to my parents. My father hasn't been able to work for years and Frederick takes care of him and mother. I don't know what will happen to them now."

She stopped, sobbing again. Sam gave her his handkerchief in a wordless gesture of sympathy, his feeling for her tempered by his own memory of isolation from the town for two weeks past.

"Your husband made you promise not to write?" he asked.

"Yes," she sobbed. "There was no one I cared to write to here but—but Charlie." She broke down again as she mentioned the murdered man's name. "I always hated this town. We had no friends. My husband is a machine for making money. He built a big house and put me in it for an ornament. I stood it for five years and then—when Charlie . . ."

Sam now knew all that was necessary, except how Jane Grimes had come to find him in the park.

"I flew to the city and rented a car to drive to Hensonville," she told him. "I just had to see Charlie again, promise or no promise. I waited until after dark so no one would recognize me, and then I drove to his apartment. When I didn't see a light I drove around town looking for him. Not finding his red car on the streets, I thought he might be out here with another woman. I was certain of it when I saw the car here. This is one of the places we came together. It's where Frederick found us and we had that terrible row. I . . ." She fell into Sam's arms as she broke down this time. He held her gently for a long time until she was calm again.

She was the one to suggest going to see the sheriff. This surprised Sam, who had feared her reaction to the idea and had been trying to find the right words to tell her what the two of them had to do. He gave a sigh of relief.

The moon was high but veiled by clouds as they drove slowly toward town. Sam hadn't raced his engine in neutral when he started the car this time. The defiance that had been his dominant characteristic for weeks was gone from him. There was no sense of triumph in anticipation of what was to come when they reached the sheriff's. Sam just felt terribly sorry for Jane Grimes. For her husband he felt nothing.

"Probably got rid of the murder weapon at once," Sheriff Tom Jackson said to Sam Bates and Jane Grimes, picking up the phone to call back the two city detectives who were working the case. The sheriff had quickly seen the import of the story told him by the couple who had come to his home and roused him from bed.

"The police knew you were innocent, Mr. Bates," one of the city detectives said to Sam hours later, near dawn, as the detectives, Sam, Jane, and Sheriff Jackson all sat around the sheriff's oilcloth-covered kitchen table with empty coffee cups and full ashtrays before them. "We never suspected Mr. Grimes though," he went on. "He must have done it, all right, but how are we going to prove it?"

Jane Grimes said little. She had cried herself out while in the car with Sam, and now she sat dry-eyed while Sam told the story. She showed no desire to help her husband.

Neither Sam nor Jane left the sheriff's house that day. They were detained there, under guard, while the sheriff and the two detectives quietly built their case against Frederick Grimes. Until they were ready to charge him, the police wanted Grimes to remain ignorant of his wife's presence in Hensonville.

Sam's car was seen outside of Sheriff Jackson's house that morning and his absence from work that day led immediately to the rumor of his arrest. By ten o'clock the rumor had flowed up and down the main street and into the bank. Grimes was not the first person who had asked Sheriff Jackson about it by the time the sheriff made his way to the bank just past noon. To his other questioners the sheriff had refused comment. He wanted them to speculate and he wanted Grimes, in particular, to become anxious. Ostensibly the sheriff was at the bank to cash a travel voucher for the two out-of-town detectives, a normal occurrence. Actually he was there to offer Grimes the chance to put his head into the hangman's noose.

"Keep it under your hat, Mr. Grimes," said the sheriff. "We think we've got our man. We're keeping Sam Bates at my house instead of the station because we're not quite ready to charge him. He flunked the lie detector test and we know he had the motive—Charlie Walsh was beating his time with Helen Pringle. We checked with a psychologist from the city, and he thinks Sam really bought Charlie's car because he subconsciously wants to get caught. What we need to wrap up the case is either the murder weapon or a confession—preferably both. Sam Bates isn't too smart, Mr. Grimes," the sheriff concluded, "and those city detectives are real good at sweating a man. We'll get him."

305

As the sheriff pushed the brass plate on the heavy bank door and went down the granite steps, Frederick Grimes watched him thoughtfully. Then he went to his private office and closed the door behind him. Grimes did not go out to lunch that day, but remained at his desk until the bank closed. Then he drove straight to the big house on the edge of town in which he had lived alone except for his housekeeper since his wife went East.

The two policemen watching his home from the woods behind it reported nothing over their walkie-talkies until past midnight.

At twelve-thirty the housekeeper's small car emerged from Grimes' big garage. Grimes, its sole occupant, drove away from town, the police making no effort to follow, knowing Grimes would watch to see if he were tailed. Instead, state police were alerted in Barton, the next town east.

Meanwhile, police watched the roads back into Hensonville.

Grimes never reached Barton, but turned off on a side road and circled back to Hensonville, the stakeout on the park road spotting him as he went by. The park had been deduced as virtually the only place Grimes could plant the murder weapon in incrimination of Sam Bates. The sheriff was already there waiting, and men were stationed along each of the spoke-like roads leading from the park's lake.

Grimes stopped along one of the side roads and for a time sat motionless in the car, listening. The only sound was the chirping of crickets. Then he quietly left the car and walked several yards from the road into the dark woods. When he returned, the beams of several strong flashlights struck him almost simultaneously. He held a small shovel in one gloved hand and a revolver in the other.

"Where were you going to plant it, Mr. Grimes?" asked Sheriff Jackson softly. "In the bushes near one of the places Sam Bates has been camping out?"

"I refuse to say anything until I've consulted my attorney," Grimes said calmly, and spoke not another word. He didn't have to. The sheriff's ruse had worked, and Charlie Walsh's murderer was on ice. The case was closed.

Sam Bates did not find his triumph enjoyable. The townspeople still turned silently away from him, although now for a different reason—their shame. Sam continued to drive the red station wagon around town, showing its black racing stripe like a flag of small-town bigotry. He asked no

306

more local girls to go out in the car with him. He roomed now at the Hensonville Inn, where Brody gave him a special monthly rate. One evening Brody suggested that he and Sam shoot pool together, but Sam said no, he had a book he wanted to finish. Brody didn't ask again.

After a time Sam was offered a transfer and promotion to another government job, in the East, near the city to which Jane Grimes had returned to live with her parents.

Sam had thought often of Jane since the trial. Now as he prepared to drive East, camping out in his red station wagon along the way, he thought of her again, and patted the faded brown stain on the front seat beside him—for luck.

The Prosperous Judds

by Bob Bristow

The partnership of Reuben and Isaac Judd had proved to be a profitable one. By word of mouth, that most reliable form of advertising, their fame had spread across the rolling hills of South Carolina. Their product was in great demand because Brother Reuben and Brother Isaac had agreed in the beginning to produce a quality drink—not too harsh to the taste, not too devastating to the liver.

"No bad liquor, Brother Isaac," Brother Reuben had said firmly the day they hauled the large drum behind a mule up the steep grade where the product was to be manufactured.

Pure water and good copper coils and a real quality corn and barley mash, the Brothers Judd agreed, were what made the old family recipe the most famous in the hills.

They began modestly. That first run two years before had been only thirty gallons, but they had distilled the drink with utmost care, a care born out of family pride, and the moment of critical evaluation came when the two of them, alone, tested the alcohol.

It was a moment of sweet discovery. The liquor was mild to the taste. It did not—as inferior moonshine did—burn like a hot sword all the way to the stomach. And once inside, the kick was a gradual flowing glow that crept to the nerves and kissed them to life. That first night of discovery had been a memorable time. Brother Reuben, deceived by the mildness of the taste, took too much and fell off the mountain, suffering three cracked ribs. Brother Isaac, intoxicated with joy, was overcome with a long-secreted love for the Widow Carrie Stiles, who lived near the town limits of Pinesboro, and narrowly missed being cut in half by the Widow's double-barreled bird gun.

But the following morning the brothers knew they had a winner. They passed around—to a select group of hill people who had indicated a liking for moonshine—some small samples. Within hours, orders began to whisper across the hills, reaching the whiskey still nestled below the great pines of the mountain.

Thus, one of a select few famous names was born in the rich tree-covered hills. And, as it is said biblically, the brothers prospered. Always seeking to perfect the product, they installed a stainless steel drum and drew water from the spring only after the rush waters of a rain had subsided and the stream had returned to its purest state.

Because the drink was superior, it was soon in great demand. The brothers asked—and got—a dear price for a gallon of the brew. They responded to prosperity by taking to wearing the most expensive overalls and brightly colored shirts.

Life was good. The Judd farm, located not uncomfortably far from the still, abounded with good, blooded Yorkshire hogs and prancing, fighting cocks.

This prosperity, as well as fame, aroused the interest of Sheriff's Deputy Satterberry. As is the custom in the region, a man elected sheriff once acquires essentially the permanence of a federal judge, at least as long as he does not tread too heavily on the interests of the constituency.

Sheriff Otis Tatum had been in office since the Brothers Judd were boys, but now, aging and becoming senile, he was little more than a figurehead. After his twelfth election, he had appointed his son-in-law to the position of deputy.

Deputy Satterberry, however, was a petty man who grew bitterly resentful toward those who acquired a wealth he would not work for. His sagging mouth drew into a tight line when he observed the shiny brass buttons on the Judd brothers' new overalls. The clusters of hogs in the shade on the Judds' front porch brought him to a seething envy. After considerable effort, Deputy Satterberry had discovered the precise location of the Judd brothers' still.

And Deputy Satterberry's proposition, reduced to its essentials, amounted to a payoff, a kickback to the law, in exchange for unmolested operation of the business. In the infancy of the Judd brothers' partnership, such a proposal would have been met with severe mountain hostility and very well might have claimed lives. But prosperity had tempered the brothers, and it seemed the choice was to pay the immoral tariff or lose the business entirely. The brothers reluctantly agreed to the deputy's terms—to pay a small sum on each gallon of moonshine.

Before this capitulation of principle, they had considered taking the matter directly to Sheriff Tatum who had always been a forthright man and who would certainly find a shakedown unsavory. But the brothers took into consideration the fact that Sheriff Tatum's mind was not what it had once been, and they could not depend on his favorable reaction.

A further consideration was that Deputy Satterberry was, through marriage, in the Tatum family, and loyalty to the family was passionately observed in the Carolina hills. If the Sheriff heard of the shakedown on a clear-minded day, he might react unswervingly in favor of his daughter's man and, once committed, would be obliged to destroy the still.

So Brother Reuben and Brother Isaac agreed to pay fifty cents on the gallon for the protection of the law. In spite of the unpleasant aspects of the agreement, as well as Deputy Satterberry's habit of visiting the location of the still to inventory suspiciously the output and make certain he was receiving his cut on the volume, the partnership continued to prosper. Without fail, Deputy Satterberry asked for a complimentary half gallon of the liquor.

But there came a day when it appeared to Deputy Satterberry that the original shakedown had been so easy he could see no reason why the brothers might not be willing to pay one dollar per gallon.

This was too much. Brother Reuben, who was the acknowledged leader of the pair, sat scratching the stubble on his chin, his face screwed down in an angry grimace. He loosened his high-top shoes and slipped a foot free, examining the lines of dirt that had crept into the wrinkles of his sockless foot. Brother Reuben was a tall man, more than six feet, and thin as a railroad spike. His head was oblong, a shock of dark hair sweeping back toward his crown. When angry, his pale blue eyes grew intent and his voice lowered to a whisper. Most wise people took a step back when Brother Reuben spoke softly.

He moved a big toe thoughtfully and peered across the fire at Brother Isaac, his elder by six years, and began to take stock of their vulnerable position.

"We might move the still, Isaac, where he can't find it."

Brother Isaac, the heavier of the two, scratched his head. "He'd find it. We'd lose this good water." Brother Isaac gestured toward the flowing spring.

They were silent as the fire crackled in the pre-dawn light and the first blue jay began to flutter high in the pine above them.

In one electric moment the brothers' eyes met across the fire and held.

310

And silently they examined the thought that had not needed words.

"It couldn't be just a *plain* killing. Not him bein' deputy and all," Reuben said.

A few feet away the clear water of the spring murmured down the hillside and the cool water condensed the liquid, drip . . . drip . . . as steadily the moonshine filled a waiting glass jar.

"That's a fact," Isaac agreed.

Reuben's face was torn with indecision. He looked around him, weighing the problem, cherishing the thing the two of them had made here on the hillside.

"It'd have to be like a accident," he said wisely.

Isaac nodded and shoved a fresh stick of kindling on the fire. "They's lots a accidents," he agreed pleasantly.

Reuben stood, knowing the problem was his. He turned his back to the fire to absorb some warmth and peered down the hillside through the narrow opening they had cut in the timber.

"He's comin' today," Reuben said to himself.

"He said he was," Isaac agreed behind him.

"That's a right steep hill," Reuben said.

He visualized the hated fat-bellied figure of the deputy laboring up the hillside later in the morning, his head bent down, his shoulders hunched against the grade.

"I got a idea," Reuben said softly.

It was ten, or very nearly, before Deputy Satterberry slammed the door of the sheriff's car on the road a quarter of a mile from the hill. The brothers thought they could hear it as they peered through a crack in the stubby forest. They took positions behind a wall of logs.

"We got to move all at once, Brother Isaac. A great push all at once when he gets close."

Brother Isaac's eyes slid as though on oiled bearings as he scanned the hillside and his mouth drew into a faint smile. "Yessir . . . yessirree," he said.

The two of them, poised with crowbars, began to breathe more rapidly as the fat man suddenly appeared at the bottom of the hill.

"Allo up there," Deputy Satterberry shouted nasally.

Reuben and Isaac remained, as was their custom, very silent.

The deputy began to climb, slowly and with effort. When he was halfway up the grade, he paused and his belly moved accordion-like as he drew in great gulps of air. At last he let his head drop and began the final assault.

Reuben waited until the deputy was no more than thirty yards from the crest, dug his crowbar deep under the stack of logs, and with a silent signal from his eyes, gave the order to send them rolling down.

The brothers reacted together, hidden behind the large stack of timber, and suddenly an avalanche was roaring down on the deputy. There was time only for the deputy to jerk his head up at the sound and dive to his left. He reached the protection of a tree and cupped his head in his arms as the flood of timber cascaded past.

Knowing instinctively that the plan had failed by a mere matter of feet, Reuben provided the brothers cover by shouting a warning. Then they watched with sad hearts as the logs rolled harmlessly toward the bottom of the hill.

Deputy Satterberry came up screaming, holding his right foot where a log had cracked against his toes. The brothers were at the deputy's aid in a moment, lifting him up, examining him in feigned concern.

"I like to got killed by that damned pile of logs. You stacked them logs too close to the hill, Reuben. That's dangerous steep, that hill . . ."

"You all right?" Reuben asked.

"Like to tore my foot off," the deputy said. "Lucky they didn't!"

"They was too close to the hill, I guess," Isaac said sadly.

The deputy limped up the hill, sat on a log, and removed his low ankle shoes and his red socks. An ugly blue discoloration surrounded his big toe.

"That's too bad," Brother Reuben said softly, thinking about the failure.

The deputy massaged the toe with much sympathy, his jowls sagging sorrowfully. He asked for a measure of liquor to relieve the suffering. Brother Reuben poured from a fresh jar and the deputy sipped appreciatively.

"How many'd you run this week?" the deputy asked, managing to get his mind back on business and away from his foot.

"Isaac was sick. We only done fifty gallons."

The deputy frowned. The dark little pupils betrayed that mathematically this volume—translated to dollars in terms of his protection—was smaller than he would have liked. He also betrayed a suspicion, born out of his own dishonest mind, that the figure was inaccurate. He slipped on his sock and limped to the small stack of boxes which contained the capped jars. There were four in each box. He made no tactful pretense that the inventory was motivated by anything but distrust.

An oily mass of unruly hair fell over his forehead as he irritably returned to the fire, removed his cap, and wiped the sweat from the brim. "That ain't very good," he said wearily.

"Well . . . it takes the two of us," Reuben said.

"You wouldn't hide out any jars on me. I'd be hard on you if you done that, Reuben. I just wouldn't abide that at all."

Reuben had more dignity than to reply. He reached into his overall pocket and drew out twenty-five dollars which he tossed with some distaste across to Satterberry. He saw the deputy surveying the money. The deputy began to smile, not touching the money at all.

"It's a *dollar* now," he reminded. "You forgot about that, Reuben."

"That's too much."

The deputy rocked back and forth on the log, his belly bulging over his lap almost obscenely. "That ain't even the question. The question is you will or you won't, and if you won't, I'll be up here before noon with ten men and this whole thing . . ." He signaled the ultimate result with a snap of his stubby fingers.

Reuben resentfully drew the billfold out and counted again. He tossed the money across the log and glowered. Before the deputy was satisfied, Reuben had fetched the customary additional bribe, a half gallon of the whiskey, and placed it at the feet of the lawman.

Satterberry picked up the money, his face glowing with victory, got up with his jug and limped away from the fire. He seemed to be looking at the scattered logs at the bottom of the hill.

"That'll be a lot of work, gettin' them logs back up here," he said. "A lot of work."

With that he retreated down the hillside, stepping over a log here and there, until he disappeared. They heard the roar of his car spring to life.

"Think he knows?" Brother Isaac asked.

"He loves hisself so much, he don't suspect anybody'd try to kill him," Reuben said. "Three steps closer and he'd never a made it," he observed, gazing down the hillside.

Brother Isaac came to his side. "What now?" he asked.

"We got to figure."

The idea came while hauling sugar on the back of the mule up toward the still.

313

"Brother Isaac . . . you know that bend in the creek where all them copperheads den?" Brother Isaac knew. "I been thinking the deputy might git hisself snake bit."

"He don't pass that way."

"That's right, but we might fix it so's they go *his* way. He wears them low-cut shoes, just right for a bite on the ankle . . ."

Brother Isaac stuck his thumbs in his overall straps, his face softening somewhat. "That's a fact," he said.

"He likes that sheriff's car all shined, and I remember he draws it in a shed behind the house so rain don't make mud of the dust. And shuts the doors good."

"There ain't no snakes in . . ." Brother Isaac hesitated as his mind functioned ahead of his words. He smiled, the whiskers matting together. "Why sure," he said.

Thus, the brothers hurriedly built a box with a hinged door and crept to the bend of the creek with forked sticks where they endured the hazards of catching several copperheads, which they deposited in the box.

Very late that night, while the deputy slept in a deep sleep induced by their own whiskey, they crept to the shed by the light of a new moon, turned the latch, and emptied out the deadly cargo. They closed the door quietly and stole away unnoticed.

It was on the mountain two days later that a horn honked from the road. They recognized the signal of a faithful customer, and from Saturday Smith they learned what had happened.

"Deputy shot hisself," Saturday Smith told them after they appeared through the bushes with a gallon of whiskey.

"Shot hisself?" Isaac asked incredulously.

The brothers exchanged perplexed glances.

"Went in his grodge," Saturday Smith said, "and they was a swarm of snakes in there. Must a made a home when fall come on . . ."

"He got bit?" Reuben interjected.

"No. He liked to stepped on one, but he seen it and drew out his gun fast. But he shot the side of the car by accident and the bullet glanced off and hit the meat of his leg. He ain't hurt bad, but it give him a scare. That'll hold him!"

"That's too bad," Reuben said with deep feeling.

"A fact," Isaac agreed.

314

Having delivered the whiskey, they retired to the still and contemplated silently.

"He's hard to kill, Brother Reuben," Isaac said, shaking his head.

"He is that," Reuben agreed.

"We'd best think on it."

The brothers fell into a brooding silence that lasted all through the rains that came during the week. The stream swelled and filled with sediment and chemicals from the heart of the mountain. Usually the brothers were cautious about the water after such a rain until the stream had time to settle and clear. But they were so obsessed with their problem that they ignored principle, and the mineral from the mountain infected the whiskey. The brothers ordinarily would have destroyed the moonshine. But the work was done, and they capped it in jars.

"We could put glass in his food," Isaac offered.

Reuben shook his head negatively and huddled under a dripping loblolly pine as the rains began to dissipate.

No solution had offered itself when Deputy Satterberry limped to the bottom of the hill that Thursday. They saw him pause cautiously to survey above before he began to climb. Apparently satisfied that no wall of timber was about to descend on him, he crept, more slowly this time, up the hill. He arrived at the fireside breathing with difficulty.

"Lot a rain," he said, peering about in a suspicious manner.

"Like to washed the still off the mountain," Reuben said.

"Sold much whiskey?"

"Roads was too muddy to haul it down. We just ran a batch is all."

"How many?"

"Little more than fifty," Reuben said. "It ain't no good."

The deputy limped to the stack of wet boxes and inventoried the stock. Satisfied, he returned to the log and sat, his leg stretched out stiffly in front of him.

"I had a spell of bad luck," he said, as though asking for sympathy.

"Heard you did."

"Hair trigger on that gun. Bullet come off the car and hit my leg. There was snakes . . ." His eyes widened. "Come in there for warmth, I figure."

"Rattlesnakes?" Reuben asked cleverly.

"Copperheads. I liked to stepped on one."

"They's mean," Isaac admitted sourly.

The deputy took out his billfold to receive the bribe, ignoring the courtesy that it should have been Reuben's turn to move first. It was a rude thing to do, to just draw the billfold out like that and wait.

Reuben pulled the money out of his overalls and counted out the proper amount, not even attempting to bargain. The deputy was pleased at this. He took the money and demanded his jug.

Reuben went to the stack and selected a jar from the bad run. Since the deputy wasn't paying, he could drink from the polluted creek run.

They watched the deputy go down the hill favoring the wounded leg.

"If a man ever died from feet and legs, we'd have got him," Isaac said.

"Brother Isaac," Reuben said softly, "we got to be direct. Next time . . . I got it figured now. Next time when he sets, you'll pull a long rifle out from behind the log and aim it on his heart. You won't have to shoot him. I'll hit him in the head with some kindling and we'll carry him off ten or twenty miles and drop him in the river. He'll show up near Savannah probably."

"Might be risky, Brother Reuben."

"Well, it might, but we ain't doin' no good just hurtin' his legs."

Thus it was agreed, after some minor refinements in the plan had been devised, that the next appearance of the deputy would be the last.

More of the seasonal fall rains hampered business. The truck which usually arrived to carry the load was not able to negotiate the muddy roads. By the next Thursday, the rains had decreased, and the brothers waited for Satterberry to make his appearance. He would use chains on the car and get it muddy, if necessary, to get his money.

The long rifle was secreted behind a log. A solid length of kindling had been carefully selected. At ten that morning the brothers waited tensely. But the deputy did not appear. At eleven in the afternoon they were genuinely disturbed, because the fearful tension engendered by the intended murder became more oppressive as time crept by. At sundown, they knew he was not coming. "You think he knew? You think maybe he's about to break up the still?" Isaac asked.

"I just rightly don't know," Reuben admitted.

Friday passed and the deputy did not appear. In fact, nobody appeared, not even the truck which usually carried the whiskey to market. And the roads had dried sufficiently for passage.

"They's somethin', Brother Reuben . . . they's somethin'."

On Saturday they could bear it no longer. The brothers dressed in clean overalls and went into the town of Pinesboro.

316

As they arrived that morning, they began to observe sharp looks of silent disapproval from the people on the streets. A wall of reserve isolated the brothers.

"I feel somethin', Brother Reuben."

Reuben nodded, studied the sheriff's car parked in front of the courthouse, the windows rolled up tightly.

"We'd best find out," he said.

They strolled to the pool hall at the end of Main Street. A brooding silence descended as they entered. Eyes examined them coldly. Reuben made his way to the counter where old Nate Toombs sold chewing tobacco and soda pop.

Nate was distantly related, having married a Judd some generations back. Nate could be trusted.

"Folks is quiet. Nate, why is they a silence against us?"

Nate lowered his voice, his white stubble of beard glistening in the light of the 100-watt bulb above his head. "It's about how Deputy Satterberry died."

The brothers exchanged glances, pleased at first; then moment by moment their faces became grave.

"He died?"

Nate bobbed his head soberly.

"How'd he die then?" Reuben asked.

Nate lowered his voice so much this time the brothers had to lean forward to hear. "On *your* whiskey."

It was a harsh thing to say, a stunning thing to say to men of the Judd reputation, but Nate accented the report with a jerk of his white head. The deputy, he explained, died suddenly and the hospital over at Hayesville cut him open and ran some tests and discovered that some deadly mineral was in his stomach.

"They found an unfinished jar of moonshine whiskey," Nate said lowering his eyes, "and there was some deadly mineral in it."

Reuben swallowed hard. He turned to face the men grouped about the pool tables, most of them his friends, his customers. He protested in his mind, but declined to speak because he knew it would be of no avail. No avail at all.

A man had died drinking Judd whiskey, and that meant the end of more than the deputy, whom they had plotted to kill. Although the bad mineral had gotten into the whiskey by accident, a distrust had been born that would not be dispelled until an entire generation of hill people died, and then not easily.

Later, Brother Reuben said softly, "It couldn't last forever."

Brother Isaac nodded, sensing that what was being offered was born of difficult truth.

"And you got to admit we ain't left with wants. If we take care, we'll never need."

"A fact," Isaac admitted.

"And," Brother Reuben began to smile, "the way it turned out with the deputy, the way he died . . . it's kind of pretty, considering what he was."

Brother Isaac's face accepted this thoughtfully, and soon he responded to the pleasure of the thought. Then together they began to dismantle the still.

The blue jay in the loblolly pine watched after them a while before fluttering to the ground by the vacated campfire. The jay cock sang out a farewell, a unique cry of laughter touched subtly with a note of bitterness.

The Dead Indian

by Robert W. Alexander

If someone should ask how I got into this fix, I'd say because of a dead phone, but strangely it is because I was a dead Indian that I might escape unscathed. The only flaw in my ingenious plan is trusting an actress. The police want me, a syndicate bookie wants me worked over or eliminated and, worse if possible, a certain disgruntled man of the underworld has specifically ordered my demise. I'm sure!

Except for the police charge, I'm innocent, even though I have the money. Before all that, I was just making a few bucks at a job, to get the right clothes and meet the right people. I'm an actor—well, I wanted to be an actor. I had a taste of it, my first and only part, just a few months ago.

I've heard it said that if a person will knock around Hollywood long enough, opportunity is bound to strike. Nobody mentioned disaster. Anyway, after bothering casting offices and agencies for a while, I happened to be in the Levine agency resting my feet when they got a hurry-up call for an actor.

Previously, my lack of experience had precluded employment. I had never been in a movie or on TV; in fact, I'd never even been in a high school play. Doris gave me the idea. She's a ravishing brunette who is ga-ga over actors. So I thought, O.K., if it's an actor she wants, I can emote with the best of them. All I needed was the chance, which is tough to come by.

Doris seemed offended when I told her. Her yen for actors didn't include me? One would think she tried to identify with actors to further her own career. Well, she's young. She'd have to fawn around me when I was a star. I didn't mind starting as a bit player, and I could learn. I mean, what yokel *couldn't* squint down the dusty trail and say, "They went that-a-way."

The man in the Levine office was desperate enough to dash out to his

319

waiting room to survey us hopefuls. I couldn't believe he decided on me! I'm rather plain.

"How quick can you get to Mervin Studios?" he asked. "They need an Indian. You got a car?"

It wasn't exactly the role I was looking for, but I said, "I could take a cab."

"You got the fare?"

"Uhhh . . ." I hedged. He shuddered, clenched his jaw, and resignedly shook his head. I guess he knew that most of us would-be's are broke and barely get by on meager night jobs, to be able to sit around in agents' offices all day.

However, my face must have fit the part because he advanced me ten bucks, had me sign an agency contract for the part, and then sent me out to the street to await the taxi he'd phoned.

At the studio, a huge one, I handed the unimpressed guard my paper. He said, "Get a hustle on. Stage three."

"Where's it at?"

My question pained him. "About a half mile straight down, you'll see the arrow. They're on their fannies waiting for you! Ya should've been on time. They'll never hire you again."

"I just got the role . . ."

"Don't tell me your troubles. Move!"

If they were in such a fireball hurry they should have had a limousine waiting—a car, at least. It was a long way. I dog-trotted down the pavement, hoping to sight a movie star, but no luck. Oh, well, I was on my way. Doris would be shocked. Someday in the near future I'd let her come along when I'm chauffeured down this lane in style.

I found an arrow pointing to Stage 3, an immense building, and picked up speed. The door was at the far end and I raced up to it, yanked it open, and dashed in. The first words that greeted me were: "Who the hell opened the door?"

An angry man in an open-collared shirt flew around a prop blocking my view. "Didn't ya see the red light?" he screamed. There was more screaming with everybody seeming to yell, "Quiet!"

I was quiet. I handed him my credentials: my paper from the Levine agency. He snatched it from me.

"The Indian!" He eyed me suspiciously. "Ugh! Well, follow me, and don't make a sound! They're reshooting the scene you spoiled."

320

The sound stage was impressive. They had an outdoor desert real enough to watch for rattlesnakes. There was a stagecoach, horses, a pretty girl in a checked gingham dress, and a suave, blue-eyed cowboy who was obviously the leading man.

Everybody greeted my apologetic smile with black glares, except the pretty girl in gingham; she seemed to have a twinkle in her eyes. Then they all ignored me, and I stood beside the assistant director who held my paper and watched them shoot the scene. It was an interesting shot of the girl getting out of the stagecoach.

I'd always thought they laboriously redid scenes over and over to get perfection, but not this crew. As soon as they filmed the girl getting out of the coach, the large director in the chair yelled, "Print it," and then they hustled the camera up to her face for a close-up. I wandered up beside the director where I had a better view.

After he yelled, "Print it," for the close-up, he whirled to the assistant director and ordered, "Shoot the Indian."

The assistant director worriedly nodded and rushed toward me, but the director was furious for any delay and screamed in my ear, "Where's the Indian?"

"I'm the Indian," I said. He looked at me in horror. Then he roared out a string of unprintable words, right in front of the gingham girl, who stonily pretended not to hear. I blushed.

Perhaps the flush on my face made me look more like an Indian. There were curses and threats for not having the Indian ready, and excuses that the Indian actor ahead of me had suddenly taken ill, gotten drunk or something. Anyway, they broke for an early lunch to let me get into costume and makeup. I quickly learned why the Indian actor before me suddenly took ill.

The assistant director rushed me to the nearest men's room and helped me strip off my clothes. I thought they would have dressing rooms, but I later learned it was a low budget picture, the whole movie to be shot in three days.

When I was stark bare, the assistant director handed me a buckskin G-string.

"It's cold in here," I told him.

"Will you hurry!" he roared. I assumed that assistant directors were allowed to yell at bit players, so I got into the buckskin and looked for the rest of my costume. There wasn't any!

321

"Now wait a minute," I complained. "There's a girl out there."

He grimaced. "Do you think an Indian would care? Now, what are you? An actor or a misfit?"

It was a case of misfit, believe me. I'm on the skinny side and the low-budget costume was loose. I showed him, and he scoffed.

"Don't worry, we'll pin it tighter after we smear on your war paint."

I shrugged. Anything for art; I wasn't going to blow my career.

He hustled me out of the lavatory and across the way to where a dainty man with white hair and cold hands applied a film of reddish mud over my torso.

The assistant director approved. Then the real shocker came when he said, "Shave his head."

"What!" I blurted. If it weren't for Doris' obsession for actors, I'd have walked off.

"Look," he argued, "did you ever see an Indian with sideburns?"

I shook my head. Frankly, I'd never seen a real Indian—not one in war paint. So he shot me the ultimatum. "The script calls for a shaven-head Indian. Do you want the part, or not?"

The makeup man clipped me clean and ran an electric shaver over my head. My reddish locks dropped to the floor; some hair stuck to the grease on my body and had to be picked off.

The director was ready for me when I got back. "What's your name?" he asked.

"Steve McKing," I said, using my stage name.

He looked like he might be sick, but he explained my part. "You're the dead Indian," he said. "You just lie down there and don't move." The assistant director placed a tomahawk in my hand and showed me where to sprawl out on my back.

I heard them clack the sound gizmo, and I kept my eyes closed. Nobody had bothered to explain the story or the plot of the picture to me. I figured I would have to pay to see it, to find out what it was about.

I heard the pretty girl in gingham pretend to get off the stagecoach again. I was lying right at her feet. Suddenly, I heard her gasp! I thought, *My god!* I opened my eyes to see if—

Everybody yelled at me for moving. All she had gasped about was at seeing a dead Indian. It was part of the story. So the second time I didn't flinch when she inhaled. I heard her say to the leading man, "I suppose you shot him?"

322

He said, "Yes'm, I did."

"But he's just a boy," she retorted.

"He'd'a split yer head with the tommyhawk," said he. "Don't trust 'em. Not even a dead one!" With that, he pushed his pointed boot into my ribs. I'd been having fits with a tickling hair in my nose, and when his boot touched near my armpit, their dead Indian jumped a foot.

I caught hell, of course, but they finally got the scene they wanted on the fourth try. That was all the use they had for me, but no one told me that. I stood around freezing until quitting time, when everybody suddenly took off and left me.

The makeup man had disappeared too, and I didn't have any way to get the greasepaint off. I couldn't even touch my clothes. I wandered around, looking, and finally the girl in gingham, who had changed to a chic mini-skirt, saw me outside the building asking passing workmen if they had any cold cream. She brought me a jar and told me where I could find a shower. Later, out at the gate, I found her waiting for some friend she had phoned to pick her up. She smiled at my nude head. I had a look at myself in a mirror, and I couldn't fault her for grinning.

"Hideous, huh?" I lamented.

"Oh, I don't know," she said, watching my eyes compare her to Doris. "You might get a lot of work with a bald head."

"Really?"

"Sure. Not many boys your age are bald. Might be smart to keep your head shaved. A lot of 'quickie' companies can't afford elaborate makeup."

"That's mighty nice of you to tell me. I'm fresh out of loot right now, but tomorrow when I get my check from the agency—"

"I'm spoken for," she smiled. I smiled back. I had figured she might be, a budding star and all. Another thing, I'm cursed with looking younger than I am. For some reason I look nine years younger than my twenty-six.

A Lincoln picked her up.

I didn't break the great news to Doris that I had worked in a picture until the next day. After I collected my check from the Levine agency, I dashed up to her apartment. She lives only a block from my one-room pad which has running water at the end of the hall. I hammered on her door and hoped it wouldn't be opened by her roommate. I was in luck. Doris opened the door, but her mouth sagged.

323

"My God!" she exhaled.

"Oh, this." I touched my skin head. "I was a dead Indian," I announced proudly, and waved my check.

"You're a dead duck! A plucked one, at that! If you think I'll be seen with you, you're nuts!"

I lost my temper. She was envious because I had gotten a part. All she had ever managed was propositions.

"You're jealous," I said.

She slammed the door in my face. Worse, my taunt prompted her to speak to Mr. Crenshaw, who hires and fires at the drive-in where I filled in on Saturday nights as a counterman. She's a carhop there.

Mr. Crenshaw took a look at my head and said, "Uh, uh. You're not working here. You'll give the customers indigestion." But I knew Doris got him to fire me. He doted on Doris with futile high hopes, and I told him, "With her you'll make nothing more than change," *after* he fired me, of course.

So, I was a dead Indian as far as Doris was concerned, and could have given up acting, except that I liked it. I kept shaving my head and making the rounds of the casting offices, and I bothered the guy at the Levine agency every other day or so. "We'll call you," he'd groan, but I knew to keep reminding him that I existed.

Naturally, I had to find new employment to make out, and that meant a night job so I could pursue my career in the daytime. My bald head was a deterrent. Finally, after I added a pair of horn-rims with plain glass lenses, I appeared the studious type—I said I was working my way through college—and I got a janitor's job in an office building, a kind of run-down building, but located near the center of town.

A fat man with a lot of phones on his desk sat in his office by himself and tipped me to burn personally all his scrap paper. He said he was in the brokerage business.

This Mr. Shelly was really a bookie—I knew it—and one night at about seven, when I was sweeping up his place, the phone rang and some guy named Miller wanted to put ten on a horse in the fifth at Santa Anita the next day. I said, "O.K.," and left a note for Mr. Shelly.

"Not on my desk top!" he stormed at me the next night. "Ya crazy?"

"Sorry, Mr. Shelly. Thought I was helping."

He calmed down after I assured him I knew he was a bookie. He lit a cigar and studied me.

324

"Tell you what, Steve," he said, using my stage name that I gave everybody. "I'm moving out of here. Like, right now. How'd you like a job? You like figures?"

"Passionately."

"Yeah, well, these are numbers, but you can spend the profits on your choice."

So there went my night work. I became an assistant bookie. Sam Shelly worked for a national syndicate, and the bookie business was no small operation. I was amazed. Sam knew a lot about horses, too. He personally booked some bets.

"Look at this," he said once. "Two hundred to win on Stella Fancy. She ain't got a chance." So he didn't write the bet in the book, nor did he relay it to the syndicate. The horse lost and he pocketed the whole two hundred.

Hm, thought I. So, when Sam Shelly was out one day and a sucker called and wagered ten to win on a hopeless long shot, I booked the bet. The damn horse won and I had to cough up three hundred dollars, my entire salary for three weeks. I had to admit it to Sam, because he personally took care of the payoffs.

"That's the way it is," he shrugged. "Take the risk, pay the penalty. But get this, Steve—not too often. And be careful who you book. The syndicate hears we're taking bets on our own, they'll break our heads."

He didn't have to worry about me doing it again.

Two weeks later, Sam happily announced we were moving again. "Hey, top spot, kiddo. How about that? The boys promoted me to luxury. Watch the type of bets we get now."

He was right. We rented a swank office on the Strip and handled what Sam said was lay-off money. In cash! Sometimes five and ten thousand dollars a bet. Sam raised my salary to two hundred a week and I was nearly tempted to give up acting.

Most of the time I was a runner. Any time the money in our safe reached fifty thousand, I took it in a locked satchel to a big hilltop home with a view of the ocean. I gave it to a Mr. Bozelli, a large bull-necked guy who was sort of uncouth, would be the word. He had dark eyes and bushy brows and all he ever did was glare at me.

"Hey, baldy," he said on my second trip. "Ya know better than to touch this." He slapped the briefcase I'd given him.

"Yes, sir," I assured him, removing my glasses and pretending to be

325

duly alarmed. The alarm didn't take much effort, but I don't know why I pretended I couldn't see very well without the fake glasses—unless I was afraid to let him know I was ogling the blonde out by the pool. Her sunsuit wasn't much more than ribbon.

I knew the blonde. She was the star of that Grade Z Western. The Levine agency told me the producer hadn't been able to get it distributed.

Mr. Bozelli said, "I'll get you the receipt for Sam." He never counted the money I brought in my presence, but went into a private office. It usually took him eight minutes. With nothing else to do, I used to clock him. Today was different.

I tore out to the pool. When she looked up, I said, "Hi, there."

"Well, hello." She was surprised. I didn't want her telling Mr. Bozelli I shaved my head. He might think I was nuts, since he didn't seem to be the type who understood actors. He might even order Sam to fire me. I explained my position to Miss Vida Lamour, after she told me her name.

She laughed. "Don't worry, Mr. McKing. Your secret is safe."

"Thank you. Uh—do you know Mr. Bozelli very well?"

"Yes." She contemplated me with amusement, obviously thinking me years her junior.

"I'm twenty-six," I said.

"Oh?" She winked. "Come on."

"Honest, I just look young." She didn't believe me. I shrugged. "There'll be no joy in Mudville . . ."

She cocked her head. "The mighty Casey struck out? Is there more than the obvious connection?"

"Casey is my real name. Steve McKing is just for the stage."

"I sort of guessed." Her brown eyes were suddenly friendly with that light of encouragement a woman can give. I whipped my wallet from my pocket.

"Would you like to see my driver's license?"

"I believe your name is Casey."

"No! My age. I'm twenty-six." A horrible thought struck me. "Uh—you're not married to Mr. Bozelli?"

"No. He's my uncle. Are you working for him?"

"Not directly. I work for a man who works for him."

She smiled. "You don't look the type. However, Casey—"

"I'd, uh, prefer you call me Steve. I started out as Steve McKing and they might not understand."

"All right, Steve—"

We were suddenly interrupted by Mr. Bozelli. "Who the hell told you to come out here?" he demanded. He grabbed me by the arm and propelled me through the house and out to the front porch where he handed me the receipt. "Don't try that again," he threatened, without allowing me to explain.

I didn't tell Sam Shelly about Vida Lamour, but that afternoon, about an hour after I got back from Mr. Bozelli's, I heard Sam answer a phone. "You want who? Twenty-six?"

"Hey! That's for me!" I yelled. I pushed the button and took the call on my line. "Miss Lamour?"

"Are you really twenty-six? You look eighteen."

"That's encouraging. Everybody used to say *seven*teen."

We chatted on a little bit, me kind of under pressure with Sam sitting there. I took the opportunity, when he was busy with a phone bet, to tell her I was going to let my hair grow. She didn't want me to.

"No, Steve. I called to see if you'd be interested in joining a theater group. We're casting a play."

Naturally, I was entirely interested, and at the tryout I won the minor part of a woman whose head was shaved by the Nazis. I was with Vida every night that week, and life was good. Then it happened. Sam Shelly caught the Hong Kong flu.

I was left in charge of the whole operation—and I was busy! I had to handle all the phone calls, and the rare cash bets that were brought to the office. One thing Sam always did with the huge cash bets was to notify the syndicate immediately. If some outfit was trying to score with a fixed race, the syndicate seemed to know, and would bet a like amount at the track to cover themselves.

There was one guy in particular who visited our office every now and then and placed some heavy bets, but Sam took care of him personally. He was a sharp dresser with slick black hair, but his piglike, expressionless eyes ruined his looks. He usually had a couple of his boys with him. He gave me the creeps, and I didn't cultivate his acquaintance.

He walked in during the second afternoon that I was alone. Both of his men were with him. He placed a briefcase on my desk and waited until I hung up a phone.

"There's ten G's on Fightin' Fool in the third at Santa Anita. Count it."

That took a while, of course, and personally accepting the wager shook me a little, too. I wasn't conscious of the time—post time, that is, and I mean *our* post time. The track had the race scheduled for 1:40 p.m. and that meant we wouldn't take any bets on the race after 1:10 p.m. Our rule was that we had to have a half-hour leeway on any bet over a thousand. I looked at the clock. It was five minutes after one, so The Greek—that's what Sam called him—had just made it.

I wrote him a receipt in a hurry, and didn't bother to answer the ringing phones. I had a number to call—but quick!—to tell them of the bet I had accepted. The Greek picked up his receipt for the bet with a stone face.

"If it wins, I'll be back at five to collect. O.K.?"

"O.K.," I nodded. Sam had that kind of arrangement with him. So I watched him leave and then rapidly dialed our center control office.

My phone was dead! I had five ringing phones, and my private line to the head office was dead! Not even a buzz. I told myself, *Calm down, boy, use another phone.* I wildly grabbed the one nearest to me. Some guy who called himself Chazz, an old customer, attempted to place five hundred on Fightin' Fool!

I told him he had a wrong number. The idiot argued with me and stoutly maintained that he recognized my voice. He demanded to speak to Sam.

"Sam's sick!" I shouted, and hung up the phone. I took time for a breath and then lifted the receiver again. He was still on the line, cursing a blue streak and yelling that he had paid a hundred dollars for the tip, and that I wasn't going to gyp him out of a bet.

I dropped that phone and picked up another one. Another imbecile wanted to place a bet and wouldn't get off the line. All I could do was take his bet: two hundred to win on Fightin' Fool!

When I finally got him off the line I called central control, but got a busy signal. Never had that happened before. I was getting sick from a knotting in my stomach. I called Sam at his apartment.

"I'm sick," he groaned.

"Sam, listen. The Greek was in. Bet ten thousand, and I can't get our office. The line's dead!"

"Ohhh, I'm dying . . ."

"Sam! Damn it! What'll I do? The line's dead!"

"Ohhh . . . jiggle it. It's a private one-way line. Sometimes it sticks. Don't bother me." He hung up.

328

Jiggle it? I shook the living daylights out of it. Then I dialed, and shook it again, and dialed.

Finally, Mac answered. That's all the name I had for him. I tried to sound calm.

"This is Steve calling for Sam. The Greek wants to bet ten thousand on Fightin' Fool in the third—"

"You know the rules. He's a minute past our post. That's final."

"You don't understand—"

"Tell him no!"

"The phone's been dead!"

"I've been sitting right here, buddy, and you got me loud and clear. Tell him we're laying off and can't handle any more."

He hung up on me!

I called Sam again, but he wouldn't answer. My hand began to feel clammy, and I noticed a decided tremble when I lit a cigarette. I debated calling Mac again and telling him how I happened to accept the bet. The syndicate might not kill me; accidents happen. I decided it was better I explain to the syndicate *before* the race was run, than to attempt an explanation afterward to The Greek.

I was reaching for the private phone when the guy who runs the elevator broke into the front office. He dashed inside to where I was.

"The vice squad!" he hollered. "I saw them come in the lobby, and I shot up here. They'll grab the other car. You got about two minutes!"

Sam paid the elevator gang a hundred a week to spot the police. They knew every man on the vice squad, and they earned a two-hundred-dollar bonus for tipping us.

We kept the bets on a roll of paper like adding machine tape. I grabbed that and the ten thousand I'd placed in our escape valise—that was all the cash I had taken in so far—and raced to the elevator with my savior.

He clanged the doors shut and we started down just seconds before the police in the next car came up. I grimaced, and the elevator boy, a guy about my age, grinned.

"Wonder who tipped them?"

"I've got a good idea," I said. Undoubtedly the customer, Chazz, was mad because I didn't take his bet. "I'll see that Sam pays you," I told him.

"Don't forget," he said. He let me off on the second floor. I knew the escape route. I walked innocently down the back stairs and whipped

329

through a parking lot. Sam had a car staked out in the second lot down. The key was in it and I was out of there in nothing flat.

I drove a few miles and stopped at a drugstore. I locked the money in the trunk of the car and went in to use the phone booth. Where does time go? It was already 1:42 P.M. on the clock in the store. The syndicate would never understand my phoning about the accidental bet *after* the race was run!

Maybe the horse will lose, I hoped. Wow! If it did lose, I was rich. I might have to split with Sam to keep his mouth shut, but five thousand? Wow! I left the drugstore and raced back to the car. I let my hopes build as I drove. After all, there were other horses in the race, and the odds were real great in my favor that it would be O.K. Anything could happen. Why, just a few weeks ago, the jockey fell off Swordfish when the horse was the favorite.

Fightin' Fool won the third at Santa Anita! Not only did he win by four lengths, but he paid $14.20. That's over six to one, and the syndicate owed The Greek over seventy thousand dollars and didn't know it.

I wondered how they'd settle it.

Actually, I'm not in bad shape—especially financially. I'll miss Vida Lamour, of course, but not for any longer than I did Doris. Down here in San Diego, where I'm residing, I met a redhead by the impossible name of Mary Jones.

I'm letting my hair grow, and I discarded the useless glasses, and even Sam hadn't known that I didn't need them. The only person now in the know—that I'm not a bald-headed unfortunate—is Vida Lamour. That's her stage name. Her real handle is Thelma Bozelli, a name I'll never forget.

I chanced a phone call to her, at the theater where we were doing the rehearsals for the play about the Nazis. I didn't go into details about the trouble I was in. I just told her that I wouldn't be able to participate in her play.

She seemed to understand. She just asked, "Where are you?"

I said, "San Francisco." Then I said, "I just called . . . well, not only to tell you I'm out of the play, but to ask you to keep your promise not to tell your uncle or *anybody* that I'm capable of growing hair."

"Oh? Are you letting your hair grow?" She laughed nicely too.

"Uh, yes. My jet-black hair is sprouting up."

"That's odd. You had fiery red hair before they cut it."

"You remember," I laughed with her. "I've, ahh . . . been coloring it a little."

"I see. Well, Steve McKing, don't fret. I wouldn't *dream* of telling about your disguise."

"It's not really a disguise," I said quickly. "It'll be me, and I'm sure hoping nobody will recognize me."

"If they do, you're a dead Indian," she said.

We both laughed again—I had to force mine—and then hung up. She's not a bad actress. I hope she doesn't think blood is thicker than the bond between bosom troupers, because if she reveals that I'm a redheaded boy of twenty-six who looks eighteen, I *am* a dead Indian.

The China Cottage

by August Derleth

"**M**y esteemed brother," said Solar Pons as I walked into our quarters one autumn morning for breakfast, "has a mind several times more perceptive than my own, but he has little patience with the processes of ratiocination. Though there is nothing to indicate it, it was certainly he who sent this packet of papers by special messenger well before you were awake."

He had pushed the breakfast dishes back, having barely touched the food Mrs. Johnson had prepared, and sat studying several pages of manuscript, beside which lay an ordinary calling card bearing the name Randolph Curwen, through which someone had scrawled an imperative question mark in red ink.

Observing the direction of my gaze, Pons went on. "The card was clipped to the papers. Curwen is, or perhaps I had better say 'was,' an expert on foreign affairs, and was known to be a consultant of the Foreign Office in cryptology. He was sixty-nine, a widower, and lived alone in Cadogan Place, Belgravia, little given to social affairs since the death of his wife nine years ago. There were no children, but he had the reputation of possessing a considerable estate."

"Is he dead, then?" I asked.

"I should not be surprised to learn that he is," said Pons. "I have had a look at the morning papers, but there is no word of him there. Some important discovery about Curwen has been made. These papers are photographs of some confidential correspondence between members of the German foreign office and that of Russia. They would appear to be singularly innocuous, and were probably sent to Curwen so he might examine them for any code."

"I assumed," said an icy voice from the threshold behind me, "that you would have come to the proper conclusion about this data. I came as soon as I could."

Bancroft Pons had come noiselessly into the room, which was no mean feat in view of his weight. His keen eyes were fixed unswervingly upon Pons, his austere face frozen into an impassive mask, which added to the impressiveness of his appearance.

"Sir Randolph?" asked Pons.

"Dead," said Bancroft. "We do not yet know how."

"The papers?"

"We have some reason to believe that a *rapprochement* between Germany and Russia is in the wind. We are naturally anxious to know what impends. We had recourse to Curwen, as one of the most skilled of our cryptologists. He was sent the papers by messenger at noon yesterday."

"I take it he was given the originals."

Bancroft nodded curtly. "Curwen always liked to work with the originals. You've had a chance to look them over."

"They do not seem to be in code," said Pons. "They appear to be only friendly correspondence between the foreign secretaries, though it is evident that some increase in trade is being contemplated."

"Curwen was to have telephoned me early this morning. When seven o'clock passed without a call from him, I put in a call. I could not get a reply. So we sent Danvers out. The house and the study were locked. Of course, Danvers had skeleton keys which enabled him to get in. He found Curwen dead in his chair at the table, the papers before him. The windows were all locked, though one was open to a locked screen. Danvers thought he detected a chemical odor of some kind; it suggested that someone might have photographed the papers. But you shall see Curwen. Nothing has been touched. I have a car below. It isn't far to Cadogan Place."

The house in Cadogan Place was austere in its appointments. It was now under heavy police guard; a constable stood on the street before the house, another at the door, and yet another at the door of the study, which was situated at one corner of the front of the house, one pair of windows looking out toward the street, the other into shrubbery-grown grounds to a low stone wall which separated the building from the adjacent property. The house was Georgian in architecture, and likewise in its furniture.

When the study door was unlocked, it revealed book-lined walls, the shelving broken only by windows and a fireplace. The walls framed what we had come to see—the great table in the center of the room, the still-lit lamp, the motionless form of Sir Randolph Curwen, collapsed in his armchair, arms dangling floorward, his head thrown back, his face twisted into an expression of agony. Beside him stood, as if also on guard, a man whom Bancroft Pons introduced as Hilary Danvers.

"Nothing has been disturbed, sir."

Bancroft nodded curtly and waved one arm toward the body. "Sir Randolph, Parker. Your division."

I went around immediately to examine the body. Sir Randolph had been a thin, almost gangling man. A grey moustache decorated his upper lip, and thin grey hair barely concealed his scalp. Pince-nez, one eyeglass broken, dangled from a black silk cord around his neck. He appeared to have died in convulsive agony, but there was certainly no visible wound on his body.

"Heart?" asked Pons.

When I shook my head, he left me to my examination and walked catlike around the room. He examined the windows, one after the other, tested the screen on the half-opened window to the grounds, and came to a pause at the fireplace, where he dropped to one knee.

"Something has been burned here," he said. "Part of the original material?"

Bancroft said peevishly, "A cursory examination suggests that someone burned papers with figures on them, as you can see. We'll collect the ashes and study them, never fear."

Pons rose and came around to the table. He stood to scrutinize it, touching nothing. Most of its top was spread with the papers from the Foreign Office; these were divided into two piles, with one sheet between them, this one evidently being the paper Curwen was reading when he was stricken. A pad of notepaper, free of any jottings, was at one side of this paper. The perimeter of the desk was covered by an assortment of items ending with a small white, rose-decorated cottage of china, with an open box of incense pastilles beside it. Curwen's chair had been pushed slightly back from the table and around to one side, as if he were making an attempt to rise before death overtook him.

"Well, Parker?" asked Pons impatiently.

"A seizure of some kind," I replied. "But I fear that only an autopsy can determine the cause of death precisely. If I had to guess, I'd say poison."

Pons looked at his brother. "You mentioned an odor on entrance."

334

"We believe the odor emanated from the incense burner," Mr. Danvers said.

"Ah, this," said Pons, his hand hovering over the china cottage. He gazed inquiringly at Danvers.

"We have tested for fingerprints, Mr. Pons. Only Sir Randolph's were found."

Pons lifted the cottage from its base, where, in a little cup, lay the remains of burned pastilles. He bent his face toward the cup and sniffed. He looked up with narrowed eyes, picked up the base of the china cottage, and thrust it at me. "What kind of scent might that be, Parker?"

I followed his example and sniffed. "Almond," I said. "They make these pastilles in all manner of scents."

Pons put the china cottage back together and picked up the box of pastilles. "Lilac," he said dryly.

"The room was locked, Mr. Pons," put in Danvers. "No one could possibly have got in, if you're suggesting that someone came and poisoned Sir Randolph."

"Child's play," muttered Bancroft impatiently. "What did he find in the papers that someone should want to kill him? Or burn his findings?"

"You're irritable today," said Pons. "There's nothing here to show that Curwen found anything in the papers."

"On the contrary, there is everything to suggest that somehow someone managed entrance into this room, killed Sir Randolph, and burned his notes."

"Why not take them along? If he were clever enough to enter and leave a locked room without a sign to betray him, he must certainly have known that something could be determined from the ashes. I believe the papers in the grate were burned by Sir Randolph himself. He tore off what was on his pad and what had accumulated in his wastebasket under the table, emptied the wastebasket into the fireplace, and set fire to the contents. The ashes are substantial. There is among them at least a page or two from the *Times*, no reason for burning which I could adduce on the part of a foreign agent. Yours is the Foreign Office approach, all intrigue and espionage."

"It is indeed," said Bancroft shortly.

Pons turned again to the china cottage. "If I may, I should like to take this back to Praed Street." He picked up also the box of pastilles. "And this."

Bancroft stared at him as if he were convinced that Pons had taken leave of his senses.

"This is bone china," Pons said, with a hint of a smile at his lips. "Of Staffordshire origin, it dates, I should say, to the early nineteenth century. This china, though translucent, will tolerate a surprising amount of heat."

"Pray spare me this lecture," said Bancroft icily. "Take it."

Pons thanked him dryly, slipped the box of pastilles into his pocket, and handed the china cottage to me. "Handle it with care, Parker. We shall examine it at our leisure at 7B." He turned again to his brother. "Sir Randolph lived alone. Surely there were servants?"

"A Mrs. Claudia Melton came in to clean the house twice a week," said Bancroft. "And there was a man-servant by day, Will Davinson. He prepared Sir Randolph's meals and tended to the door. He has come in, if you wish to question him. If so, let us get about it at once."

Bancroft signalled to the constable who stood at the threshold, and he led us out of the room to the rear quarters. In a combination kitchen and breakfast room, there sat waiting a middle-aged man who, immediately on our entrance, clicked his heels together, standing like a ramrod.

"Mr. Davinson," said the constable, "Mr. Solar Pons would like to ask you some questions."

"At your service, sir."

"Pray sit down, Mr. Davinson."

Davinson regained his chair and sat waiting expectantly. His eyes were alert and conveyed the impression of youth the rest of his body belied.

"You were Sir Randolph's orderly in the war?" asked Pons abruptly.

"Yes, sir."

"You had reason then to know his habits very well?"

"Yes, sir."

"He seems to have been addicted to the burning of incense."

"He has burned it for as long as I've known him."

"You will have had occasion to ascertain how many pastilles a day he customarily burned."

"Sir, he released the fragrant smoke only when he retired to his study. This was usually in the evening. He seldom burned more than three in an evening, and commonly but two."

"His favorite scent?"

"Lilac. But he also had pastilles scented with rose, almond, thyme, and, I believe, lavender. He always had a good supply."

336

Pons took a turn down the room and back.

He stood for a few moments in silence, his eyes closed, his right hand pulling at his earlobe.

"Sir Randolph was a reclusive man?"

"He saw very few people."

"Whom did he see in the past fortnight?"

Davinson concentrated for a moment. "His niece, Miss Emily Curwen. She had come to London from her home in Edinburgh and came to call. That was perhaps a trifle over two weeks ago."

"No matter," said Pons. "Go on."

"Mr. Leonard Loveson of Loveson & Fitch in High Holborn. That was a business matter. Sir Randolph held a mortgage on their place of business."

"Sir Randolph held other such mortgages?"

"I was not in Sir Randolph's confidence, sir, but I believe he did."

"Go on, Mr. Davinson."

"Well, then there was a great-nephew, Ronald Lindall, the son of Miss Emily's sister, also from Edinburgh; he was at the house six days ago, paying a courtesy visit, I took it."

"Anyone else?"

"Yes," said Davinson hesitantly. "There was a legal gentleman two days ago, all fuss and feathers. They had words, but briefly. Sir Randolph soothed him and sent him off. I believe the matter concerned another of Sir Randolph's mortgages."

"He was a hard man?"

"No, sir. Quite the contrary. More than once he remitted interest due him—even cancelled it. And on one occasion he forgave a small mortgage. No, sir, he was far too easy a man to deal with. Some of them took advantage of him."

Pons took another turn around the room. "Of these people, which were familiar visitors?" he asked.

"Mr. Loveson."

"You had not seen Miss Emily before?"

"No, sir. Sir Randolph had spoken of her, but she had not visited at any time that I was in this house."

"You admitted her?"

"Yes, sir. Sir Randolph never answered the door. If I had gone, unless he had an appointment, he did not answer the door at all."

337

"Will you cast your mind back to Miss Emily's visit? How did she seem to you?"

"I don't follow you, Mr. Pons."

"Was she composed—sad, gay, what?"

"She seemed to be a trifle agitated, if I may say so. But that was when she left, Mr. Pons. When she came in she was very much a lady."

"She and her uncle had words?"

"I could not say." Davinson was suddenly prim.

"Mr. Lindall, now."

"He was a somewhat truculent young man, but apologetic about disturbing Sir Randolph. They had a pleasant visit. Sir Randolph showed him about the house and garden, and he took his leave."

"Mr. Loveson. Do you know, is the mortgage a large one, presuming it has not been settled?"

"I don't know, but I had the impression that it is quite large." Davinson swallowed and cleared his throat. "I must emphasize again, Mr. Pons, that while Sir Randolph did not take me into his confidence, I was able to come to certain conclusions about his affairs."

"One could hardly expect otherwise of a companion of such long standing."

Davinson inclined his head slightly as if modestly accepting faint praise.

"The gentlemen from the Foreign Office," Pons said then. "Did you admit them?"

"No, sir. They came after I had gone to my flat."

"You answered the telephone while you were here. Do you recall any appointment after your hours during the past two weeks?"

"The foreign gentleman, three nights ago."

"Did he leave his name?"

"No, sir. He asked to speak with Sir Randolph. He spoke in a German accent. Sir Randolph was in his study. I made the signal with the buzzer, and Sir Randolph took the call. I stayed on the wire just long enough to be sure the connection had been made."

"You heard their conversation?"

"Sir, only enough to know that Sir Randolph was very much surprised—I took it, agreeably. Afterward, he came out and instructed me to prepare some sandwiches and chill some wine. So I knew he expected someone to come in during the evening. I assumed it was the foreign gentleman."

Pons nodded. "Your leaving arrangements were by your choice, Mr. Davinson?"

"No, sir. That was the way Sir Randolph wished it. He never wanted to be valeted, didn't like it. But he needed someone to do the ordinary things in the house during the day."

"You have your own key?"

"Yes, Mr. Pons."

"Sir Randolph was secretive?"

"Only about his work. He was a gentleman who, I should say, preferred his own company to that of anyone else. He treated me very well. Indeed, if I may say so, I should not be surprised to find myself mentioned in his will. He hinted as much to me on several occasions, and that ought to be proof enough that he was not unnecessarily secretive."

"Thank you, Mr. Davinson. I may call on you again."

"I want to do anything I can to help, sir. I was very fond of Sir Randolph. We were, if I may say so, almost like step-brothers."

"Was that not an odd way of putting it?" asked Bancroft, when we were walking away from the kitchen. "One says, 'we were like brothers.' Step-brothers, indeed!"

"Probably not, for Davinson," said Pons. "I fancy it was his way of saying they were like brothers one step removed on the social scale, Sir Randolph being a step up, and he a step down."

Bancroft grunted explosively. "You've frittered away half an hour. To what conclusions have you come?"

"I daresay it's a trifle early to be certain of very much. I submit, however, that Sir Randolph was murdered by someone he had no reason to fear. He appears to have been a cautious man, one not given to carelessness in the matter of his relationship with the public."

"You have some ingenious theory about the murderer's entrance into and exit from the locked room, no doubt," said Bancroft testily.

"I should hardly call it that. Sir Randolph admitted him, and Sir Randolph saw him out, locking the doors after him. Until we have the autopsy report, we cannot know precisely how Sir Randolph was done to death."

"We are having the papers gone over once again."

"A waste of time. You Foreign Office people think in painfully conventional patterns. I submit the papers have nothing to do with it."

"Surely it is too much to believe that Sir Randolph's possession of these papers at the time of his death amounts only to coincidence?"

"It is indeed an outrageous coincidence," said Pons. "But I am forced to believe it."

"Is there anything more here?" asked Bancroft.

"If possible, I should like to have a copy of Sir Randolph's will sent to 7B without delay."

"It will be done."

Back at our quarters, Pons retired with the china cottage and the box of pastilles to the corner where he kept his chemicals, while I prepared to go out on my round. When I left 7B, he was in the process of breaking apart one of the scented pastilles; when I returned two hours later, he had broken them all apart and was just rising from his examination, his eyes dancing with the light of discovery.

"Sir Randolph came to his death by his own hand."

"Suicide!"

"I have not said so. No, one of the pastilles contained cyanide. It was prepared and placed among the pastilles in the box on the desk, unknown to him. Since he used not less than two pastilles a day and not more than three, and the box contains normally two dozen pastilles, we can assume the poisoned pastille was placed there not more than twelve days ago. From the ashes in the china cottage it is possible to determine that the cyanide was enclosed in inflammable wax, and this enclosed in the customary formula. Sir Randolph fell victim to a death trap which had been laid for him by someone who both knew his habits and had access to his study."

"I thought it poison. What was the motive?"

"It was certainly not the papers, as was evident the moment I concluded that the incense burner was the source of Sir Randolph's death. That faint odor of almond, you will remember, was indicative."

"His estate then?"

"We shall see. Only a few minutes before your return a copy of Sir Randolph's will arrived. I was about to examine it."

He crossed to the table, took up the sealed envelope lying there, and opened it. He stood for a few moments studying the paper he unfolded. "An admirably clear document," he murmured. "To his faithful servant, Will Davinson, twenty-five hundred pounds. To Miss Emily 'who is otherwise provided for,' the sum of five hundred pounds. To Mrs. Claudia Melton, two hundred pounds. The bulk of his estate distributed equally among five charitable institutions. All mortgages forgiven!"

340

"There is certainly not much in the way of motive there," I said.

"Murder has been committed for as little as ten pounds," said Pons. "And less. But hardly with such care and premeditation. I fancy the stake was considerably more than two or five hundred pounds."

"Davinson has motive and opportunity."

"He could hardly deny it," observed Pons with a crooked smile.

"He knew he was mentioned in the will. He told us as much."

"Rack up one point against his having planned Sir Randolph's death," said Pons.

"I recall your saying often that when all the impossible solutions have been eliminated, then whatever remains, however improbable, must be the truth." Parker continued, "Davinson spoke of a foreigner, a German, who visited Sir Randolph only a few days before his death."

"We have only Davinson's word for it," said Pons.

"If not the papers from the Foreign Office, we seem to be left with only Sir Randolph's estate for motive," I pointed out, with some asperity.

"His estate seems to be well accounted for."

"The mortgage holders!" I cried.

"I have thought of them. Even before I saw this document, I suggested that some inquiry be set afoot about them. But I venture to predict it will be disclosed that Sir Randolph did not hold many unpaid mortgages, and that the total sum involved is not as large as Davinson, for one, believed."

"The man Loveson?"

"I have not forgotten him. His will very probably turn out to be the largest outstanding mortgage. He may have had motive in addition to having opportunity. The probability, again, is remote, for it must surely have occurred to him, should any thought of killing Sir Randolph have crossed his mind, that his motive would be instantly perceived. Moreover, we have Davinson's word for Sir Randolph's lenience with his debtors, and this is given adequate support by the terms of Sir Randolph's will, forgiving his mortgages. No, there is something else here of which we have as yet no inkling, something that induced his murderer to go to great pains to prepare a deadly pastille, secrete it among those on the table during the time of his visit with Sir Randolph—or his secret entry into the house, if it were that—and then be safely away when his victim by chance selected the poisoned pastille for use. It was all very carefully premeditated; there was nothing impulsive about it. That is why, patently,

341

the papers have nothing to do with the matter, for whoever put the pastille into the box did so well before even Sir Randolph knew that he would be sent the papers for examination. By the same process of deduction, the foreign visitor lacked motive—if there were such a visitor."

"And if not?"

"Then, I fear, we should have to put Davinson through it. But there is little reason to doubt Davinson's story. A foreign visitor to Sir Randolph is not unlikely. And Davinson does not seem to me to be capable of so elaborate a plan."

"Who then?"

"We must consider that Davinson was gone by night. Sir Randolph was alone. He could have given entry to anyone he pleased, regardless of what Davinson believes."

"Well, then, we get back to motive."

"Do we not?" So saying, Pons sank into a reverie, from which he stirred only to eat, with a preoccupied air, a lunch Mrs. Johnson sent up. He still sat, smoking pipe after pipe of his abominable shag, when at last I went to bed.

Pons' hand at my shoulder woke me while it was yet dark.

"Can you spare the day, Parker?" he asked, when I sat up. "We have just time to catch the four o'clock from King's Cross for Edinburgh."

"Edinburgh?" I queried, getting out of bed.

"I have an unyielding fancy to learn what the late Sir Randolph and his niece had words about. We lose a day traveling later. The four o'clock brings us into Edinburgh by one-thirty this afternoon. We shall have ample opportunity to make our enquiries of Miss Emily Curwen. You will have hours to sleep on the train."

"Miss Emily!" I cried. "For five hundred pounds? Preposterous!"

"Unlikely, perhaps, but hardly preposterous," retorted Pons. "Poison, after all, is primarily a woman's weapon so she is a suspect."

Pons had already summoned a cab, which waited below. As soon as I had dressed and made arrangements for my locum tenens to call on my patients for the next two days, we were off for King's Cross station, which we reached just in time to catch the train for Scotland.

Once in our compartment and northward bound out of London, Pons sank again into cogitation, and I settled myself to resume the sleep Pons had interrupted.

When I woke in the late morning hours, Pons sat watching the lovely countryside flow by. We had crossed the Scottish border, and soon the familiar heights of Arthur's Seat, the Salisbury Crags, the Braid Hills and Corstorphine Hill would come into view. Here and there little pockets of ground mist still held to the hollows, but the sun shone, and the day promised to be fine.

The tranquil expression of Pons' face told me nothing.

"You cannot have been serious in suggesting that Miss Curwen poisoned her uncle," I said.

"I am not yet in a position to make that suggestion," replied Pons, turning away from the pane. "However, a curious chain of events offers itself for our consideration. There is nothing to show that Miss Emily visited her uncle at any time previous to her recent visit. Then she comes, they have words, she hurries off, distraught. Does not this suggest anything to you?"

"Obviously they quarreled."

"But what about? Two people who have not seen each other for many years, as far as we know, can hardly, on such short notice, have much to quarrel about."

"Unless there is a matter of long standing between them."

"Capital! Capital, Parker," said Pons, his eyes twinkling. "But what ancient disagreement could exist between uncle and niece?"

"A family estrangement?"

"There is always that possibility," conceded Pons. "However, Miss Emily would hardly have come, in that case, unannounced and without an invitation to do so."

"Perhaps, unknown to Davinson, she had been invited to come," I said.

"Perhaps. I am inclined to doubt it. Miss Emily yielded to the impulse to confront her uncle to ask some favor of him. His failure to grant it angered her and she rushed off."

"That is hardly consistent with the premeditation so evident in the careful preparation of a poisoned pastille," I couldn't help pointing out. As usual, it was superfluous.

"Granted, Parker. But there's nothing to prevent such premeditation in the event that the favor she asked her uncle were not granted."

"What could it have been that, failing its granting, only his death would serve her?" I protested. "If a matter of long standing, then, why not longer? No, Pons, it won't wash, it won't at all. I fear you have allowed your latent distrust of the sex to darken your view of Miss Emily Curwen."

Pons burst into hearty laughter.

"Where are we bound for? Do you know?"

"Miss Emily lives in her father's house on Northumberland Street, in the New Town. I took time yesterday to ascertain this and other facts. She and her sister were the only children of Sir Randolph's brother, Andrew. Her sister married unwisely, a man who squandered her considerable inheritance. Both the elder Lindalls are now dead, survived by an only son, Ronald, who is employed in a bookshop, on Torpichen Street. But here we are, drawing into Edinburgh."

Within the hour we stood on the stoop of the house on Northumberland Street. Pons rang the bell three times before the door was opened, only a little, and an inquiring face looked out at us there.

"Miss Emily Curwen?"

"Yes?"

"Mr. Solar Pons, of London, at your service. Dr. Parker and I have come about the matter of your uncle's death."

There was a moment of pungent silence. Then the door was opened wide, and Miss Curwen stood there, unmistakably shocked and surprised. "Uncle Randolph dead? I saw him within the month. The picture of health!" she cried. "But forgive me. Come in, gentlemen, do."

Miss Emily led the way to the drawing room of the old-fashioned house, which was certainly at one time the abode of wealth. She was a woman approaching fifty, with a good figure still, and betraying some evidence in the care she had taken with her chestnut hair and her cosmetics of trying to retain as much of a youthful aspect as possible.

"Pray sit down," she said. "Tell me of uncle's death. What happened? Was it an accident?"

"Perhaps, in a manner of speaking, it was," said Pons. "He was found dead in his study."

"Poor uncle!" she cried, unaffectedly.

She seemed unable to fix her eyes on either Pons or myself. Her hands were busy plucking at her dress, or lacing her fingers together, or carrying her fingers to her lips.

"Perhaps you did not know he left you five hundred pounds?"

"No, I did not." Then her eyes brightened quite suddenly. "Poor, dear uncle! He needn't have done that. Now that he's gone, I shall have it all!"

344

"Somewhat over a fortnight ago you called on your uncle, Miss Curwen."

"Yes, I did."

She grimaced.

"You found him well at that time?"

"I believe I have said as much, sir."

"You left him, upset. Was he unkind to you?"

"Sir, it was the old matter. Now it is resolved."

"Would you care to tell us about it?"

"Oh, there's no secret in it, I assure you. Everyone knows of it here in Edinburgh." She tossed her head and shrugged, pitying herself briefly. "Uncle Randolph was as hard a man as my father. My older sister, Cicely, made a very bad marriage in our father's eyes. He had settled her inheritance on her, and when he saw how Arthur wasted it, he made certain I could never do the same. So he put my inheritance, fifty thousand pounds, in trust, and made Uncle Randolph guardian of the trust. I could have only so much a year to live on, a pittance. But the world has changed, and everyone knows that it is not so easy to live on a restricted income as it was twenty-five years ago when my father died. But now all that's over. Now that Uncle Randolph's dead, what is mine comes to me free of his or anyone's control."

"You must have had assistance, Miss Curwen," said Pons sympathetically.

"Oh, yes. My nephew, my dear boy! He's all I have, gentlemen. He has cared for his old aunt quite as if I were his own mother. I've been very much alone here. What could I do, what society could I have, on so limited an income? Now all that is changed. I am sorry Uncle Randolph is dead, but I'm not sorry the restrictions on my inheritance are removed."

Pons' glance flickered about the room, which looked as if it had not quite emerged into the twentieth century. "A lovely room, Miss Curwen," he observed.

"My grandfather planned it. I hate it," she said simply. "I shall lose no time selling the house. Think of having fifty thousand pounds I might have had when I was in my twenties! Oh, Mr. Pons, how cruel it was! My father thought I'd do the same thing my sister did, even after I saw how it went with them."

"I see you, too, are given to the use of incense, Miss Curwen," said Pons, his gaze fastened to a china castle.

"Any scent will serve to diminish the mould and mildew, gentlemen."

"May I look at that incense burner?" persisted Pons.

"Please do."

Pons crossed to the mantel where the china castle rested, picked it up, and brought it back to his chair. It was an elaborate creation in bone china, featuring three lichen-covered turrets, and evidently three burners. Carnations adorned it, and a vine of green leaves, and morning glories. Its windows were outlined in soft brown.

"A Colebrook Dale marking on this Coalport castle identifies it as prior to 1850 in origin," said Pons.

Miss Curwen's eyebrows went up. "You're a collector, sir?"

"Only of life's oddities," said Pons. "But I have some interest in antiquities as well." He looked up. "And what scent do you favor, Miss Curwen?"

"Rose."

"One could have guessed that you would select so complimentary a fragrance, Miss Curwen."

Miss Curwen blushed prettily as Pons got up to return the china castle to the mantel, where he stood for a few moments with the opened box of pastilles in his hand, inhaling deeply the scent that emanated from it. He appeared to have some difficulty closing the box before he turned once more and came back to where he had been sitting. He did not sit down again. "I fear we have imposed upon you long enough, Miss Curwen," said Pons.

Miss Emily came to her feet. "I suppose you will take care of such legalities as there are, gentlemen?"

"I fancy Sir Randolph's legal representatives will do that in good time, Miss Curwen," said Pons.

"Oh! I thought . . ."

"I am sorry to have given you the wrong impression. I am a private enquiry agent, Miss Curwen. There is some question about the manner of your uncle's death; I am endeavoring to answer it."

She was obviously perplexed. "Well, there's nothing I can tell you about that. I know he was in what looked like perfect health when I last saw him."

She did not seem to have the slightest suspicion of Pons' objective, and walked us to the door, where she let us out. From the stoop, we could hear the chain being quietly slid back into place.

"I must hand it to you, Pons," I said. "There's motive for you."

"Poor woman! I'll wager she's dancing around by herself in celebration now," he said as we walked back down to the street. "There are pathetic people in this world to whom the possession of money is everything. They know little of life and nothing of how to live. Presumably Andrew Curwen was such a one; I fear Miss Emily may be another. One could live well on the income of fifty thousand pounds if one had a mind to, but Miss Emily preferred to pine and grieve and feel sorry for herself, a lonely, deluded woman. I shall be sorry to add to her loneliness, but perhaps her wealth will assuage her. But come, Parker, we have little time to lose. We must be off to the police. With luck, we shall be able to catch one of the night trains back to London."

Inspector Brian McGavick joined us when Pons explained his need. He was in plain-clothes, and looked considerably more like an actor than a member of the constabulary.

"I've heard about you, Mr. Pons," said McGavick. "This morning, on instructions from the Foreign Office. I am at your service."

"Inspector, you're in charge here. I have no authority. I shall expect you to take whatever action the events of the next hour or two call for." He outlined briefly the circumstances surrounding the murder of Sir Randolph Curwen. By the time he had finished we had arrived in Torpischen Street.

"Let us just park the car over here," said Pons, "and walk the rest of the way."

We got out of the police car and walked leisurely down the street to a little shop that bore the sign, *Laidlaw's Books*. There Pons turned in.

A stout little man clad almost formally, save for his plaid weskit, came hurrying up to wait on us.

"Just browsing, sir," said Pons.

The little man bowed and returned to resume his place on a stool at a high, old-fashioned desk in a far corner of the shop. The three of us began to examine the books in the stalls and on the shelves, following Pons' lead.

Pons soon settled down to a stall containing novels of Sir Walter Scott and Dickens, studying one volume after another with that annoying air of having the entire afternoon in which to do it.

In a quarter of an hour, the door of the shop opened to admit a handsome young man who walked directly back to the rear of the shop, removed

347

his hat and ulster, and came briskly back to attend to us. Since Pons was nearest him, he walked directly up to Pons and engaged him in conversation I could not overhear until I drifted closer.

"There is merit in each," Pons was saying. "Scott for his unparalleled reconstruction of Scotland's past, Dickens for the remarkable range of his characters, however much some of them may seem caricatures. I think of establishing special shelves for each when I open my own shop."

"Ah, you're a bookman, sir? Where?"

"In London. I lack only a partner."

"I would like to be in London myself. What are your qualifications?"

"I need a young man, acquainted with books and authors, capable of putting a little capital into the business. Are you interested?"

"I might be."

Pons thrust forth his hand.

"Name's Holmes," he said.

"Lindall," said the young man, taking his hand.

"Capital?" asked Pons.

"I expect to come into some."

"When?"

"Within the next few months."

"Ample time! Now tell me, Mr. Lindall, since I am in need of some other little service, do you know any chemistry? Ever studied it?"

"No, sir."

"I asked because I saw a chemist's shop next door. Perhaps you have a friend there who might make up a special prescription for me?"

"As a matter of fact, I do have. A young man named Ardley. Ask for him and say I gave you his name."

"Thank you, thank you. I am grateful. In delicate little matters like these, one cannot be too careful."

Lindall's interest quickened. He ran the tip of his tongue over his lips and asked, "What is the nature of the prescription, sir?"

Pons dipped his hand into his coat pocket, thrust it out before Lindall, and unfolded his fingers. "I need a little pastille like this—with cyanide at the center, to dispose of old men and middle-aged ladies."

Lindall's reaction was extraordinary. He threw up his hands as if to thrust Pons away, stumbled backward, and upset a stall of books. Books and Lindall together went crashing to the floor.

"Oh, I say! I say now!" called out the proprietor, getting off his stool.

348

"Inspector McGavick, arrest this man for the murder of Sir Randolph Curwen, and the planned murder of his aunt, Miss Emily Curwen," said Pons.

McGavick had already moved in on Lindall, and was pulling him to his feet.

"You will need this poisoned pastille, Inspector. I found it in a box of rose pastilles in Miss Emily's home. You should have no difficulty proving that this and the one that killed Sir Randolph were manufactured for Lindall at his direction." To Lindall, Pons added, "A pity you didn't ask after my Christian name, Mr. Lindall. Sherlock. A name I assume on those special occasions when I feel inordinately immodest."

In our compartment on the 10:15 express for London Pons answered the questions with which I pelted him.

"It was an elementary matter, Parker," he said, "confused by the co-incidence of Sir Randolph's possession of the Foreign Office papers. The death trap had been laid for him well before anyone at all knew that he would see the papers in question. This motive eliminated, it became necessary to disclose another. Nobody appeared to dislike Sir Randolph, and it did not seem that any adequate motivation lay in the provisions of his will.

"We were left, then, with Miss Emily's curious visit, angrily terminated. She went to London to appeal to her uncle for an end to the trust. She came back and complained to her nephew—her 'dear boy' who is 'all' she has—her designated heir, as an examination of her will will certainly show. In a fortnight, familiarized with Sir Randolph's habits by Miss Emily, he paid him a visit on his own, managed to slip the poisoned pastille into his box, and was off to bide his time. He had had two made, one for his aunt, and felt safe in slipping the other into her box of pastilles. He might better have waited, but he had not counted on the death of Sir Randolph being taken for anything but a seizure of some kind. He under-estimated the police, I fear, and greed pushed him too fast. 'The love of money,' Parker, is indeed 'the root of all evil.' "